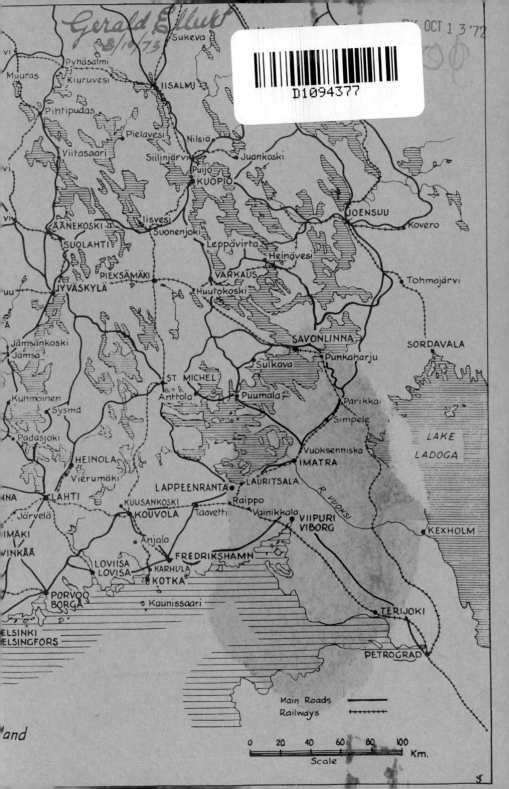

GIVE
ME
THE
DAGGERS

GIVE
ME
THE
DAGGERS

CATHERINE GAVIN

WILLIAM MORROW & COMPANY, INC.

New York   1972

To Eeva Kilpi

AUTHOR'S FOREWORD

This book was prepared in all the cities in which the action takes place.

In Helsingfors (Helsinki) I discussed the character of General Gustaf Mannerheim, later the Marshal of Finland, with Dr. Eino E. Suolahti, Professor of History at the University of Helsinki, who kindly read some of the relevant chapters in typescript.

In London I had an illuminating talk about the Finnish timber trade with Mr. John Benn, a member of the Price and Pierce Group of Companies, which has been connected with the timber industry in Finland for the past seventy years.

In Zürich Madame Marie-Louise Kessler, proprietor until 1971 of the Veltliner Keller, allowed me to use both the name of her restaurant and something of her own personality in the fictional Maria Matter.

In Seattle and Vancouver I found the historical collections invaluable, and back in London I discussed my impressions of both cities with the American author Luree Miller, a native of Seattle.

In Lima the influence of Mr. John Harriman of Librerias ABC greatly expedited my research at the National Library of Peru.

To all of the above my grateful thanks are due.

*   *   *

This novel is a compound of fact and fiction. Thus, it is true that General Mannerheim was in Aberdeen on November 11, 1918, but he did not meet a Canadian called Tom Fleming there. What he says to Tom in the story is based on the opinions published in his own *Memoirs*.

Similarly, the action at the fictional Sainte Elodie which so painfully impressed Tom Fleming took place in fact, and was reported in *The Times* newspaper.

The major cities in Finland in 1918 are given their Swedish names in the text; both the Swedish and Finnish names are given in the endpaper maps.

PART ONE

Infirm of purpose —

1

"THE CHIEF WILL SEE YOU NOW, Mr. Fleming," said the man in naval uniform. "Would you like to leave your coat out here?"

"Sure. Thanks." Fleming got up stiffly. He laid his new civilian overcoat and hat on the leather sofa, saw his gloves on the floor, stooped awkwardly to pick them up, and shot a glance at the girl at the corner desk. She was typing industriously. Since the first shocked look when he came in, she had not raised her eyes from the page in her typewriter.

"This way, please." At the end of a short corridor a heavy door was opened, and Fleming passed alone into the room which was one of the nerve centres of a country at war. The ceiling lights were still burning, although a red December sun had struggled clear of the fog and was gilding the roofs and turrets of Whitehall. A reading-lamp on the desk had its cone of light directed on a foolscap sheet of typescript, the shade almost concealing the face of the man who briefly acknowledged Fleming's entrance.

"Sit down, Mr. Fleming. Very good of you to accept my invitation so punctually."

"Colonel Henderson said you wanted to see me right away, sir."

"But you weren't obliged to come at all, you know."

The quizzical tone was wrong, he realised, for the visitor hitched his chair away from the desk as if to take advantage of the shadow cast by the lamp, and was silent. The Chief began to talk smoothly about Fleming's journey up from Scotland, asking for Colonel Henderson and the other medical officers at Dykefaulds, until he saw that the young man was sufficiently at ease to accept a cigarette, and even to lean across the desk towards the proffered lighter. Then the Chief saw the ruin of what must have been a pleasant face, caused by a raised welt running crimson from Fleming's upper lip, which it slightly distorted, across his left cheek to the corner of his eye.

11

"I don't have to tell you, Mr. Fleming," he began, simultaneously with the snapping shut of his lighter, "that everything said inside this room must be regarded as completely secret."

"Of course, sir."

"Colonel Henderson tells me that after your last board declared you unfit for military duty, you made arrangements to take up a temporary position with a timber firm in Finland. I was rather interested to hear about that. Would you tell me how it came about?"

"Through my family in Canada, sir," said the young man, with what was meant to be a smile. It twisted his upper lip still further, and the thickness of the ridge on his cheek became more painfully pronounced. "Timber is our business. My father founded the firm in Vancouver about thirty-five years ago, and now we're concerned with every branch of the industry from logging to turning out the paper for Canadian bank-notes."

"I understand your brother, Mr. Graham Fleming, is very well known in Ontario for his contribution to the war effort."

"I believe so, sir."

"And you were in the administrative side of the business too?"

"Only for about six months. My brother started me in the Toronto office early in 1914. Before that I was in the woods, right from the time I finished high school. Lumberjack, camp foreman, timber cruiser—I liked the outdoor life best."

The Chief consulted his typed notes. "But you were in Vancouver when you enlisted in August 1914?"

"I was home on vacation, sir."

"You went overseas with the First Canadian Division for training and landed in France in the following February." The Chief looked over his spectacles at Fleming. "You were mentioned in despatches after Second Ypres, and served with distinction until you were wounded last summer at Sainte Elodie."

"I sometimes wish I'd been killed there, sir."

"Eh?" The Chief scowled. "Did you let the newspaper nonsense upset you to that extent? You may be sure your conduct at Sainte Elodie was militarily correct, Mr. Fleming, otherwise you wouldn't have received a decoration. That reporter fellow was only out to make a cheap sensation; really, Lord Kitchener is missed in more ways than one. He detested all war correspondents on principle—wouldn't allow any of 'em within five miles of his own HQ."

"I'm inclined to sympathise with that," said Fleming drily, and it was the Chief's turn to smile. He was pleased that a crack of irony had appeared in the tense façade of the Canadian's composure. When he regained his confidence, he might be the ideal man for the job in Finland.

"Was it your father who put you in touch with the firm in Helsingfors?" he asked.

"Not directly, sir. Our own company is represented here in London by a firm of selling agents, Messrs. Ballantine and Macaulay. Both the partners have been very kind to me, ever since I was training on Salisbury Plain in '14. It was Mr. Ballantine who came up with the Helsingfors idea. They have a representative of their own in Helsingfors, a Mr. Baker, an elderly man. He's in poor health and pretty much confined to the house this winter, so I'm to take his place for six or eight weeks, visiting the saw-mills and making sure all the deliveries will be ready for First Low Water."

"And are *you* fit for that sort of exertion?"

"I can walk all right now."

The Chief looked down at the page beneath his hand, on which the words "severe intra-abdominal lesions" were underlined, and wondered if the internal wounds had marked Captain Fleming more deeply than the scar across his face.

"I don't enquire," he said, "why a man invalided out of the army should want to spend a winter in Finland instead of going home to Canada; presumably you have good and sufficient reasons for that. But—how much do you know about the state of affairs in Helsingfors?"

"Not very much, sir, I'm afraid."

"Didn't you have access to the newspapers at Dyke-faulds?"

"We saw *The Times* and the *Glasgow Herald* every day. But there wasn't much in the papers about Finland, except when there were strikes and rioting at the time of the Bolshevik revolution."

"That was last month. But I can tell you one item which you'll read in your *Times* tomorrow morning." He paused impressively. "The Grand Duchy of Finland, the Russian Grand Duchy, has ceased to exist. The cabinet has made a declaration of independence, and the Diet, as they call their parliament, ratified it last Thursday by a narrow majority."

"Meaning the Finns don't want to be a part of Soviet Russia, sir? Well, good for them."

The Chief took off his spectacles and rubbed his eyes. "I hope so," he said. "But I'm afraid the Social-Democrat opposition, which *is* in sympathy with Soviet Russia, is bound to make trouble for the government. However, that's not the point. At this moment the declaration of Finnish independence poses one more problem for our own cabinet."

"I'm sorry to be stupid, sir," said Fleming, "but I really don't quite understand."

The Chief looked at him. The daylight had grown brighter inside the room, paling the lamps which had burned all night, and the young Canadian had ceased to be a dark shape in the shadows beyond the desk. Now that he had partly overcome his desperate self-consciousness and sat more easily in his chair, it was possible to assess the physical advantages which still remained to him: the well-shaped head, the powerful shoulders and the long muscular limbs. His hands, in which the Chief had noted a slight tremor, the last effects of shell-shock, were steady enough as he reached for an ashtray and stubbed out his cigarette.

"No need to apologise," the Chief said kindly. "A man who's been on active service for the past three years can't be expected to have a grasp of Baltic politics. Just let me explain that the first, the vital thing to remember, is the importance *to us* of the Bolshevik revolution. No matter what it means inside Russia, or even to Finland, Lenin's success in Petrograd may make all the difference between victory and defeat for the Allies. For if the negotiations he and his gang have opened with Germany should end in an armistice, then the German High Command will be free to hurl all their forces against us in the west."

"Yes, sir, but isn't that where the Americans are supposed to come in?"

"Of course we all hope and believe that the United States will turn the tide. But their war machine has been mortally slow in starting, and there's only a token force of American troops in France so far. That's why a Russian armistice could be disastrous—on top of all the reverses of the past few months."

Fleming nodded. He knew the whole sorry story: the French army mutinies, the Italian rout at Caporetto, the new British attack at Cambrai which had begun so well and was fast turning into a retreat. It was December 1917, a time of disaster for the Allies.

"Now Finland," continued the Chief, "has served both the Empire and the Bolsheviks as a useful springboard since the war began. Torneå, at the head of the Gulf of Bothnia, was used by ourselves for getting medical supplies to the Czar's armies via Sweden—and by Lenin for running propaganda material and Bolshevik agents into Russia. Lenin himself was hiding out in Finland over the past few months. And at the same time most of the Russian aristocrats and politicians with any sense began using Finland as an escape route soon after the March revolution. There are Russian refugees stranded in Finland still."

"And you want me to help them, is that it, sir?"

"Hardly," said the Chief. "I'm sorry to disappoint you, Mr. Fleming, if you've jumped to some romantic conclusion to this interview. I'm not sending out a one-man mission to rescue the Imperial Grand Duchesses from Tobolsk. They're beyond help or hope, I fear. Whatever Kerensky's merits, he may have signed the Imperial family's death warrant when he despatched them east to Siberia instead of south to the Crimea."

"But I thought Kerensky was on our side," protested Fleming. "When he was at the head of the provisional government, they wanted to carry on the war."

"Exactly, and that's why our government wants to get him out of Russia alive. Lenin and company aren't by any means firm in the saddle yet; there are several fighting forces ready to take arms against them, and the cabinet believes Kerensky is the only man who can rally them all to the White cause. That's as may be; what *I* want is to bring out two of my best agents, who've been with Kerensky ever since he was on the run. And that I believe I can do, with your help, within the next few weeks."

He was watching Fleming closely. He saw the carefully controlled hands begin to shake again.

"Will you, when you get to Finland, meet a third man of ours and carry out any instructions he may give you, and will you, as soon as you reach Helsingfors, look for what we call a safe house, where our agents can take shelter until they can cross to Sweden?"

15

"I don't know what to say, sir. I want to help, but after all—why me?"

"Because you've got the perfect cover story. Ready-made, and absolutely true."

"Couldn't they use my room at the Society House Hotel, where Mr. Ballantine arranged for me to stay?"

"Too public, too many Russian refugees, and probably Bolshevik agents among them, too."

"But how can I find the sort of house you mean, sir? I don't know a living soul in Helsingfors. Would the British consul help?"

The Chief sighed. "We very seldom operate through the consulates," he said. "You mustn't bring Mr. Grove into this, unless you have to. Go and pay your respects to him in the normal way, but otherwise make yourself as inconspicuous as possible."

"If I can."

The tone of bitterness left no doubt of Fleming's meaning. The Chief looked squarely at the wounded face, and said, "That will improve in time, you know."

"So the doctors say."

"Count your blessings, my boy. You might have been lamed for life."

"Sir," said Fleming desperately, "if it was something I could do on my own, I'd jump at the chance, I'd take it like a shot. But to have two men dependent on me in a foreign land, where I can't speak a word of the language and hardly know my way about, that's quite another story. If I hesitate, it's only because I'm afraid of letting you and your agents down."

"I don't think you'll do that," said the Chief quietly. "Do you accept the mission, Mr. Fleming?"

"To meet your man and take my orders from him, certainly. But as far as finding a—a safe house, do you call it? I can only promise that I'll do my best."

"I'm very much obliged to you." The Chief reflected. "I think I ought to explain more fully about the need for a place of refuge. Until the Bolsheviks seized the power, our agents in Russia were nearly as safe as before the abdication of the Czar. In any case they were absolutely safe as soon as they crossed the border into the Grand Duchy. But now the situation has changed. Crossing the frontier has become extremely dangerous, and the unrest in Finland itself doesn't help. Incidentally, you said you 'hardly knew your way about Finland'. I thought you'd never visited the place before?"

"Oh no, sir, but Mr. Ballantine sent me a map, and a lot of details about the different saw-mills."

"Excellent. Well, if you've identified the towns on your map, I can tell you that there's a Russian garrison in every one of them, and in a good many country areas as well. The Russians hold the Åland Islands, in the Gulf of Bothnia, and their entire Forty-second Corps is at Viborg, the town nearest to Petrograd. There are twenty thousand mutinous Russian sailors in port at Helsingfors, in addition to a large garrison. They are all enthusiastic supporters of the Finnish Red Guards, who led the rioting and occupied the Senate House in Helsingfors only a few weeks ago."

"What's the Finnish army doing about all this?"

"There is no Finnish army," said the Chief. "It was disbanded by the former Czar and his ministers many years ago. I want to impress upon you that Finland is now to all intents and purposes in the power of the Bolsheviks, and is no longer a safe country for any known British agent."

"Will the Finns *stay* in the power of the Bolsheviks?"

"There are three million Finns in Finland, and two million Russians in Petrograd alone, Mr. Fleming. What do you think the Finns can do? Now, I believe you meant to leave for Stockholm on the seventeenth. I have to ask you to leave from Hull tonight."

Fleming had been taking orders for too long to show any surprise. He only said, "Still sailing for Stockholm, I suppose?"

"Yes, and not under luxury conditions, I'm afraid — in a Swedish cargo boat whose skipper sometimes obliges us in an emergency. The Gulf of Bothnia will be iced in any day now, and you must cross from Stockholm to Helsingfors as fast as you can. I'm sorry if this upsets any personal plans for your stay in London.'

"I hadn't got around to making any, sir. I was going to take a girl out to dinner tonight, but I can telephone and call it off."

The Chief was slightly surprised. Colonel Henderson's report had indicated that Captain Fleming, unlike most of the other inmates of Dykefaulds, had shown no interest in girls.

"I know you're not married," he said. "Are you by any chance engaged?"

Fleming laughed for the first time. "Not to anyone, and not by any chance to Nancy Macpherson! She's just an old friend from Seattle—her father and mine did a good deal of business together, when they were younger men."

"What's her father's name?"

"James J. Macpherson, sir."

"The president of the Equator Steamship Line?"

"Carrying passengers and freight from Seattle to Callao and intermediate ports," said Fleming. "He was planning to open a service to Japan when war broke out."

"I'm sorry about your dinner engagement," said the Chief, thinking that the son of Arthur Fleming and the daughter of James J. Macpherson, sitting down to dine, would represent a fair proportion of the capital and enterprise of the Pacific North-west. "Perhaps you can see Miss Macpherson earlier today?"

"I'll try, but she's with the US Canteen Corps, so she's got a job to do too. And I'll have to see Mr. Ballantine first, I guess. This is only the tenth, and he's expecting me to be in London for a whole week yet."

"What are you going to tell him about your change of plan?"

Fleming reflected. "I'll tell him Mr. Baker's feeling worse, and wants me to go on to Finland right away."

"You'll do," said the Chief. "And will you, with equal discretion, arrange with Mr. Ballantine that your first trip outside Helsingfors shall be to the Broberg Saw-mills near the falls of Imatra?"

When their conversation ended fifteen minutes later the Chief wished Fleming luck, and walked to the door with him. It was only then that Fleming realised the man was a cripple.

2

THE FOG CAME DOWN again over London later in the day. It seeped into shops and offices, and every time the doors leading to Piccadilly and Arlington Street were opened the yellowish-grey vapour writhed into the Ritz Hotel. Tom Fleming was coughing as he stopped beside the Piccadilly entrance to buy an evening paper from the shivering vendor under the Ritz arcade. The news was certain to be bad, but he was a quarter of an hour early for his appointment with Nancy Macpherson, and the paper would make a useful screen against any shocked eyes in the Ritz. He had already seen shock in too many London faces when they looked at his.

A grey-haired waiter greeted him at the top of the steps leading to the Palm Court.

"Good afternoon, sir. Table for one?"

"For two, please."

"This way, sir."

But Tom Fleming turned away from the indicated table to one beside the net-veiled window at the far side of the room, partly concealed by palms in a gilded tub. The place was only half full, and nobody paid any particular attention to him.

"Would you care to order anything, sir?"

"No thanks, I'll wait for the lady."

"Very good, sir."

Tom spread the evening paper wide. The tragedy at Halifax, Nova Scotia, was still on the front page, with the death roll rising to the ten thousand mark. Sabotage was suggested as the reason for the explosion of a munitions ship in Halifax harbour, which had laid half the great Canadian seaport in ruins. The Million Pound Tank in Trafalgar Square had raised not one but three million pounds for the War Loan in three weeks. Father Bernard Vaughan had spoken on behalf of the war effort from the top of the tank.

Tom lowered the paper cautiously and looked around. The

Palm Court was one place that hadn't changed since his last Blighty leave, except to grow a little shabbier, the chandelier lights dimmer, the carpets very slightly frayed. The two marble pillars at the top of the steps still seemed to be supporting the whole weight of the British Empire, and there were fresh flowers on the tea-tables to compensate for margarine and rationed cakes. But the guests were either much older or much younger than Tom remembered. The only other man in civilian clothes was a white-haired old party entertaining two dowagers of the pre-war era, whom Tom studied appreciatively. In their furs and lace frills they reminded him of his mother and any one of her cronies, sitting over the teacups in what Vancouver society knew as The Hotel. There were four second lieutenants, determinedly gay, sitting where some tables had been pushed together and enjoying what looked very like a schoolroom tea. Their companions were very young girls; two of them, Tom saw with amusement, had tucked their pigtailed hair inside their dresses and were pretending to be grown up. He supposed they belonged to the new breed of flappers, and that the older girls, the real party girls whom he had enjoyed taking out, had given up tea at the Ritz for the duration. They would make their appearance at dinner-time, rested, scented, fresh for the evening at the theatre and the supper club which helped their escorts to forget that a subaltern's expectation of life at the front was now estimated at ten days.

Tom wondered what he would do if one of those boys were to turn round and say:

"D'you see that fellow in the corner, with the messed-up face? That's Fleming, the Canadian murderer. Killed six of his own men and got away with it, how about that?"

He forced himself to think, instead, about the girl on her way to meet him. She had been very pleasant on the telephone, as willing to agree to the change of plan as in the days when she was always ready to play Calamity Jane to his Wild Bill Hickok in the long carefree holidays they shared in the Canadian woods. The Macphersons and the Flemings spent their vacations together for many years before the war, and Tom's older sisters, Isabel and Dorothy, were always ready to make a pet of little Nancy, and felt hurt when she preferred rough games with Tom. By the time she was ten, and he fourteen, Tom's sentimental mother was calling them "the little sweethearts" and "just made for each other", and within a few years there had been sweethearting of a clumsy kind at picnics and beach parties. When Nancy was eighteen and Tom twenty-two there had been an exchange of breathless kisses at a country club dance which seemed to hold a promise for the future. But soon after that Nancy entered Washington University in Seattle, and, as if assailed by measles, came down with a fine attack of adolescent socialism.

Tom Fleming thought—and unwisely, often said—that Nancy's socialism was fed and fanned by her history instructor, a woman called Kathleen Donovan. Dr. Donovan's classroom lectures were consistently slanted to the left, and in city politics she was a dedicated supporter of the Industrial Workers of the World, known to their opponents as the Wobblies. In this he was less than fair to Nancy, for Seattle, that rumbustious young city, had always bred strong-minded women, and Nancy, like her predecessors, had the courage of her own convictions. Delightfully aware that she was annoying her father, she spoke at street corners in support of Eugene V. Debs, the socialist candidate for the Presidency of the United States in 1912, and destined to be no more successful than in 1900, 1904, and 1908. She came out strong for the Wobblies in the Potlatch Day riots of 1913, and after being in the thick of the excitement in Skid Road was arrested on a charge of assaulting a policeman, fined, and bound over to keep the peace.

As long as Dr. Donovan and Miss Macpherson confined their militancy to Seattle, a young man like Tom Fleming, uninterested in politics, could afford to laugh at both of them. But in the summer after the Potlatch riots something more serious took place. Nancy had come to Vancouver to be a bridesmaid at Dorothy Fleming's marriage to Harry Carlson, one of James J. Macpherson's most promising young executives, and Tom returned from Toronto to be the best man. He was inclined to thank God that the wedding was safely over before the row began, the row that had been brewing on the Pacific coast for at least seven years, as opposition to Asiatic immigration mounted in Seattle and Vancouver. This time it was Vancouver's turn. Four hundred Sikhs aboard a ship called the *Komagatu Maru*, chartered by a Punjabi agitator, were refused permission to land at Vancouver, and disturbances broke out along the waterfront. Nancy Macpherson, naturally, was on the side of the Sikhs;

21

Tom, with those whose slogan was "Keep British Columbia British". She called him a racialist, he called her a half-baked Red, and flung out of the house to go camping with two other young men on the Fraser river. The story ended ignominiously enough when HMS *Rainbow* intervened, and the Sikhs were escorted aboard another vessel for deportation to Hong Kong. Two weeks from that day the world was at war, Tom Fleming had enlisted, and was marching through Vancouver with his regiment to entrain for eastern Canada. Nancy was standing with his parents on Granville Street to watch the boys in kilts go by, and he was grimly pleased to see that she was crying.

She hadn't cried at Shorncliffe, though, when she saw him swathed in bandages and lying in a hospital bed. He had been so heavily sedated on that day three months ago that all he could recall was the touch of cool hands and a voice that took him back to happy times, certainly no tears. Nor did he think she would flinch at the sight of him today.

Tom Fleming felt weary and nervous. After the quiet months in hospital the roar and pace of London were exhausting, and so was the sense of having been not so much spoken to as spoken at by both the Chief and Mr. Ballantine. The Chief's exposition of Finnish politics had required concentrated thought, and then there followed two strenuous hours at Ballantine and Macaulay's office in Cheapside. Mr. Ballantine had clearly been annoyed at having to find time in a busy day for an interview with young Fleming, and to pack into that interview the leisurely review of the Finnish timber industry he had intended to spread over a whole week. Tom's mouth was dry. He hoped Nancy wasn't going to pay him out for standing her up on the dinner date by being late for tea.

She came in on the stroke of five, with a smile for the old waiter and an eager look in the direction he indicated. Tom stood up. She came across the room with nothing but gaiety in her face and gave him both her hands.

"Tommy! Am I ever glad to see you!"

"It's wonderful to see you, Nancy. You're looking great."

"So're you," she lied, and took her place on the banquette beside him, making a little business of taking off a leather satchel she wore over her shoulder and laying it on a chair. The waiter took their order for tea. Tom was aware that without looking at anyone but him Nancy had attracted the attention of everybody in the room. Americans were in fashion, and she was unmistakably an American, and a very attractive one, from her wide felt hat with a turned-up brim, to the toes of her polished and high laced boots. Light blue flashes on the shoulders of her olive-drab blouse bore the words "US Canteen Corps", while the blouse itself was worn over a shirt and tie of the same light blue and belted with a heavy dark brown belt. The flappers in their party dresses sulked as the boy lieutenants stared admiringly at the pretty girl in uniform. Nancy was a long way from being beautiful, but a tilted nose and a short upper lip gave her an alert, vivacious look, and her blue eyes were brilliant under a curly fringe of dark brown hair.

For the first few minutes, while the waiter put the tea things before them, with one plate of cucumber sandwiches and another with slices of a pallid cake, their talk was inconsequent, turning on the health of their relatives and the latest news in a letter from Dorothy Carlson, with whom Nancy had always kept in touch. They were both trying to renew their old friendship, held only by a tenuous thread of letters and field service cards across three years of war. Then Fleming said, "Now let me look at you properly. Remember at Shorncliffe Camp, I'd only about half an eye to see you with?"

"Yes, I remember. You were a pretty sick boy at Shorncliffe," said Nancy, and then, as his amused gaze swept over her: "Tom Fleming! What are you grinning at?"

"I can't help it," he said, "it's that comic-opera uniform. A US campaign hat, a British officer's Sam Browne belt, and let's see, a London bus conductress's boots. You haven't worn a get-up as good as this since we played Mounties and redskins, and you were Minnehaha the faithful squaw."

"I didn't *invent* the Canteen Corps uniform."

"Whoever did might find herself in trouble with the Provost Marshal one of these days."

"I'm very proud to wear it." Nancy changed the subject. "Say, did you really get your discharge, up there in Scotland?"

"Discharged, demobbed, back in civvy street—you name it, Nan, I'm out."

"I thought you'd have to go back to Canada, Valcartier or some place, to be discharged."

"I guess they couldn't wait to see the last of me."

"I was so surprised when I heard you were going to Finland. Does it mean you're going right back to Scotland tonight?"

"No, why? I'm sailing in a Swedish boat from Hull."

"I thought you might be leaving from Aberdeen. Haven't you got a cousin up there who runs a steamship line?"

"Oh, you mean John Endicott? What a memory the girl has! I don't know if the Tarras Line's still operating, they took one hell of a pounding from the submarines last year. Anyhow, Tarras goes in to Bergen and Christiania, not Stockholm."

"And you didn't get to see Mr. Endicott, while you were at this Dykefaulds?"

"I only got to go in to Glasgow twice, to shop for my civvy gear. We had to go in groups of three, with an MO along to nursemaid us; it wasn't exactly fun."

"Tom." She wrinkled her brow. "What sort of convalescent hospital was it really?"

"It was a high-grade looney-bin, if you want to know."

Nancy was deeply shocked. But she had the courage to attempt a smile, and say, "Well, that's water under the bridge now, isn't it? Are you looking forward to Finland? What exactly are you going to do up there?"

"I wrote you, just a temporary office job in Helsingfors."

"You don't need a temporary office job anywhere. You've got your own job waiting for you back in Canada."

"Do you think brother Graham's waiting to kill the fatted calf, back in Bloor Street?"

"Why shouldn't he be? And he's only your half-brother, after all."

"He's the effective partner in Arthur Fleming and Son. Son, singular."

"Go back and have them make it plural."

"Not while Graham's in his present frame of mind."

"Wasn't he pleased about your decoration?"

"Who told you anything about a decoration?"

"It was in the *Official Gazette*," she said defensively. "Anybody could have read it. But actually your mother sent me this."

Nancy opened the workmanlike satchel, took a frayed newspaper clipping from one pocket and handed it to Tom. It was cut from a Vancouver morning paper and read:

MILITARY CROSS AWARDED TO
CAPTAIN THOMAS FLEMING
SEAFORTH HIGHLANDERS OF VANCOUVER

Word has been received here that the military authorities have approved the immediate award of the Military Cross to Captain Thomas Fleming, younger son of Mr. and Mrs. Arthur Fleming, Rubislaw House, Vancouver.

At midnight on August 15, Captain Fleming led a raiding patrol of one NCO and five ORs to destroy an enemy post in front of his company position at Sainte Elodie on the River Scarpe. When the patrol was about twenty yards from the post the enemy opened fire and Captain Fleming received facial wounds. He ordered his assault group forward under heavy fire from not one but three enemy outposts, each in platoon strength. The Canadian patrol engaged the enemy with hand-grenades and small-arms fire until their ammunition was exhausted. Severely wounded before dawn and unable to withdraw from his entrenched position, Captain Fleming set his patrol an example of endurance to which they fully responded until their company advanced and occupied the enemy's front-line trenches.

Mr. and Mrs. Arthur Fleming said today at Rubislaw House

"Where's the rest of it?" said Tom.

"The rest of it? That's all *I* saw."

Tom smiled his twisted smile. A photograph of himself in uniform, taken before his regiment embarked for Europe, had been inset in the new paragraph, which described his parents' anxiety and pride. Someone, with the shrivelling tact he must get used to, had cut it from the printed page.

"What rot they write," he said. "Entrenched position, I like that! We were pinned down in a shell hole, all that night and half the next day. You say my mother sent you this?"

"Yes, and Dorothy did too."

"They've been very active. But you should have seen the story in the Toronto *Star!*"

Nancy was silent. "Maybe you *did* see it?" he persisted. "But mother wouldn't have sent that one on, nor Dossy, bless her heart. Who did?"

"It was my father, Tom. It ran in the *Post-Intelligencer*."

Tom Fleming winced. "Well," he said. "I knew it was a case of British Columbia papers please copy; I didn't know I'd hit the headlines in Seattle too."

"Tommy, it was ages ago, it's all forgotten now."

"No it's not."

"It will be soon. And I could *kill* that Limey war correspondent."

Tom almost smiled again at the sight of the small clenched fists. "At least the guy was up front, since he got as far as the field hospital; I reckon he deserved to get a story. And Rennie, poor kid, had a right to express his own opinion—before he died."

"To tell a newspaperman the whole patrol would have been saved if you'd surrendered to the German officer?"

"It was the truth, Nan, as far as Rennie knew it."

"But the way it was written up! It made you seem like a monster!"

"Perhaps I am," said Tom. "That's the very word Private Rennie's mother used when she wrote to tell me what she thought of me. Sergeant Fowlie's widow just said I was a murderer."

"They didn't realise how badly you were hurt yourself."

"They only knew the whole patrol was dead, except for me."

"Do *you* think any of their lives would have been saved if you'd surrendered?"

"That's what I'll never know."

"But you weren't *supposed* to surrender! Your colonel must have thought you did the right thing, or you wouldn't have got the MC for it!"

"Oh, the gongs come up with the rations, you ought to know that by now."

"But have you actually got it? The medal, I mean?"

"Good Lord, I haven't got it on me, what do you take me for? I sent it home to Dad and Mother."

"They'd be thrilled, of course. But Tom, when did you get to go to Buckingham Palace? I thought you went straight to Scotland when you left Shorncliffe."

"It wasn't a Palace job, this one. The Prince of Wales came down to Shorncliffe Camp and held a hospital investiture."

"Isn't he *divine*?" breathed Nancy.

"He's a nice little guy. Now, that's enough about me, Nancy; tell me about you, and what goes on at your canteen."

26

Fun, said Nancy, with the anxiety in her eyes changing to a sparkle, fun was what went on all day at her particular branch of the US Canteen Corps. She hoped soon to be promoted to the Victoria Station branch; she was *dying* to get out to France. It was fun to be in London, and the air raids were exciting, last Thursday the anti-aircraft guns began at five in the morning, and she and her room-mate, Linda, sat around in their bath-robes drinking coffee till the raid was over. They worked in shifts at the canteen, the supervisor was a mean old thing but the other girls were good sports, and then, it was a privilege to wait on so many of the boys who'd given up everything to come over here and join in the struggle for democracy.

"That's quite a spiel, Nancy, you should be back in the States selling Liberty Bonds," approved Tom. "It's taken your dough-boys three years to get off their backsides and into the struggle for democracy; our First Division sailed for Europe less than eight weeks after the war began."

"Say, did you ever hear of the Declaration of Independence?" asked Miss Macpherson with spirit. "We didn't have to get into a British row just because Canada did. But now we're in we'll win the war, you'll see!"

"That's up to Black Jack Pershing," said Tom indifferently. "Let's hope he does better in France than he did in Mexico. He couldn't even catch Pancho Villa, remember?"

Nancy refused to rise to the bait. "I'm very glad to be helping out," she said, "even if it *is* only serving doughnuts to doughboys."

"I'm surprised your father allowed you to take a job like that. He's up to his eyes in business, I suppose?"

"Dad? Yes, and living in terror of a possible strike on the Seattle waterfront."

"He was probably glad to get you off to Europe before he found you on a picket line outside the Equator piers."

So far, Nancy had taken his surliness meekly enough. She knew intuitively that in his bitterness and humiliation Tom Fleming was making his old playmate into a whipping-boy. But now there was angry colour in her cheeks as she retorted, "Don't make me out a Red, please, Tom."

"A pinko, then, a parlour pinko. Remember the good old Wobbly days when Kathleen Mavourneen had you out on Skid Road singing 'The Red Flag'?"

27

"Kathleen Mavourneen? Oh, I remember you used to call her that, poor old Donovan. I haven't seen her for at least two years."

"Whatever happened to the great Dr. Donovan?"

"She got fired from her university job. Or rather, they just let her go when her contract expired, she never had tenure."

"Fired because of all that Wobbly stuff?"

"Of course that was the real reason. But they got her out on a technicality, for giving false information. When she applied for the instructorship she said she was a single woman, and it turned out she'd been married."

"Divorced?"

"No, she was a widow, that was just the point. Her husband was a Russian revolutionary, a Nihilist or an anarchist or something, and that was a bit too much for Washington U to take."

"I'll bet," said Tom. "Did she clear out of Seattle?"

"She got a job writing for a little pacifist weekly, published somewhere in back of Skid Road, but it folded when we got into the war. Then I heard she did leave town, but I don't know where. I'm through with all that," said Nancy positively. "From now on in, I believe in my country, right or wrong."

"The great awakening," said Tom. "What made you change your tune?"

"The two revolutions in Russia, as much as anything. You know, Tom," said Nancy, "I was *glad* when the Czar was forced to abdicate, and I believed the provisional government would do great things. A liberal government in Russia at last! Then when Alexander Kerensky became prime minister, the first socialist ever, that was better still. He seemed to be so full of reforming ideas, and at the same time true to the Allies, and then what happened? Lenin seized the power, and now there's murder and looting and destruction in Russia, and maybe famine and civil war to come. Everything that's happening now in Russia happened in 1789 in France, and all because the liberals started something they couldn't complete or control, and made it possible for the real terrorists to come to power."

"You may well be right," said Tom. His throat felt cramped; it was somehow ominous that this pretty girl, in the sheltered surroundings of the Ritz, should have mentioned Kerensky's name.

"I wish you weren't going to Finland, Tom."

28

God! was it possible she was reading his thoughts? "Why so?" he said.

"Because there's going to be a struggle between the Reds and the Whites there too."

"I don't suppose anything much can happen to a big guy like me between now and the first of February."

Nancy looked round at the emptying Palm Court and spoke urgently. "Tom, promise me you'll go back to Canada as soon as this job's done. They're all longing to see you again."

"Including brother Graham, who says men at his club have been 'questioning' him, whatever that may mean, about the story in the *Star*, and that stuffed shirt husband of Isabel's, who's afraid his political career will be ruined by my 'unfortunate publicity'?"

"They don't matter a damn, Tom. Think of your mother! She's longing to have you home to fuss over, and feed you up, and get you really fit again—"

"I don't want to scare her out of her senses with a face like this."

"Scare her! Your own mother! And darling, it isn't bad, not really *so* bad, and it's certain to get better—"

"I don't believe it."

That "darling" had slipped out in spite of Nancy's control, but Tom seemed unaware of it.

"Tom, why don't you grow a moustache?" she said.

The insensitive little bitch! Tom's overtaxed nerves snapped. "Did my mother put you up to trying to get me to go home?" he said.

"Nobody puts me up to anything, you know that."

"And nobody pushes me around, you know that too."

"I think it's time for me to be going," said Nancy Macpherson. "You mustn't miss your train."

"It doesn't leave till seven." But he signalled to the waiter to bring the bill. There was nobody left in the Palm Court but the children in uniform, who sat laughing and talking, extracting the last crumb of enjoyment from their tea party. Nancy felt blindly for her gloves and pulled them on. She was stunned with disappointment. She had hoped against hope that Tom Fleming's nerves had healed along with his body, but even in her inexperience she knew that this neurotic, impatient man was far from being healed.

29

"I really am sorry about tonight," he said, when the waiter went away in search of change. "I was planning to take you somewhere very nice for dinner. Only this thing came up—"

"Oh, it all worked out quite well," she said coolly. "About an hour after you called, two American officers we know stopped by the canteen and invited Linda and me to a première tonight. Lily Elsie and Owen Nares are opening in *The Charm School*, it ought to be sensational."

"I bet you get a lot of invitations, Nancy."

"Sure."

"You must be having a wonderful war."

"Let's go," she said, and led the way across the room, where the waiters were switching off the lights, and down the steps. An attendant helped them both into their overcoats.

"I'll take you back to the canteen, or wherever you want to go," said Tom. The doorman whistled for a taxi.

"I'm going home to Earl's Court to change," said Nancy, "and you're going to King's Cross. So we'd better say goodbye right here. Good luck to you in Finland, Tom!"

"Good luck to you too. Have fun at *The Charm School*."

"Thanks." In his morbid sensitivity, Tom thought she would shrink away if he tried to kiss her. He patted her uniformed shoulder, put her into the taxi, and watched her drive away through the London fog.

"You're in luck, sir," the doorman commented, as a second taxi deposited its fare at the entrance to the Ritz. "Often a long wait between cabs on a night like this." Tom tipped him in silence. "King's Cross," he told the driver. He was on his way to Finland.

But halfway along Piccadilly his heart smote him. That Nancy—she was a cute kid really; she had looked so pleased and eager coming into the Palm Court, and what had he done but slap her ears down and snub her for nearly everything she said? Kidding her about her crazy uniform and her pinko politics, and sneering at the tardy Yanks! "I can't leave her like that," he thought, and seeing a flower-shop still open on Charing Cross Road he told the driver to pull up and wait. There were not many blooms to choose from at that hour on a December night, but the salesman produced a pottery bowl with a dozen pink hyacinths, sturdy and sweet, just coming into flower. He promised that for taxi fare and a five bob tip his messenger would get it to Nancy's Earl's Court hostel within an hour. Tom wrote hastily on the card provided:

Dear Nancy, I'm sorry about this afternoon. I don't know what got into me. Please forgive me, and write me at the Society House Hotel, Helsingfors. Love, Tom.

He felt a good deal better after that—well enough to go with assurance about the routine which had meant such an effort at Glasgow only the night before, of getting his suitcases from the cloakroom and having a porter take them to the train. There was still time to go to the saloon bar for a drink.

The place was crowded. There was room for one more at the bar, but the bar had a plate glass mirror behind it, and Tom Fleming took his glass and perched on a windowsill, beneath a window which freely admitted the fog well mixed with railway engine smoke and dirt. There were sandwiches on the bar counter, but although he had barely touched the food at the Ritz, and restaurant cars on the trains now belonged to the past, he was not tempted to eat. The double Scotch and soda made his head spin a little after so many abstemious months, but also it did him good, and made him think more confidently of his promise to the Chief, and the coming rendezvous at the falls of Imatra. He noticed that the drinking being done was quick and heavy, as if other civilians like himself were trying to drown anxiety. The service men on the platform outside the bar were in uproarious spirits. There were a good many bluejackets among them, for the Scotch express was waiting to take men back from leave to the Fleet in Scapa Flow, and Tom's train to Hull would carry liberty-men returning to the destroyer flotilla lying off Parkeston. The noisiest group were soldiers bound for the Dovercourt garrison, some absorbed in farewells to their sweethearts and wives, but most armed with bottles of beer, and singing:

There's a dear old lady, Mother Britain is her name,
And she's all the world tae me—

Tom Fleming pricked up his ears. He knew the song; had heard Harry Lauder sing it in a show called *Three Cheers* at the

Shaftesbury Theatre almost exactly a year before. It had been a real show-stopper, with a detachment of the Scots Guards marching on to the stage for the finale, and the audience going into a frenzy of applause. Tom Fleming had clapped and cheered too, quite under Harry Lauder's spell, though even then he knew that the sentiment of the song was exactly what had sent himself and twenty thousand other young Canadians off to war. He was not bitter about that; what he remembered bitterly was the way that theatre evening had ended, after supper at the Trocadero, after the close-embraced taxi drive back to the girl's flat in Bayswater—in her bed, in her arms until the winter dawn. He had her telephone number, but he would never call that girl again, or any other like her, for desire was dead in him, and in the evasive answers of the doctors he read confirmation of his own fear that his internal wounds had been severe enough to deprive him of his manhood. He sat on his windowsill devoid of feeling, listening to the song, and guessing the redcaps would come along to interrupt the singing. The wonder was, after three years of a desolating war, that there was no derision in the unharmonious voices. They were belting the song out straight, with as much conviction as if these tired men in khaki weighed down with rifles and equipment were all before the footlights of the Shaftesbury:

> When we all gather round the old fireside
> And the fond Mother kisses her sons,
> A' the lassies will be lovin' a' the laddies—
> The laddies who fought and won!

3

THE ARRIVAL OF THE daily train from Petrograd was a matter of great interest to the citizens of Helsingfors in the winter of 1917. True, the interesting passengers were usually jostled about in a crowd of Russian soldiers, but there was always someone of note to be pointed out and stared at by the railway station loungers. It might be a group of the local Social-Democrats, swollen with importance at having been summoned to a conference with Lenin or another of the People's Commissars at the Soviet headquarters in the Smolny, or better still it might be one of the Commissars themselves, come to demonstrate his comradely affection for the Finnish workers. Once it had actually been Joseph Stalin, a rising young Bolshevik who had given a stirring address to the Social-Democratic Party Congress just before the declaration of independence. Between the revolutions of March and November, almost every day saw the arrival of a group of refugees, some hysterical with relief at having got out of Russia alive, others still quelled into silence after their long interrogation at Bielostrov frontier station.

For some of them, Finland was destined to be, at least for a time, the end of the journey. Those who had been clever enough to transfer funds to France, and who had influence in Paris, got visas from the French consulate in Helsingfors and continued on their way—the most fortunate of all to their own villas on the Riviera. Those who attempted to proceed to Britain were less fortunate, for Czarist refugees were not welcome there. King George V was the former Czar's first cousin, but that did not influence Lloyd George's cabinet, who had decided that the arrival of Nicholas II and his family in England would cause enough strikes in the docks, mines and munitions factories to destroy the whole war machine. There had been too many stories of Russian pogroms and the Pale, the knout and the Black Hundreds and the prisoners in Siberia to make the Romanovs, or even their adherents, acceptable in Britain.

The refugees who owned houses in the pleasant surroundings of Helsingfors, used in pre-war days as summer holiday homes, made off in that direction as inconspicuously as possible, took down the shutters and were still there when the November revolution erupted in Petrograd.

On the afternoon of December 18, when the train from Russia was as usual hours late, it carried one passenger conspicuous in any company, and never more so than at that moment. He was travelling in some degree of comfort, though the red plush and lace curtains of his "soft" carriage were woefully stained and torn, and even, since he was accompanied by his orderly, in some degree of military style. Amazingly, he was dressed in the uniform of a general in the Imperial Russian Army, in which he had served all his life, and which, even after the March revolution and the Czar's abdication, he had not considered leaving while Russia was still at war.

His name was Gustaf Mannerheim.

He was a man of fifty, usually taken (and secretly proud to be taken) for ten or even fifteen years younger. On this bleak December day, with the last of the light turning to a sullen grey the innumerable creeks and bays surrounding Helsingfors, he looked older than his age, with deep lines carved in his handsome face and new wrinkles round the eyes he had never closed during the tedious trip from Petrograd. For if he shut his eyes he saw at once the great pool of blood spreading across the railway platform at Mohilev, where his train had stopped on the long journey from Odessa. His old friend, the Imperial Chief of Staff, had been shot dead there by a rabble of soldiers when he came by appointment to meet the Bolshevik Commander-in-Chief. Blood was the motif of Mohilev, where Nicholas II had bidden farewell to his mother and his staff before departing for his imprisonment at Czarskoe Selo.

Whenever he thought of Mohilev, Mannerheim remembered the Czar's coronation day. He had been one of the four officers of the Chevalier Gardes who stood motionless on the steps of the throne, helmets in one hand, drawn sabres in the other, during the long ceremonial of the crowning. Such splendour, such piety, such autocracy, to end in a railway carriage halted at a wayside station!

In the Russian capital, as at Mohilev, Mannerheim had looked

34

calmly into the grim face of revolution. Ignoring Lenin and the comrades of the Smolny, he had spent a week in Petrograd, hearing the names of officers he had served with, shot dead by their own men, seeing houses where he had been welcome burned to the ground. But never, even among men who hated and feared the Bolsheviks who had supplanted Kerensky, had he heard that they were prepared to overthrow the Bolsheviks and bring Kerensky back, or to deliver the Czar and his family from their Siberian prison. The fecklessness inherent in the Russian character plunged the survivors of the November days into a torpor of inactivity. For Gustaf Mannerheim, always a man of action, there was only one personal solution. Still wearing the general's uniform which any Bolshevik might have taken as an incitement to murder, he applied for and received a travel permit under the only description which now fitted him: a Finnish subject on his way home.

He was a Finn by birth, although he had lived outside his native land for thirty years. His family had come from Sweden, four generations back, and it was by its Swedish name that he thought of his boyhood's home as Villnäs, which the Finns called Louhisaari. The estate had passed into the hands of another branch of the family, and the Mannerheims of his own generation were scattered now. The general's eldest brother, a Finnish patriot, resisted the Russification of his country so vigorously that he had been expelled from Finland, and died in exile. A brother and sister went to Sweden, another brother emigrated to South Africa. But there were two sisters still in Helsingfors, and General Mannerheim would have a roof to shelter him on this troubled night.

A roof above his head, and little else. He leaned his elbow on the windowsill, sunk his chin in his cupped hand and considered his position. He had never thought of himself as a lonely man, for his charm and intelligence had gained him many friends, but no close ties bound him to domestic life. For years he had lived separated from his Russian wife, and his two daughters, young ladies now, had, like their mother, gone to live abroad. Since the outbreak of war he had had no home of his own. His personal possessions and household goods were in storage in Poland, where he had served for seven years, and he thought regretfully of the souvenirs of a great ride across Asia in his younger days. The temple horns from Lhasa, the prayer rug given him by an old lama, and the Buddha he carried home on the pommel of his saddle would probably never be seen again.

Up ahead he could see the lights of Helsingfors beyond the Tölö lake. The train ran through the freight yards, came alongside the platform and pulled up with a jerk that almost threw Gustaf Mannerheim from his seat. He stretched his tall body wearily, put the white fur hat squarely on his head, and stepped down into his country's future.

There had been chaos at the Finland Station when he left Petrograd, and there was chaos in a milder form at Helsingfors, for a train from Åbo on the west coast had arrived ten minutes earlier, and all the new arrivals were being marshalled through a check-point set up by the Red Guards. In the complaining crowd there were many who glanced sideways at the tall man in Imperial uniform followed by an orderly carrying his military valise. Tom Fleming, who had just arrived from Åbo, recognised the uniform, for he had once seen a party of Russian general officers on a visit to the French front, and he too looked with interest at the man whose face showed no impatience as he stood in line, and no emotion when the Red Guard behind the trestle table scanned his travel permit with astounded eyes. General Mannerheim walked away with his orderly behind him and disappeared into the gloom of Helsingfors.

✳   ✳   ✳

The manager of the Society House Hotel saw Tom Fleming carrying his suitcases across the Railway Square. It was almost quite dark, and raining, but the lights from the tramcars fell upon the cobbles, and the stranger was clearly visible, advancing from the dark to the light and disappearing into the dark again while the manager looked on. He was standing at the window of his private office, keeping an eye on the two Red Guards who had been lounging outside the door of the hotel for the past hour. The capital had been fairly quiet since the November rioting, but there had been disturbances in Åbo for the past forty-eight hours, and two armed Reds were perfectly capable of bursting in and demanding the contents of the petty cash box for the workers' cause. The manager sighed, and went out to the front desk to act as receptionist. Tom Fleming was making his way in by the revolving door.

"Mr. Fleming from London?" conjectured the manager, with a professional smile. "Welcome to Helsingfors! We've been expecting you for some days, sir; would you be good enough to register?"

"The trip took longer than I reckoned on." The newcomer slouched over the desk as he completed the complicated registration form, his face partly concealed by the loose flaps of a large fox cap. The beginning of a dark moustache was visible on his upper lip.

"I have a nice quiet room for you, Mr. Fleming," said the manager, taking down a key. "Number one hundred and twelve, one of our rooms with private bath, as you requested."

"Fine."

"And Mr. Baker asked me to hand you this letter as soon as you arrived. Will you come this way?"

They went through an empty lobby to the lift, passing the entrance to a dark and silent restaurant. The lift rose up through a dimly-lit region of broad landings where huge sofas and closed doors added to the general effect of desolation, and Tom said, "Not very busy, are you?"

"These are our banqueting floors, sir, and not many banquets are being given in Helsingfors these days. This way, please."

Room 112, at the far end of a corridor, was large and chilly, with two long windows and a high ceiling. The manager expressed the hope that Mr. Fleming would be comfortable.

Tom said, "I hope the restaurant isn't permanently closed?"

"Oh, certainly not, sir, but we have a staff problem at present, and close in the afternoons. A table d'hôte supper will be served from half past seven to nine; or, if you wish, I'll have bottled beer and sandwiches sent up to you directly."

"Don't bother," said Tom. "I had some food at a way station on the trip from Åbo."

The manager was about to speak, but a young porter came in with Tom Fleming's bags, and he thought the better of it. To evince too much interest in the latest news from Åbo might perhaps not be discreet. He bowed himself out, taking the porter with him, and Tom sat down in one of the two stiff armchairs, tossed his fur cap on the bed, unbuttoned his overcoat, and opened Mr. Baker's letter.

December 12, 1917

Dear Mr. Fleming,

Welcome to Helsingfors! I am sorry not to greet you in person, but my health has deteriorated in the past two weeks, and I leave tomorrow for Gothenburg to undergo an operation. I trust you will find no insoluble problems at the office, where I shall hope to join you by the end of January. I have asked Miss Sandels to give you the keys of my apartment. If you would like to occupy it during your stay, I hope you will feel at liberty to do so. With all good wishes,

> Yours sincerely,
> James P. Baker.

Tom read this letter with dismay. It was too bad that the lie he told Mr. Ballantine had in fact come true, and that he had missed the old gentleman by a matter of days. Mr. Baker must have been arriving at Stockholm just as Tom's Swedish freighter, her captain roaring drunk, was wallowing round The Skaw. And then "Miss" Sandels; he hadn't bargained for a woman in the office, since the names of Mr. Baker's two Finnish clerks had been given to him as S. Sandels and N. Hirn. He got up and took his coat off, first removing his travelling flask from an inside pocket. He was not hungry, but the situation called for a drink.

In the little bathroom, which had obviously been partitioned off the bedroom, the water in the Cold tap was exceedingly cold, and so was the water in the Hot. Tom mixed whisky and water in a tooth-glass, took out his cigarettes and went back to the bedroom to look for matches. It was absolutely silent in room 112. He opened the dark brown curtains and looked out. There was nothing to be seen but the unlit windows of a few old wooden houses built round a small deserted courtyard, which accounted for the enveloping silence. After the days of smashing and shouting in Åbo, Tom found it very soothing. He sipped his drink and felt more cheerful. In spite of all the delays, he had got to Helsingfors with four days in hand before the meeting at the falls of Imatra.

He looked round the room appreciatively. It was not luxurious, but the large brass bed had a feather mattress, and was set between two marble-topped commodes each holding a small brass lamp with an orange silk shade. The top and the foot of the bed were padded with quilted satin in a rich shade of reddish brown, and the bedspread, over a down quilt of the same satin, was made of white crocheted lace. Just such a bed, he remembered, stood in one of the guest-rooms of Rubislaw House, having once belonged to his grandmother.

All at once he decided to go out. There was a telephone on the dressing-table, and unless the line was out of order it should be possible to telephone the J. P. Baker office and announce his arrival, for the business day had still an hour to go. But the probability of finding a Finnish speaker on the other end of the line, and some restlessness after an incredibly slow train journey, drove Tom downstairs and out of the hotel. He had an excellent sense of direction, and having bought a street map of Helsingfors while in Stockholm, had a very fair idea of the way to go. A railway map of Finland, and a Service pistol in a shoulder holster completed Tom's simple preparations for his new job.

"Mr. Fleming!" The anxious manager hurried after him as he put his hand on the revolving door. "You'll be careful if you're going out? Please be sure to show your papers to any Red Guard who may challenge you. You'll know them by their red armbands."

"I know how to identify them, thanks." Red armbands— he'd seen plenty of those in the streets of Åbo, and there were several groups of men at the street-corners of the Railway Square equipped not only with the armbands but with rifles slung on their shoulders, the bayonets fixed. Nobody challenged him, however, and he passed under the heavy Teutonic buildings of the square, through streets where there were some lighted shops, until he reached the Swedish Theatre at the top of the Esplanade. And here for the first time Tom Fleming became aware of the harsh beauty of Helsingfors in winter, with the black boughs of the leafless trees etched against the glow of light in the sky where his map had told him that the harbour lay. The Esplanade was a short but handsome avenue, with a central alley flanked by ornamental gardens dividing the north and south sides where the lights were going out in shops and office buildings and a number of Finnish business people were hurrying on their homeward way. Half a dozen Russian soldiers in filthy grey overcoats were arguing noisily outside the door of the Hotel Kämp. Tom crossed over to

39

the garden side to avoid them, passing the statue of a man on a pedestal among the dark trees, and crossing back almost at once to find the address he had been given on the North Esplanade. The number was above a narrow passage running between two shops into a courtyard very like the one beneath his bedroom window. But here there were signs of life, for several offices were lighted in the floors above the yard, and at ground level the steamy, uncurtained windows of a cheap restaurant revealed a score of Russians in tattered naval uniforms. They were drinking and singing, and though the windows were tightly closed a strong smell of cabbage diffused itself in the cobbled yard.

The name of J. P. Baker & Co. was painted up, with others, beside a flight of stairs opposite the eating-house. Tom Fleming climbed two flights and saw a crack of light beneath a door. He knocked, said "May I come in?" and opened it at once. A young woman rose from behind her typewriter to greet him.

"You must be Mr. Fleming, sir," she said. "Welcome to Helsingfors!"

"Why thanks," said Tom. "You're Miss Sandels, I suppose?"

"Sophie Sandels," she said with a little bow.

Tom looked around him. They were in a small outer office, furnished with two desks and four bentwood chairs, a hat-rack, a wooden stand for coats and a wall telephone. The window looked down on the courtyard and the sailors' restaurant. The woman facing Tom was at first sight severe, with light brown hair strained away from her pale face into a tight knob at the nape of her neck, and two sleeve protectors of black oilcloth, reaching to the elbows, gave her white shirt-blouse an almost military look. But her smile was shy and pleasant, and it occurred to Tom that she looked like a young woman in any one of the little French towns where the Canadians had gone into rest billets—the schoolmaster's daughter, perhaps, or the *curé*'s niece, better educated and more modest than the village girls who were all over the troops from the word go. He had seen girls like her standing in the background in some little square in the early days, when the Allied troops were greeted with wine and roses and shrill French cheers: diffident girls, smoothing down their Sunday aprons, hardly daring to join in the hurrahs.

"I'm glad to know you," he said, "but where's Mr. Hirn?"

"Mr. Hirn." She looked discomfited. "He left about an

hour ago. He recently joined the fire brigade and had to attend a drill this afternoon."

"The fire brigade!" said Tom. "D'you get many fires in Helsingfors in winter?"

"There's always a fire risk where there are so many wooden buildings."

"Well, all right," said Tom, "never mind that now. I've had a letter from Mr. Baker. I'd like to discuss it with you. Shall we sit down?"

"Let me take your coat, sir. Would you care to go into Mr. Baker's room? It's rather cold this evening, I'm afraid."

Tom realised that the scanty heat in the radiators was supplemented, in the outer office, by a portable oil stove.

"Let's stay here," he said. "I was sorry to hear Mr. Baker had to undergo an operation. But why in Gothenburg?"

"It seemed the wisest plan. His housekeeper left him at the time of the rioting in November and went home to her family in the north, and so the apartment wasn't very comfortable. Mr. Baker's daughter is married and lives in Gothenburg, and she persuaded him to have his operation in the Sahlgrenska hospital there."

"I wish I'd got here in time to see him. But the crossing from Hull was delayed, and then there was the stopover in Åbo—"

Sophie Sandels said quietly, "Was it really very bad in Åbo last weekend?"

Tom shrugged. "Some local hooligans went haywire, and did a pretty thorough job of smashing windows and looting all the shops. The rail traffic was at a standstill, and the police didn't seem to be much help."

"The Red Guard in Åbo threw the chief of police and the provincial governor into prison when the strike was on."

"Looks as if they're still inside, then. It was the foreign consuls who saved the situation: they appealed to the Ukrainian troops in the city to restore order."

Sophie Sandels closed her lips on what might have been a scornful word. She said, "I'm glad you got here safely, Mr. Fleming. Are there any particulars about the business you would like me to give you now?"

"Let's leave all that until the morning, Miss Sandels. Do you live near here?"

41

"Oh, not very far away. Just over the hill, on the other side of Union Street."

"Maybe I ought to see you home. There are a lot of drunks around, and that rabble downstairs seem to be celebrating something."

"I'm quite accustomed to walking home alone." But Sophie made no further protest; she put on an unbecoming dark green hat with an elastic band which snapped beneath her coil of hair, pulled off the sleeve protectors and allowed Tom to help her into a heavy coat. She took up an umbrella.

"Was it raining when you came in, Mr. Fleming?"

"Just a little."

"You're well equipped for a Finnish winter," she said with the hint of a smile for his furlined coat and heavy boots.

"I bought all this gear in Stockholm. I thought I'd be wading through snow in Helsingfors."

"You will be soon." They went downstairs, past the shouting Russians, and out into the North Esplanade. Tom saw a droshky pulling up at the door of the Hotel Kämp. "Here's a bit of luck," he said, "a cab! Hey, driver!"

The driver heard the shout and waited for them. Tom hurried Sophie along the pavement. The soldiers he had seen earlier had moved away into the gardens where the statue stood, and one of them was vomiting copiously at the foot of the pedestal.

"Oh, that really is too bad!" said Sophie Sandels, but Tom told her abruptly to give the driver her address. His only comment was, "The Russian officers don't seem to keep much discipline."

"They've shot their officers . . . Oh! He's taking us the long way round."

"Doesn't matter." All he wanted was to get her home, out of this sinister half-darkness, those streets in which ordinary life was so strangely overlaid with danger. "D'you live with your family, Miss Sandels?"

"All the family I've got left. My little sister and I share a small flat near the Kaisaniemi park."

"Does she work in an office too?"

"Yes, in a bank. I wanted her to go to university, but it just couldn't be managed." They were now driving along a broad street laid with tram lines, a street of tenement houses with little shops at street level, obviously a much poorer quarter than the

North Esplanade. The droshky turned right and stopped almost at once in front of a three-storey apartment building.

"Thank you for bringing me home, sir. Do you want the man to take you back to your hotel, or may I—" Sophie hesitated— "may I invite you to have a cup of coffee with my sister and me? Lisa always gets home first and has the coffee ready."

The brief spurt of energy which had driven Tom out of his hotel room was long since exhausted. To chat, to rest for half an hour was very tempting. "I'd like that," he said, "just so you stop calling me sir."

The lobby of the building was lighted by a gas jet, and so feebly that Tom bruised his shin on a toboggan, left by some child in the hopeful expectation of snow. There was a baby's perambulator beneath the stairs. "We live here," said Sophie, opening a door on the first landing. "Do come in, Mr. Fleming . . . Why! the place is in darkness!"

Close at hand they heard the striking of a match.

4

SOPHIE SANDELS MUST HAVE turned up the bead of gas inside a wire-shaded bracket, for suddenly an incandescent burner glowed with white light. Tom found that they were in a tiny lobby, with pegs for hats and coats and a shelf for overshoes, and doors opening to the right and left. "Let me take your coat and hat, Mr. Fleming," she said clearly, and, hanging them up, opened the door on the right. The room beyond was lit only by two candles, whose tiny flames had just caught alight, and a fair-haired boy and girl were sitting, stiff and self-conscious, in horsehair armchairs on each side of the hearth. The girl's face looked as if it had been pressed, only a moment before, against the boy's rough jacket.

"I didn't think you'd be back so early," blurted out the girl, and the boy, much more composed, got up and bowed. "Good-evening, Miss Sandels," he said.

"Are you economising on paraffin?" said Miss Sandels coldly. "Lisa, this is Mr. Fleming from London, you knew he was expected at the office."

"Welcome to Helsingfors, sir. Mr. Baker told us all about you." The pretty fair-haired girl dropped a little curtsy and gave Tom her hand. He thought the curtsy was a deliberate guying of a schoolgirl's manners. Little monkey, he thought with amusement, they were petting, and big sister's mad.

But big sister, serenely enough, was explaining, "Mr. Fleming, this is Mr. Heiden from Switzerland, a new neighbour of ours."

The boy, who had unobtrusively put on a pair of spectacles, bowed over Tom's offered hand and said in the European way:

"Boris Heiden."

"I made the coffee, Sophie," Lisa said.

"Then please go and put the cups and saucers on a tray."

As she spoke, Sophie Sandels was lighting a paraffin lamp of the old-fashioned student variety, and explaining to Tom that the gas and electricity pressures had been so low since the strike that she

44

had gone back to using lamps and candles for much of the time. She placed the lamp on a round table, covered with a green felt cloth, which occupied the centre of the living room. By its light what had been shadowy in the candles' glow sprang to sharper life: the walls papered in a dark green striped with black and covered with photographs and watercolours, the china plates arranged on an oak ledge which ran round the room about a foot beneath the ceiling, a canterbury and a bookcase with glass doors. Tom was invited to sit on the horsehair sofa, the place of honour in any Finnish parlour of that time.

"Boris, put some logs on the fire if you want to make yourself useful!" said Lisa pertly, and followed her sister from the room. Tom heard Sophie's voice, speaking in a foreign language, raised rather sharply above the chink of teaspoons and china. The other guest, with a smile at him, dropped to his knees beside the square tiled stove and opened its little door.

A large wicker basket filled with birch logs stood on the empty hearth beneath a mantel, draped in swags of crimson cloth finished with a ball fringe, on which the lighted candles stood. On the wall behind them, hung rather high, was the coloured picture of a blonde girl clutching something to her breast against a background of rocks and a stormy sea. Heiden took two logs from the basket and placed them inside the white glazed stove, which was decorated with trails of wild roses in pink and green. As the flames leaped up Tom saw his face more clearly.

It was a nondescript face, with blunt, slightly Slavic features, and the chin was covered with wispy blond hair like a boy's first attempt at a beard. Both the Sandels girls were tall, and Heiden was no taller than Lisa and slightly built, but his body was muscled and compact, and the movements of his hands were neat and economical. He wore a jacket and trousers of some rough dark material like frieze, the trousers being tucked into high boots reaching to his knees. His expression, when he smiled at Tom, was placid and friendly.

"That thing gives out a lot of heat," said Tom, nodding at the stove.

"Old-fashioned, perhaps, but very useful in the winter. As Miss Sandels said, the heat in this building isn't up to much just now."

"Do you rent an apartment here?"

45

"Oh no, sir, I'm only a student. I share a room with another man in Mrs. Rentola's apartment on the floor above."

"At the university, eh?"

Heiden stood up. "Shall I leave the stove open?" he said. "The firelight's cheerful. Yes, I enrolled at the university at the beginning of the session, but classes have been irregular for the past two months, and I'm trying to earn a little money by freelance journalism."

"Using what language?"

"German. I've got some useful contacts with the Swiss newspapers."

"And you're studying— ?"

"Political science."

"Well!" said Tom, "I envy you your languages. What a break for me that you all speak English so well!"

"We have to!" said Lisa, coming in with the coffee tray. "Mr. Fleming, what language are *you* going to speak in the logging camps?"

"You'd be surprised," said Tom. "I've got quite a vocabulary of logging German. My father employs a lot of Galicians, and I picked up a bit from them."

"Galicians?" said Heiden. "In Canada?"

But before Tom could explain Lisa Sandels interrupted with a spoilt child's imperiousness: "My sister is making some—some pieces of bread for you, Mr. Fleming. She says you've had a long journey, and must be hungry. We're all to take our places round the table and have some coffee while we wait for her."

"I hope she's not going to a lot of trouble."

The coffee was excellent, and Lisa poured it with a flourish intended to show off a slender wrist. She was a strikingly pretty girl, with large grey eyes and very fair hair cut short, springing out round her face in waves that foamed, or so Tom thought, like a lemon soufflé.

"You work in a bank, do you, Lisa?" he said.

"Yes, in the Private Bank. I don't like it much."

"Lisa likes going to the Biograph show better than banking," Boris Heiden said.

"I don't blame her."

Sophie Sandels carried in a second tray and put two plates on the round table. One held squares of rye bread piled with hard-boiled egg and anchovies, the other, little stars of hot pastry stuffed with a prune mixture, a specialty, she said, of the Christmas season now beginning. "They were already made, and I warmed them in the oven," she told Tom, "just to celebrate your visit. You haven't had much of a welcome to Finland so far!"

"I think this is a great welcome, Miss Sandels. I was hungrier than I realised," said Tom. He didn't want to hack through the tale of the Åbo rioting again, so he told them a funny story about his two days in Stockholm, waiting for the boat, and going to Rolf's cabaret one night to see a performance by well-known British variety artistes, intended to be a machiavellian piece of British propaganda in that pro-German city. Lisa giggled, always glancing at Heiden to see if he thought it funny too, and Miss Sandels laughed aloud. She looked younger in her own flat than she had done in the office, with her hair slightly ruffled and her face flushed from the heat of the gas stove. Tom felt cheerful and at home. The Chief's phrase, "a safe house", came to his mind. This was a safe house, although not in the Chief's sense; not for a fortune would he ask those two nice girls to shelter British agents, or become involved in any intrigue whatever. He simply felt relaxed, taken for granted, not stared at but accepted, and he leaned back in his chair, enjoying the mingled scent of good food and birch logs and of the white Roman hyacinths which grew, fragile and tall, in a ceramic bowl on top of the canterbury. Then Heiden rose to offer cigarettes, and Tom saw his dark shadow on the wall.

"You had an interesting journey from London to Helsingfors," said Heiden, and Tom answered, "I sure did. And oh, say" (remembering) "just about the most interesting thing was right at the end, when my train came in tonight. I saw a man get off the Petrograd train, wearing a Russian general's uniform, as bold as brass with his soldier-servant at his heels, and he sailed past the Red Guards at the check-point with his nose in the air. Mannerheim, I heard them call him." He was not prepared for the effect upon two of the company.

"*Mannerheim!*" said Heiden, and stood stock still with a spent match in his hand.

"General Mannerheim!" Sophie sprang to her feet; her face was radiant. "Here in Helsingfors tonight! Home in his own country in her hour of need!"

"Oh, Sophie, how you love to dramatise," said Lisa.

"Miss Sandels is a patriot," murmured Heiden.

"Good for you," said Tom to Sophie, and she blushed.

"You'll have to tell me about General Mannerheim," Tom continued. "I'm afraid we didn't hear much about him on the western front."

"Nobody heard much about him on any front," said Boris Heiden, and Sophie flung out, "For shame, Mr. Heiden! General Mannerheim has been in action ever since 1914, in the Carpathians first, and then in Bessarabia. His record is as good as any general officer's in the Russian army."

"Perhaps." Heiden made his hostess a little bow. "But I doubt if a Czarist general will last very long in Helsingfors. Remember, he was a *général à la suite* to the former Czar, and married the daughter of the Chief of Police of St. Petersburg: I don't know how he got out of Petersburg alive."

"I don't know how you know so much about the Russian court," said Tom.

"My late father held a minor post at court." Heiden turned to Tom. "In fact I was born in St. Petersburg, which we must now call Petrograd. My mother and I took Swiss nationality some years ago."

"Baroness Heiden has a beautiful house in Zürich," Lisa put in.

"I resent what you said about the general as a soldier." Sophie stuck to her point. "In 1905 he fought bravely at Sandepu, and again at Mukden. If he had been the Commander-in-Chief instead of Kuropatkin, Russia might have won the war against Japan."

"I wonder you can bear to mention it," said Lisa, but Sophie appeared to pay no attention.

"You've been in Helsingfors how long? three months," she said to Heiden. "You can't possibly know how much respected the Mannerheims are, or how much a part of our national history. If Gustaf Mannerheim wishes, he can rally powerful friends and followers here. Because he never forgot his friends, Mr. Heiden; even my poor father in his misfortunes; for years we had his cards of greeting, and oh! now I remember—"

She knelt down before the canterbury, and took out an inlaid mahogany box. "We keep our special treasures here," she said, looking up at Tom—and now he saw that her eyes were a beautiful dark grey—"we have a picture of the general, which belonged to our father."

Sophie got up and laid the picture underneath the lamp. It showed a strikingly handsome young man in a white uniform, wearing a helmet and high jackboots, and carrying a sword. It was signed in a bold hand: G. Mannerheim.

"The helmet was silver, and the supervest was scarlet, emblazoned with the Order of Saint Andrew," Sophie said. "Mustn't he have looked magnificent?"

"I guess so," said Tom, "but he doesn't look very like the gentleman I saw getting off that train tonight."

"This photograph was taken nearly thirty years ago! He was only an ensign in the Chevalier Gardes then."

"The splendour of a vanished age," said Heiden softly, and Sophie retorted, "The splendour of today! And tonight, the night he came home to Finland, I'm going to put his picture in the place of honour."

She set the old photograph on the mantelpiece between the candles, under the picture of the girl alone on a wild seashore, and said softly:

"Mannerheim! *Sans peur et sans reproche!*"

Tom glanced instinctively at Heiden. Behind the concealing spectacles he caught a gleam of pure hate in the young man's eyes.

"I'm sure Sophie thinks we ought to drink a toast to General Mannerheim," said Lisa, "but there isn't any wine. Let's have another cup of coffee instead."

"I've had two already, and I mustn't outstay my welcome," declared Tom. "Time to be going!"

"I'll see you on the way to your hotel," said Heiden.

*   *   *

In not much more than an hour the evening had grown colder. Tom tied the earflaps of his fox cap tighter, and was surprised to see that Heiden walked along bare-headed, with his ungloved hands in the pockets of a short leather jacket. They turned to the left when they emerged from the side street where the sisters lived, and almost at once had to step off the pavement to avoid being jostled by a crowd of men going purposefully in the same direction.

49

"Hey!" said Tom, half stumbling in the gutter, "what's going on? There's a whole lot more folks around here than there were not so long ago!"

"This is Union Street, one of the main streets of the city. Most of those men have come over the Long Bridge from the workers' quarter, probably from the Workers' House itself. You may be going to see a demonstration, Mr. Fleming, on your very first evening in Helsingfors."

The tone was lightly mocking, and Tom grunted in reply. He was half a head taller than Heiden, and looked down suddenly at the Swiss under the light of a street lamp far brighter than Lisa's candles. It struck him that Heiden was an older man than he had thought. In spite of the boyish profile, the boyish wisp of beard, there was a hardening of the skin round the eyes and ears which told its own story. As if aware of his scrutiny, Heiden changed the subject.

"Charming girls, our hostesses," he said.

"Very."

"I was most fortunate in meeting them, so soon after I came to Helsingfors."

"I'll say you were."

"I hope Miss Sandels wasn't too much upset by what I said about Mannerheim. I only wanted to curb her enthusiasm—to prevent her, if I can, from making the mistakes her father made in 1905—"

"You're speaking as a student of political science?"

"Of political science, of course."

"I don't see what the hell Miss Sandels's political opinions have got to do with you."

They went up the slope of the hill, and the imperturbable Heiden pointed out the old Russian Orthodox church. "Where the Czars used to worship when they came to Helsingfors as Grand Dukes of Finland," he said. "They used to drive here at top speed to hear a Te Deum, and give thanks for having sailed down the Gulf from Petersburg without being blown to pieces by their loving subjects."

Tom laughed unwillingly.

"There's a Russian cathedral now, near the North Harbour. But the old place has a large congregation still; I went there only last Sunday with Lisa Sandels and her sister."

"The Sandels girls go to the Russian Orthodox church?" said Tom, surprised.

"I'm sure Miss Sophie calls it *Finnish* Orthodox," murmured Heiden. "But yes, that's their communion." He halted Tom with a touch on the arm. "You know, theirs really is a tragic story. Their father had a high place in the civil service, that is, the Russian service; the family lived in a handsome house near the Observatory Hill, and the older daughter, at least, had every possible advantage. Then Nicholas II, with the complicity of his ministers, began his policy of Russification. No Finnish constitution, no Finnish army, *Finis Finlandiae!* Whereupon Mr. Sandels is overcome by patriotism, loses his job, his house, his money, and ends on straw as a tallyman down at the docks. As Miss Sandels will end," he ended on a savage note, "if she continues to put her trust in Mannerheim."

"How do you know all this, Heiden? You're a newcomer to Helsingfors."

"My landlady told me all that, and more too, in twenty minutes by the clock."

Tom grunted. "Well, good for those two girls. At least they had the gumption to get out and earn their own living . . . Hey! Is this your demonstration?"

They stood at the top of a noble square, with a statue in the middle, beneath a broad flight of steps leading to the Lutheran cathedral, the great Nikolai Kirk upon whose white walls and blue star-studded cupolas now flickered the light cast by a hundred torches. On either side, the perfectly proportioned Empire façades of the University and the Senate House were enclosed by the fourth side of the square, a line of government buildings, behind which rose the glow Tom had observed from the Esplanade, cast by the riding-lights of nearly two hundred Russian ships of war in the great outer harbour. There were lighted windows in the Senate House, in front of which two city policemen stood on guard.

Two policemen, confronting a thousand men in high boots and leather jackets like Heiden's, wearing flat working-men's caps or fur hats and cheap scarves or mufflers twisted round their necks. Some were carrying torches, all were equipped with the armbands and the fixed bayonets of the Red Guard, and they were drawn up in a ragged formation facing the Senate House. A hum of talk rose from the ranks.

51

"What do you think of them?" Heiden asked.

"They seem orderly enough. What's going on inside?"

"At a guess, an anxious gentleman named Per Svinhufvud is telling the Senate about a speech he means to make to the assembled Diet, possibly tonight, certainly in the immediate future. It will be one of his usual predictions of doom and disaster, followed by an emotional appeal to the Great Powers to recognise the independence of Finland. Mr. Svinhufvud is a realist, or he ought to be, for the Czar sent him to Siberia for three years, and that should have taught him realism—he knows perfectly well that the first recognition to be won is the recognition of Russia. The Powers won't move without it; and if Mr. S. didn't know it already, every Allied consul left in Helsingfors has been telling him so for the past two weeks. And that's not my landlady's gossip, Mr. Fleming: it's been in all the newspapers."

"So you think even an independent Finland is still dependent on the Russian favour?"

"Absolutely . . . Are you cold? The temperature is dropping, we'll have snow before midnight."

"I'm cold and tired," said Tom. "As a demonstration, this doesn't compare with the last two nights in Åbo. What the hell do those chaps think they're doing?"

"Tonight they're only here as a reminder. Last month they broke in and occupied the Senate House, they're not quite ready for a repeat performance."

"Well, I'm going home," said Tom. "And I hope you know where you are, because I don't believe we're anywhere near the Railway Square."

Heiden laughed. "It's not very far away. I imagine your droshky took you the long way round, but if you go back down Government Street—here, to the right—you'll be outside the Seurahuone in five minutes."

"The— ?"

"You'll have to learn a few words of Finnish, Mr. Fleming, if it's only the name of the Society House. You won't mind if I don't come any further? I'd like to stay and watch awhile."

"Sure, I'll be all right. See you around, maybe. Good night."

"Good night."

52

Tom looked back after he had gone a dozen paces in the direction of the hotel. Heiden was still standing on the corner, looking across the square, with his hands deep in the pockets of his leather jacket. Fleming remembered the dark shadow which had fallen across the green wallpaper in the friendly parlour, and looked for a similar shadow on the freezing cobbles of the square. But Boris Heiden was standing midway between two street lamps, and cast no shadow where he stood.

5

THERE WAS NO REMAINING trace of any demonstration when Sophie Sandels walked along Union Street on her way to work next morning. She was half an hour earlier than usual, for she wanted to reach the office before the cleaner left to make sure the private room was comfortable for Tom Fleming, but already the street sweepers were at work with their twig brooms, removing the night's snowfall from the cobbles. Snow lay on the head and shoulders of the statue in the middle of the square. It was a memorial to the Czar Alexander II, whom some Finns called "the good emperor" because his policy towards the Grand Duchy had been so much more humane than that of his two successors. He had freed the serfs in Russia, but that had not saved him from death by an assassin's bomb.

If Sophie had been in a mood to remember, the symbols of death were close about her as she swung down the slope towards the gardens of the Esplanade. Bobrikov, as brutally repressive a Russian governor-general as Finland ever knew, had died in the Senate itself at the hands of a Finnish patriot called Eugene Schaumann, who then committed suicide; and Bobrikov's murder had ushered in the whole train of reprisals which had kindled the latent patriotism of Sophie's father and a thousand others. But her thoughts were not on violent death that morning. It was still, of course, pitch dark, but the stars were shining, and the thought of Mannerheim's return to Helsingfors gave a new buoyancy to her spirit and her step. The tramcars running across the foot of the square were full of office workers like herself, beginning the business day, and all, for the moment, was ordinary and peaceful in Helsingfors.

There was a supplementary electric fire in Mr. Baker's room, not very powerful, but less pungent than the paraffin stove, and Sophie switched it on while the charwoman dusted the empty desk and opened the window to let in a breath of the fresh snowy air. She was checking the ink well and pen nibs when she heard

54

a heavy step on the staircase, and the charwoman, opening the door to leave, stood aside for the entry of Mr. Nikolai Hirn.

He stared to see Sophie in the private room.

"Don't tell me Mr. Fleming's here at last!"

"Yes!" said Sophie. "He arrived yesterday afternoon, less than an hour after you left, Nikko!"

"Good heavens."

Nikko Hirn took off his sealskin hat and knitted gloves. He was a tall, unwieldy man with a jovial red face, now unusually solemn as he asked, "Did he enquire for me?"

"Of course he did. I told him you'd gone to a fire brigade drill. He seemed rather surprised, but he took it very well."

"If Mr. Baker approved, I don't see what Fleming's got to say."

"I'm sure he won't say anything, he's a very nice man, but I think he'd better know the truth, Nikko. After all, he's been a soldier himself—"

"Hey hey," said Nikko, diverted, "did you know Mannerheim was back?"

"I did," she said, glowing, "Mr. Fleming saw him coming off the Petersburg, I mean the Petrograd, train. What a blessing!"

"*Ja*," said Nikko Hirn deeply, "we shall have a leader now. Does Mr. Fleming speak any Swedish?"

"What do *you* think? But you'll get on with him, I know, he's very pleasant and informal, I suppose in a Canadian sort of way. He took me home in a droshky last night, so I asked him in for coffee, and he seemed glad to come up and spend an hour with us. Lisa said afterwards that he was stupid, but I don't agree; he was only rather quiet, and making up his mind about a lot of new things."

"What sort of things?"

"Well—Boris Heiden was there, alas, and Mr. Fleming made it perfectly obvious that he wasn't impressed by *him*."

Nikko grinned. "That was a pretty good start, as far as you're concerned. But look here, Sophie" (he had divested himself of his overcoat and galoshes now, and was sitting at his own desk) "has it ever occurred to you that this Mr. Fleming may not be entirely what he seems?"

"What *do* you mean?"

"I mean, why should Mr. Baker hire a man with Mr. Fleming's

55

background—and pay him next to nothing, we both know that—to come to Finland for such a short time, *just* to visit saw-mills and write reports? With no Finnish, obviously, and now you say no Swedish too? The whole thing arranged through London, with heaven knows who behind Ballantine and Macaulay, eh? Isn't it just possible that Mr. Fleming might be a British agent, keeping an eye on our friends across the border?"

"I suppose it is possible," said Sophie slowly, "but I don't think so. You'll understand as soon as you see him. His poor face is even worse than Mr. Baker was told, and maybe he—" She held up her hand with a warning gesture, for she had recognised Tom Fleming's step on the wooden stair.

Introductions followed, and almost before Nikko had offered the ritual "Welcome to Helsingfors!" the post arrived. Among the letters there was one from Mr. Baker's daughter in Gothenburg, which Sophie translated, announcing that her father's operation was safely over, and the doctors very pleased with his condition. This good news broke the ice of the first morning, and the Canadian, bringing his chair into the outer office and lighting a cigarette, cheerfully asked the two regular members of the staff "to put him wise to the whole operation".

As they talked (Sophie frequently helping her colleague with an English translation) Tom Fleming studied S. Sandels and N. Hirn. He had expected Mr. Baker's staff to consist of two junior clerks, both boys, and behold! one of them was a charming woman of about thirty, and the other a man nearer forty-five than forty, who could certainly not be rebuked by a newcomer from London for taking time out for fire-fighting drill. But a bigger surprise was the extent of J. P. Baker & Co.'s business, which had not been fully explained to him by Mr. Ballantine. Mr. Baker was much more than the representative of a London firm of selling agents. He had built up a business on his own account in hand-sawn timber bought directly from peasants in the interior of the country, and exported in the same steamers as carried the machine-sawn timber from the inland mills to British and continental ports. He was a major shareholder in the company which owned these vessels, registered as the Sampo Line, and had recently bought a half share in a processing firm producing pulp and cellulose. Nikko Hirn had been delegated to handle all these subsidiary interests in Mr. Baker's absence, while Tom would

56

look after the Ballantine and Macaulay account. This gave him an excellent opportunity, just before the early luncheon break, of announcing that he would visit the Broberg Saw-mills first.

"I think you're very wise, Mr. Fleming," said Miss Sandels, "to get the longest journey over and done with. It *is* a long way to Imatra, you know; it's not very far from the Russian border." She was aware of Nikolai Hirn's speculative eye, and added hastily, "I only hope the train will run on time, or run at all!"

"I'll take a chance on that," said Tom, "get me a ticket for the east-bound on Friday morning, please. But first off, put in a call to Mr. Broberg himself and make sure he'll be on hand to see me."

"Certainly, sir. Mr. Baker's a very old friend of Mr. and Mrs. Broberg, he always enjoys spending the evening at Imatra manor."

"But I can't impose myself on them, a total stranger; call the Valtio Hotel and get a room for me for Friday night."

"Should I ask them to send a sleigh to meet you at the main-line station?"

"Please do."

It seemed a little early to go out for lunch at eleven o'clock, but Tom deferred to the custom of the country, and asked Nikko Hirn to be his guest. Nikko was a widower, living in a modest pension in the Third Line of Berghäll, across the Long Bridge; he said he often ate in the taverns and cafés of the waterfront, and suggested one not far away on the South Quay. When they went out Tom Fleming saw Helsingfors by daylight for the first time, with the façades of its miniature palaces tinged with rose by the winter sun shining through a frosty mist from the harbour, and every branch of every tree in the Esplanade sheathed in ice. He felt invigorated as they walked the few blocks to the South Quay. The little restaurant, furnished with booths for the diners and tables covered in clean coarse linen, was directly opposite a red brick, covered market, from which excellent fish was bought by the proprietor. Fish, potatoes, a piece of cheese and some good coffee made the simple meal.

After it was over they walked along the wharves, and Nikko pointed out which doors, in a series of red-painted doors, were closed over the entrance to the Sampo Line piers. They could only catch a glimpse of the timber ships, with broad green lines round their hulls, lying at anchor. Nikko explained that most Finnish merchant ships normally left their home ports in winter, before the ice closed in, and earned their keep by tramping between the North Sea and the Mediterranean ports. The war had put a stop to much of this trading, and since the Russian warships came to Helsingfors—said Nikko—their mutinous crews were so suspicious of any harbour traffic that no Finnish vessel dared leave the port at all. There were Russian sailors on guard at all the dock gates, and Tom and Nikko faced levelled rifles when they tried to approach the Sampo Line wharf.

"But where the devil *are* they?" fretted Tom, for the South Harbour held nothing but fishing boats, a ferry steamer, and the passenger boats to Stockholm, which only ran in summer.

"They're lying out in the Kronberg firth, one of the finest landlocked harbours in Europe, with the only passage in under the guns of Sveaborg." Nikko pointed out the fortress islands in the bay, which the Royal Navy had ineffectually bombarded in the Crimean War. "The Russians rebuilt the fortifications years ago," he said. "More than once they trained the guns on Helsingfors; what do you bet, if we went out in a rowboat, we'd find the guns pointing at the city today?"

"No takers." They walked back in silence to the office, and Tom started to go through the back files relating to all the mills he was to visit. He was disgusted to find, as the early darkness fell, and the tap of Sophie's typewriter came hypnotically from the next room, that he was increasingly restless. The walls of Mr. Baker's room seemed to be closing in on him, and he only remained quietly at his desk by an effort of will. It was nearly three and a half years since any sort of office discipline had been imposed on him, and he remembered how he had chafed at the routine of the Toronto office after the free life of the western woods. It had not occurred to him that after three years in the trenches he would find a warm, dry office and a job he understood so hard to take. He was glad when the hands of his watch stood at half past four.

"Let's call it a day," he said to Sophie. "I'd like to stop by Mr. Baker's flat on my road home, if it's not too far out of the way. I expect he asked you to let me have the keys?"

"He did," said Sophie, getting up, "I put them in the office safe. And it's quite near your hotel, in fact it's in our own locality, near the Kaisaniemi park, but more secluded."

They walked through light flurries of snow, chatting as they went, and Sophie explained that Mr. Baker was an old friend of her family, who had employed her as his secretary seven years before, when her predecessor left to be married. "Before that I worked in a bank, like Lisa," she said, "but I much prefer working for Mr. Baker. Poor man, he had a bad time during the last few weeks. That fool of a housekeeper never even gave notice, she was so terrified during the November riots that she simply packed her bags and ran away; and then he felt so ill. I'm glad he's gone to Gothenburg, to Mrs. Jarrel."

Tom agreed. Nikko had told him that Mr. Baker had been suffering from a prostate complaint, and that he had been terrified, too, before he left for Sweden; Tom wondered what condition the flat would be in. They entered a very quiet street not far from the station, behind the National Theatre, it was only not a cul-de-sac by virtue of ending on the verge of the Kaisaniemi park, which stretched desolate and unlighted at the far end of the little street. Two belated urchins, one of them in tears, were trailing home with their toboggans.

The apartment buildings had been constructed in a heavy monumental style to match the theatre and were obviously lived in by prosperous tenants. Tom and Sophie could feel the warmth as soon as they opened the street door on a tiled lobby, and it was still warm when they entered Mr. Baker's flat, one of two on the ground floor of the building nearest to the park. The electricity had not been cut off, and the flat came alive at once.

"Is this the living room?" said Tom, pushing open the nearest door.

"The dining room. How empty it looks, without the silver and the Sèvres china in the cabinets! He had all his valuables taken to a strong-room." The glass-fronted cabinets indeed looked empty, the six chairs for the dining table were ranged against one wall. There was, however, a comfortable array of bottles on the sideboard.

"Liked his glass, did he?"

"In moderation. We'd better look into every room, he was dreadfully afraid of burglars."

The living room was more welcoming, although the velvet drapes had not been drawn, and the white muslin curtains embroidered in pale colours were transparent against the wood of the closed shutters. The walls were panelled, and the floor was of polished brown wood—not parquet—partly covered with two Finnish rugs. An incongruous note was struck by two bamboo rocking-chairs, one on each side of the beautiful porcelain stove, and there was an upright piano in one corner of the room.

They looked into three bedrooms, each, except for the bed, furnished like a sitting room, and the bed-linen was woven of the finest flax, lace-trimmed, embroidered and initialled. "Mrs. Baker was a wonderful housewife," commented Sophie. The bathroom was very old-fashioned, but the water ran hot in the taps and also in the kitchen sink. The only room which showed signs of neglect was the kitchen, where the taps and burners of the gas cooker were spattered with grease and the copper pans on the wall were turning green.

"What do you think of it, Mr. Fleming? I know Mr. Baker rather hoped you'd live here and look after the place."

"It's far too big for me. I don't want to be bothered with a housekeeper and all that for such a short time; I'm really better off at the hotel."

But he smiled when he said it; he was very satisfied with Mr. Baker's unoccupied apartment.

"It's beautifully warm," said Sophie enviously, "but I suppose it really is too big. This kitchen alone would keep a daily woman busy."

Tom nodded. His eye had been caught by a coloured picture above the cooking stove. "Isn't that the picture you've got above your mantelpiece?" he said.

"Like at least ten thousand other people. It used to be the most popular picture in Finland—*The Attack*, it's called. You see, the fair-haired girl *is* Finland, holding our Code of Laws—look at the *Lex* on the book, and the double-headed eagle is snatching it away from her—"

"The eagle being Russia, of course."

"Russia, robbing us of our Constitution. I wonder what it's doing in the kitchen. Did you know Mrs. Baker was a Finn? While she was alive it always hung in the dining room, above the sideboard."

"Perhaps she was a patriot, like you."

"She was indeed." Sophie had taken off her woollen gloves and was twisting them nervously.

"You were very kind to defend me last night," she said, "when Boris Heiden jeered at my patriotism."

"He was only kidding you a little bit."

"Kidding?"

"Making fun of you."

"I don't understand that kind of fun . . . But it made me think you might listen sympathetically to something Nikko wanted to tell you at lunch-time, only you went to a restaurant with booths, and he was afraid you would be overheard."

"I'm listening," said Tom, "let's go back to the living room and sit down. But take your coat off first, Sophie, else you'll catch a chill when we go out."

The Canadian informality took Sophie by surprise. There was colour in her cheeks as she allowed Tom to take her coat, and lay it on one of the rocking-chairs, while she sat down on an imitation Chippendale settee which stood by a small tea table. Tom Fleming pulled a chair up and sat down thankfully. He had to admit that standing for any length of time still tired him more than walking.

"Right!" he said. "What does Mr. Hirn want to tell me that he can't get around to saying for himself?"

"He wants to explain about the fire brigade."

"You mean the drill he took time out to attend yesterday?"

"Yes. He told Mr. Baker he was going to join, and Mr. Baker quite approved it—"

"Well, that's all right then, if they must have their drills in office hours. I'd have been sorry to think he was just soldiering on the job."

"Soldiering!" said Sophie, and caught her breath. "Oh, Mr. Fleming, that's exactly it. 'Fire brigade' is only another name for the Defence Corps, or Civic Guards, or White Guards they're sometimes called. There must be a group of volunteers in every town in Finland now—organised to protect the people against the Reds."

"Are they armed?" It was his instinctive reaction: he had seen a thousand Reds with rifles and bayonets outside the Senate, if the Whites were similarly armed there would be bloodshed.

"All the farmers have shotguns, and most of the townsmen have pistols or revolvers."

He could have told her that he had seen no sign of a Defence Corps in Åbo, where the Reds had had it all their own way till the Ukrainian troops took over. But he hated to disillusion a woman whose face had grown youthful with the force of her own feelings, the mouth softer, the grey eyes darker and more brilliant. He said, "The Reds have Russian weapons behind them, I'm afraid. Shotguns will be as much use as scythes and pitchforks against machine-gun fire, if it comes to a showdown."

"I thought—from what you said last night—that you sympathised with us."

"My dear girl, I do; but I think you were carried away last night, just because General Mannerheim had come back to Finland."

"It means we have a leader now."

"In Mannerheim? He may be all you say he is, but he's got no army and no arms; what can he do against the Reds and the Russians together?"

"David had no arms and no armour when he went out against Goliath."

"David had the right fire-power, a sling and a pebble, I learned that in Sunday School. Come, Sophie, this is pure fantasy. I'm all for a Defence Corps to keep order, for the police don't appear to be up to that, but the future of Finland will have to be settled by negotiation, not by street fighting and barricades—"

"You don't understand us yet," she said proudly. "You don't know what our resources are, either of the spirit or the fact. You think of Finland as a little lost, forgotten country up here on the edge of darkness: you don't realise that this is the moment when at last we can realise *ett Finlands varldsdrömma*—"

She had dropped into Swedish, but Tom understood in part, and, half fascinated, half repelled by her passion, he tried to calm her by saying prosaically:

"I think you've allowed Heiden to get under your skin."

This, of course, had to be put into other words for Sophie, and even made her laugh a little. She accepted a cigarette, and admitted that Heiden's attentions to her sister were causing her anxiety.

62

"You two girls had a row about him after we left last night, didn't you?" said Tom.

"A row?"

"Quarrel, argument, difference of opinion."

"I spoke to her sharply, I must admit; it was so embarrassing to come home and find them sitting in the dark together. But there's no saying anything to Lisa these days, she seems to be infatuated with him. And of course she's more than ten years younger than I am; she thinks of me as her old maid sister, always criticising and spoiling sport. If I were married, Lisa would feel differently, but—the man I loved was killed thirteen years ago at Mukden, during the war with Japan."

"Was he a Russian?"

"Oh no, he was a Finn. Michael's background was just like General Mannerheim's: he was educated in the Finnish Corps of Cadets at Fredrikshamn, and then joined the Russian army, but of course he was only a lieutenant when he was killed."

"And General Mannerheim was his commanding officer."

She looked up, startled. "How did you guess that?"

"From something Lisa said, about wondering how you could bear to mention it, or remember it—something like that."

It was just what she had thought, he wasn't stupid at all. He could listen, and observe, and put two and two together and make four. She said, "Yes, that surprised me, what Lisa said. She was only eight when it happened, and we haven't spoken of it for years."

"So she's going on twenty-one now, eh? Maybe you should ride her on a looser rein for a bit, and see if she cools off on Heiden."

"I'm ashamed to bother you with my personal problems."

There was so much distress in her voice that Tom got up and pressed her shoulder, saying, "Don't worry, Sophie. Relax, and try to think about yourself for a change."

It was a casual touch, like the pat he had given Nancy Macpherson when they parted in London, but the feel of Sophie's slim shoulder beneath his hand roused feelings so long dormant that he involuntarily tightened his grip, and she looked up at him in surprise. Tom released her.

"Come on," he said, picking up their coats, "I'll walk you home across the park. It's the short cut to your place, isn't it?"

"It cuts off the corner, certainly." She followed him out of

Mr. Baker's flat in silence, and waited while he locked the door.

"Shall I put the keys back in the office safe, Mr. Fleming?"

Under the hall lamp their eyes met in another sort of awareness.

"Don't bother," said Tom Fleming easily, and dropped the key ring in his pocket. "I'll take charge of them for the time being."

6

THREE MORNINGS LATER Tom Fleming pushed open a balcony window in the Valtio Hotel and listened to the roar of the Imatra falls.

He had been conscious of the sound even in his sleep, for the deafening noise, audible long before the sleigh from Imatra manor drew up in front of the hotel, had reverberated through his dreams and kept him on the edge of wakefulness the whole night long. Yet he had expected to sleep well, for the visit to the Broberg mills had been exhilarating. Driving in the hired sleigh from the railway station, and then in Mr. Broberg's magnificent cutter to the nearest logging camp, his lungs had been filled with sparkling pine-scented air, and although the rain forests of British Columbia, with their vast stands of fir and cedar, did not wholly resemble these Finnish woods where the evergreen boughs drooped under their weight of embossed snow, he had the easy sense of being in familiar surroundings. Everything was known to him, from the high, conical waste-burners of the saw-mills giving off their smoke plumes above the river to the smell of newly felled trees at the logging site. Equally familiar was the hospitality, more formal but as lavish as the Candian style, which he had enjoyed in Mr. Broberg's cheerful home.

But the roar of the falls had made him dream, again and again, of an opening barrage on the western front, and he woke too early, trembling with nerves because this was the day when he must prove himself in the carrying out of the Chief's mission. All he had to console him, as he went into the big Edwardian bathroom of what must have been a splendid suite, was the thought that his staff work had been good. "Be at the east side of the falls of Imatra, by the bridge, at ten o'clock on the morning of the twenty-second," the Chief had said. It was only half past seven, and the falls were at a garden's distance, underneath his window.

The process of shaving was unexpectedly calming to his nerves.

His beard had always grown quickly, and already, after less than two weeks, his moustache had made very respectable progress. No doubt about it, Nancy had hit on the right idea: the distortion at the side of his mouth was hidden by the new dark hair, and as a bonus the welt seemed to be flattening out near his eye. He scraped his chin smooth, finding it possible to look at himself without revulsion, and took a tepid shower. The fittings in the bathroom were quite modern, probably dating from 1912, for the Valtio Hotel had been a favourite holiday resort of the Russian aristocracy, and, the Chief had said, it was now full of Russian refugees. The silence of the place, and the emptiness of the lobbies and salons when he checked in the night before, meant nothing; so much he had learned from his few days in the Society House. The Russians were there all right, holed up behind locked bedroom doors, but oh boy! when the supper bell rang they came in and cleaned out the dining room faster than he'd ever seen happen in any logging camp.

When the simple breakfast was eaten Tom Fleming was ready to go, and it was still too soon. Here, a hundred and fifty miles east of Helsingfors, daybreak had come sooner than in the dark streets of the capital, and he could see the sun outside, shining through a curtain of snowflakes hardly distinguishable from the blown spume of the falls. All that flying white would be a useful curtain as he made his way across the garden, and would hide the eccentricity of a traveller who wanted to visit a famous tourist attraction like Imatra so remarkably out of season. White— that was the cover name of the man he was about to meet. "You can call him White because he'll be wearing white," said the Chief, "and there's no danger of any impersonation, because White has very strongly marked, Byronic features, and wears"— the Chief's nose twitched—"sidewhiskers. He'll be given your name and description, and I see no need for any password nonsense. You're not likely to be interrupted in the forests of Imatra."

As a precaution against interruptions, Tom was carrying the Service Webley in its shoulder holster. He was perfectly willing to take orders from Mr. White, but after his experiences in Helsingfors he was determined to assert himself a little: to be an agent, even if a minor one, but not a tool. As he strapped it beneath his armpit and buttoned his jacket carefully his mind

66

was still worrying at the problem of the "Byronic" looks of Mr. White. There had been a portrait of Lord Byron in one of his schoolbooks, but all Tom could conjure up was the image of a supercilious young man in an open-necked shirt, very much in need of a short-back-and-sides. It was not a useful identification.

"You'll have a sleigh on hand for me about noon?" he said to the desk clerk as he paid his bill. "I don't want to leave Imatra without seeing the famous falls."

The clerk registered no surprise. "Please be careful as you go, then, sir," he said. "The path by the river is frozen solid since the thaw, and there are heavy drifts on the east side, I hear. Not that you'll want to cross the bridge anyway, few people do in winter, except the foresters."

"Not much of a bridge, is it?"

The clerk shrugged. "Our summer visitors used to say they felt safer in the olden days, when they crossed in a box worked by a pulley. You must come back in summer, sir, and enjoy the picnic parties by the ford."

"That sounds like fun."

The man was right about the paths, they were frozen solid even inside the hotel grounds, and Tom put his feet down cautiously in the heavy rubber-soled boots he had bought at the Nordiska Company's shop in Stockholm. The roar of the falls grew appallingly loud as he crossed the garden. He looked back once at the hotel, a true Czarist relic of pepperpot towers and balconied bay windows, and saw no sign of life except wood smoke rising from the chimneys. It was as desolate as the river path, where strange little iron summerhouses, locked under their cones of snow, spoke of the Romanov Augusts which would never come again. He arrived without slipping at the bridge.

And now, averting his eyes from the bridge itself, Tom saw that the falls of Imatra were not falls but rapids, immensely long, caused by a narrow gorge through which the Vuoksi river surged on its way from Lake Saimaa to Lake Ladoga on the Russian frontier. The winter season had until then been so open that although the rocks beneath the cliff where Tom stood were frozen over, the mighty river itself was running free, boiling and seething down its half-mile slope within a granite chasm. The Vuoksi was yellow, with tawny and golden glints beneath the white foam, and Tom was suddenly reminded of the contrasting clear, glacial water, the malachite green of the Thompson in his home province of British Columbia. What he looked upon might have been dazzling in summer; alone, on a December day, he looked at the Imatra falls and shuddered.

The bridge he had to cross was merely a double row of planks, roughly nailed together and swinging above the torrent at its narrowest point, which still was over twenty yards in width. A rope attached to slender posts served as the handrail, and rope and planks were sodden with blown spray. When Tom set a cautious foot on the planking the narrow bridge swayed from end to end and the rope rail sagged and then tightened in his hand. The gigantic river waves leaped high enough to wet his trousers to the knee. The toe of one boot struck heavily against a double width of rope tied round the planking, and as he stumbled he almost lost his balance. As he recovered himself he knew he was in the grip of vertigo.

Tom Fleming had never had a very good head for heights, but this was a matter of depth, not height. This was a matter of looking down into a swirling icy cauldron, with the cold spray breaking over his feet and legs, and beneath the spray a whirlpool of gilt and umber pierced by cruel rocks. He began to tremble, as when he was first shell-shocked. His jaw stiffened and his limbs slowly locked. With a huge effort he forced himself to look at the opposite bank, and saw nothing but a blur of ever-greens, the white boughs bending and beckoning as if in a gale. Gripping the rope rail as if his life depended on it, he forced himself to put one foot before the other and inch slowly forward. To cross the bridge took more than ten minutes, and when he was safely on the far bank he found that his face was wet with sweat. The spruces were standing motionless in a flat calm.

He took off his glove to wipe his face with his handkerchief, retied his fox cap and plunged into the forest. The path, if it existed, was snowed over, and there were drifts, marked with delicate animal tracks, beneath the trees. But he had put the rapids of Imatra behind him, and in a few minutes he found himself in a forest clearing where a man stood watching him from the lee of a clump of birches. A man dressed in a short white sheepskin coat with a hood attached, who moved forward to meet him in a curious shuffling walk.

68

"Captain Fleming, dead on time! A very sporting effort, congratulations!"

They shook hands in silence, for Tom had not complete control of his breathing, and as if he sensed this White went on, "Sorry I couldn't come over to the Valtio to meet you, but we thought it better not. Couldn't risk running into some dear old pal from Petrograd, the place is crawling with them still. When did you get to Helsingfors?"

"Tuesday afternoon. I only had two full days there, but I think I've got you what you wanted."

"Good man! Come further in among the trees, we don't want to be snowed under."

There was no danger of their being seen in that snowy wilderness, but the thickly embossed boughs gave some protection from the falling snow, and White pushed back his hood. Tom saw the "Byronic" face described by the Chief, with the heavy dark brows and sidewhiskers giving drama to a conventionally clean-cut face. He said, "How did *you* get here, if I'm allowed to ask?"

"On those," White looked down at his feet, and Tom saw that he was wearing snowshoes. "I came by the Lake Ladoga route, with a guide and a party of rich frightened Russians who daren't face the official border crossing. Our man guaranteed to put them aboard a train on the Finnish side, and they've got to make their own way to Langinkoski."

"That's near Kotka, isn't it?"

"You've been doing your homework. Yes, on the Kymi river, Czar Alexander had the fishing rights there, and a lot of *dachas* were built round the Imperial lodge. How long it'll be a refuge, God alone knows, but at least they're safe for the time being. What have you got for *us*?"

"Something pretty good," said Tom, "the only problem is, how long will you want it for?"

"How much did the Chief tell you about the job in hand?"

"Nothing, except that it had to do with Kerensky. He said you would give me my instructions."

"Right. The first point is, Kerensky has been found. He's been in hiding in the forest near Novgorod, and our men have been with him all the time. Second, he's determined to return to Petrograd, not merely to go underground and wait until we can pass him through to Finland safely, but to make a public appearance at the next meeting of the Constituent Assembly."

Tom whistled. "After putting up a fight against the Bolsheviks and then going on the run for the past two months?"

"Obviously it's suicide. But he's pig-headed enough to try it, in which case we'll have to get our men out alone, unless Mr. K.'s Petrograd friends persuade him to throw in his hand. So that puts a time limit to Operation Kerensky: not before New Year's Day and any time after the fifth of January, the date when the Constituent Assembly opens at the Tauride Palace."

"Good," said Tom, "because the safe house I found for you isn't available indefinitely. The owner is in hospital in Sweden, but he may be back in Helsingfors by the end of January; that should work out all right."

"Doesn't he *know* you—"

"Not he," said Tom, and White, with his dark face creasing in a soundless laugh, saw that his nonchalance was not feigned. Three years of billeting orders, of requisitioning, of making free with other people's homes in the evacuated areas behind the lines, had taught Captain Fleming a fine disregard for property.

"Where is this place?" he said, and listened intently while Tom described the location of Mr. Baker's flat, its seclusion and its convenient nearness to a large park and the freight yards where all trains slowed down before entering Helsingfors station, allowing men reluctant to pass the check-point to drop from the train and hide among the sheds and piles of timber."

"Ideal," he said briefly. "You brought the keys, of course?"

"I had a second set cut on Wednesday. I'm keeping one myself."

"Quite so, but we shall need your telephone numbers, at the hotel and at your office too."

"All right." Tom scribbled the numbers in a page torn from his pocketbook. It was so cold that he had to blow on his fingers before he could hold the pencil steady; White beat his arms once or twice across his breast. Something in the movement, and in the look of the man in his white coat with the hood falling on his shoulders, reminded Tom of the naval officers he had seen on watch aboard the transport which had brought the Canadian volunteers to the war in Europe. That White was, or had been in the navy, he was suddenly sure.

He handed over the slip of paper and the two keys. "The big one opens the street door," he said, "I suppose it's locked at night, but it was open when I was there. And there's no porter."

"Better and better."

"One thing, s—Mr. White. If the whole operation blows up, and your men get nowhere near Helsingfors, how am I to know? What do I do then? How do I contact you?"

White considered. "The operation could only blow up in two ways, east of the border," he said. "If Alexander Kerensky is captured by the Reds on his way to Petrograd, they would either kill him out of hand or hold him incommunicado until they stage his trial as an enemy of the people. If he's taken in public, say when the Assembly meets at the Tauride Palace, that of course is world news, and the American correspondents would break the story."

"Why not the British?"

"Because I fancy we'll be pulling up our stakes and clearing out before too long. Now the Soviets have signed an armistice with Germany, the Ambassador is almost bound to ask for his passports, and request safe conduct for all his staff to Finland en route for Britain. Well, not all," he corrected himself, "somebody's got to stay and mind the shop. But communication direct with Petrograd will be impossible . . . Let's do it this way," he said, "if my colleagues haven't contacted you within one month from today, that's by January the twenty-second, you must alert the British Minister at Stockholm. Cable 'goods undelivered', or something like that."

"What if I can't communicate with Stockholm?"

"Why shouldn't you?"

"Because a month from now there could be civil war in Finland, Reds against Whites, and the Reds being the stronger side, they could capture and destroy the state communications system at the very first go-off."

"God!" said White. "A civil war! Is this your—hypothesis, after one week in Finland?"

"It's an opinion strongly held at the British consulate in Helsingfors, Mr. White, I paid a courtesy call there on Wednesday. And from what I've seen of the Finns themselves, it's not a hypothesis, it's a probability. Last evening Mr. Broberg told me every man in his concern would go out armed with an axe

71

or a peavey-hook rather than allow the Russians to occupy Karelia."

"They expect the Russians, the Bolsheviks, to support the Finn Red Guard?"

"Yes, and they're quite calm about it. I couldn't help remembering while Mr. Broberg was talking, that the Chief told me in London there were three million Finns in Finland and two million Russians in Petrograd alone."

"And nearly two hundred million Russians in the Empire at the last pre-war census," White groaned. "It's like the slaughter of the innocents."

"David and Goliath, that's the way *they* like to look at it."

"I suppose the Chief told you, this is none of our business? That our great anxiety is the prospect of a lasting peace between the Soviets and our enemies?"

"He certainly did."

"What I can't get out of my mind is the Russian ships iced in at Helsingfors. Have you heard anything about those?"

"Their crews are very much in evidence, but the ships are held in the ice out in the Kronberg firth. Nearly two hundred of them, I was told."

"Including thirteen Dreadnoughts and fourteen 'Novik' class destroyers. If those are handed over to Germany by the terms of an eventual peace treaty—after the ice melts—and appear in the North Sea, what then?"

"The Royal Navy might have to fight another Jutland, that's what."

The man in the white sheepskins looked narrowly at Fleming, as if he scented sarcasm, but he only said, "We'd better walk up and down, it's freezing. What else did you glean in your busy days in Helsingfors?"

"I met one fellow I'm not sure about. He claims to be a Swiss national, but he was born in St. Petersburg, where his father had a job at court. His name's Heiden."

"Igor Heiden?"

"No, Boris, at least that's what he's called."

"Heiden. That's a Baltic German name, and the Baltic barons pretty well ran all the Imperial administration that worked efficiently. Baron Heiden, does that mean anything?"

"His mother seems to be a baroness."

"Baroness Heiden. No, it's the name *Igor* Heiden that sounds

72

right. Before my time, though, I've only been in Russia for the past two years. What does your Heiden look like?"

"Like anybody you don't notice in the street."

"But you think he might be a Russian agent?"

"With a Swiss passport? Possibly."

"Keep your eye on him, then, and I'll try to get a line on the family. Now I must be off. My guide's waiting, not very far away, and you've got to get home to Helsingfors." They walked back towards the Vuoksi river, and the roar of the rapids, blurred only by the screens of trees, came menacingly to their ears.

"I did a quick reconnaissance, before you came along," said White. "That's a ramshackle bridge you had to cross."

"I'm not looking forward to the return trip, I can tell you."

"You'll find it's not so bad, the second time."

They shook hands and parted. Before he started walking in his own tracks, still visible, down the steep descent to the river bank, Tom looked round. White was waiting by the clump of birches and raised his hand in salute. Then the white coat and hood faded into the white tree trunks and disappeared.

*   *   *

Tom Fleming had a long, cold wait at the little country station before he was able to board the train to Helsingfors. It came in crammed with soldiers, who looked at him suspiciously as he clambered aboard by the first door that would open, finding himself in a "hard" coach of indescribable filth, with Russian troops standing three deep between the seats. Tom was inured to troop transports in France, from the Channel packets and the overcrowded military trains to field ambulances and army lorries, but even the ambulances with their smell of death and soaked field dressings were fragrant compared to the sour stench of this Russian train. He stood wedged in between the sweating, unwashed bodies, breathing through his nose and wondering how many of the lice he saw crawling on the collar of the man next to him would be transferred to his own clean clothes.

Burning wood, and proceeding at less than the normal speed of twenty-five miles an hour, the train from Petrograd crept slowly towards Helsingfors. Tom Fleming was afflicted by a rising sense of nausea. The vertigo of the bridge crossing, the bitter

cold in the forest, combined with the weakness which long standing caused in his abdomen and groin to increase the sickness.
He was doubtful if he could hold out for the four or five hours'
ride into Helsingfors, and was trying to inch his way towards
the window when the train ground to a halt, and orders were
yelled which emptied every carriage at the double. Tom Fleming
was pushed down to the platform by sheer weight of numbers,
staggered, regained his balance with difficulty, and collapsed
against a stack of timber piled for railway engines at the far end
of the platform.

"Mr. Fleming! Are you are all right?"

The English words came to him from far away. Still holding
himself upright by his clutch on the logs, he opened his eyes and
recognised Boris Heiden.

"I'm fine," he said. "It's nothing—nothing at all."

"Here, sit down for a minute." There was a broken bench
not far from the timber, piled high with soldiers' packs and bed-
ding rolls. Heiden, without concern, swept the whole pile to the
ground. On top, Tom saw his own small suitcase, which someone
must have thrown out of the train.

"Here, drink this." Heiden was holding a handsome silver
flask with a crest on it. He filled the cap and handed it to Tom.
It contained brandy, strong and reviving.

"Thanks, Heiden. What place is this?"

"Kouvola junction. The train stopped to let the men eat,
and to wait for the connection from Kotka."

"Were you aboard the same train as me?"

"No, I came from Helsingfors." He bent forward, and the
wispy beard almost brushed Tom's ear as he murmured, "Going
to Langinkoski . . . old friends of my mother's . . . needing help.
How are you feeling now?"

"Much better, thanks to you." And since some word of
explanation was required, Tom added, "I've been at Imatra.
Rather too long a trip for the first time out."

"Perhaps you've been doing too much." There was not a trace
of guile in the candid hazel eyes behind the glasses. "Do you
feel up to coming indoors now?"

"If there's room."

There were places for two, instantly, in the barn-like room
which had once been a comfortable dining room at the statutory

74

main line stop for food. It was of course seething with troops, crowding round the samovars and at the same time clutching the rifles they dared not lay aside while their NCOs were watching, but there was no food on sale. Each man had his own provisions. The soldier on the extreme end of the bench where Tom and Heiden found places was gnawing a whole herring, and, his hunger partly satisfied, he carefully put the uneaten half back in the inside pocket of his grey coat and took out a handful of sunflower seeds. Heiden gave Tom's arm a friendly grip. "I'll get some tea," he said.

Tom watched the crowd round the samovar melt away with the same alacrity as the places on the crowded bench had been vacated. Mr. Heiden, in his unassuming workman's clothes, was being remarkably effective. "*Tovarichi*," he called the soldiers, but there was nothing comradely in his manner, and he got instant service at the samovar. On his way to Langinkoski—that was the place White had named as a refuge for Czarist refugees near Kotka. It was plausible enough.

Heiden came back carrying two clean glasses of milkless tea. The soldier with the herring had quietly moved away; the two civilians had the bench to themselves now, and room to breathe. Tom found his cigarettes and offered them to Heiden.

"Are we making a long stopover here, do you know?"

"Only until the train comes up from Kotka—assuming it ever starts . . . What do you think of the Russian army, Mr. Fleming?"

Tom had been looking around him, head quite clear now and nausea gone. Most of the men still in the dining room reminded him of the immigrants whom his father and other Canadian employers lumped under the name of Galicians, that conglomeration of Ruthenians, Slovenians, Rumanians and south-east Europeans generally, who shared Slav features and German as their common tongue. "Judging by this lot, eh?" he said.

"They're as good a sample as any."

"Right now they need a good RTO to sort them out."

"What's an RTO?"

"Railway Transport Officer."

Heiden smiled. "Those men are not too fond of officers, of any sort. What I meant was, how do they compare with your Canadian troops?"

75

It was Tom's turn to smile. "They don't," he said. "Our chaps were an élite corps—shock troops, any fancy name you like to call them. They were hand-picked for the toughest jobs on the western front, and they allowed—*we* allowed, that only a few of the British divisions were our equals."

"Which were they?"

"The two Scottish Divisions, Highland and Lowland, and the Guards of course."

"How about the French troops?"

"I didn't have much to do with them."

"Not at any time?"

"At Vimy Ridge, when their native troops were on our flank."

"The Germans were using gas, weren't they?"

"That's right."

"The French troops broke under the gas attacks, and the Canadians held the line?"

"We took the Ridge, sure, but I tell you it wasn't the French themselves, it was their North African troops. Zouaves and Turcos, they panicked under gas."

"But the Canadians didn't?"

"We'd had our first whiff at Second Ypres. That's when we learned to use field dressings soaked in a bicarb solution as emergency gas masks. It worked pretty well."

"Do you think the rout of the troops from French North Africa was a pointer to last year's French army mutinies?"

"They weren't very serious."

"Oh, come, Mr. Fleming! Not serious, when sixteen army corps were affected, and sixteen men were executed?"

"Sixteen agitators were executed, by order of the government, and then General Pétain stopped the rot. I've got to hand it to you, Heiden, you never let up on your political science studies, do you?"

"I'm interested in the reactions of men under duress. Now *you've* been exposed to great stress lately, haven't you?"

"Take a look at me."

"You interest me so much, Mr. Fleming. You seem so proud of belonging to a *corps d'élite*. I take it you joined the Canadian army as a volunteer?"

"I did."

"There was no conscription in Canada?"

"Not in August 1914."

"And you rose from the ranks?"

"No, I was commissioned, second lieutenant, when I enlisted. Say, what are you getting at?"

"I'm only trying to understand what made a young man like you rush to join in a war which would obviously be fought thousands of kilometres from your own home. Was it to defend Canada . . . or the British Empire?"

"Partly it was to fight for the old country—for an idea we all inherited from our fathers and mothers. And partly it was to prove I was as good a man as my brother."

"Ah—!" The nondescript face relaxed in a smile. "He was a soldier too, your brother?"

"Hell, no! There weren't any wars when he was twenty. He came in for the big adventure, the gold rush of 1898. You've heard of it?"

"In the Klondike—certainly."

"Graham took off for the Yukon, over the Skagway trail. He made a good strike on Minóok, took out about ten thousand dollars' worth of gold dust, and came back to Vancouver quite the local hero. At least I thought so. I was eight."

"And so you wanted to be a hero too?"

"I wanted to go one better than Graham Fleming."

"Remarkable," said Boris Heiden, and his voice was quite sincere. "This is something we have in common, Mr. Fleming. I too had a brother, a writer, whom I thought of as a hero—"

"Was his name Igor?"

Tom Fleming had spoken impulsively; he was unprepared for the effect on the young man. Boris Heiden's face flushed, his lips seemed to grow fuller and his eyes to grow as wide as a cat's behind his spectacles.

"Now how in the world could you know that?" he said.

"I can't say," Tom replied lamely. "It just seems to me that sometime, some place, I heard the name Igor Heiden."

"In Seattle?"

"I can't remember where. Igor Heiden—so he was your brother? Could I have read anything he wrote?"

Heiden looked over his shoulder. The Russian soldiers were fed, after their fashion, and were outside gathering their equipment off the platform. The dirty shed which had once been a restaurant was almost empty. Even so, Heiden lowered his voice.

"Some of his articles were translated and published in North America before the war. Poor Igor! What he wrote was eloquent, visionary I suppose you would say, calling for world peace and the brotherhood of man. Tolstoy was his inspiration, Prince Kropotkin was his own teacher. Many people thought he had a brilliant future."

"So what happened to him?"

"You mean you don't know?"

"No, I don't."

"He died young."

Outside on the platform they heard a bell strike once.

"That means the connecting train is coming up from Kotka. Better get aboard, Mr. Fleming; you don't want to stand all the way to Helsingfors."

"You bet I don't." This time he got a corner seat, and while the troops piled in around him was even able to lower the window and say goodbye to Heiden.

"Many thanks for the tea and brandy. Some day soon I'll do as much for you."

"I'll remember." Heiden took a cloth cap from the pocket of his leather jacket, put it on, and sketched a salute as the Helsingfors train pulled out. And all the way to the capital Tom Fleming chewed at one tiny problem, unimportant but unforgettable: the mention of Seattle.

*   *   *

It was still with him next morning, the assurance that Heiden could never have thought of Seattle in connection with himself. Lisa Sandels had said, "Mr. Baker told us all about you," which he assumed to be her polite way of saying "We knew you'd been in hospital, we knew about your face and we don't mind." but even if Ballantine and Macaulay had sent Mr. Baker a record of Thomas Fleming's life from the date of his birth in 1891, there could have been no possible mention of himself in connection with Seattle. He had never lived there, never worked there, the only tie-up was his family's friendship with the Macphersons.

So why Seattle?

He was disturbed enough to go that day, in the too-early

lunch break, to the university library, in the hope of finding some clue to the life and work of Igor Heiden. He was not experienced in library techniques, and it took the woman librarian on duty and himself some time to arrive at the word "bibliography" to explain what he wanted, which was a list of magazines publishing translations from the Russian in the United States and Canada. They decided on the period 1910 to 1914, and while the librarian went through the files Tom walked quietly round the reading room looking for reference works in English. It was a small masterpiece by Carl Ludwig Engel, the architect of all the glories of the Senate Square, and Tom found its proportions satisfying; walking softly, not to disturb the students bent over their books, he was almost sorry when the librarian motioned him up to her desk. She was apologetic, she could find no translations, inside the period, of articles by the writer he mentioned. He hardly noticed that she looked at him with an odd expression, but was intent on thanking her and getting back to a desk with the biographical dictionary he had found. It had struck him that something might be learned about Igor Heiden from his mentors. Tolstoy, Tom Fleming knew, was a novelist, though what the man had written he could not have said, except a book about Anna Somebody which his sisters Isabel and Dorothy had been forbidden to read. But Prince Kropotkin, now!

It took Tom some time to track Kropotkin down. In the past week he had heard so many names, difficult to pronounce and impossible to spell (Per Svinhufvud, Kullervo Manner, Jaakko Rahja, Karl Enckell) that he confused Igor Heiden's teacher Kropotkin with Kuropatkin, the Russian C-in-C in the Japanese war. But he found him at last, not dead but very much alive, this anarchist prince, dedicated, so the dictionary said, "to the total destruction of the bourgeois world by the propaganda of the deed, and the use of dynamite, the gun and the dagger."

7

LISA SANDELS SAT ON her own bed in the little bedroom she
shared with her elder sister, and watched Sophie studying
her reflection in the dressing-table mirror. It was Christmas
Day, and the sky above Helsingfors was so dark and full of snow
that Sophie had set a lighted candle on each side of the glass.
In their soft glow her face was young and pensive.

"You do look nice, Sophie!"

Lisa herself looked pretty and gay in a thick scarlet sweater
and matching knitted stockings; her navy blue serge skirt was
short. Sophie had put on her best dress, seldom worn, of dark
red velvet cut low at the neck, and with an uncertain hand was
trying the effect of various lengths and colours of lace around her
throat.

"Which do you think?" she said.

"It's best without any lace at all," said Lisa.

"Honestly? You don't think it's cut too low in front?"

"With a skin like yours? Not a bit."

"Maybe I should at least wear mother's necklace."

"That great heavy old thing? Do, if you want to lunch at the
Seurahuone looking like a character from the *Kalevala*."

"Perhaps you're right." The Nordic skin was dazzling
against the garnet velvet. Sophie smiled.

"Mother's earrings!" Lisa exclaimed, "you can wear those!
They'll give you colour, since you won't wear lipsalve, silly girl."
Lisa's own mouth was painted as bright as a geranium, it brushed
her sister's hair, now released from its tight knot and swathed
becomingly round Sophie's head, as she hooked the barbaric
Russian earrings through the pierced pink lobes. "Now a dusting
of powder and your lace-edged handkerchief, but *not* with lavender
water on it, Sophie, please! Stand up and turn around. You're
lovely! It's a shame you've got to take your pretty slippers off and
put your boots on to go outdoors."

"I'll take my Christmas slipper-bag, darling." It had been

Lisa's Christmas present, and she looked pleased; as for the boots, they were part of a woman's routine in Helsingfors in winter, when everyone had to carry her indoor shoes and clump through the snowy streets in the heavy boots which ruined the appearance of the smartest dress. Lisa had a Christmas present from her sister too, and was going to carry a new pair of skates to attach to her old lacing boots. She shrugged quickly into her rough little blue coat and picked up a knitted tam o' shanter.

"What time'll you be home, Sophie?"

"Oh, not very late." Sophie paused in the act of winding her mother's "fascinator" carefully round her head. "Look, Lisa, I could have coffee and cakes for you and Mr. Heiden any time after five, if you'd like that."

"*Mister* Heiden! I wonder what your Canadian friend would say to that! He called me Lisa when he'd only known me for about five minutes!"

"Well, Boris, then. Remember I don't know *him* very well. But tell him he'll be welcome here on Christmas Day."

"You're sweet, but I think Mrs. Rentola means to have coffee for all of us upstairs, and we're going to play games in the evening."

"Well, then, have fun, but do be careful at the harbour, that's all I ask."

"Don't *fuss*." Sophie Sandels was not demonstrative, but now she kissed the girl, so eager to be off to her skating party and her Boris, and Lisa, glowing, said, "I'm so glad you're having a Christmas party too! You and Mr. Fleming'll be like Beauty and the Beast."

"What a horrible thing to say!" Sophie sprang to her feet, and the spoilt child saw she had gone too far.

"Oh, I didn't mean to be nasty," she said, "but honestly he does look terrible; if Mr. Baker hadn't warned us I think I'd have shrieked out loud the night he walked in here—"

"I wonder you care to remind me of that evening," said Sophie, tight-lipped. "Mr. Fleming's face isn't nearly as badly disfigured as he thinks it is; and you know he was wounded fighting for his country."

"Boris says Canada's not a country. It's a Dominion, part of the British capitalist-imperialist world system, which is no better than the Russian Empire in its treatment of subject races."

"Boris talks a lot of rubbish." The moment of sympathy had passed. The two girls parted on the landing without further words, Lisa to run upstairs and Sophie to go down and start walking towards the Railway Square. When she reached the broad street where the trams ran she saw candles in all the dingy, uncurtained windows, and on the other side children were shrieking in the park as they tried out their Christmas sleds. There were still a few Christmas trees in the corner of the square where the tree market had been.

She felt that her luck was in when she arrived at the Society House, for Tom Fleming was not waiting by the reception desk, and she had time for the awkward business of getting the boots off and the black satin slippers on, before he came out of the lift and hurried towards her.

"Merry Christmas, Sophie! You look stunning!"

"Merry Christmas, T-Tom!"

She stumbled over his Christian name, which made him laugh, and say how glad he was to see her, and by the warmth of his welcome she judged that he was homesick on this day of a home festival. Even before they entered the restaurant he was asking if Sophie knew of any reason for delays in the cable service. He had sent Christmas greetings to every member of his family, but not one reply had arrived so far, and he couldn't help feeling cut off—

"No Christmas greetings from your relatives at all?"

"Just one message from a friend in London." It had read "Merry Xmas Tommy lots of love from Nancy", that exasperating but efficient girl having correctly worked out the transmission time between London and Helsingfors.

"How pretty everything is!" The Society House, though handicapped by rationing, had made a big effort for Christmas 1917. There were wreaths on the walls, a vase with a single tulip on each table, and a small string band playing in one of the curious little balconies which overhung the big dining room. Every table was occupied, for even the most timorous of the Russian refugees had ventured downstairs for the Christmas dinner, served at the unusually early hour of two o'clock. On the table reserved for Tom lay a parcel in Stockmann's distinctive wrapping, with a small bunch of violets knotted in the ribbon bow.

"For *me*?"

"Don't open it now," said Tom, lowering his voice conspiratorially, "it's half a dozen pairs of silk stockings. I only hope I got the right size."

"Six pairs!" Sophie's eyes were as wide as a child's. "Lisa has one pair, but I, never—*six*! How terribly extravagant—and how kind!"

"With my Christmas wishes. Now, a drink!"

He ordered vodka, and led her to the table of hors-d'œuvres in the middle of the room, which held half a dozen kinds of fish, eel and pickled salmon, cold reindeer tongue and many other delicacies. The hot dish which followed was roast goose, and Tom had ordered a bottle of burgundy. After that the waiter brought pancakes with cloudberry jam, and coffee.

"Brandy?" said Tom. "Or something sweet, like Benedictine?"

"Could I have that liqueur from Danzig, with the little gold flecks in it? My father used to let me have a tiny glass of it, when we came here for treats long ago. But we never had a feast like this!"

"We've both been on short commons long enough to enjoy it." The liqueurs came, and Tom chose a cigar with care. "How's Lisa spending her Christmas?"

"Vera Rentola organised a skating party for this afternoon. About a dozen of them went off together, including Boris Heiden, I'm afraid."

Tom resisted the temptation to say "So he's back from Kotka, is he?" He had not mentioned, in the office, that he had seen Heiden at Kouvola junction.

"Where do they skate?" he asked.

"The Skating Club has an area marked off for its own use on the South Harbour, once the ice is bearing. They use fir trees in pots to mark the boundaries, and they waltz carrying torches to band music—it's really a pretty sight. I only hope the Russian sailors won't be wandering around drunk this year."

"Do you go in for skating?"

"I used to like ski-ing better, out at Alphyddan, and best of all, when we could get horses, there was riding on the sea, as we used to call it, after the harbours froze. Now that was fun!"

"I'd like to try that sometime."

"Forbidden, while the Russian ships are here. But we mustn't

83

think about such things today. Tell me about your Canadian Christmases. Did you go to church, as Lisa and I did today?"

"Sure we went to church, after we opened all the presents Santa Claus had brought." He began to tell her about Christmas in his childhood, and helping his sisters Isabel and Dorothy to decorate Rubislaw House with evergreens and deck the tree with the baubles and spangles and the gold angel brought out every year from the great camphorwood chest in the attic. He was enjoying Sophie's rapt attention, and the picture she made in her dark red dress, turning the little bunch of violets in her hand. The wine had given her colour, and the exotic earrings added a new dimension to her narrow face.

"After the plum pudding, and the snapdragon and all the rest of it, we three kids were turned out to play while the grown-ups had a nap. We usually collected some of our own gang from the neighbourhood, and played tag round the barns and stables to keep warm until tea-time, and then we were all set for a big Christmas tea. Isabel was the eldest, she got to cut the cake."

"Your parents must have a big house, with all those attics and barns and stables."

"And an ornamental lake with a Japanese bridge across it, leading to a little Japanese teahouse where my mother and the girls entertained their friends."

"So your father has a really big estate in Canada?"

"No, it was a real small lake," laughed Tom. "Rubislaw House is built on a ten-acre lot, and it's only twenty years old. We had a pretty nice villa before that, where I was born, but Grandma Fleming went right on living in her first Vancouver home. It was a little clapboard farmhouse with a tumbledown porch at one end and the barn at the other. They built it in I guess 1860, when Vancouver was called Coal Harbour, or maybe it was Gastown, anyway it was long before the railroad came in. I've seen a lot of wooden houses in Finland like the old Fleming farm."

"Your grandfather was a farmer?"

"He kept a cow. I figure he could turn his hand to most things, old Sandy Fleming. He began life as a quarryman in Aberdeen, Scotland. Then he tramped to London and made some money in business, and that's how he got to know my mother's father, Arthur Tarras. And the long and the short of it was that he persuaded my grandmother to marry him and emigrate to Canada."

"A quarryman? You mean he dug the stone from quarries?"

"Aberdeen granite; yes, that's right."

"In Russia such a man would have been a serf."

"Yes, well, we don't go in for serfs in Scotland. But don't you think my grandma was a heroine? After all, he'd always had it pretty rough, but she was raised a real young lady, with a maid, and accomplishments and all, and she just hotfooted it off to Canada with him, long before the country was opened up. My dad was born at Winnipeg when it was still Fort Garry, just a Hudson's Bay trading post, with Indians roaming around, and all. And grandpa wouldn't stay put in Fort Garry. He'd heard about the gold strike on the Fraser river, so off they went to the Cariboo fields where British Columbia first began, and then they settled down on the Gastown farm."

"You're proud of them, aren't you, Tom?"

"I sure am."

"Did you know them, your grandparents I mean?"

"Not my grandfather. But I was sixteen when Grandma Fleming died, grown-up enough to realise what a grand old girl she was. Granny Bell, I used to call her."

"She must have loved you very much."

Tom grinned. "Being Scots she never said so, but she proved it in some very practical ways." In fact old Mrs. Bell Fleming, a shrewd speculator in Vancouver real estate, had set up a handsome trust fund for her favourite grandson.

The bandsmen were beginning to pack up their instruments, the Christmas dinner at the Society House was over. Sophie sighed as she rose to go. "It's been wonderful," she said, and slipped her violets through the ribbon of the parcel which held her Christmas gift.

Walking her home across the frozen square, it was so slippery that Tom tucked her arm securely through his own. "It's like seeing a girl home from dancing class," he said, indicating the slipper-bag beneath his other arm, and Sophie laughed happily. "Listen, the snow's screaming!" she said as they gained the pavement by the park and the packed snow squeaked beneath their boots. They could hear music and laughter from the Rentolas' flat even before they came beneath the windows.

"Safe home and enjoying themselves, thank goodness," Sophie said, as Tom held the street door open for her. He followed her into the dark entrance hall.

"Thank you for a happy time, Tom."

In the merciful darkness where his face was hidden, he took her in his arms and kissed her. It was meant to be a light kiss, a signature to Christmas, but Sophie's lips clung to his, and suddenly Tom Fleming was kissing her with passion, with a sudden and joyful awareness of virility restored.

*   *   *

The Christmas peace lay over Finland, but only for a day. As soon as the holiday ended political activity was resumed by both sides: by the Reds, as the Social-Democrats were already known, and by Mr. Svinhufvud's government and the moderate party, who were increasingly referred to as the Whites. Nearly three weeks had passed since the declaration of independence, and in spite of all appeals to the Powers it had become clear that no country would acknowledge Finland's independence unless Russia did so first. Finland had been a Russian Grand Duchy for over a hundred years, and before that a possession of Sweden, and it was not easy for the European powers to visualise the little country as a sovereign state. As for the President of the United States, Mr. Woodrow Wilson, who had been such a prolific writer of Notes to the belligerents before the United States entered the war, he was understood to be hatching a programme of Fourteen Points for peace, which included freedom for Russia to determine her own political and national policy, but said nothing about the lands formerly (or still) under the Russian yoke.

So in Finland both the Whites and the Reds looked to Petrograd, where Vladimir Ilyich Lenin was already as powerful as any Romanov Czar, and the trains to Petrograd were crowded with delegates eager for an audience with the autocrat of the Smolny. Lenin, of course, had his personal agents inside Finland, including one Glasunov, the Helsingfors president of the "Rayon" group, a soldiers' revolutionary committee with its headquarters at Viborg. Glasunov was named on December 24 as Soviet Russia's official representative in Finland, whereupon Kullervo Manner, the leader of the Social-Democrats, went posting off to put his own point of view to Lenin at the Smolny. He came back subdued: the great man had berated him for the lost opportunities of November, and advised him to take the power by force next time. A few days later it was the turn of the Whites, and Mr. Svinhufvud left for Petrograd with two of his cabinet colleagues. With intentional rudeness, the Finns were kept hanging about in the corridors of the Smolny for many hours. Cold, hungry, humiliated and weary, they had to wait until the last moments of the old year before a document was put into their hands, signed by Lenin, Trotsky, Stalin and others, promising that the Soviets would recognise and ratify the independence of Finland . . . with reservations.

When the government spokesmen returned to Helsingfors, and these reservations were made known, there was fierce indignation among the Whites. For Lenin had refused to withdraw the Russian garrisons from Finland, thus making it clear that he considered the new state to be as much a part of Russia as the Grand Duchy had been, or at the very best a satellite of the Soviets. There was to be no release from the odious presence of the Russian troops, bullies and troublemakers in every town or village under their occupation. In self-defence, more and more "fire brigades" or groups of Civic Guards were forming, but as yet they lacked a leader. The Military Committee, composed of senior officers the youngest of whom had last worn Finnish uniform thirteen years before, was not very militant, and although General Mannerheim was said to have joined it, he had so far proved nothing but his ability to travel unmolested on the Helsingfors-Petrograd railway line. He made no speeches or public appearances, spending a quiet week in the home of his brother-in-law, Michael Gripenberg, and visiting his handsome eldest sister, the matron of the Surgical Hospital. It was left to rumour to spread the story of his daring journey from Odessa to Helsingfors. The Whites greatly enjoyed it, and were all the more disconcerted when, at the end of his quiet week, General Mannerheim returned to Petrograd as coolly as he had left it.

Tom Fleming spent most of the ten days after Christmas in visiting logging centres and saw-mills in Ostrobothnia, the province north-west of the capital bounded by the frozen Gulf of Bothnia. He went as far north as Gamla Karleby, for long a centre of the tar industry, and spent two days in and around Vasa, the provincial capital of Ostrobothnia. Everywhere he went he was assured that felling and hauling were going ahead at the usual rate, and that "under peaceful conditions" floating would start as usual when the ice on the lakes and rivers broke up. Tom was impressed by the progressive methods he saw in operation: the new types of saw, the extended use of timber flumes, and above all the understanding of conservancy in the land where timber was called green gold. In the early days of logging in British Columbia trees had been felled wastefully, and the reckless "slash and burn" tactics had destroyed the small trees and young growth. Tom Fleming dictated a letter to his father with an account of Finnish forest management and his own views thereupon, which was typed in triplicate by Sophie so that a copy could go to Graham Fleming at the Toronto office.

The news of Mr. Baker continued to be good, and he expected soon to be released from hospital and allowed to convalesce in the Gothenburg home of his daughter, Fru Jarrel, near the Lorensberg park. Tom sent full reports of his trips to Mr. Baker. He was dictating to Sophie Sandels, and that was all; Mr. Fleming and Miss Sandels behaved so correctly in the office that the eager kisses of Christmas afternoon might never have been exchanged. Nor did they meet outside the office, for Tom was not prepared to rush his fences. The secret assurance that he was capable of sexual response was enough to carry him over the next few days, when his general physical condition improved steadily in the bracing conditions of the forest life. It seemed as if his near collapse by the timber pile at Kouvola station had marked the very end of his long illness after being wounded at Sainte Elodie; from that day on, his strength returned. He could stand without weakness, walk farther, work for longer hours and, when he did spend time in the office, it was without the claustrophobia and restlessness which first afflicted him in Mr. Baker's room. He came to know the streets and lakes of Helsingfors, and often compared it in his mind with Vancouver. The two cities were almost the same in population, but although Helsingfors was not an ancient capital it had been laid out by a great planner working with a great architect, and Vancouver as yet had nothing to show half as splendid as the palace of the Czar-Grand Dukes, now standing empty by the South Harbour, or the house on the South Esplanade—palatial in the purity of the lines drawn by Carl

88

Ludwig Engel—formerly the Residence of the Russian Governors-General. The New Year came in, Gustaf Mannerheim returned unostentatiously from Petrograd, and as the days grew longer the red of the sunset grew deeper on the walls of the palace and the Residence.

In those days Tom Fleming began to know and appreciate the Finns. He had come among the last people in Europe likely to be dismayed by, or comment on, his marred face, and in the forest world they took him quite for granted. As his skin grew more weatherbeaten by the winter cold the vicious scar began to pale, and the flourishing moustache completely covered his upper lip. He adapted easily to the extreme cold and to the pleasures of the steam bath, for every house he stayed at had its sauna. He took very kindly to food ranging from *filbünke*, curds sprinkled with powdered ginger, to reindeer steaks and fish trapped through holes in any of the thousand frozen lakes which reminded him a little of his own Kootenays. In Ostrobothnia he found that if the saw-millers who spoke no English phrased their Swedish very simply, and he spoke his "Galician" German slower still they could understand each other in business terms, and the spirit of these men Tom understood very well indeed. Every parish had its tale of violence, theft and murder perpetrated by the Reds. Every township had its own defence corps which, judging from the sounds Tom sometimes heard in the forests, was eager to blaze away its whole supply of ammunition on target practice.

He was persuaded by a hospitable client to spend the first Saturday night of the new year in the country, and so was in the train on the way back to Helsingfors when the Red Guards made their first big move since the November attack on the Senate House. This was the occupation of the former Residence, now housing the Ministry of Labour, and easy to execute on a Sunday which was also a holiday, the Feast of the Kings. The classic centre of the city was deserted when the Red Guards marched along Union Street from the imposing House of the Workers, built a few years earlier by the hands and the contributions of the working men themselves. The Workers' House occupied a whole corner block just north of the Long Bridge, with a view across the creek towards the Tölö lake, and underneath its mock-medieval tower it held sixty rooms and five great halls, one being the largest in the whole of Finland. The House, however, was not large enough

89

for the extremists among the Red Guards, who were growing tired of Manner and the Social-Democrats, and wanted to proceed to open revolution. The little Residence was seized in the name of the Red Staff, neither police nor militiamen opposing, and the token force of fifty which went in had increased, by Monday morning, to a rabble of four or five hundred, plundering, investigating, destroying, spitting, eating, much as the Petrograd mob had done when the Winter Palace fell.

"Well, they've got their Smolny," said Nikko Hirn sourly, looking across the Esplanade at the Residence, where the Red Flag had now taken the place of the Russian double eagle. "That's what it's for, you know: just for the comrades to play at being Lenin and Trotsky, and harass all of us here in the business district—swine!"

"Could be," said Tom laconically. Privately he thought the seizure of the Residence was much more than a gesture: the Red Guards were getting ready to force a real showdown. But he didn't say so, because Sophie was in the room with them, like every other office-worker whose own window did not face on the Esplanade on that Monday morning. Everyone safe inside his office was looking across, or up or down the street at the Residence, and the Red Guards on sentry duty at the door, who made a great business out of crossing their bayonets in front of any caller whose credentials did not satisfy them. There was a great deal of coming and going at the new Red stronghold, and once Tom was certain he saw Boris Heiden talking to someone at the door. But after all he couldn't swear to it, the distance across the gardens, between the trees, was too great, and then, Heiden in his flat cap and high boots looked just like anybody else.

At the lunch hour there was a big demonstration, mostly led by the young, singing "Arise, ye prisoners of starvation!" up and down the two sides of the Esplanade. But there was no violence, and Tom and Nikko even stopped to listen when a French comrade, a woman, appeared at one of the windows of the Residence to sing the *Internationale* in her own language.

> *C'est la lutte finale, groupons-nous, c'est demain*
> *L'Internationale sera le genre humain!*

The avenue, between the tall houses, was rolling with sound as a thousand voices took up the song. Tom and his companion pushed their way down to the little fish restaurant by the covered market without exchanging many words. There were still some stalls open on the Market Square in front of the empty palace, and Nikko bought five crocuses, three white and two blue, from a woman who was just blowing out the lamp which protected her flowers from the frost. Tom saw them later in a glass on Sophie's desk, and Sophie looked as if she had been crying.

"Come and have dinner with me tonight, Sophie," he said, when the depressing day came to an end at last. "We'll get something to eat at the hotel and maybe go to the Biograph and cheer ourselves up."

"The Biograph!" She looked dismayed, as if a visit to the cinema was somehow unthinkable on such a day. "I'm sorry. It's very kind of you, but I promised to have supper tonight with two women friends—girl artists we know, they have a studio near the Athenaeum."

"All right, but let's have some coffee first at Fazer's, you can manage that, can't you?" he coaxed. "It's on your way, mine too, and you look so cold. Is that stove working?"

"The woman forgot to bring any paraffin today."

"If she hasn't got her wits back by tomorrow you'll have to work in the other room." He took her arm protectively as they went into the street. There was a blaze of light from the new Red Staff Headquarters at the Residence, and an important coming and going of messengers; they were playing the Smolny scene right up to the hilt. Sophie turned thankfully away in the opposite direction, but before they were abreast of the Hotel Kämp she whispered to Tom that she would like to go into the gardens for a moment. They crossed the street and stood in front of the statue where they had seen the Russian soldiers sprawling on the night Tom came to Helsingfors.

He knew now, because Sophie herself had told him, that it was the statue of Johan Ludwig Runeberg, Finland's national poet. The words on the pedestal were the words of the national anthem, which he had written, and the female figure was intended to represent Finlandia. Tom was not surprised when Sophie reverently laid her posy of blue and white crocuses at the base of the statue, beside a few other bunches, whitening under the falling snow. He was decidedly taken aback when, looking up at the statue of an elderly man in a frock coat, she began to recite a few lines of poetry:

> Pillar-high in the pleasant garden,
> Straight he stands, like a banner furled,
> Seer-king and passionless warden
> Over a little northern world.

Sophie did not raise her voice, and there was nobody but Tom to hear her as she repeated one or two more stanzas while he stood beside her in the snow. Then she put her arm through his again and looked up at him expectantly, Tom finding nothing better to say than:

"Did he write that?"

"Runeberg? No, Tom, it was written *about* him." But she smiled for the first time that day, and they walked quickly—it was not very far—to Fazer's, the leading tea-room of the capital. Like all public places at that time it was half empty, but one of the charms of Fazer's was a fine log fire, and Tom secured a table as near to it as possible. When he came back from hanging up their overcoats he found Sophie holding out her chilled hands to the blaze.

"You know, you're a remarkable girl," he said when the coffee and cakes were brought. "I don't know anybody else, man or woman, who would start reciting poetry to a statue on a snowy night."

"Canadian ladies don't say poetry in the park?"

"No, they don't. I do know one American girl who would say poetry, or sing a song, or make a speech, any time, any place it took her fancy." He remembered that that girl had sung "The Red Flag" on Skid Road in her radical days, but it was not the time to say so.

"What's her name?"

"Nancy Macpherson." He had almost said "Calamity Jane", before he remembered the impossibility of explaining Wild Bill Hickok to the Finnish girl.

"Nancy's an enthusiast, like you, only she has a new enthusiasm every five minutes, and they don't always last. Right now she's a patriot, solid for Old Glory and the US army and My country right or wrong."

"Is she *in* the army? In France?"

"I don't think they're enlisting women yet," said Tom drily. "She's working in a soldiers' canteen in London. I know she hopes to get to France."

"She must be quite young, then?"

"Twenty-two."

"And pretty?"

He was going to say "Yes, quite," when he remembered the round face under the rough dark curls, and the brilliant blue eyes, the face he couldn't even remember seeing for the first time, the face of always, and he said, "*Very* pretty," and changed the subject.

"Sophie," he said, "would you repeat that last verse you said by the statue? Something about 'the conflict nigh'?"

"Of course:

> Through him the heroes of ancient story
> Hearten their sons to the conflict nigh:
> To live and labour for Finland's glory,
> In her free service proud to die."

"Is that the verse?"

"Yes," said Tom, and sighed. "That's what I thought you said. And you believe in it, don't you? 'The conflict nigh' and 'proud to die' and all that stuff?"

"Stuff?"

"Yes, Sophie. You mustn't get carried away with it. If there's a conflict, your side's going to lose, and the dead aren't proud, they're only dead—I've seen 'em."

"Our side is going to lose? The Reds win? Never!"

"For *God's* sake," he said to the sudden fury in her face, "I don't want the Whites to lose and the Bolshies win. But you can't have any idea how long it takes to put an army in the field, and the Whites haven't even got the nucleus of an army, just a bunch of defence corps scattered up and down the land. Take what happened to the Canadian Division. We were shipped overseas in jig time, just about three weeks after I enlisted in Vancouver, and then what? We had to spend nearly five months of rain and mud on Salisbury Plain, in England, training to *be* soldiers, before we were ready to go to France and kill or be killed. Your Mannerheim may be all you say he is, but if he were Napoleon and

93

Wellington rolled into one he couldn't win without a staff and a body of professional officers, and that's what Finland hasn't got!"

"Oh, but we have," she said.

"Come again?"

"You've never heard of the Jäger Battalion?"

"Sounds like a German outfit to me."

"And that's what it is—at present," said Sophie in all innocence. "For as long as three years Finnish boys have been escaping to Germany for military training, to be ready for the day when Finland would be free from the Russian yoke. There are two thousand now, and they've already been in action on the Russian front. Very soon they'll come back to Finland as the officers you say yourself we'll need."

"Just let me get this straight," said Tom Fleming. "You say they were in action on the Russian front?"

"Yes, two years ago. They've been stationed at Libau on the Gulf of Riga for the past twelve months."

"Never mind that. They were fighting against Russia on the *German* side?"

"Yes, certainly . . . But what's the matter? Why do you look like that?"

"I don't suppose I look any worse than usual," he said brutally. "You can't expect me to grin and congratulate you on your reinforcements from Germany. Don't you realise I've been fighting the Germans for the last three years?"

It was not very far to the street where Sophie's artist friends lived, and Tom had his irritation sufficiently under control to bid her a cheerful good night at the corner. But Sophie was nearly in tears as she hurried down the little street, and when she stopped to compose herself before ringing the bell she was not thinking of the Jägers, nor of Tom's unexpected reaction to the idea of Finnish troops trained in the German army. She was saying to herself, and desperately:

"Young and very pretty! Only twenty-two, and very pretty! Oh, my God, if I were only ten years younger!"

8

EVEN BEFORE THE RED occupation of the Governor-General's Residence Tom Fleming had one silent pre-occupation: his anxiety whether, or when, the two British agents would arrive in Helsingfors. The assembly at the Tauride Palace in Petrograd, which Kerensky was determined to attend, was to have opened on the fifth of January, while Tom was in the country, and from that time he never returned to his hotel, or entered the office, without asking if there had been a telephone message in his absence. At last, and late in the day after their talk in Fazer's, Sophie tapped on the door of the private room. and said,

"Telephone for you, Mr. Fleming. An English gentleman, I think. He didn't give his name."

"Thanks." Inwardly cursing Mr. Baker's system of having the only telephone in the outer office, he took up the receiver and said, "Thomas Fleming here."

The voice which came over the wire was deliberately subdued. "My name's Black, Mr. Fleming. Mr. White said you were expecting us."

"You bet!" said Tom enthusiastically. Out of the tail of his eye he saw Nikko Hirn get up from his desk and stretch, his broad, rather Mongolian face one vast yawn, as if the "fire brigade" had been on duty all night long. "You're not alone, I hope?"

"We're both at the flat," said the voice, "but there's been a spot of trouble. Could you come over?"

"Sure!" cried Tom, still with false jollity, "be with you right away! Good to hear from you!"

"Miss Sandels," he said, reaching for his coat, "some pals of mine blew into town. Could you hang on for half an hour or so? I'll call you back."

"Certainly, Mr. Fleming," she said, looking bewildered by the slang which sounded phoney even in his own ears, like some corny dialogue in a road company performance of *The Girl from*

Calgary. He didn't want Sophie and Hirn to catch on to anything, and yet he dared not lose his only line of communication in this foreign city. He almost ran across Alexander Street, past the Athenaeum, across the Railway Square, and arrived winded at Mr. Baker's door.

He let himself in with his own key. The living room door was ajar, and a voice said, "Fleming?" as he crossed the tiny hall. He said, "Yes, it's Fleming," and went in to confront one of the largest men he had ever seen.

Tom was six foot tall, but this man was at least six foot six and built in proportion, with shoulders like a barn door. His long hair was dirty and tousled, and he wore a moujik's blouse with one button of the neck band missing and a sheath knife clasped to the belt. His heavy greatcoat had been spread on the wood floor, with another coat on top, to make a bed for a young, bearded man who lay there with his eyes closed, his lips blue, his breathing quick and shallow. His boots had been removed, one trouser leg slit to the knee, and the giant, who had straightened up to greet Tom, bent again to his task of washing the leg clean of dirt and blood. It was the left leg, and the unconscious man's left arm had been wrapped loosely in a gauze bandage, already dyed with blood. A tin basin stood on the floor, half full of red-stained water.

"What happened, for God's sake?" said Tom.

"The Reds caught up with us this side of Borgå and hunted us down with a motor lorry," said the big man. "I got a knock from the bumper and landed in the ditch, but poor old John got crushed against the wall of some factory or other—"

"But how did you get here?"

"A fellow came by in a waggon and gave us a lift into town as far as the bridge."

"And then?"

"Then I carried him on my back across the park."

"Good Lord!"

"He wasn't very heavy."

Tom felt the feeble, irregular pulse, touched the cold, moist skin and looked at the bared leg. "You should have told me it was a case for a doctor," he said, "that's a compound fracture, at the very least."

" 'fraid so. White said you would know—"

The hell of it was that he didn't know; it was a contingency which White had never mentioned, and Tom Fleming had not had the wit to foresee.

"I'm going to phone," he said. "Have you got enough of that gauze stuff? There's a first-aid box in the bathroom."

"That's where this came from."

In Mr. Baker's flat the telephone was in the dining room. Tom picked it off its handstand and dialled the office number. Sophie answered immediately, as if she had been standing waiting for the phone to ring.

"Sophie? Tom. Is Mr. Hirn still there?"

"He left just after you did. Is anything wrong?"

"Just wanted to make sure you were alone. Now listen, can you give me the name of a reliable doctor, someone who can speak English?"

"Reliable?"

"Somebody who won't talk."

He heard her gasp. "Have you hurt yourself? Tom! Where are you?"

"I'm all right. I'm at Mr. Baker's flat. A man here needs a doctor badly."

"Shot?"

"He's been in an accident. Two compound fractures, or I miss my guess."

"I'm coming at once." The line went dead, but Tom continued urgently: "Sophie! No! Stay right where you are! Just give me the number!" The line buzzed; she had hung up on him.

He went back to the living room. "It's all right," he said, "help's on the way. How is he now?"

"He's coming round, I think."

"We ought to keep him warmer." Tom stripped off his own overcoat and laid it gently on the injured man. He felt the radiators beneath the windows, not as hot as when he first visited the flat, and saw with relief that the stove was set with logs and kindling. They blazed up as soon as he threw a lighted match among the wood shavings.

"Bill!" said the man on the floor suddenly, "Bill! Who?"

Tom again knelt down beside him, and gently said, "A friend. Everything's fine now, and you've got a Blighty one, what do you say to that?"

The injured man said, "Water."

"Better wait until the doctor comes, John old boy," said Black. "He won't be long. Will he, Fleming?"

"I don't think so. But a Finnish girl will get here first, and please remember, Black, her name is Sophie. You don't need to know her last name, or any more about her. By the way, what's John's name? Green? Or Redding?"

"Why not Brown?"

"As good as any. You look as if *you* could use a drink yourself. Why don't you get whatever you want from the dining room?"

He felt himself in command of the situation, for the first time since he took his patrol out at Sainte Elodie. He pulled up a chair and sat down to watch the man who had relapsed into unconsciousness, not taking his eyes off him until Black put a dram of neat whisky in his hand.

"Hadn't you better tell me a bit more?" he said. "What happened after you got out of Russia? How did you get side-tracked down to Borgå?"

"We weren't sidetracked. We went that way on purpose. We left Petrograd by the same train Kerensky did, and attracted all the attention we could at the Red check-point at Bielostrov. John looks enough like Kerensky to pass for him—you'd have taken them for a pair of Nihilist students by the time we left the forest."

Tom's first impression when he knelt down beside the injured man had been: he looks like Boris Heiden. The hair was far longer, but of the same light colour, and there was the same wispy beard, the slight but strong limbs—and there he had stopped himself with the thought that he had Heiden on the brain. He agreed now that Black's friend looked very like what Tom could remember of the photographed face, big-nosed, small-chinned, distinguished, of the former president of the Russian provisional government.

"So you were running interference for Kerensky?" he said.

"Yes," said Black, "and it worked! Mr. K. came right through on the train without any trouble, and he's safe with friends in Helsingfors now. I rang up his contact before I telephoned you."

"And what did you do? Jump the train?"

"Yes, as soon as we were sure the Reds were excited enough to start searching the compartments. We made a spectacular departure, borrowed a couple of bikes and started in the direction of Borgå. We wanted it to look as if Mr. K. and friend were on their way to join the Grand Duke Kiril at Haikko manor.''

"And then the truck caught up with you?"

"That's it."

"You were damned lucky they didn't come back to make sure they'd finished you off."

"Don't I know it! But there were just too many people about for them to risk it, unless they wanted trouble with the local Whites. There was a big printing-works, or something of that sort, not far away, and the waggon that picked us up was coming from there. The back was piled with books for Helsingfors.''

"There's a big publishing company—" Tom began, and then broke off. He had heard Sophie's ring at the door of the apartment building.

She was standing on the doorstep, with the light of the solitary street lamp on her anxious face, and beside her was a young man in a dark overcoat and hat, who clicked his heels and bowed to Tom in silence.

"This is a friend of mine, Mr. Fleming," Sophie said. "May we come in?"

"Of course." Beyond them, in the street, he saw a discreet limousine, with no red cross or hospital identification, but big enough to hold the stretcher which two men were now unfolding through a rear door.

"This way, doctor," said Tom. Sophie touched his sleeve. "You can trust him," she said. "We thought it better not to bring an ambulance. I told him there'd been a car crash—will that do?"

"There was, as a matter of fact."

In the living room the young doctor was already examining his patient while Black stood silently by. At last the doctor straightened up and signed to the two attendants to carry the injured man out. Then he spoke to Sophie in Swedish, and Tom was glad to see that she smiled and nodded, before he spoke in English to the two young men. "These road accidents are most distressing," he said. "Your friend is suffering from a fractured scapula, do you say shoulder-blade? and a compound fracture of the shaft, do you say shaft? of the tibia. Also of course from shock and loss of blood. I take him now to my clinic, do you say clinic?"

99

"Nursing-home," said Sophie.

"Nursing-home, at this address." He laid a card on the little table. "That is my name, and my patient's is—"

"John Brown, of London," said the man called Black.

"Quite so. He will be much better by the day after tomorrow, and you may visit him. Good night, madam; good night, gentlemen!" He was about to leave when Sophie spoke again, and with a nod he took a bottle from his bag and handed it to her.

"Good Lord, that was quick work!" said Black as the door closed behind him. "Miss Sophie, you were wonderful—"

"Hush up a minute," said Tom curtly. He went back to the street door, listening to the purr of the limousine's tyres on the snow as it turned the corner into the Railway Square, and looking up and down the street. Not a window shutter had been opened, not a light was to be seen except the street light. It seemed as if the strange doings at Mr. Baker's flat had been ignored by every other resident of that quiet neighbourhood.

He went back to find Sophie laughing in the relief from nervous tension, and pretending to bully the admiring giant. "Now you must wash your face, Mr. Black," she was saying. "There's some hot water, and you must get clean, and then dab all those bruises and grazes with surgical spirit, I made the doctor leave some for you. Then I think you should try to rest."

"I'm all in," said the big young man. "Haven't closed my eyes for twenty-four hours. Can I use any of the rooms? Just for a couple of hours?"

"I hope you're going to sleep all night," said Sophie. "Try!"

*   *   *

"Thanks, Sophie," said Tom awkwardly, when they were alone. It made him uncomfortable to see her standing there, staring at him, and then round the room which she must have seen so often, now so strangely altered. The birch logs blazed in the porcelain stove, the muslin curtains trembled in a slight draught from behind the closed shutters, all the spindling furniture was in its place. Only the bamboo rocking-chairs had been pushed aside to make room for three overcoats, two of them stained and tattered, and for a kitchen basin full of water stained with red.

"Those men are British agents, aren't they?" she said.

"Yes."

"Come out of Russia?"

"Look, Sophie," Tom Fleming said, "the less you know about all this, the better. I was a skunk to bring you into it, but I had to get a doctor in a hurry, and—"

"Don't apologise," she said, "I knew something like this would happen, as soon as you told me you were going to keep the keys."

"Mr. Baker," he said. "Do you think he'd mind? Those chaps needed shelter—"

"He'll be glad," she said confidently. "Mr. Baker never hid his White sympathies . . . but you, Tom! oh! when I look back on the sermons you preached to me about fire-power, and what it takes to make an army, and all the time you were on our side, fighting for us, believing in our cause—" She began laughing, so hysterically that he took a step towards her, to warn her to be quiet, and with that she made to fling herself into his arms, tripped on the overcoats and was caught by Tom before she reached the ground. Embraced, they sank down together, he kissing her frantically, each conscious only of the other and the warmth of the fire and a vicarious escape from danger. It was then, totally aware of Sophie's body pliant against his own, that Tom heard a heavy knock upon the door.

She heard it too. She started up, dragging him with her, and they both froze into silence. The knock was repeated, and something was said in a man's gruff voice.

"What did he say?"

"He said 'Open up!' " whispered Sophie. "Can it be the police?"

"I'll find out," said Tom. "No, you stay here, Sophie, I'll handle this myself." He shut the living room door firmly, and in the little hall transferred the Webley from his shoulder holster to his jacket pocket.

He opened the outer door on a man and a woman, both carrying rifles with fixed bayonets, and the armbands of the Red Guards. The woman, for good measure, wore a red feather in her black felt hat, and was smoking a cigarette. The man had a tawny beard, clipped to a point, and a black caracul cap with the ear-pieces tied on top of his head. He growled out something in Finnish when Tom appeared.

"*Was wollen Sie?*" said Tom with a show of authority. "*Ich bin Kanadier, was ist los?*"

101

The girl laughed sarcastically. "*Kanadier! Kanadier!*" she imitated him. Then from behind her back she produced a cocoa tin covered in red paper, with a slit in the lid, and shook it under his nose. "For the workers' cause!" she said in English. Tom gave her a few coins and shut the door. He heard the Red Guards laughing in the lobby. There was no sound of footsteps on the stairs; they were not begging from any of the other tenants in the house. The front door shut with a bang.

"Who was it, Tom? I heard you speaking German." Sophie was trembling now, all her courage gone in the dread of discovery. "Was it the police? What did they want?"

"Now, only two Red Guards, asking for money as usual. I gave them a couple of marks just to get rid of them."

"Two men?"

"No, a man and a woman, a real fly-by-night with a beat-up red feather in her hat, and a cigarette."

"What did the man look like?"

Tom described him, and saw her gesture of dismay. "Those two were hanging about on the North Esplanade when I left the office tonight. Oh Tom! Do you think they followed me here?"

"Nonsense, you're imagining things." He made her sit down in the rocking-chair and wait for ten minutes, till she was calm, and then he went out and checked every doorway in the quiet cul-de-sac before he would allow Sophie to come out and start on her homeward way. When they were in the broad street with the trams she breathed more freely, and he stood at the corner and watched until she was safely inside her own front door. Then he went quickly back to the flat and put more logs on the fire. He glanced into the nearest bedroom. Black had taken his boots off, and was stretched out on a sofa with his moujik blouse rolled up for a pillow, and his long legs dangling uncomfortably over the end. Tom took the quilt from the bed and spread it over the sleeping giant. It was still only seven o'clock.

It was not quite nine when he shook Black's shoulder, and the young man opened his eyes at once: wide awake, clear-headed, and, throwing aside the quilt, he came to his feet in one quick movement. "Time?" he said.

"Just on nine. Sleep all night if you like, but you said two hours as if you meant it—"

"I did. Thanks, Fleming, I must be on my way."

"Take time out to shave and eat first. There's hot water in the bathroom."

There was also food in the kitchen, which was warmer than the cheerless dining room, and where Mr. Baker appeared to have been hoarding some of the tinned eatables Tom had got to know only too well in Flanders. There was hot soup from a can, and a Maconochie's beef stew with vegetables, with a hot grog to begin with and a pot of coffee at the end.

"It's a banquet," said Black, eating the stew ravenously. "You're a pretty good hand in the kitchen, Fleming."

Tom laughed. In his logging days, his father had started him on the lowest rung of the ladder, as camp chore boy; any number of temperamental camp cooks had sworn at him and thrown cast-iron pots at his head until he learned how to put a decent meal on the table. He was not hungry himself, but he drank a mouthful of grog thirstily, and asked Black what he planned to do.

"Now we know Mr. K's all right, I've got to get out to Sweden, no time to lose," he said. "What's the chances of going through by Åbo?"

Tom was positive that the Åbo route was out. The port was iced in to the extent that even the icebreakers were staying in harbour, and the town itself was more or less in the hands of the Reds. Black risked being picked up if he had to stay in Åbo, waiting for a steamer, for any length of time.

"Except that they think I'm dead, old boy, dead in a ditch outside Borgå," said Black. "They won't have troubled to send any description of me on ahead. But I can't risk any delay, the way things are in Petrograd. I'll have to go round the Gulf by Torneå and Haparanda, hell!"

"There's a train out to Torneå at eleven o'clock," said Tom. "Cigarette?"

"Thanks. Eleven. That means about noon tomorrow at Torneå. Lie up all day and cross the river after dark, h'm . . . at least I can telephone to Stockholm from Haparanda. Twenty-four hours. I wish I had the nerve to try the Kvarken!"

"What's that?"

"It's a strait in the Gulf of Bothnia, running roughly from Vasa to Umeå in Sweden, which is on the main railway line to Stockholm. In summer it's a steamer route. But in winter, if a man can get to an offshore island called Björkö after the Gulf freezes hard, it's possible to cross the Kvarken and reach Sweden on foot. I know one chap who did it twice, but it's a hell of a risk unless you've got a reliable guide, and I've no contact in Vasa to put me on to one."

"Don't crowd your luck too far," said Tom. "You two got away with your lives at Borgå; just make sure of getting safely to the Swedish side. Now tell me about the way things are in Petrograd."

Whereupon Black, pouring himself another cup of coffee from the shabby enamel kitchen pot, told Tom something of his travels with Kerensky after the former prime minister had fled from Petrograd. Their last hideout had been in a forest cottage near Novgorod, from which late on New Year's Day they had emerged to catch the Petrograd train at Bologoye halt, and arrived without challenge in the capital. There Kerensky's friends had finally persuaded him that an attempt to address the Constituent Assembly would be suicidal, and they were proved right: Lenin's desperadoes not only dissolved the gathering in the Tauride Palace by force of arms, but entered the hospital where two members of the former government were lying, and bayoneted them to death. The Bolsheviks had entered on a reign of terror and the British Ambassador had asked for his passports, while Kerensky, accompanied by one friend, escaped by train to Helsingfors.

"So that's the story," Black concluded, stretching and yawning. "God! I'm going to sleep for forty-eight hours when I get to Stockholm! Except for poor old John in hospital, we didn't do too badly. By the way, the British Minister in Stockholm will settle his bills, of course; just get in touch with him as soon as you can. I'll tell him what a thundering good job you've done, and the Chief too . . . By the way, did I hear voices outside when I was giving myself first aid?"

Tom briefly told him about the Red Guards' visit, and Sophie's fear that she had been followed to the house. A comical expression of dismay appeared on the big young man's face.

"My dear fellow, I'm afraid it means you're blown," he said. "Goodbye to our safe house in Helsingfors!" He took the keys of the flat from his pocket and laid them on the kitchen table. "Well, it was only for this one time, and thank God it worked! But now you must keep away from the place yourself, you and your friend Sophie. I'd hate to think of anything happening to that splendid woman."

"Yes, but what about if you can't get across the border at Haparanda?" argued Tom. "What if you have to turn back to Helsingfors? You'd better come and share my room at the hotel, until you can get out through Åbo."

"If I don't cross at Torneå-Haparanda it'll be because I'm underneath the ice," said Black. "And from what you tell me the Whites will have to fight their way into Åbo before anybody on their side can get out. What about yourself, Fleming? If war starts here, will you try the Torneå run?"

"I hadn't thought about it." It was a half-lie, he had been forced to think, by the evidence which lay all round him, of the likelihood of war in Finland, but the thought of actually leaving had never crossed his mind. "A lot of people seem to pin their faith to General Mannerheim, but what can he do without any weapons?"

"Mannerheim went back to Petrograd two weeks ago to ask the French Military Mission to give him arms," said Black precisely. "The French have a large supply of arms at Murmansk, dumped there before the Czar's abdication. Murmansk is a hell of a long way from Helsingfors—yes, I knew you were going to say that" (nodding at Tom, who was about to interrupt), "but the question of transport didn't even arise. General Niessel turned him down flat, and Mannerheim came back here empty-handed."

"So that was why he made a return trip to Petrograd," said Tom. "You heard all this at the Embassy, I suppose?"

"Not on the spot, no, we didn't pay a courtesy call," said Black with a grin. "We were sticking pretty close to Mr. K. But White was in touch with me, and he passed on the news—oh, Lord! I nearly forgot to deliver a personal message for you from White. You were asking about a chap called Igor Heiden?"

"Boris Heiden." Tom's mouth was dry. "Boris was the fellow I told White about."

"Yes, well, Boris was Igor's younger brother."

"He told me that himself, within hours after I saw White at Imatra."

"Right! They were the sons of a Baltic baron called Alexander Heiden, a big noise in the finance department during the old Czar's reign. There was some scandal about him too, though not enough to affect his place at court, and anyway he died in '99, long before Igor got himself into trouble. Our Igor, if you please, was one of the gang who tried to assassinate Stolypin, the prime minister, at his dacha outside St. Petersburg in the summer of 1906. They were all rounded up, and Igor Heiden was condemned to death and hanged."

9

LONG BEFORE THE NIGHT train pulled out on its long run
to the far north, Sophie Sandels had persuaded herself that
she must have imagined being followed by Red Guards from
the North Esplanade to Mr. Baker's flat. Lying in her darkened
bedroom, listening to Lisa's even breathing, she argued with herself that she hadn't even seen the two people Tom had handled so
briskly at the door. "*Ich bin Kanadier*"—that must have taken them
aback—and there was no reason why they should have been the
same two who were hanging round the cabbage-scented eating-
house in the courtyard less than an hour before. Heaven knew the
Esplanades, North and South, had been crawling with Red
supporters since Sunday's occupation of the Residence, and among
them were plenty of men with caracul hats and women flaunting
red feathers. Sophie was furious with herself at making a fuss,
after showing the practical good sense which had brought a
doctor to help two Englishmen in trouble. For half an hour she
had lived in the heat of a desperate event which, although it
concerned two British agents, Sophie could only too easily equate
with Finland's bid for independence, and then she had relapsed
into being as nervous and excitable as Lisa was apt to become for
far less cause. But Tom had stood between her and the imagined
danger. On that delicious thought she fell asleep smiling, to
awake next morning on a still happier thought, that now there
was a secret which they shared.

Tom, when they met at the office, was grave and preoccupied.
He had spent the whole night at the Baker flat, leaving it exactly
as he had first seen it except for the small quantities of food and
drink consumed, and although he told Sophie that Black had
left Helsingfors, he refused to name his destination. Instead,
he told her to telephone at once to the nursing-home, before
Nikko Hirn arrived, and find out how the man called John
Brown had spent the night. The news was not good. The Englishman had suffered from the extreme cold and exposure of his

107

journey into Helsingfors, and the onset of pneumonia was to be dreaded. Visitors were absolutely forbidden for the present.

"Now you remember that, Sophie," said Tom sharply. "Even when he's better, I don't want you going off to that place to ask for him."

"But it's so near, just off the Tölö road, behind the National Museum."

"Doesn't matter where it is, I don't want you to be seen around there. First for your own sake, then for Brown's, and right now he's too sick to give a damn for flowers or kind enquiries. If anything goes wrong, that doc knows where to find us, and meantime you keep out of it, understand?"

Sophie was not dismayed by his abruptness. She had seen Tom Fleming changing from the self-conscious, diffident young man who had arrived in Finland, back into his former character of the competent young army officer, and she was fascinated by the change. But lacking the key to his character she failed to realise that just as his body and nerves were being restored by a return to the forest life, so the encounter with the British agents had revived much of his former energy. Tom was perfectly willing to act as cook and bottlewasher—for one evening—to two Englishmen on the run. But he envied Black, who had so coolly made his getaway on the late train to Torneå, back into the world of daring from which Tom Fleming now seemed to be excluded; and when, thirty-six hours later, a telegram arrived from Swedish Haparanda saying "Merchandise arrived in good condition" he almost regretted that the adventure of the British agents was so quickly and almost tamely over.

He had been planning a trip to Kotka before the end of the week, but until Brown was out of danger Tom thought it wiser not to leave Helsingfors. In any case a rail ticket on the main line, eastbound, was becoming impossible to obtain. The line to Petrograd was all but closed to civilian traffic, and Kotka, where some of the largest timber businesses in Europe were located, was now celebrated as the centre of one of the largest refugee communities in Finland. The Russians who had fled to their own dachas round the pavilion built for the Czar Alexander III at Langinkoski, near the mouth of the Kymi river which every spring carried three million logs from the lake systems down to Kotka, were becoming terrorised by the presence of the Russian

XLII Corps at Viborg. They had begun to move west, on to Helsingfors, and hotels which had been half empty before Christmas were now crowded to the doors. Even the businesslike Finns became infected with the fatal Russian habit of endless talk and speculation, and the office of J. P. Baker & Co. was only one of a thousand in which all commercial activity seemed to be grinding to a halt.

For just one week, the second week of 1918, a kind of euphoria blanketed that part of the Helsingfors population which supported the government. The invasion of the Residence had been a severe shock, but it had not been followed by violence, and within a day or two began to seem unimportant compared with the news arriving from the outside world. This news came through diplomatic channels and was reported in the national press: it had nothing to do with the progress of the Great War on the continent or at sea, and indeed Finland seemed curiously remote from the world war. It was the recognition by the Great Powers of Finland's independence, so ardently desired, so miserably associated with the decision of the Soviet Commissars, which was now being announced day after day. The neutral Scandinavian kingdoms and three of the belligerents, Germany, Austro-Hungary, and their enemy France, all in that euphoric second week of January officially assented to the independence of the sovereign state of Finland. Britain sat on the fence, calling Russia still her ally while ordering Sir George Buchanan and his embassy to return to London, but Greece recognised independent Finland and so, as the week ended, did neutral Switzerland. It was the official realisation of what Sophie Sandels had called "Finland's world's dream" of being henceforth a separate entity and a partner of the western powers.

For just those few days, the gratification and importance were so great that any thought of coming danger was overlooked. An independence festival was hurriedly arranged for Sunday, January 13, to take place in the National Theatre, and the city was ransacked for flowers and flags to decorate the stage and the auditorium. The celebrations, of course, were open to anyone who could obtain a ticket, but as the improvised programme took shape it was clear that most of the celebrants thought they were scoring a strong point over the Reds, and that this Sunday's festivities were a tit-for-tat for last Sunday's occupation of the

Residence. So the battle lines between Reds and Whites were ever more clearly drawn, and Tom Fleming said as much to Sophie when she asked him, shyly, if he would care to join "his Finnish friends" at the great gathering in the theatre.

"I'll join *you*, if you'll let me," said Tom, "but you know I won't understand a word of it from beginning to end."

"I believe the music will be very fine."

"All right, let's go listen to the music," said Tom. He was in a relaxed mood. John Brown was out of danger, and Black, of course, must have reached Stockholm and be on his way to London. Alexander Kerensky appeared to be safe in his Helsingfors hideout, wherever it was; at least, there had been no announcement of his arrest. Music, then, for Tom Fleming and his Finnish friends: he asked Sophie to get the best tickets available "and one for your sister, too, if she cares to come."

But Lisa tossed her head and said *if* she went to hear a lot of silly speeches she would go with her own friends rather than play gooseberry for her sister and Mr. Fleming. Sophie only smiled. She was in a private but very feminine flutter about what to wear at the theatre: for Finland's first great national occasion her best velvet dress was not too grand, but then the colour! Impossible to celebrate Finland's independence in the enemy red! She had very little finery, and after sponging and pressing a long black skirt, also made of velvet, she went to an expensive little shop on Alexander Street and bought what the saleswoman called an evening blouse. It looked quite different from the severe shirt-blouses she wore in the office, being made of jade-green chiffon and cut on soft clinging lines, but this revealed the ridge of her long whalebone corset, so that Sophie left the shop with two wisps of lace, one of which held up a pair of the silk stockings Tom had given her for Christmas. Lisa was out when she dressed, and Sophie studied her reflection earnestly in the candlelit mirror. The jade green made her skin more dazzling than ever, and brought out auburn highlights in her straight pale brown hair, but was there a first wrinkle on her forehead, the beginning of tiny lines at the corner of her eyes? Brow, eyes, and firm jawline were faultless in the mirror; the recollection helped Sophie, now so scantily clad, to bear the cold as she hurried to join Tom at the National Theatre.

This theatre had been for more than two generations an integral part of Finland's search for a national identity. Built long after the beautifying hand of Engel had passed from Helsingfors, it was not in itself pleasing to every eye, being part of the heavy Teutonic structures which stood around or near the Railway Square, but its value lay in its symbolic purpose, the search for poetic truth leading the seekers far beyond the boundaries of the former Grand Duchy of Russia. Shakespeare, Schiller, Molière had all been played in translation from the time the National Theatre was opened, and Finnish dramatists had showed convincingly that their native language was rich and valid in the expression of emotion. Nearly fifty years of Finnish history had had their focus on that stage, in that auditorium, and even Tom Fleming felt the excitement in the audience as he led Sophie Sandels to their seats in the stalls.

"Oh, Tom, isn't it wonderful!" she whispered, when he helped her to take off her coat and said, "What a pretty thing this is!" as he touched the soft full sleeves, caught in tight bands at her wrists, of the jade-green chiffon. But the wonderment was not in Tom's praise, much as she enjoyed it: the wonderful sight was the great golden Finnish Lion, framed in white pillars and surrounded by the flags of the three Scandinavian kingdoms and of France, Russia and Germany. "I needn't have worried about wearing red," she murmured, for red was one of the dominant colours in the auditorium. The decorators had worked with the colours of the old Lion Flag of Finland, red and gold, and the auditorium was hung with swags and drapes in those colours, while between the stage and the stalls a mass of red and yellow tulips stood outlined by the laurels of victory. It was a sight which Sophie Sandels had never thought to see, and the tears came to her eyes. Tom took her hand and held it tightly. He fully understood that for a patriot this was a tremendous moment, although he could hardly match Sophie's mood of exaltation. She would have liked the places of honour in front of the massed flowers to be filled by kings and emperors, each in his robes and crown to do honour to Finland, and if Gustaf Mannerheim, miraculously twenty-five again, could have strode on to the stage in the white uniform of the Chevalier Gardes, she would have thought his silver helmet and silver-handled sword entirely appropriate to the occasion. But instead of young heroes in shining armour the guests of honour were four worried, middle-

111

aged men in business suits, the consuls of France, Sweden, Denmark and Norway, and the even more anxious and apprehensive gentlemen who were the elected Senators of the new state of Finland . . . and there were too many empty seats among those reserved for members of the Diet.

"I wonder if we can see Lisa, she said they would be in the gallery," said Sophie, as a soft musical overture was played, and both she and Tom turned round to look up at the high rows where most of the younger people sat.

"It's easy to spot Lisa; look, over to the left," said Tom. The very fair, fluffy hair made Lisa Sandels easy to identify, and she had taken off the woollen tam o'shanter which she now waved cheerfully at her sister. She was sitting in the front row between two young men, both wearing leather jackets, both wispily bearded, both, as it happened, leaning forward on their folded arms. It was not easy to say which one was Boris Heiden. His talent for melting into the background was very clearly demonstrated on this night when the eyes of everyone in the theatre kept returning to the golden Finnish Lion, and to the field of flowers from which, in the slowly warming atmosphere, a sweet scent of spring was rising.

The programme began. The speeches were too long, but the phlegmatic Finns listened and applauded earnestly. A clergyman, a professor, a woman writer, an historian celebrated the independence of their country with a wealth of clichés about freedom and unity and civilisation. The music, on which Sophie Sandels had counted to save Tom from boredom, was uninspired, consisting chiefly of the national anthems of the countries represented by their consuls or their flags, and she could hardly blame Tom Fleming when she saw his jaw set with annoyance at the singing of "Deutschland über Alles". But then came music by a great composer, when the "Jäger March" was played for the first time in public, and the melodies of Sibelius gave lustre to the song of praise of the young Finns who had escaped from Russian tyranny to train as fighters in the cause of freedom. The orchestra concluded with Finland's own national anthem, and Sophie was only one of the many who were in tears as Runeberg's words were sung by the audience standing. Our land, our land, our fatherland: at last it had a meaning.

"Now we'll go back to the hotel and get some supper," said

Tom, when they were again breathing the clean snowy air of the January night.

"I don't think I can eat anything after that."

"Oh yes, you can. Patriotic songs give anyone an appetite, I found that out in London," said Tom cheerfully. He had not been bored in the theatre, in spite of the interminable speeches, but he was determined to get what remained of the evening on to a less heroic plane. So he told Sophie how badly she needed powder on her pretty nose, and made her laugh: she was quite gay by the time they reached the Society House, and she went off to change into her slippers and repair the ravages of emotion.

Tom himself went straight to the restaurant. He had seen a good many of the excited people from the theatre trekking across the square in the direction of his hotel, and was not surprised to find that not a single supper table remained available. The head waiter could promise nothing in less than an hour. Even the little lounge outside the restaurant was crammed with men and a few women, supping on sandwiches and beer, and the lobby beside the reception desk was packed with new arrivals. Tom had to fight his way back to Sophie at the cloakroom door.

"No food for an hour yet, I'm afraid," he said casually. "Will you come up to my room and have a drink?"

"Yes, I'd like to." She was as casual as he was, as if going upstairs with a man to his hotel room was something Sophie Sandels did every night of her life, although he could tell by her heightened colour and the quick rise of her breast under the green chiffon that she was excited by her own daring. They went up in the lift past the banqueting rooms, now invaded by whole families of refugees, and in his own corridor Tom told the chambermaid on duty to bring two bottles of "English soda" to Room 112. He stood aside to let Sophie enter, praying at the last moment that the maid had not arranged the bed for the night, with his pyjamas folded across the pillow.

The maid must have been interrupted in her work, because the white lace bedspread had been removed, and lay neatly folded over the foot of the brass bedstead. But the eiderdown in its queer reddish-brown cover was drawn closely up to the padded bedhead, and the orange shaded lamps were lit. Tom pulled forward one of the two stiff chairs, and asked Sophie if she cared to sit beside the lamp, but she was too nervous to sit down at once.

She roamed round the room, touching the brass door handle, which was oddly cast in the shape of a fish, and looking with curiosity at Tom's belongings strewn round the telephone on the dressing-table. He had a weakness for that kind of clutter, possibly in a reaction against the stringency of trench life, and the hotel maids declined to cope with it more than once a day. On the green cover of the table were two fountain pens, loose pages of timber calculations, an unopened packet of tooth powder and a number of small items like collar studs spilt out of a red leather box in an earlier attempt to find his gold cufflinks. A double leather travelling frame, scratched and battered, held photographs of his father and mother.

"Your parents?" Sophie asked.

"Yes. Taken quite a while ago, before the war."

"You're very like your father."

"Sort of a Scots look, would you say?"

"Perhaps."

Sophie set the leather frame down as an elderly maid came in with the soda and tall glasses. The woman had curtsied and left the room before it occurred to Tom that it was the first time anyone had commented on his looks since the action at Sainte Elodie without driving him into an agony of embarrassment.

He fetched a bottle of Scotch from the little closet opposite the bathroom which did duty as a wardrobe, and poured, first a weak drink for Sophie and then a stiffer one for himself.

"*Skål!*" said Sophie, touching the glass to her lips.

"*Skål.*" He thought she might sit down then, but Sophie was still restless. She looked critically at the bare walls, the sombre curtains, and peered out at the dark courtyard before settling down at last in the chair beside the lamp.

"Don't like the Scotch?"

"Oh yes, I . . . It's very nice. It's an acquired taste, I should think."

"Probably." Tom grinned. Sophie put her glass down quietly on the marble-topped table. The yellow liquid took on darker shades beneath the orange lamp, the jade-green blouse faded to olive against the rust and brass of the big bed. "You look wonderful, sitting there," said Tom. "The colours are just right for you. Like a modern painting—"

"Are you interested in painting?" she said, surprised.

"My sister Dorothy and I used to dabble in watercolours, when we were kids."

"Those artist girls I know say these are the kind of colours Finnish designers will be using before very long. Browns and dull greens and barbaric yellows."

"But you prefer the red and the gold, don't you, Sophie?"

"I did tonight."

"I know you did."

He produced his cigarettes, and when he had lighted hers, Sophie Sandels said, "Tom, what was the matter in the theatre? What was worrying you?"

"Nothing. It's tough when you don't understand what other people are saying—"

"It was more than that, wasn't it?"

"All right then, Sophie; here it goes." He came and sat close to her, on the edge of the bed, putting his empty glass beside her full one on the bedside table. "That show tonight—I know you thought it was the greatest ever, but it felt all wrong to me. Those men you pointed out were members of the government, so fine, that's great, but where were the leaders of the Social-Democrats? Where were any of the Russians? It was a White festival, not an independence festival; it was a victory celebration, victory in a war that hasn't yet been fought, and if it *is* fought—"

"Yes?"

"It'll be a civil war, and no country fights a civil war without taking two generations to recover."

"Have you become a pacifist since you left the army?" It was the most cutting thing she had ever said to him, and Tom scowled.

"Not me, no; but I knew a lot of guys in hospital who went that way, and I don't blame them. Some of them were far worse off than me."

"I'm sorry."

"It's all right." He took the hand she had impulsively held out to him and began to fidget with a heavy gold bracelet on her wrist.

"Sophie, I've tried so hard to make you understand what war's about. If the Whites fight the Reds in Finland, either the Russians will come in, and then your cities will be wiped off the face of the earth like Ypres, and Amiens, and Arras, or else the Germans will come in on the White side, and the Allies might—mind you, I only say *might*—make Finland a new battle-ground against Germany; and whichever way it goes, you just can't win. I want to see the war in Europe fought to a finish, and the Germans whipped. I don't believe in an arranged peace, or an armistice, I believe in unconditional surrender, but my God, Sophie, if we could put the clock back to June 1914, don't you think every civilised person in the world would vote for mediation between Austria and Servia, so that the murder of two people at Sarajevo shouldn't mean the death in battle of heaven knows how many millions more?"

"And where do the clock hands stand for Finland?"

"Well past the eleventh hour."

Sophie did a totally unexpected thing. She laid her free hand against Tom's scarred cheek and whispered, "Tell me what happened to *you*."

He understood immediately. She was incapable of taking it in, as an abstract. The names of the ruined towns he knew so well meant nothing to the Finnish girl. What she wanted was the personal experience: tell me about Tom Fleming's war.

He said, "You mean tell you about what happened at Sainte Elodie?"

"Was that where . . . I don't even know where Sainte Elodie is."

"It's a village, I mean it was a village, on the Scarpe. The enemy was holding it in strength, and we advanced as far as the perimeter one afternoon last August. Later I was ordered out on night patrol." He broke off. "I'm damned if I ever told anyone the story before!"

"Not anybody?"

"Not to tell it word for word. Sure, I dictated a report to my commanding officer—I couldn't see very well then—but that was a routine thing, by the manual. Then I had to answer questions at Dykefaulds about my reaction to this and my reaction to that, and of course I would have been questioned at the court martial—"

"You were court-martialled?"

"Hell no, I was decorated. I mean if there had *been* a court martial. Like some newspapers said there should have been."

Sophie said no more. Bewildered by Tom's confused beginning, she tried hard to follow his quick, still not quite familiar English speech, keeping her eyes on his, and all the time aware that his nervous fingers were pressing the links of her bracelet into the flesh of her thin wrist.

"Something we Canadians specialised in was night raider work. I mean the whole Division did well at it, and the Vancouver Seaforths were among the very best. Guys like me, who'd been bred up to the woods and hunting, got to have a special feel for it, going out in small groups and raiding the enemy lines in darkness. We were trained in bomb and bayonet work, though I never cared for the bayonet much; a good pair of wire-cutters and a couple hand-grenades used to suit me fine. We all wore privates' uniforms, with the badges of rank sewn on in back of our tunic collars—that was in case we were taken prisoner, Sophie—and we had our faces and hands blackened before we lit out. In the winter of '15, in the dark of the moon, I used to reckon on just ten minutes for a fast in-and-out to Jerry's forward trench, and back with three or four prisoners all ready to tell their story. Sure, we were all good at it . . . in the winter of '15.

"But this was 1917, and summer, and the nights were short. Not that that made any difference. I took men who knew the job inside out, but we never got up to Jerry's lines. He had three forward posts where I'd figured on one, and the whole lot of us were wounded and pinned down in a shell hole in the first four minutes. That's when I was hit in the face. But I don't think any of the men were killed outright. In fact I know they were all alive at dawn.

"That was when the enemy sent out an officer under a flag of truce. They saw him well enough from our own lines, even without binoculars. He came right up to the edge of the shell hole and asked who was in command. I said, me. I'd been wounded again and I couldn't hear him very well, but I said, me."

"He spoke English?" Sophie breathed.

"Perfect English. And he said—I remember every word— he said, 'Captain, my men have been disturbed all night by the screaming and moaning of your wounded. I call upon you to surrender, and allow us to give them the medical care we give to all our prisoners of war.' "

"And—?"

"I told him to go to hell. He asked me again, maybe twice again, and each time he used that word 'disturbed', as if the Huns hadn't got a decent night's rest because of us. So finally he went back under his flag of truce, and the barrage started up again . . . I don't remember much about the morning. Once or twice I thought I could hear larks singing, but it might have been one of my men crying . . . Then the Canadians advanced about noon and the stretcher-bearers got us out and back to the field hospital."

"How long had you been lying helpless there?"

"About twelve hours."

"And your men?"

"I was the sole survivor." It was impossible for Tom Fleming to go on. He had tried to paint for Sophie the true face of war, its savagery and its pain: he was literally incapable of describing the bitter aftermath of poor Rennie's dying confidence to the war correspondent looking for a sensation, about the German officer so generously offering medical help to the wounded, and the stubborn young Canadian refusing it on behalf of them all. The papers had made him out to be the villain of the piece, and yet Tom knew that not all the headlines from Halifax to Vancouver would stick in his brain (he had begun to forget the worst of them already) like the unforgettable words of the German officer—

My men have been disturbed all night by the screaming and moaning of your wounded.

"Poor Tom! Oh, poor Tom!" He was just aware of Sophie's voice, muted and sweet, and the forward, embracing curve of her shoulders and breast as she leaned towards him. He looked down at the hand he held.

"Your wrist, I've hurt your wrist," he said stupidly. The white flesh, blue-veined, was ringed with the marks of her chain bracelet, reddened and grazed with streaks of blood.

"It doesn't matter, my poor love, it doesn't matter." Then his head was between Sophie's breasts, and her arms were round his shoulders, while with hands suddenly eager he loosened the dark velvet skirt and the soft chiffon and, at last, the long strands of her shining hair. Then the feather bed and the goose-down pillows enveloped them, and in the body of Sophie Sandels Tom forgot the action at Sainte Elodie.

10

THE CONSUMMATION OF SOPHIE Sandels' desire was like a
dam bursting. Tom Fleming's passion fully matched it, but
Tom's sexual deprivation had lasted for months only, while
Sophie had lived through many years without love since the
death in battle of the first and only man to possess her. They
were greedy lovers, snatching at the fleeting present as violently
as if they knew there was no future for them, and during the
week following the independence celebrations they hardly dared
to see each other in the daytime hours. Alone with Sophie in the
office, Tom knew himself capable of taking her (and she consent-
ing) on the floor of Mr. Baker's private room, and so he was careful
to keep Nikko Hirn, who sometimes looked at them with
thoughtful eyes, close to his ledgers and his desk. Twice Tom
left the city on visits to logging centres which were profitless
except as an exchange of news about the political situation. Once
he went in Nikko's company to Riihimäki, only two hours away,
and on another day was able to get a rail permit to Lahti, where
there were six or seven important mills. The return journey
should have taken just over three hours, and took five because of a
blizzard, which made Sophie—waiting for him in the lounge of
the Society House—say delightedly that with the frozen snow
on his fur cap and the blown snow on his coat, Tom looked like
a white bear from the northern woods.

They met in the lounge every night and went straight to the
restaurant for supper. Then they took the creaking lift upstairs,
where no one seemed to notice them, for the lift boy, the floor
waiter, the chambermaid on duty in the little service room beside
the lift had more personal concerns in those anxious times than
the relationship of a man and a woman who walked so quietly
down the long corridor to Room 112. Every bedroom in the
Society House held its own secrets now: its refugees, its conspira-
tors, its moneychangers and its foreign newspapermen, and the
walls hummed with words which drowned the whispers of two

lovers embracing in the old-fashioned brass bed beneath the embroidered linen sheet and the red-brown quilt.

At some time before midnight, while they dressed, Tom would telephone to the hall porter, and when they went downstairs a droshky would be waiting at the door, the grumbling driver an anonymous bulk of furs and snow. And those dark drives, so quickly over, were the climax of the evening for Sophie Sandels, when she lay in Tom's arms and watched the snow falling in the street outside, knowing herself warm and cherished in the freezing cold of the Helsingfors night.

He wanted, of course, to load her with presents, and she, equally of course, refused to accept them. "But what could I tell Lisa?" she objected, when Tom spoke of a black astrakhan coat which had taken his fancy in Stockmann's window. He felt inclined to say, "Tell her to go to hell!" but had to content himself with buying fur gloves and silk scarves for Sophie, and sending flowers and chocolates to the flat for both the sisters. Lisa, apparently, made no comment beyond "How nice!" She had become unusually silent and withdrawn.

Their passion was heightened by the imminence of war. Tom's occasional adventures in France and England had taught him that a girl's appetite for love was stimulated if an air raid was in progress, or if a soldier had to leave his rest billet before daybreak to get back to the line. Sophie Sandels had no such experience, but she had lived so long on the knife-edge of anxiety for her country that she responded feverishly to all the rumours of war which swept through the city in the days following the premature rejoicings at the National Theatre. As her fever translated itself into explicitly sexual terms, Tom remembered his mental image of Sophie, when he first saw her in the timber office, as a Frenchwoman in one of the towns behind the firing line.

He was not in love with her. He was overwhelmingly grateful for her generosity, which had proved that he was still a man, that the wounds which had made the doctors shake their heads and reply evasively to his anxious questions, had not destroyed his masculinity for ever, and he was grateful, too, for her docility in love. For Sophie never, after the first night when he had purged himself of the guilt of Sainte Elodie, came to him in compassion, never again opened her arms in the maternal gesture which cradled his head upon her breast. From that night on, he was the dominant partner, and she withdrew into a charming shyness which it was his delight to overcome.

Tom Fleming believed, because he wanted to believe it, that Sophie was not in love with him. He was sure she must feel, as he did, that theirs was a purely physical relationship, and that their two natures neither meshed nor matched. It was not the five years' difference in age that came between them (although Tom sometimes remembered, and despised himself for remembering, that Black had called her "that splendid woman" instead of "that lovely girl") it was the lack of a common past and a common interest. Tom had experienced three years of war, but all he had seen and done as a soldier had not made the deep impres sion on his nature that her country's wrongs had made on Sophie Sandels. His youth in Canada had been so pleasant, a prolonged enjoyment of sport and work outdoors and a happy family life, while her girlhood in Finland had been shadowed by all the consequences of her father's defiant stand against the Russification of his country. She had grown up at a time when Finnish women dressed in black or sombre colours, and all the traditional gaieties and sociability of Helsingfors had been subdued. Her life had made her strong and tender, but not light-hearted, and at that grim moment of Finland's history she positively thought it wrong to laugh. She was a hero-worshipper, and he was not a hero: Tom privately thought her true ideal was the young Gustaf Mannerheim, dressed in the uniform of the Chevalier Gardes.

In civilian clothes, impeccably groomed, and once again apparently bearing less than the weight of his fifty years, General Mannerheim's tall figure was now often seen in the streets of Helsingfors. He had joined the Military Committee of former officers of the disbanded Finnish army; he called upon the head of the government, Mr. Svinhufvud, and other Senators; he had meetings with old friends of his schoolboy and cadet days. Quietly, and without forcing the issue, he was emerging as the hope of White Finland. On the very night of the independence festival, the Diet had taken the decisive step of voting, by a small majority, to establish "a strong force for the preservation of order in the country" which in fact meant the welding together of all the White Guards, Defence Corps and "fire brigades" in the land, and this considerable task was to be entrusted to Gustaf

Mannerheim. He accepted it on one condition, that no armed intervention was to be sought from any other Power. He would welcome foreign volunteers, he hoped to obtain, by purchase, foreign arms, but he was adamant on one principle, that the salvation of Finland must come from within. This being promised, Mannerheim announced that he would begin his operation in the province of Ostrobothnia, where the yeoman farmers had already organised efficient defence groups. Taking no more risks with the Red Guards at the station, he left Helsingfors for Vasa with forged travel papers in the name of Gustaf Malmberg, trader, by the night train on January 18.

Although the general's departure was discreet, it was soon known in Helsingfors that Vasa was to be the rallying place for the "strong force" to be called the Civic Guards, and Tom Fleming, while still hoping for mediation rather than a declaration of war, got out his railway map and applied his own knowledge of the logging world to Mannerheim's choice of a terrain. The soldier in him applauded, because it was obvious that as well as the loyalty of the farmers of Ostrobothnia, there were valuable strategic advantages in the choice of Vasa. The town was a port, iced in at present, but after the thaw offering short lines of communication with Sweden, and through two important junctions linked with the entire railway system of Finland. If General Mannerheim, who had no arms and no armour, could commandeer sufficient rolling stock, he would be able to move his Civic Guards from the Gulf of Bothnia to within twenty-five miles of Petrograd.

The news of Mannerheim's safe arrival at Vasa spread through the capital on Thursday, the nineteenth, and Tom expected Sophie to be in one of her heroic moods when she came to his hotel that evening. But she appeared in the lobby with a face so pale that Tom departed from what had become their habit by making her sit down in the lounge and drink a small glass of spirits before going into the restaurant for supper. The meal had begun, and there was hardly anyone in the lounge to overhear them.

"You've heard, I suppose?" she said miserably. "The war's started. In Karelia, at Viborg of all places, and Mannerheim so far away, at Vasa!"

"I heard something about it this afternoon." Tom's tone was

deliberately flat. "But the man who told me—well, his English was on a level with my German, so I don't know yet if I got it straight. What happened exactly?"

"Oh, the Russian garrison was at the bottom of it, of course. They'd been selling rifles, old Japanese rifles taken in the 1905 war, to the Defence Corps in Viborg. Anything to earn a rouble on the side! And then they, what do you call it, they double-crossed the Whites and told the local Red Guards where the arms depot was, with the Defence Corps sentries guarding it. They shot it out together, but I'm afraid the Reds won."

"First blood to them, then," said Tom laconically. "But the way I heard it, there's been fighting elsewhere in the area."

"Yes, at several other points on Lake Ladoga and along the Vuoksi river. Just about where you went on that first trip to Imatra."

"Well, if those loggers of Broberg's got into it, I bet they gave as good as they got."

"But Tom—Karelia, and Mannerheim gone off to Vasa! I thought he would stay here in Helsingfors and defend the city."

"We'll have to rely on Nikko and his 'fire brigade'," said Tom, in a vain attempt to make her smile. "Try not to worry too much tonight, dear. There won't be any reliable news from Viborg till tomorrow."

He emptied his glass as a hint to Sophie that it was high time to be going in to supper if they wanted anything to eat. But Sophie sat still, looking more wretched than when she first came in, and Tom was moved to ask, clumsily enough, if there was "anything wrong".

"Tom, it's Lisa."

"What's Lisa done now?"

"I had a terrible scene with her after I got home this afternoon. She was crying when I went in, and it was a long time before I could get her to tell me what she was crying about. Oh, you've probably guessed—it was Boris Heiden."

"They've had a row?"

"A quarrel? I only wish they had! No, it was far worse . . . Tom, you know my sister has a job in the Private Bank?"

"Sure, she told me, that first evening at your flat."

"Of course she's only a junior. She has nothing to do with the

123

customers yet. But the other day she had to type some documents which showed that the bank president had deposited fifteen million marks in General Mannerheim's personal account at Vasa."

Tom whistled. "Fifteen million, eh? Over three hundred thousand dollars; it'll buy a lot of hardware. But that Lisa! What a damned little fool to blurt it out, even to you . . . Sophie, don't look so scared! Are you trying to tell me she told Boris Heiden?"

"Yes, she did. She says he's always asking questions about the bank—ever since she told him what a lot of bank clerks knew, and some of the public too, that the gold reserves of the Bank of Finland were taken to Kuopio at the time of the troubles."

"Where's Kuopio?"

"In the lake country, far away from here."

"Anywhere near the Russian border?"

"No," said Sophie, and then, fearfully, "why do you ask me that?"

Tom answered with another question. "Is Heiden still rooming at Mrs. Rentola's?"

"Yes, he is. Oh, how I wish, I wish to God we'd never seen him!"

Sophie was shaking as Tom had shaken in the grip of shell-shock. But his hands were warm and steady over hers. "Calm down, darling," he said. "There mayn't be any real harm done after all. Of course, if the depositors of the Private Bank don't cotton on to the idea of a big loan to Mannerheim the president could find himself in trouble—"

"And Lisa would lose her job."

Tom realised that this was the crux of the matter. The loss of Lisa's salary would be a blow to the tiny Sandels budget, and this alone was the reason for Sophie's terror at the betrayal of a bank secret to Boris Heiden. He set to work to reassure her. She would say no more about it, *he* would keep the secret, and Boris Heiden was a mere busybody, he liked to think he was in the know, but he was quite unimportant, there was nobody he could pass on his bits of gossip to. At least not in Helsingfors, he added silently.

Sophie was consoled into smiling at last. "Tom, you're such a comfort to me!" she said gratefully.

"Is that all I am?"

*   *   *

He was her lover, not her comforter, but Tom Fleming could never bring himself to say he loved her. Yet this was the one thing Sophie required of him when she was in his bed, totally his, and he was transported by the sense of his restored manhood and its approaching, unbearably exquisite climax. Then she would whisper —having learned, so quickly, how to alter the rhythm of her embrace, to delay the pleasure—"Say you love me! Say you love me!" and that was what Tom had never said, in his own language, to any woman in his life.

Why, he didn't know. Perhaps the words were too important for any of his casual conquests. He had muttered *"Je t'adore!"* in Paris, but that didn't count, it was part of Paris leave, and nothing but an expected compliment to the girl in his arms. In Helsingfors, with a girl who was anything but casual, it was far too serious. He evaded the issue by getting Sophie to teach him "I love you" in Swedish. And that, he saw, made her very happy—so happy and responsive that he sometimes wondered if she could hear a soldier, long dead at Mukden, speaking with his lips, or if when her eyes were closed in the last transports, she pictured another face than his. He was always conscious of his own scarred body, and careful, when they lay at peace, talking and smoking, to turn the right side of his face towards her. When they embraced he buried his head in the pillow, on her shoulder, in her hair—anything to keep the marred left cheek from contact with her face. But once, when they fell into a light sleep, Tom dreamed an exceedingly erotic dream about Nancy Macpherson, in which her lips were pressed to the scar of Sainte Elodie, her breasts flattened beneath his weight. He woke assured that she was the woman in his arms, and felt himself ready for the act of love. It was only when he heard Sophie's familiar whisper in the unfamiliar language, "Say 'I love you,' say it, *kära* Tom!" that desire wilted, and in an access of shame he got up and hunted for his cigarettes.

This happened in the evening of the day after fighting had broken out between Whites and Reds in Karelia. It was a Sunday, and Tom Fleming had spent some anxious hours trying to decide what, if anything, he ought to do about Boris Heiden. He suspected the Swiss of being a Russian agent, but what had he got to go on beyond suspicion? Heiden's elder brother had been hanged for his part in the attempted assassination of the Czar's prime minister, but did that necessarily mean that Heiden himself was a revolutionary? He had wormed information about a loan to Mannerheim out of a silly infatuated girl, but if he passed that information on to Lenin in person, what would be the benefit to the Red cause in Finland? So Tom argued with himself, feeling that for the first time in his life he was irresolute, unsure, and above all completely on his own in a strange and troubled country. He remembered the Chief's calm assurance and White's confidence, and wished he could talk to either one of them about the Heiden problem. As it was, his only contact in Helsingfors was the man called John Brown, and before he took Sophie home that Sunday night he made her tell him exactly how to reach the nursing-home where Brown was lying.

He went there at twilight on the next day. It was a forlorn neighbourhood, just beginning to be developed for the better as part of the residential complex behind the new Museum, but still dingy with old run-down wooden houses and patches of neglected garden. The granite of which Helsingfors was built showed itself in huge irregular outcrops waiting to be blasted level to make new streets, and among the boulders some very small children were playing at soldiers—playing with a fierce, silent vigour leading to bruised cheeks and bloody noses which was unlike any children's play Tom Fleming had ever seen. The nursing-home was in one of the new streets, a complete, three-storey house distinguished from its neighbours only by a brass plate bearing the name of the doctor who had come to the rescue of the British agents. An elderly Finnish woman answered Tom's ring. It was not easy to make her understand, but presently Tom saw the doctor in a small consulting room and was told that Mr. Brown was making as good progress as could be expected.

"I'd like very much to see him," said Tom.

"I believe he's asleep at present. This is not our regular visiting hour, sir."

"I don't want to disturb Mr. Brown, but it's really important that I see him today—"

Finally he persuaded the young man to take him to Brown's room. It was very small, containing nothing but a hospital bed, a washstand, a chair, and the apparatus for keeping Brown's broken leg in traction. The Englishman was not asleep, but his eyes and voice were dulled, and Tom thought it likely he was under sedation. He did not recognise Tom Fleming, and Tom remembered that he had been unconscious for nearly the whole time they were together in Mr. Baker's flat.

"I just wanted to know how you were getting on," he said awkwardly.

"Fine . . . Soon be up and around again, won't I, doctor?"

"You're getting on very well indeed."

"I'm rather anxious to get in touch with Mr. White," said Tom.

"Is *he* in Helsingfors?"

"Well, that's just it, I don't know where he is."

Brown's heavy eyes closed. He murmured something which sounded like "staying behind", and the doctor motioned Tom away from the bedside.

"He really isn't able to talk to you today."

"I guess not. Take care of him, doctor."

"We're doing that. And I shall let your friends in Stockholm know as soon as Mr. Brown is fit to travel." They were in the highly-polished, disinfectant-scented corridor now, and the Finnish woman was opening the front door.

"I suggest we keep in touch by telephone, Mr. Fleming. We want to keep this as a safe house, and we shall have to take precautions about all foreign visitors in future. You understand, I hope?"

He said he did, and walked away between the granite rocks and the ugly clapboard houses, more baffled than ever. White was "staying behind"; from what White himself and the man called Black had let drop, that meant in Petrograd, perhaps in the soon to be deserted embassy. Tom was worried enough to think of going to Petrograd himself, but also realistic enough to know that he might be held indefinitely at the Russian frontier post of Bielostrov, now a camp of human flotsam and jetsam thrown up by the Bolshevik tide. The only travellers from Helsingfors allowed to proceed to Petrograd were the anxious Senators who still hoped to prevent widespread hostilities in Finland by an appeal to the Commissars at the Smolny, and even they travelled at the risk of their lives on a line where every trigger-happy Russian soldier thought himself entitled to shoot a bourgeois on sight.

The fighting had died down in Karelia, and from Mannerheim there came no sign of action. The Whites, the Reds, the Senators, the general, were all in the melting-pot together, and the hand that stirred the brew was still Lenin's. He had his key men in Helsingfors: Colonel Svechnikov, who had come from XLII Corps at Viborg to be military adviser to the Red Guards, Glasunov, and Izmailov, the chairman of the Russian sailors' committee which had raised the black flag of anarchy at the harbour. All three, and many more, were fanning the flames of what Trotsky himself declared to be the Finnish Revolution, part of the great upheaval which had shaken Russia so short a time before. When Senator Svinhufvud was forced to spend a long night aboard a Russian ship frozen in the harbour, called to account by Izmailov and his drunken sailors for the "aggressions" of the Whites, the government realised at last that mediation was impossible. Lenin was sending rifles and Marines to help the Finnish Reds, and Izmailov had personally threatened to raze the capital to the ground.

It was Glasunov, Lenin's mouthpiece, who gave the order for a total mobilisation of the Red Guards at midnight on January 26. All next day, a Sunday, a red lamp burned in the tower of the House of the Workers, where every window was illuminated. Bells pealed and trumpets sounded as arms and ammunition were issued at every Russian depot from the great lion-yellow barracks near the harbour, another Engel masterpiece, and the old wooden hutments of the Cossack headquarters out on the Tölö road. There was singing, there was the usual rabble milling in the Senate Square, but there was no outbreak of fighting. Respectable citizens stayed at home behind locked doors and hoped for the best, and Tom Fleming had no difficulty in making his way to Sophie's flat in the late afternoon. He went expressly to warn her to stay at home until the city should be calmer, though in the face of the general mobilisation that time seemed far away, and he found her much concerned with Lisa, who was huddled over the stove nursing a heavy cold.

"How's your beau these days, Lisa?" he asked, while Sophie was in the kitchen.

"My— ?"

"Mr. Heiden."

"I have no idea." She tossed the cornsilk hair, hanging now as limply as a sick dog's coat.

"What, isn't he still rooming upstairs at Mrs. Rentola's?"

"He moved out last Monday to the Students' House. That's where he wanted to live when he first came here, and now they've found a room for him."

"I see." Lisa said no more, and after she had drunk a cup of coffee declared she had no appetite for the early supper and would be more comfortable in bed.

"She's looking rotten," said Tom when she had gone. "Sophie, this town's no place for you two girls just now. Isn't there some place out in the country you could go to for a bit? Don't you have any relatives who'd be glad to have you visit them?"

Sophie shook her head. Their only living relative was an old cousin of their mother's, a retired farmer who lived in a modest cottage about twenty miles out on the way to Åbo. He and his ailing wife lived on the produce of their garden and little farmyard, and could never afford to feed two extra mouths at such a time.

"I'll give you all the money you need to pay for your keep out there."

"Have *I* given you the right to offer me money?" Sophie said fiercely. She was as independent as any Finn of them all.

"Don't get mad, darling, you know I only want you to be safe."

"Nowhere is safe now," she said, and it was true. "But who's going to bother about us, two women living quietly in a back-street flat? I've laid in plenty of food. If we must, we can stand a siege until Mannerheim comes in—"

"Oh, don't be silly, Sophie. If you won't go out to this old cousin's, would you consider moving into my hotel? I'll give up the room to you and Lisa, and make that manager chap find some sort of bunk for me—"

"Who's being silly now?" It was no use; she refused to move from her own home, and there they spent a sad and anxious evening, now and again hearing Lisa cough or sigh in the room next door, both so aware of her nearness that caresses seemed impossible, and Tom left Sophie at last with only one long kiss which reminded them both of Christmas night. He hurried back across the square, feeling responsible for her and for her future in a way he had never felt before.

When he returned to his hotel he found the place almost deserted. There were only three elderly men in the lounge, talking in lowered voices, and the manager with a long face told Tom, as he handed over his bedroom key, that Tammerfors, one of the country's most important industrial towns, had been taken over by the Reds in the course of the day. With that news to digest, it was long before Tom Fleming slept, but he was sound asleep at three in the morning, when General Mannerheim, who had spent a week in controlling and organising his eager bands of farmers, struck his first blow for liberty. It was a magnificent piece of bluff, for the recruits he sent against the Russian garrison in Vasa and the Red strong points on the loop railway were hardly armed at all. Only the front ranks of each White detachment carried their own shotguns, or whatever other weapons they possessed. But within a matter of hours they were armed with the weapons of their enemies, for the shock tactics of surprise and utter determination carried the day; and almost before the winter morning broke not only Vasa but the important railway junction of Seinäjoki had passed, with Lapua, into the hands of the Whites.

As part of Mannerheim's operation the telephone lines to Vasa had been cut, and so news of the first victory had not reached Helsingfors when the phone rang in Tom Fleming's bedroom at half past six. He stumbled out of his bed, feeling for the telephone in the litter on his dressing-table, and trying to switch on a lamp with the other hand while the operator told him she had a local call for him, coming in on a bad line. At last, after a good deal of buzzing, the voice of Nikko Hirn was heard, saying something about an emergency.

"It must be, to have you call me at this hour," said Tom. "What's up, Nikko?"

The line went dead, and then Nikko came through again, saying "must see you . . . come to your hotel?"

"I'll expect you in half an hour," said Tom, and hung up. There was no point in prolonging the conversation; apart from the bad line, he had noticed before that Nikko's English was never as good on the telephone as when they were talking face to face. Tom shaved and dressed hurriedly and went downstairs. It was still only ten to seven, but two waitresses were already moving ponderously round the restaurant, and knowing their usual slow service he went in and ordered coffee to be set ready on a corner table. Through the glass door he saw it being brought at the same moment as Nikolai Hirn came in.

"Is it raining?" he asked in surprise, seeing the Finn shake wet drops from his heavy coat.

"*Ja*, it thawed in the night, and the streets are a mess. The trams are running, though, I caught one at the Long Bridge."

"Come and have coffee, then." Tom felt they were talking to impress the night clerk, who was still on the desk, and the night porter, waiting for his relief to come. Nikko was blessedly phlegmatic: he didn't look like a man bringing bad news, but Tom was sure the emergency was real and urgent. Even in the empty restaurant it took time to get him to the point, for first he had to explain that he had been calling from a newsagent's shop in the Third Line, that the newsagent was an old friend, etc., and then the waitress loomed over them with breakfast rolls and butter, and Nikko became absolutely silent until she had withdrawn behind the service door. When Tom's patience was nearly at an end, he said in a rush of words:

"Last night, late, a man came to see me at my boarding-house. One of *them*, you understand, a Social-Democrat for many years, high in the party. But now, I think, afraid, as some of them are afraid, of the Bolshevik element, of a civil war. He and I went to school together, long ago . . . He also knew, and much respected, the father of Miss Sandels."

"Go on."

"He came to me because last night, in the House of the Workers, he saw a list of names. A Black List. Listing those denounced as enemies of the people, to be liq—liquor—"

"Liquidated?"

"Killed. Nearly all men, not many women on the list. But Sophie Sandels is one of them."

"My God!"

"*Ja*," said Nikko simply. "Is bad."

"But for God's sake, man, why?" Tom pushed his chair back violently. It was all he could do not to push the table over too, sweep the crockery to the floor, make some wild physical gesture to relieve his alarm. "*Sophie* an enemy of the people? It doesn't make sense! Are you sure this man wasn't fooling you, just for

131

the hell of it? How about *your* name? You're a known White, aren't you on their damned death list?"

"He said not. He thought perhaps Miss Sandels was because her father was so very—very Finn, one of the Active Committee in his time—"

"He's been dead for seven years. And she never took any part in politics, did she?"

"I've *known* her for seven years, and always the same as she is now: quiet, busy, with some close women friends, artists and teachers mostly, not political talkers—"

Tom Fleming was hardly listening. Vivid and clear, there came to his mind a picture of Sophie on the first night they met, planting General Mannerheim's youthful portrait on the mantel-shelf under the picture of Finlandia resisting the double-headed eagle, and saying with such pride, "Mannerheim! *Sans peur et sans reproche!*" And he remembered the hate in Heiden's eyes, lit by the blazing birch log in the open stove.

"It doesn't matter now, I mean why her name got on their bloody list," he said. "The thing to do is get her out of here and into some safe house, safe place I mean; only last night I tried to make her go away. Nikko, there's no time to lose, I'll have to go and get some money."

He was talking at random, but a plan was forming in his mind as he ran upstairs three at a time, not waiting for the lift, to get his outdoor garments. The nursing-home, that "safe house" where Brown lay—the friendly doctor would take her and Lisa in for a few hours, until Tom could hire a car and drive them himself to that cousin in the country . . . and then where? Where to find a refuge in a land where the Red network was everywhere, and powerful? He rejoined Nikko, it was nearly half past seven, and not a droshky to be seen in the Railway Square.

His bank was in the North Esplanade, in the next block to the office. It would open at eight, and he would be waiting on the doorstep—*if* it opened, on the day after the Red mobilisation; Nikko was saying they had nine battalions, fully armed, in the capital alone. The street-cleaners had not come on duty, for the streets, usually brushed clear of snow, were deep in the slush of the overnight thaw, and Runeberg on his pedestal in the Esplanade garden was being lashed by a thin, driving rain.

"Trouble ahead," said Hirn laconically. There was a great

crowd of Russian sailors, waving their arms and shouting, where the harbour area began at the foot of the Esplanade.

"I hope to God the bank opens," said Tom. He was pulling off his glove to look at his wristwatch when Nikko caught his arm. It was ten to eight and still very dark.

"There's a light in the office!"

They were almost abreast of the office building, and a faint light, coming from the outer room, was shining through Mr. Baker's uncurtained window.

"The Reds, ransacking," said Tom. "Or else— ?"

The same thought was in both their minds. They ran through the courtyard and up the familiar stair. They could hear Sophie's voice before they reached the landing: she was talking, louder than usual, and in Swedish, on the telephone.

"Sophie! What the devil are you doing here?" Tom managed to get out. She was just hanging up the receiver, and stood staring at the two of them, Nikko as breathless as Tom Fleming, and swearing at her in his fright. It was clear that Sophie, too, had come to the office in a hurry, for instead of the hat she always wore in the street she had twisted round her head one of the beautiful scarves she had allowed Tom to give her. It was the olive-green one with the intricate pattern of rust red and orange, his brain registered; he had chosen it because she said these were the colours Finnish designers would be using soon, and the colours were fast, he saw, although the scarf was soaked with rain.

"I told you last night you were to stay at home," he said, and she replied defensively, "I came to telephone for a doctor— Lisa's very ill—"

"You came *here* to telephone?"

"All the shops are shut in our district—"

"The nursing-home doctor?"

"No. Our family doctor. He'll be with her in an hour—"

"We haven't got an hour," Tom told her brutally. "Sophie, your life's in danger. Don't argue, don't question me, just do as I say. Nikko, be a sport and go see if the bank's open, and what those bastards are up to down at the harbour."

"Tom, you must tell me what has happened!" Sophie burst out as soon as they were alone.

"Don't talk to me, I tell you! Get on the phone again and call that nursing-home. Tell them you'll be there in half an hour and

133

they're to book you in under any name you like except your own. And you're to *stay* there till I take you out—"

"But Tom, I can't leave Lisa!"

"*Telephone!*"

She obeyed him, and he understood enough Swedish now to know that she was repeating his instructions, but when the call was completed nothing could shake her from the refusal to leave Lisa. Even Nikko, returning to say the bank had posted a notice saying "Closed for business", could not persuade her to do more than hurry home, with themselves for escort, make Lisa rise and dress, and then, with her sister, take refuge in the nursing-home.

The Russian sailors were moving slowly up the Esplanade, and a crowd of Red Guards were on their way from the Residence to join them. From somewhere on the waterfront, probably near the former imperial palace, Tom heard the chatter of machine-gun fire. But Union Street, at the Esplanade end, was clear of troops, and they hurried up past the University, along the side of the Senate Square. The usual rabble was congregating outside the Senate House, and now for the first time they heard real noise, not animal shouts but organised slogans:

"Fire the Senate!"

"Death to the Senators!"

"Down with the Butcher Guard!"

"Don't be frightened, Sophie," said Tom. "Give me your hand, and Nikko, take her other arm." They were almost pulling her along through the slush. She was wearing galoshes, Tom saw with the same clarity as he had registered the details of her scarf, and in her haste she must have left her gloves at home.

"Your hands are cold," he said, and terrified though he could see she was, she smiled at him.

"Cold hands, warm heart!"

Then there was a burst of rifle fire behind them, and looking back they saw the Russians shooting at some White Guards running up Government Street into the Square. The passers-by were screaming and beating on the doors of locked shops, only to keel over in the yellow slush as the bullets found their marks.

"Run, Sophie!"

"The hospital!" said Nikko. "Must—be open!"

Tom saw what he meant. There was no hope now of reaching Sophie's flat unmolested, for along the far side of Union Street, advancing from the Long Bridge, came a mob of Red Guards, marching in a ragged formation with their rifles in their hands. Sophie recognised the man in the front rank, and turned with a scream to fling herself against the bolted door of the university library. Tom saw him too, and recognised the red beard, the black caracul cap; he tore open his coat to get at the pistol in his shoulder holster. But the man was quicker: he levelled his rifle with a great shout—

"An enemy of the people!"

He fired, and Sophie Sandels fell, shot in the side, and then Nikko and Tom were firing together, while the Red Guards stormed forward and machine-gun fire rattled round the Senate Square. Two young doctors from the hospital, wearing their white coats and Red Cross brassards, rushed into the thick of the crowd, to make a path for Tom, carrying Sophie. They dragged two or three of the wounded Reds into the shelter of the hospital. Tom knelt down on the stone flags of the old lobby and lowered his light burden gently to the ground.

"You'll be all right, darling!" he tried to say. Her scarf had fallen off, and her hair was trailing loose over his arm. She spoke to him, but she spoke in Swedish, and the only word he really heard was "Lisa", before the nurses took her away from him, and the machine-gun bullets were spraying the street outside.

He was only in the way in that place, for the great doors were opening and shutting steadily to admit new victims of the workers' revolution. The place had once been a military hospital, and now swarmed with soldiers again as the casualty wards were filled. Tom saw an old wooden settle and sat down beside two weeping women. He found that he had Sophie's scarf in his hands, and he was twisting the wet silk, which clung to his fingers as her living hair had clung when the nurses lifted her out of his arms. The scarf had been wet, but warm from her neck, and presently it grew so cold in that anteroom of death that Tom himself was cold and quite prepared when Nikko Hirn reappeared beside him and shook his head.

11

A FEW DAYS AFTER THE morning on which the revolution burst in fury over Helsingfors, Tom Fleming sat in a slow, wood-burning train on the second lap of a cross-country journey to General Mannerheim's headquarters.

In the same compartment were two elderly men returning from an auction sale at Björneborg, which, being Finnish speakers, they called Pori, and a young woman with two small tow-headed children. None of them paid any more attention to the foreigner with the scarred face than he did to them, but if interrogated they would have said that the man was well dressed, had no luggage but a small valise, and appeared to be interested in the view from the window, from which he never took his eyes. In fact Tom saw nothing of the landscape, which at that stage of his journey was pleasant but monotonous, as the train moved through the farming parishes of Ostrobothnia, with here a farmhouse painted red and white, here a frozen lake and there an icebound river to break the undulating plain of snow. He saw nothing but his goal, the White GHQ at Seinäjoki station, where he would join the fight with Mannerheim and avenge the death of Sophie Sandels.

The psychiatrists who had treated Tom Fleming at Dykefaulds would have diagnosed that their former patient was now on the verge of a severe mental breakdown, and might—for the science they professed was only in its infancy—have prescribed a return to hospital care and a course of occupational therapy such as book-binding or woodcarving. Tom himself was vaguely aware of his condition. He knew that he was suffering from intermittent amnesia, for there were huge gaps in his memory of the day of Sophie's death and the days following. His first memory was of lying face down on his bed in the Society House, writhing in pain, and burrowing his face into the pillows in the hope of finding some last trace of Sophie, some faint scent of the stuff, smelling like spring birch trees, that she used to wash her hair.

But the hotel's laundry service was excellent, the linen freshly washed and ironed, and everything of Sophie was gone from the bed where he had been her lover.

He thought this memory belonged to the first night, and then there was a gap which filled slowly with the grey light of early afternoon. He was standing with a little group of people dressed in black in a desolate place not far from the seashore, which he knew to be a graveyard because of the crosses, although these were crosses of a shape he had never seen before. There were words spoken which he couldn't understand, and people who stared at him whom he couldn't recognise, except the faithful Nikko who had seen to everything, and the girl with her foaming hair confined by a black mourning veil, who clung to the arm of the bewildered old man who was going to take her home. Tom took her hand, and called her "Lisa, poor Lisa!" but he couldn't remember what she said in reply. The only voice he could hear was Sophie's, in the last coherent words she spoke to him, "Cold hands, warm heart!" When that scene grew dark, he could still hear her voice, and now he was in an unidentified room with Nikko, and there was a bottle with glasses on the table between them. He was asking Nikko, and he was sure not for the first time, what Sophie had said, in Swedish, at the very end, and Nikko was patiently repeating that her poor voice was so low, he hadn't heard very clearly, but he thought it was "Tell Lisa," or "Take care of Lisa"—something like that. It was certainly then, across the table with the vodka bottle, that Nikko Hirn had said something more positive: "You gave her much happiness, Tom. Remember that."

Of the public events which took place on and after that fatal January 28, Tom Fleming remembered exactly nothing. He knew, because he heard people talking about it, that the Reds and their Russian allies were in complete control of Helsingfors, as of other major cities of Finland. They had stormed the Senate House, scattered the Senators and the members of the Diet—many of whom were now in hiding—had taken control of the banks and the government offices, and had seized the entire communications system. It was an entirely successful coup d'état, and the only factor to set against it was a proclamation, the last act of the Senate, declaring that the Civic Guards were now the White

Army of the legitimate government, and that General Mannerheim was that army's Commander-in-Chief.

From the little wooden house with prim lace curtains in Ylihärmä which he called his headquarters—in any other circumstances it would have only been a command post—General Mannerheim directed increasingly successful operations against the Russian garrisons. He had eight thousand rifles now, with ammunition, and a number of pieces of light artillery, and he used these to push his troops south and east, and also to secure his rear in the north. At the beginning of February, after hard fighting, Uleaborg was liberated, and almost at the same time, Torneå. The White Army now controlled all the territory from Vasa to the Swedish land frontier.

Just when he decided to volunteer for the White Army, Tom Fleming could not exactly say. He had an idea there had been long talks with Nikko, who after trying to dissuade him had given him a letter of introduction from his own section commander to a Captain Holsti, a former officer in the disbanded Finnish Guards. He had the letter in his pocket ("Captain Thomas Fleming, MC" were the only words he could read of it) and that in itself was proof of the conversations which must have taken place. But the talks he could remember, word for word, were the talks at the British consulate, when he had persuaded the officials to place signs saying "British Property. Under the Protection of HBM Consul-General" on the now padlocked doors of Mr. Baker's flat and his office, closed for the duration. Signs in English, Finnish, Swedish and Russian—Tom was rather proud of that last touch.

After that there was only the round-about journey, beginning with the long trip west to Björneborg. The Red Guards at the station were turning away passengers to Vasa, because so many men and boys were trying to leave Helsingfors to join Mannerheim, but a Canadian businessman going to Björneborg met with no hindrance, and after a wait at the seacoast town Tom was able to continue his journey east and north. The farming people all got out at the second halt, and he had the compartment to himself. It was easy, then, to hear the voices which other people's conversation sometimes drowned.

Cold hands, warm heart.

You gave her much happiness, remember that.

138

The hands now cold in death, the fleeting happiness all in the past—the words which brought such thoughts were not as hard to bear as those other words which cut through all the gaps in Tom Fleming's memory, like a flame still flickering in a burned-out house:

My men have been disturbed all night
by the screaming and moaning
of your wounded

＊　　　　＊　　　　＊

Promotion came quickly in the White Army in February 1918. Captain Holsti had become Colonel Holsti by the time Tom reported to him at Seinäjoki station, where the Finnish officer shared a room which had once been the preserve of the local station-master. He was a stout elderly gentleman, arrayed in the old Finnish Guards uniform worn before he passed on to the reserve list in 1897, with the two lowest buttons of the tunic undone to accommodate his paunch, and wearing an unmilitary pair of rubber fishing boots. "My English it is all forgot," was his greeting to Tom Fleming, "but you are very welcome to Seinäjoki, captain. You come from Canada to join us; this is far."

Tom said, "Thank you, sir," respectfully, and the other occupant of the cramped little office looked up and grinned. He was younger than Tom Fleming, with a shock of fair hair and a boyish face, his uniform consisting of a blue fisherman's jersey with a turtle neck, worn over tweed trousers, and a white band bearing the word *Suomi* on his arm.

"This is Captain Keiller, from Gothenburg," the old colonel introduced him. "He . . . moves the trains. He speaks good English. Is best you work with him."

"Sir," said Tom, still respectfully, "I'd hoped to be assigned to combat duty."

"Maybe so, maybe so," prosed the colonel, "but this letter tells you were much wounded, not soon ago, is better you not fight early, no?"

Captain Keiller spoke rapidly in Swedish, received a nod of assent, and stood up.

"I'm going to take you to the mess, Captain Fleming." he

said cheerfully. "Got to get you some hot food and a billet, and then we'll have a *dekko* at the paperwork, right?"

"Fine," said Tom. He realised that he was hungry; he was long past feeling tired.

They got rid of Tom's valise at the "billet", which was no more than a pallet bed set beside three others in a commandeered school classroom, and went on to the "officers' mess"; a local restaurant where the Finnish proprietor did not respond cheerfully to Captain Keiller's shout of *"Koi hai!"* All that was available between meals, he said, was tea and flatbread; Captain Keiller told Tom they would have to settle for a cup of *chai*. His curious choice of words was soon explained, for over the teacups Captain Keiller, chattering faster than Tom had heard anyone talk in slow-spoken Finland, laid bare the whole story of his life. He was the despair, he said, of a most respectable family of merchants in Gothenburg, who had sent him to high school in Dundee, where they had relatives who were prepared to take him into their jute firm. One year of jute in Dundee had been enough for young Karl Keiller (who liked to be called Charlie) and the Scottish relatives had shipped him out to another branch of the family in Bombay. Equally bored with jute in Bombay, he joined the Indian Army force sent to fight in German East Africa in 1914, enjoyed soldiering and chasing General von Lettow, after the capture of Dar-es-Salaam, into "Portuguese East", and there was smitten by what he described as some infernal bug. He had been back in Gothenburg for only a few months when "this jolly little show blew up in Finland", and believed in all modesty that he was the first man from Sweden to join Mannerheim.

His varied experiences had given Charlie Keiller a remarkable command of army slang, both Indian and British, and Tom felt his spirits rising as he listened to the story, punctuated by hearty bursts of laughter from the narrator. He had known and liked a lot of men like Keiller on the western front, the cheery ones, the ragging-in-the-mess types, and he had been missing that kind of company. He was aware of the delicacy with which Keiller asked for none of the reasons which brought an ex-officer of the Canadian army under the banner of White Finland. Nor did Karl explain that the Keillers had been soldiers of fortune for nearly three hundred years, ever since the younger son of a Perthshire laird left home to make his fortune in the army of Gustavus Adolphus when the Protestant champion led his Swedes into Europe. There had been a Keiller in the ring of officers round Charles XII, when the eighteen-year-old King of Sweden saw the Russian standards dipped to him in surrender at Narva, and yet another, a robust and cheerful young Keiller like his descendant, had found favour in the army and the arms of Catherine the Great. The Charlie of 1918 was a throwback to his soldier ancestors, but his attitude to war was not romantic: it was strictly practical.

"I know you want to have a bash at the Russkis, *ek dum!*" he said. "So do I. But we'll have to carry on with that dear old dug-out, Colonel Holsti, until the Swedish officer volunteers get here. We're useless at the front at present. I couldn't give the words of command in Finnish, and I bet you couldn't either; can you even sling the *bat* in Swedish?"

"A word here and there."

"Well, there you are! Here at GHQ we're needed, the C-in-C is short of junior officers, and we'll have to stick to admin. until the guerilla phase is over." He added oracularly, "You'll think it's worth it when you meet him."

"He's really good, is he?"

"Terrific with the troops, and nothing fazes him."

"Is he here now?"

"Up at Ylihärmä. It's on a spur line, he may come down on the staff train in the evening. And talking of trains—"

They went back to the railway station. A message had arrived in their absence, saying General Mannerheim was on his way to Vasa and would not return to GHQ that night. This caused the irrepressible Keiller to mutter to Tom, so low that Holsti failed to hear, "Trouble with the Senators!" For although the head of the government, Svinhufvud, had gone underground in Helsingfors, four members of the Senate—enough, by law, to make decisions in the government's name—had escaped from the capital and made their way into Ostrobothnia soon after the Red coup d'état. Whether the Commander-in-Chief was glad to see them remained unknown: urbane as ever, he welcomed the dishevelled gentlemen, told them he intended to win the war in fourteen weeks, and returned to his military duties. On February 5 Svinhufvud himself attempted to escape from Helsingfors by air. With the complicity of two young Finnish officers who had served in the Russian Naval Air Squadron he was actually airborne in a Farman Kone OL I when it was discovered that the Russian sailors guarding the hangars had drunk all the spirit intended to keep the water from freezing in the aircraft's cooler. The pilot landed safely, and the president of the Senate went back into hiding; it was left to Captain Keiller to sum up the fiasco as one more transportation problem solved.

As Tom settled down to the routine duties of an assistant RTO, he began to appreciate Mannerheim's remarkable talent for making bricks without straw. The man had nothing, as modern warfare was understood: no air support, no tanks, very few mechanised vehicles, not even cavalry. There were plans to raise one cavalry regiment, but all the available horses were required for the transportation of Russian army prisoners of war to the frontier north of Lake Ladoga, an operation which was Captain Fleming's assigned duty at the railway station. Yet the directives which came down through the echelons at GHQ were so phrased that they might have been written in the great days of the Imperial War Ministry at St. Petersburg. The area under Mannerheim's control was divided into four corps commands, the general staff was formed, the regiments took shape with the same impressive speed as Tom Fleming himself had seen the Canadian Expeditionary Force created at Valcartier. But alone in his spartan compartment in the staff train, Mannerheim wrestled with two problems which the Canadian generals had not had to solve: the tactful handling of his high-spirited yeoman farmers, quite unaccustomed to the chain of command, and of his middle-aged field officers, whose military science was as rusty as their jealousy of each other was keen.

It was a situation which might have meant trouble with troops of more effervescent blood than the Finns. But the man at the top of this curious structure was absolutely confident in the outcome. Mannerheim was not only a cavalry general called upon to lead infantry over a very difficult terrain. He was a commander who had led Russian troops accustomed to follow their officers blindly (until the day they rose and struck those officers down) and he was now leading guerillas whose Finnish mother tongue he spoke with difficulty, and who were the last men in the world to be the slaves of any officer, even their Commander-in-Chief.

But in spite of his thirty years in Russia Mannerheim was a Finn at heart as well as a Finn by birth, and behind the façade of his perfect manners he was as stubborn, as cunning and as determined as any farmer in the ranks.

From the window of the improvised railway transport office Tom Fleming had more than once witnessed the activity which accompanied the arrival or departure of the staff train in which Mannerheim travelled up and down the front. But the general did not visit the office itself until a few days after Tom's arrival, when everyone at GHQ had been cheered by a successful White advance in Central Finland resulting in the capture of Kuopio, the town to which the Bank of Finland's gold reserves had earlier been taken. Karl Keiller and Tom were working out the rail plans necessary to send reinforcements to the hard-pressed White front in Karelia, possible—on paper at least—now that a whole central province had been liberated, when an ADC announced the arrival of the commanding general.

Colonel Holsti and the two young men came instantly to attention, and while greetings were exchanged in Swedish, Tom had a moment to study the man he had last seen alighting from a train at Helsingfors on a rainy December night. Tom now wore, like Keiller, a turtleneck sweater with the white armband which bore the one word Finland, but the general's own uniform was hardly more elaborate, and was concealed by a long khaki trenchcoat, with a big fur collar, which fell to the tops of his field boots. He carried a walking-stick and his binoculars were hung on a strap round his neck. Tom was tall, and so was Captain Keiller, but General Mannerheim was taller still, and a white fur hat gave him added inches: he carried himself very erect and with an unselfconscious dignity.

"Sir," said Colonel Holsti in English, "may I present our Canadian volunteer officer, Captain Thomas Fleming, MC?"

"Captain Fleming!" said the general. "A pleasant and friendly name to me. The original owners of my boyhood's home were Flemings, as I recall. They were of Scottish descent; are you?"

"On both sides of my family, sir."

"And where did you win your decoration?"

"At Sainte Elodie on the Scarpe, sir."

"Ah! Third Ypres! You took part in a great battle, Captain Fleming. I'm glad you've come to join us in our war of liberation."

His English was stiff and formal, but perfectly correct, and he politely continued to talk in that language while he examined the detailed railway map pinned on the wall.

"Your quarters here are very cramped, gentlemen," he said, "but you are making a most valuable contribution to our communications system; I congratulate you."

"These officers are very anxious to be assigned to combat duty, sir," said Colonel Holsti. "And so am I."

General Mannerheim brushed his clipped, dark moustache with the back of his forefinger, and smiled. "We old soldiers don't care about being relegated to the rear, do we, Holsti?" he said. "But I think I can gratify you all by sending you into action soon. The enemy has given us a welcome breathing space— thanks partly to ourselves, and partly to brave men in Helsingfors —but obviously he is preparing to attack our front in depth, and will attempt to cut it if he can. Captain Keiller, you will report to Colonel Wetzer at three o'clock this afternoon."

"Sir."

When the general left—his ADC had been standing outside on the platform, there being no room for a fifth person in the office—Karl Keiller murmured, "What did I tell you?" with a wink at the colonel, who had been glowing at Mannerheim's equation of them both as "old soldiers". Tom nodded; the general was as good with officers as he was with troops, and the graceful introduction of the Fleming name and the Scots background had pleased him more than he cared to admit. The Canadians were not overly impressed by generals, except their own, but the Finnish general was impressive, and without being overbearing, made a strong projection of power. Tom sat down to his lists and timetables with renewed energy. It was slow work, for every plan he drew up had to be translated into Swedish by Captain Keiller, but it was the only work he had been fit for when he arrived from Helsingfors. It had dulled his nerves and deadened the memory of Sophie, and now there was the prospect of action ahead, the final test of the manhood she had renewed.

*   *   *

They went into action in the Vilppula sector, in the lake country south of the vital railway junction of Haapamäki, the objective of Colonel Svechnikov, once the adviser to the Red staff in Helsingfors, and now commanding two battalions of Russians and Red Guards. Compared with Third Ypres, it was a battle in miniature, for Colonel Wetzer, commanding the Whites, had only a thousand rifles and some light artillery. Nevertheless the roar of four field-guns was enough, on the first day, to make Tom Fleming experience renewed symptoms of shell-shock, and he was in mortal fear of displaying open cowardice. By his second day at the front—which was the sixth of an action bitterly contested over a line thirty miles long—he had adapted to a new kind of trench warfare, improvised like everything else in this struggle for freedom. These were trenches which were merely ditches beside the highway which straggled through the lakeland, trenches without parados or firing step, and for parapet merely an earthwork on which rifles could be rested. The Whites were on the defensive here, and even when reinforcements came up from Seinäjoki were in no position to attack. The battle for Vilppula was fast becoming a stalemate and an ominous indication of the future of the war.

In spite of this Tom began to believe in what he had told Sophie was impossible, the ultimate victory of the Whites. Perhaps he was swayed by the strong personality of Mannerheim, backed up by the dogged determination of the yeomen soldiers in the Vilppula trenches, but he undoubtedly felt a renewal of the will to win which inspired the volunteers of 1914, in the days before gallantry turned to despair in the Flanders mud. To make war in the snow was a new experience for Captain Fleming, but after a few days it seemed to him that one of his old skills could be profitably used in the new conditions. He suggested this to Karl Keiller, and after a short discussion they went to their command post in a little lakeside farm, and asked permission to speak to their section commander. He was a young major, a Swedish-speaking Finn, and he listened to what Keiller had to propose while Colonel Holsti, who was also present, sat scowling and poking the logs in the wide, raised hearth. The farm room was just as it had been evacuated by the farmer and his wife, with two covered-in beds, a spinning-wheel pushed into one corner, and *knäckebröd*, made of both corn and rye, hanging on strings from rafter to rafter.

"So!" said the major. "The Canadian captain wants to take

out a night patrol and capture Russian prisoners for interrogation, and you wish to volunteer to accompany him, am I right?"

"Yes, sir."

"An irregular and dangerous proceeding," said Colonel Holsti.

"Captain Fleming is very good on night patrol, colonel; that's what he won his medal for."

"Be sure to tell him," said Tom in English, "that we *know* there's a Russian forward post in the birches, at two o'clock on the target, south of the lake."

"I have told him. He says how many men do you need?"

"Six," said Tom confidently. He was eager to be on patrol again, and this time with the Finns; he wanted to fight his private battle with the ghosts of Sainte Elodie. The young major over-ruled Colonel Holsti's objections: *he* was the section commander, he said decidedly, and the raid was worth a trial. In less time than Tom and Keiller had expected, four men were detailed to go out on patrol and stood grinning and nodding while Keiller explained what was required of them.

This time there were no blackened faces and hands, no disguised uniforms, but each man put on the long white hooded coat which had just been issued to the troops and took a second cloak folded and fastened to his belt. They had no hand-grenades, but were armed with pistols and knives, and as soon as they started their slow crawl across the snow Tom Fleming knew that these Finnish soldiers were potentially better than any Canadian woodsmen who had ever been on patrol with him. Their hunting instinct, primitive and deep, was kindled like his own, and in almost total silence they followed his lead, using every patch of shadow, every snow-covered tussock of reeds by the lake, in an enveloping movement on the Russian post in the birch thicket. The operation was a complete success. The Russians had no time to utter a shout when the Finns were upon them, and the extra cloaks—only four were needed—wrapped round their heads and bodies. Tom ordered scarves to be used as gags for the four prisoners, who with knives between their shoulder blades were ready to crawl, sprawl, scramble back to the Finnish lines as best they could, and without noise; they were not allowed to stand upright until they reached the door of the little farmhouse. There they were pushed into the living room, under a heavy guard, and there the muffling

146

cloaks and scarves were pulled from their heads and shoulders.
Three Russian soldiers, stupefied by cold and fear, looked dumbly
at their captors. The fourth man stooped to brush the snow from
his thighs and knees and straightened up to stare at Tom, out of
breath and triumphant, with his pistol in his hand.

"Good evening, Mr. Fleming," said Boris Heiden. "I claim
the protection of the Geneva Convention; you have assaulted a
war correspondent."

"*Heiden!*"

"You *know* this man?" exclaimed Colonel Holsti.

"Ah, you speak English, colonel," said Heiden. "Excellent!
Yes, Mr. Fleming and I have met before."

"Colonel Holsti!" said Tom, recovering from his astonish-
ment, "this man's name is Boris Heiden. He was born in St.
Petersburg, and I believe him to be a Russian agent. Captain
Keiller, I call you to witness that we captured him in a Russian
forward post, wearing civilian clothes. Under the Commander-
in-Chief's ruling, he can be shot as a spy."

Heiden smiled. He looked much the same as when Tom saw
him at Kouvola junction, though he had exchanged the leather
jacket for a heavy knee-length coat warmly lined with caracul,
and the cloth cap for a fur hat with ear flaps which he now
unfastened. The wispy beard had been trimmed and he wore no
spectacles. He was as unruffled as when Sophie Sandels found him
sitting in the dark with her young sister.

"Mr. Fleming, or is it Captain Fleming once again?" he
said, "knows quite well that though I was born in Petersburg, I
am now a citizen of Switzerland. So far from being a spy, I'm
here on the Russian front as a war correspondent. I can show you
my Swiss passport, and my accreditation from the editor of the
Neue Zürcher Zeitung."

His hand moved to the breast of his jacket, and Tom, swinging
up his pistol, said, "Hold it! Somebody search him first!"

Karl Keiller ran his hands inside and outside Heiden's overcoat. He was carrying a service pistol in the right hand pocket.
Keiller laid it, with a leather wallet, on the table.

"You were quoting the Geneva Convention," said Tom grimly.
"It prohibits a war correspondent from carrying firearms."
He handed Heiden's pistol to the Finnish section commander,
who, with his men still guarding the soldier prisoners, was

looking on amazed at the scene. Keiller spoke quickly to him in Swedish, and the Finn, nodding, went off with the prisoners and their escort to another room.

"Please examine my credentials, sir," said Heiden to the colonel. "Examine all the contents of my wallet."

There was very little to examine except the Swiss passport, a ration book issued in Helsingfors, some rouble notes and Finnish marks, and a letter from the famous Zürich newspaper.

"It's in German," said Colonel Holsti with a groan. "Put it into Swedish, Captain Keiller, be so good."

"Just a moment," said Tom. "Read it in English too, will you, Charlie?"

The letter, read in two languages, was signed by the deputy features editor of the *Neue Zürcher Zeitung*, thanked Mr. Heiden for his interesting article on the coup d'état in Helsingfors, for which payment was enclosed, and offered a similar fee for any articles on the war which might interest Swiss readers. Tom laughed harshly. "A war correspondent!" he said, "Heiden's no more a war correspondent than I am, and I've had some experience of the breed. He's a freelance, that's all he is: an accredited war correspondent would be carrying a press card and a movement order from his GHQ, and he wouldn't be in a forward post without a conducting officer. Did any of those poor moujiks look like an officer to you?"

"The Russian line is fluid," Heiden said. "My conducting officer decided to remain at their command post."

"But Mr. Heiden is a Swiss citizen," said Colonel Holsti. "Captain Fleming, by what right do you such charges make, that he should be a spy?"

"I don't give a damn what kind of citizen he is," said Tom. "He's got a good cover story, but it's not the whole truth. This man's brother was a Russian anarchist, a revolutionary, hanged in 1906 for his part in the plot to murder Stolypin. He arrived in Finland just before the Bolshevik revolution, posing as a student. I saw him myself in the company of Russian troops at Kouvola. He didn't call himself a war correspondent then, but they knew him all right; they got out of his way like a lot of scalded cats—"

"Cats?" said Colonel Holsti. "For God's sake, what *cats?*"

"Someone should translate for the colonel," said Heiden, amused. He picked up one of the stools set round the heavy farmhouse table, drew it close to the fire, and sat down. Colonel Holsti sat down heavily in the farmer's wooden chair on the other side of the hearth.

"Sir," said Heiden earnestly, "it's not a crime to enrol at Helsingfors University as a graduate student. Nor yet to travel by train to Kouvola junction, where I found Mr. Fleming suffering from some sort of fit, and incidentally did my best to care for him. He hasn't told you, perhaps, that he recently spent some time in a mental hospital in Scotland—"

"That's a lie!" said Tom.

"—and has not a stable personality. It's true my brother was involved in the plot to kill Stolypin in August 1906, but Igor Heiden paid for his folly with his life, and gentlemen, does that make me an anarchist?"

"You told me you thought your brother was a hero," said Tom.

"Because he died heroically, without complaint or appeal to the tyrant. To the tyrant," Heiden repeated, still addressing himself only to Colonel Holsti. "Since when has a patriotic Finn like you, sir, despised the would-be murderer of a Russian tyrant? Don't you all revere the memory of your young hero, Yevgeni Schaumann, who assassinated one of your worst oppressors the Czar's governor-general, Bobrikov? Shouldn't Igor Heiden be equally honoured? Don't you remember how Stolypin persecuted the Finns, and worked to bring the Grand Duchy under the Czar's autocracy? Don't you remember that in the first two months he was prime minister, six hundred political prisoners were hanged, and the hangman's noose itself came to be called Stolypin's necktie? The bombs they threw that day at his dacha on Apothecaries' island were in reprisal for the man's brutalities—"

"Some reprisal!" said Tom Fleming. "Your heroes didn't get Stolypin, but they killed thirty-two innocent people, and injured God knows how many more. Yes, Heiden! I know the whole Stolypin story now. He was murdered a few years later, in the theatre at Kiev; had you anything to do with that?"

"Of course not," said Heiden. "In 1911 I was a student in Zürich."

"Along with Lenin and Trotsky, and all the other *tovarichi*?"

"Now that does enough, Captain Fleming," said Colonel Holsti. He had been visibly shaken by the appeal to the memory of Eugene Schaumann. "I shall talk with an interpreter to the Russian prisoners. They shall know Mr. Heiden's account of his conducting officer, and after that we shall decide what must be done."

"You go with him, Charlie," said Tom as the door closed. "That old fool will bitch up the whole thing if he can." Karl Keiller nodded and went out. He had been a silent witness, with a far graver expression than Tom had seen him wear before.

Tom himself shrugged off his wet cloak, changing his pistol from one hand to the other as he did so. He stood beneath the swinging oil lamp, watching Heiden, who tilted his stool against the wall and clasped his hands behind his head.

There was no sound in the country room but the ticking of an old clock on the wall. It was a friendly sound, like the crackling of the logs in the big fireplace, and comforting, too, was the faint fragrance of tea from the peasant samovar, made by placing one rough teapot on top of the other. Heiden said lazily:

"Now that I've been searched, may I smoke a cigarette?"

"Go ahead."

Heiden took cigarettes and matches from an inner pocket and inhaled luxuriously. "Do they read Shakespeare in the Canadian backwoods?" he asked. "Do you know the lines which so perfectly describe you? 'Infirm of purpose! Give me the daggers!' You stand trembling there—yes, I can see your hands shaking—but you're bold now, because you've got a weapon in your hand; and yet you daren't use it, daren't fire on me. Here I am, quite at your mercy, and we're alone, no witnesses, you could tell your fat colonel I was shot while attempting to escape—"

"We don't shoot prisoners in the White Army," said Tom.

"My dear Fleming, what a jewel you are. How beautifully predictable! What an example of the theory of conditioned reflexes! Like Pavlov's dogs, you salivate when the bell rings, but your bell is the honour of the regiment, the Canadian Army, now the Butcher Guards. Do you remember at Kouvola station, boasting to me about the Canadians in France? No fighting men to touch them, you said, except two British Divisions and the Brigade of Guards. And now you're one of Mannerheim's bully-boys, and proud of that as well. It's an odd situation for the hero of Sainte Elodie."

"I didn't know that story got into the Swiss papers too,"

said Tom. "But it doesn't matter. I said we don't shoot prisoners. We do, under martial law, shoot spies."

"And that's exactly what I meant when I called you infirm of purpose. You haven't got the nerve to pull the trigger yourself, but you're prepared to give the word of command to a firing squad."

"I hope I get the chance," said Tom. "You bastard, it was you who put Sophie's name on the Black List, and got her killed."

"As an enemy of the people?" said Heiden in polite surprise. "Sophie Sandels? But Lisa herself told me her sister was killed in a scuffle between the workers and the Butcher Guards on the day the revolution started. I was sorry to hear it, of course. But really in some ways the poor girl was very indiscreet—"

"She admired Mannerheim," said Tom. "That first evening, I saw the hatred in your eyes."

"How very theatrical," said Heiden, but the spark of hate was in his eyes again. "You've been talking like a fool tonight, Fleming. You can't prove a single thing against me, even in a court of enquiry, if that old fool—as you rightly call him— dares to hold one; and I don't think he'll risk an appeal to the Swiss government, which so recently recognised the independence of Finland. So why don't you admit—"

The door opened, and Captain Keiller came in, followed by two of the Finns who had been guarding the Russian prisoners. He did not look at Tom. He had Heiden's passport in his hand.

"Mr. Heiden," he said, "Colonel Holsti wants to see you in the other room. Go with these two men, please."

Heiden for the first time seemed at a loss. He rose and flung the butt of his cigarette into the fire. "Am I under arrest?" he said.

"You are." The Finns fell in on each side of Heiden; he squared his shoulders and walked out.

"What happened, Charlie?" said Tom eagerly. Keiller shrugged, and, going over to the samovar, poured two cups of tea for Tom and himself. "You were right about the moujiks," he said, drinking thirstily. "They'd told the major as much as they knew about their troop dispositions, before Holsti went in. Then we all tried—and the major's Russian's pretty good—to get some information about Heiden. They knew nothing about him, except that their sergeant brought him forward about an hour before our patrol turned up. So there's still no proof that he's a bona fide war correspondent."

"I told you he was a spy!"

"I know you did, Tom old boy," said Keiller. Tom had never heard him speak so seriously, or without using any Indian Army slang. "But Holsti's impressed by the Swiss passport. Says all hell will break out if we shoot a Swiss national by mistake for a Russian spy. Anyway, the thing's too big for Holsti. He wants to get Base to hold the baby, and by good luck a truck came down from Base while we were on patrol. I'm to take Heiden back to Haapamäki as soon as they can get the driver out of the mess tent."

"I'd like to be the conducting officer," said Tom.

"You'd never get Holsti to agree to that. No, Tom, it's better I should go. I'll hand him over to the Field Judge tomorrow."

"You're not taking him alone?"

"Hell no, with the driver and two guards. Tom, I think you should try to take it easy for a bit—"

"Do *you* think I'm mentally unstable, Karl?"

"Of course not, old chap, but you've been under a hell of a strain. First Red Helsingfors, and now this! Is that the truck I hear?"

"Charlie, for God's sake take care of yourself. That devil thinks he's going to get away with it, and you've heard him talk— all that about his brother and Stolypin, he made it sound like some great feat."

"Yes, well, they'll sort it all out at Haapamäki."

"Can I look at his passport?"

"It seems genuine enough."

"Born St. Petersburg 1888. Some student—rising thirty! Address Villa Heiden, Dolder Allee, Zürich—I'll remember that. You're not going to let him have it back, are you?"

"My orders are to hold it until we get to Base. So long, Tom, see you tomorrow."

Tom Fleming was alone with the ticking clock. He expected the major and Holsti to come back, but the sound of voices from the next room faded into the farmyard and was hushed. There was nothing to be seen from the window. By the time Tom opened the front door the old Renault truck had turned and was on its way back to Base. The rear light was twinkling like a little red eye of derision in the drifting snow.

12

AT THE BEGINNING OF March General Mannerheim knew
that his hour had come. It was the time the Finns called
Maaliskuu, the month when sap rises, and the dazzling sun
on the snow was a warning that though the ice still held on lakes
and rivers the thaw, impeding all troop movements, was not very
far away.

The defensive phase of the war which had followed the first
guerilla raids could not be indefinitely prolonged. The men who
rallied to the cause of White Finland back in January had worked
miracles: they held the main railway still, and in spite of continu-
ing pressure in the Vilppula sector had never lost the vital
Haapamäki junction. In Karelia, at a time when Mannerheim
was able to send only twelve rifles and no reinforcements, two
thousand Whites had by courage alone held the line of the Vuoksi
river against a Red offensive mounted by ten thousand men.
Repeated White attacks in the central provinces drew off the
enemy's onslaught in the east, but his reserves were building up in
an alarming way.

Throughout the whole of Finland there was now much suffering. In Helsingfors and all the south there was a real Red reign of
terror, and even north of the enemy front there was, as Tom
Fleming had warned Sophie, the especial bitterness engendered
by a civil war. For the farm workers the summer of 1917 had been
"the summer of the proletariat". Red agitators had urged them
to pay no rent or taxes, serve no masters, and by harvest time
many of them enjoyed watching angry farmers stooking their
own corn. There had been Red militancy in the autumn, corn
ricks set alight, cattle lamed, murderous shots fired in the dark
of the moon. Now there were reprisals. Summary justice was
meted out by the Field Judges of the White Army and the
local commandants, and there were graveyard executions and
deportations to the prisoner camps in the north. Food grew scarce,
and meals were reduced to potatoes and the salt brine from pickled

sprats: salt codfish and sour milk became a luxury. The two warring armies fared little better than the peasants, but at least the Whites were better clad now, with rough grey uniforms and white fur hats. The Swedish Brigade wore brown.

For General Mannerheim had got his reinforcements. Although the Swedish government refused aid to Finland, except the offer of mediation in a war which, it was declared in Stockholm, the Finns could never hope to win, over five hundred young Swedes enlisted in the White Army, many of them assisted in their journey by a group called The Friends of Finland, organised by General Mannerheim's brother Johan. Among them were eighty-four army officers, immensely valuable to the general in their professionalism. With a smaller number of Danish and Norwegian volunteers they formed the Swedish Brigade, and within days of their arrival at Vasa the Finnish Jägers began to return to their native land.

These young men, whose clandestine departure for military training in Germany had fired the imagination of so many of their countrymen, arrived in two detachments. The vanguard brought with them Russian war supplies purchased in Germany, beyond price to an army which had gone to war armed only with a few sporting rifles and shotguns. The first Jägers brought forty-four thousand rifles, nine million rounds of ammunition, sixty-five machine-guns and even some field guns, and they were followed on February 25 by the main body of 1,130 men. The effect on the whole army's morale was tremendous, for the arrival of a fit and eager body of trained men was exactly the tonic the weary freedom fighters needed. General Mannerheim held his first grand parade, with a brass band playing, and also made his first public speech in Finnish, on the day he welcomed and reviewed the Jägers on a snowy city square in Vasa.

It was not only the weather and the reinforcements which decided Mannerheim to pass to offensive action. On March 3 a series of events took place destined to influence the whole course of the war. On that day Senator Svinhufvud, in hiding since his abortive attempt to leave Helsingfors by air, made his getaway by sea aboard a Russian icebreaker whose captain was willing to take a bribe, and landed at Reval on the other side of the Gulf of Finland. On that same day, the Treaty of Brest-Litovsk was signed, after long haggling and even a resumption of hostilities between Soviet Russia and Germany. For Russia the Great War was finally over, and there was nothing to stop Lenin from sending massive reinforcements to the Finnish Reds.

But the event of March 3 which most affected Mannerheim was a telephone call to his headquarters from the Senators at Vasa, telling him that the Finnish government had asked Germany to intervene to crush the insurrection in Finland. This development, a violation of the promise made to him in January, so infuriated Mannerheim that he was on the verge of resigning his command, and it was perhaps the only time in that hard winter that his officers saw him in a rage. But his cool and lucid brain mastered his temper: he saw the advantage to his army if the Germans agreed, as part of the bargain, to sell him arms and equipment, but he insisted, and successfully, that the German contingent must place itself under his command. He knew, however, for the sake of Finland's self-respect and his own, that he must win a decisive victory before the Germans could arrive.

Preoccupied with these grave matters, the general had no time to discuss problems of discipline occurring beneath Corps level, especially since he had personally selected his four corps commanders and had every confidence in their judgment. It is doubtful if Colonel, soon to be Major-General, Martin Wetzer, commanding II Corps, ever received a report on what harassed field officers came to call the Keiller Affair, which at no time went higher than Brigade level, although a Canadian volunteer officer was demanding a court martial for himself to bring certain facts into the light of day. The Keiller Affair was strangled at birth, either at Base or at Army Rear, and only the testimony of two bewildered Finnish privates, conveyed through an interpreter, remained on record as a version of what really happened on the snowy night when Charlie Keiller escorted Heiden to Base at the railway junction.

For Captain Keiller never returned to the command post at Vilppula. Tom Fleming waited thirty-six hours before he began to make enquiries, and in the meantime Colonel Holsti had turned surly, and was muttering about troublemakers and barrack-room lawyers and fairy stories about Russian spies. The language barrier seemed to stretch impenetrably between Tom and anyone who might have helped him, including the Finnish major who had authorised the night raid, but when he tracked down the

155

soldier escorts, now returned to their unit, he gave the matter no rest until an interpreter was found, who took down in writing what the senior soldier said.

Transcript.

Pte. Järvi: Him and me went up to Base in the Renault with Captain Keiller and the foreign gent. They talked their heads off in the truck, the two of them—

Capt. Fleming: In what language? English? German?

Pte. Järvi: They sounds the same to me, sir.

Capt. Fleming: Never mind. Go on.

Pte. Järvi: Well, we come to Base, sir, and Captain Keiller says, "Wait here", and he took the foreign gent in to see an officer.

Capt. Fleming: Do you know which officer?

Pte. Järvi: No, sir. But they was with him about an hour.

Capt. Fleming: Let me get this straight. When Captain Keiller told you to "wait here", were you posted as sentries, or what?

Pte. Järvi: The lads give us tea and cigarettes. Then Captain Keiller came out with the foreign gent, who was smiling, and he says, "It's all right, Järvi, we're going up to Rear. Just you come with us to the station and I'll see you get a billet all right."

Capt. Fleming: How could they go up to Vasa at that hour of the night?

Pte. Järvi: There was a supply train going back empty at o-one hours, sir. We put Captain Keiller's valise in the guard's van, and then he dismissed us, and we went off for a bit of kip.

Capt. Fleming: So you didn't actually see them start? You weren't there when the train pulled out?

Pte. Järvi: No, sir.

Nobody, as far as could be ascertained, had seen them start, nobody had seen them arrive at Vasa. Army Rear disclaimed all knowledge of the vanishing travellers, but a day or two later a Swedish national called Karl Keiller was sworn in as a member of the Swedish Brigade and sent to the front in Central Finland as a member of a reserve battalion. Of Boris Heiden no trace was found, but Colonel Holsti, now thoroughly alarmed, assured Tom that he must be somewhere in Vasa and would soon be found by the military police, who had been given his description.

"I knew this would happen!" said Tom furiously. "He got

round Charlie on the way to Rear, probably knocked him out in the end, and jumped out of the train. A supply train, empty, with no witnesses! And he's not in Vasa now, I tell you: he got out across the Kvarken, over the ice to Sweden, and Charlie's lying low because he daren't face a court martial. Hell, I'll ask permission to go up to Vasa myself—"

Permission was withheld at Base. Base, facing a storming Red attack, was sick of the Keiller Affair, of which the only immediate result was the transfer of Holsti to a minor branch of the Quartermaster's Department at Vasa, where he supervised such activities as counting socks and mufflers for the troops. Base would have willingly transferred Captain Fleming out of the area too, but a young officer, professionally trained and seasoned, was worth his weight in gold on that front, and at Corps level it was known that a great set battle was in preparation.

This was the battle for Tammerfors, a town of fifty thousand inhabitants which was rapidly overtaking Åbo as the second city of Finland. Built on an isthmus between two lakes, it had an enormous power potential in the river down which, by means of a natural slope and artificial rollers, logs could be floated to the harbour at Björneborg, and besides the timber trade many other industries had been developed in and around the town. It was a clean, well-planned little city at the beginning of the century, with no slums, but with some overcrowding in the workers' quarters and sporadic labour disputes in the factories on hours and rates of pay. Early on, the trade unions and the Social-Democratic party had made a useful alliance in Tammerfors, which became an easy prey of the Reds in January 1918. One of the worst atrocities of the war, called the Suinula massacre, took place there on January 30, when a detachment of about eighty White Guards, surrendering to the Reds, were shot down by their captors in cold blood, and when General Mannerheim made Tammerfors his objective, he issued an Order of the Day forbidding any White reprisals for the outrage at Suinula. He was preparing, for the first time in this campaign, to fight a set-piece battle in the tradition of Clausewitz, moving his troops forward in a wide ring to envelop the Red concentrations in the outlying districts, and then drawing the battle lines closely round Tammerfors itself.

The first phase of the operation was completed by March 21, and on that day GHQ moved forward to Vilppula. No man at

Mannerheim's headquarters then knew that on the same day the Germans were launching the massive attack in the west which the Allies had dreaded ever since Lenin came to power in Russia. The Treaty of Brest-Litovsk had rid Germany of all commitments in the east, and the Germans were now free to carry out the Ludendorff Plan, which was to anticipate the arrival of the US troops in strength by a series of crushing blows along a sixty-mile wide front south of Arras. Starting at St. Quentin, the first phase of the plan was alarmingly successful. The British line was driven in to a depth of forty miles. The French lost Bapaume, Peronne, and other towns in Picardy, and only the arrival of their reserves— almost the last in a country drained of men—checked the German advance towards the sea.

Ludendorff at St. Quentin used gas in support of his terrific bombardment by six thousand guns. At Tammerfors, in "the little country on the edge of darkness", as Sophie Sandels had called it, there was no gas. The Whites had thirty-five field guns, the Reds thirty, and the Whites had one hundred and forty machine-guns, twice as many as their opponents. The total number of men engaged was probably not more than fifty thousand. Yet the soldiers who fell in the Armageddon of Flanders were no braver, and no more dead, than their counterparts who died outside Tammerfors on "the bloody Maundy Thursday" when the flower of the 2nd Jäger Regiment and the Swedish Brigade fell while taking the key position of Kalevankangas. Tom Fleming was fighting in Wetzer's corps, wearing in his white fur hat the sprig of fir adopted as a badge by the Whites. Since the new artillery arrived from Germany, his nerves were becoming hardened to the once familiar sound of howitzer shells, known in Flanders as "coal-boxes", which had come over in groups of four in the methodical German "strafe" at dusk and dawn. There was no method of that sort in the battle for Tammerfors, stubbornly defended by the Reds, and no time to dig trenches: what dug-outs existed were merely earthworks covered by sacking. There the exhausted attackers of Maundy Thursday took what rest they could during the weekend when new reserves of men and material were brought up. In all, nine days passed before Tammerfors surrendered on April 6, after nearly seventy-two hours of hand-to-hand fighting inside the city, street by crumbling street, house by ruined house. It was the bloodiest encounter Tom Flem-

ing had ever known, but he came through it with only minor
bruises and abrasions requiring treatment at a first-aid post. When
free to do so he went in search of the Norwegian ambulance
where volunteer doctors and nurses were caring for the survivors
of the gallant Swedish Brigade. It was not difficult to get news
of the Karl Keiller sworn in at Vasa towards the end of February.
He had fallen at Kalevankangas and was buried there. A sergeant
under treatment for a leg wound, still in the brown tweed coat
with the cheap fur collar of the Swedish Brigade, with the blue-
yellow-blue diagonal stripe on the white armband, described
Corporal Karl Keiller exactly: a short, red-haired mechanic
from Malmö, without a word of English to his name.

Next day, being Sunday, a thanksgiving service for the victory
was held in Tammerfors. It followed a review at which the
bishop and clergy and the city councillors greeted General
Mannerheim and thanked him for their liberation from the Red
terror. The watching ranks saw that their imperturbable commander was moved by this tribute. But he was as cool as ever
at the church service which followed, sitting upright in the first
pew, alone except for a private looking for a place to sit, who
pushed his way in beside him. It was a quiet scene after the days
of strife, and Tom Fleming was not the only man who looked at
the general in speculation:

"I wonder what he's thinking about now."

✻   ✻   ✻

He thought, late that night, in the staff train:

*I must have been asleep for an hour or more. Switch on the reading light.
No, by my watch it was only ten minutes. Leave the light on.*

*I'm in my own coupé, and the train isn't moving. This is Tammerfors.
The berth is narrow and hardly long enough, and there's barely room for
my uniform on the door and my shaving tackle above the washbasin. But
I've never objected to cramped quarters. This little room is very different
from the Czar's suite in the Imperial train. Probably the sort of thing
they gave to the valet on duty.*

*I've been received by the Czar aboard the Imperial train, he in the
Cossack caftan he affected, the rest of us in parade dress with decorations,
and every carriage on the train as ornamental as a palace. That was at
Mohilev, where I saw the blood spreading across the platform. The blood
shed by the Bolsheviks.*

Did I use the right words in my Order of the Day, I wonder? "This is the greatest battle ever fought in Finland. This is the victory of the whole world over the Russian Bolsheviks, and their doctrine of world revolution and the destruction of civilisation." The victory of the whole world, perhaps exaggerated? What would Foch and Haig have to say to that?

But they're fighting the Germans. I am not. No longer. Was I able to convince those British diplomats from the Petrograd embassy that even though the Germans intervene in Finland it doesn't mean the Finnish Army is fighting on the side of Germany? Or was that mere sophistry? They were glad to have my safe-conduct to Torneå and the Swedish border.

Did they notice that I'm a little deaf? It's not always easy to conceal from strangers, especially when one has to speak in English. But I can hardly hear at all on the left side. That happened at Mukden, in the cannonading.

Thirteen years ago, and tonight my body aches from head to foot. Rheumatic pains in my ankles, and in this knee broken in five places, when was that? When I was thirty-four. Even after that I was able for the ride across Asia, the wonderful time. In Kashgar they named me Ma-da-han, "the Horse that Leaps through the Clouds".

Poor horse . . .

I was nearly asleep then. What time is it? Tomorrow there are eleven thousand prisoners of war to be got away somehow to the north. And fed. And Karelia to be liberated. And Svinhufvud is here, full of his performance in Berlin.

Was I wrong to speak of our victory over Bolshevism? My enemies could say I'm planning to carry the war across the border into Russia. I know better than that. The Whites in Russia are not organised for victory. Kolchak can't win alone, nor Kornilov with the Don Cossacks nor Dietov in the Urals, nor the Czech Legion. And my task lies in Finland.

This was what the fortune-teller meant, that evening in Odessa. She Sleep.

*   *   *

After the fall of Tammerfors it became clear that the incredible victory was almost won. General Mannerheim and his Finns had worked out their own salvation. The Russian troops were being herded into prisoner-of-war camps and the Red Guards were melting away as quickly as the winter snow. It was *Kelirikko*, the season of the thaw, which came as early in 1918 as the occasional rainy and slushy days of the winter seemed to predict, and though the resulting sea of mud slowed up marching men and wheeled traffic on the unmetalled roads of Finland, mobility by water gave a new advantage to Mannerheim. The ports began to open. Björneborg on the Gulf of Bothnia was liberated a week after Tammerfors; Åbo reopened for traffic; the German Baltic Division landed without difficulty at Hangö. At the same time the Russian sailors who had terrorised Helsingfors so long quietly weighed anchor, and the fleet faded away up the Gulf of Finland into the Kronstadt mists, where they would pose a new problem for the Allies in the months to come.

On April 10, GHQ moved forward to St. Michel, and the little town, commanding half a dozen lakes and miles of hilly woodland, became the staging point for the twenty-four thousand Finnish troops assembling for the liberation of the much enduring province of Karelia. The troop trains rolled across Central Finland on the long road from Haapamäki junction, east of Lake Saimaa and down to St. Andreae, and from there barges on the Vuoksi river carried the men to a point due east of Viborg. Their first objective was the liberation of the ancient city where the first shots of the war had been fired, but they also hoped to stem the tragic mass movement, accompanied by pillaging and arson, which began as soon as the civilian Red leaders in Helsingfors, seeing the war was lost, made plans to lead their supporters into Russia.

To St. Michel, on a sunny April day, came Major-General Rüdiger von der Goltz, commanding the German Baltic Division, to pay his respects to the Commander-in-Chief. The latter received him with the proper military courtesies, his real feelings, as usual, being hidden behind his mask of perfect manners. Others in his entourage were not so affable, but after all the argument it did not appear that the German contribution to the war would be a large one. Colonel Brandenstein had crossed the Gulf of Finland from Reval with only two thousand German troops and eight guns, and the Baltic Division, with eighteen guns, was only seven thousand strong. Yet the two German commanders wore an unmistakable air of elation in those April days, for in Flanders Ludendorff had delivered a second smashing blow at the British front, opening a new salient and taking Armentières.

Mannerheim ordered von der Goltz to proceed at once to the liberation of Helsingfors, and after two days of fighting outside and inside the city the Red Guards capitulated. They had now no leaders. The Peoples' Commissars had fled to Viborg, and Comrade Lenin had not stretched out his protecting hand. All he would promise, if Viborg was invested, was to give them the means to escape to their spiritual home in Russia.

It was at St. Michel, too, just before the final advance on Viborg, where his grandfather had been governor seventy years before, that General Mannerheim held an investiture. Quite early in the independence campaign he had instituted an order of awards for bravery, to be known as the Liberty Cross and the Liberty Medal, and on this April morning he conferred the decorations on a number of officers and men who had distinguished themselves at Tammerfors. Tom Fleming was one of the officers. He didn't understand a word of the citation, but the Cross was a pretty thing, white enamel picked out in gold, and the investiture itself was no more alarming than the simple ceremony at Shorncliffe Hospital when the Prince of Wales had laid the MC on his pillow. General Mannerheim had been all polite formality with his undesired German allies; he had the knack, with his own troops, of keeping a ceremonial occasion dignified but informal. He spoke a few words of congratulation to Tom in English.

"I am told you are a forester in your own land, Captain Fleming?"

It wasn't quite true, but then the top brass never did get things like that quite right. Tom unhesitatingly replied "Yes, sir," eyes front.

"When you are home in your own woods, wear the fir sprig for Tammerfors."

"I will, sir." And that got to him, he knew it would stay with him, like "Cold hands, warm heart", it made him buy paper and envelopes in one of the little shops that afternoon, and write a short letter to his parents. There was no excuse for silence now, with Helsingfors free the mails were going out again, but when he had finished a letter to Vancouver no more communicative than the field service postcards he had sometimes sent from France, Tom Fleming filled several pages which he addressed to Nancy Macpherson in London. He didn't read them over, but sealed the envelope as soon as he had finished with "Love, Tom";

he had a hunch that Nancy, of all people in the world, would be able to read between the lines.

The pincers movement round Viborg began on April 20. Tom Fleming missed the siege which followed, and the heaviest of the fighting, his unit being part of a detachment ordered to cut the main line to Petrograd at Perkjärvi. This prevented the Peoples' Commissars, now themselves refugees, from escaping to Russia by train, but before the beleaguered city surrendered to the Whites Comrade Lenin kept his promise of rescue. Kullervo Manner, Colonel Svechnikov (he who fought in vain to cut the White line at Haapamäki) and other rebel leaders were taken off from Viborg in a steamer and two yachts, and up the Gulf, at Kronstadt, they were cheered by the sailors of the Russian fleet who had been their right-hand men in the terrorising of Helsingfors. The greetings of the Soviet Commissars were more perfunctory. They had another escort in view, for another band of travellers, and on April 27 the former Czar, Nicholas II, and the Imperial family started on their last journey from Tobolsk to the House of Special Purpose in Ekaterinburg.

Manner and his Reds fled from Viborg before the worst of the fighting, which left liberated Viborg in much the same ruins as Tammerfors. At last the flag of a free Finland was hoisted on St. Olaf's Tower, and on May 1, the traditional date of spring festival and renewal through all the northlands, General Mannerheim held a thanksgiving service in Viborg's fifteenth-century cathedral, desecrated by the Russians and for two hundred years used by them as a military storehouse. Once again, at the review which followed, Tom Fleming listened at attention to a proclamation of which he understood nothing. Later in the day some of it was translated for him:

"With your blood, gallant soldiers, Finland has now gained a position of equality with the other nations of Europe. The Finn can walk proudly, the master in his own house."

He knew that Mannerheim's words meant the realisation of Sophie Sandels's dream, and the old pain, partly anaesthetised by the battles he had fought, drove Tom to write one letter more, to Helsingfors. He had to wait for an answer until the mopping-up operations in Karelia were over, some of them as bitter as any

in the war, and the White Army regrouped for its first peacetime
duties and the victory parade through Helsingfors. On the evening
of May 15 he was outside the city, sharing a bottle of vodka with
two officers of the Swedish Brigade, when a boy of about fourteen,
wildly excited at seeing the liberators, brought him Nikko Hirn's
reply.

Discipline was so far relaxed for this one night that many
people had made their way beyond the city limits, looking for
sons, brothers, sweethearts in the ranks, and hoping to begin the
rejoicings over the nightmare's end. It was easy for Tom to lose
himself in the crowd and read his letter alone at the edge of the
wood near which they were bivouacked. The woods were carpeted
with windflowers, delicately shaded in blue and white, there were
new tassels on the larches, new green leaves on the birch. The
long tender twilight foretold the white nights of midsummer,
and in the distance, down one of the long creeks, Tom could see
the white sail of the first pleasure boat. He opened the letter
and read:

Dear Tom,
Your letter from Viborg tells you safe and well, as me. Mr.
Baker came to-back last week and he is well. Your friend Mr.
Brown is gone to England. Some Senators also hided in that
clinic, the doctors told the Reds there was smallpox, and none
of them dared enter.

Tom, you should stop to blame yourself for Sophie's death.
If who to blame, is me, for that I went not to you that Sunday
night but waited until morning. But I believe it was in
Sophie's stars to die. She thought more of the Finland's world's
dream than of each day's life.

You demand if I have any news of the man Heiden. Such as
I have, is bad. Lisa Sandels is missing since three weeks.
She left the old people, saying she must arrange about the
flat, tables, chairs, &c, and this they agreed. But in Helsingfors
she tell Mrs. Rentola she shall leave for Stockholm where Mr.
Boris Heiden waits to marry her. We are not to know if this is
true.

Soon I hope you and I can talk together. Tomorrow I watch
with Mr. Baker from the office window.

Truthfully, Nikolai Hirn.

164

The birds were twittering sleepily in the larches above the noise of the happy camp when Tom Fleming crumpled the letter in his hand with the sick sensation that as Finland's war was ending, his own began. Heiden was still alive, and even still in Stockholm: he had crossed the ice of the Kvarken, but not with Charlie Keiller. Ever since he heard the description of the second Keiller at Tammerfors he had been sure that some day, when the snows melted, the body of the gay and impudent Karl Keiller would be found. Heiden wins again, he thought mechanically. Heiden, here I come.

The march into the cheering city next morning was every soldier's dream of glory. The crowds, the flowers, the banners, the handsome general riding on his beautiful horse Neptune, while Mayor von Hartman waited, silk hat in hand, to greet the liberators, were all in the great tradition of a hard-won victory. It was just three and a half months, as Mannerheim had prophesied, since he began the war no one expected him to win, followed by a few farmers, most of them unarmed, and now he was leading sixteen thousand disciplined men into the free capital of their country. Some of the rustic troops were seeing Helsingfors for the first time. For Tom Fleming the sight of the city in May sunlight was like a mirage. He had only known Helsingfors in pain, darkness and cold, and now between the young green of the trees and the shimmering blue of the harbour the perfect façades of cream and pearl and grey seemed the epitome of light and freedom. The Senate Square was crowded with the citizens, climbing round the Good Emperor's statue, standing on tiptoe on every step leading to the great cathedral. From where Tom stood at the south side of the square he could see the top windows of the Senate House where General Mannerheim would be received when the bouquets were presented and the speeches over. He could see in the distance the library door against which Sophie had beaten in vain. There were now a hundred people crowding on the stones where he lifted her up: the hospital where she died he could not see. In the middle of the square the conqueror was speaking:

"You were a handful of poorly armed men who, not hesitating before an enemy of infinite numbers, began the struggle for liberty in Ostrobothnia and Karelia . . . Our country is free.

From the tundras of Lapland, from the remotest skerries of Lapland to Systerbäck, the Lion Flag is flying . . . Today, for the first time for more than a century, we have heard the roar of Finnish guns from Sveaborg . . ."

The crowd, applauding, shifted and swayed like a cornfield as a passage was made for the general and his staff, the cabinet, the dignitaries, to walk up the huge flight of steps to give thanks in the cathedral. In the square, orders were shouted, feet stamped, hands slapped rifle butts as the troops saluted and moved off to re-form for the final act of the day's drama. General Mannerheim was to take the salute in front of Runeberg's statue.

For Tom Fleming the sense of unreality continued. He knew he was himself, wearing a now familiar grey uniform, with the Liberty Cross up, and the fir sprig for Tammerfors in his white fur hat. But at the same time—as the grey ranks passed the Swedish Theatre and swung on down the North Esplanade—he was the Fleming who had come this way first on a wet night in winter, and again on a black January morning to the sound of machine-gun fire. Now the bands were playing. He forgot that Mr. Baker, whose home he had appropriated, and Nikko, that good friend, would be watching from their office window like the hundreds of other watchers whose cheering filled the summer air. Under the green boughs he saw Runeberg's statue where Sophie had laid her pathetic flowers, blue and white, the national colours, when the plinth was deep in snow. He saw Mannerheim on Neptune, tall in the saddle, towering above the marching men. The sight made him remember that poem she recited, something high in the something garden, how did it go?

> Straight he stands, like a banner furled,
> Seer-king and passionless warden
> Over a little northern world.

His head swung right, his hand swung up: in Mannerheim Tom Fleming saluted the land that Sophie Sandels loved.

PART TWO

— Give me the daggers

13

THERE WAS A MOVEMENT under the white honeycomb spread in the darkened, airy bedroom, and a girl's voice called, "Who is it?"

"*C'est Gaston, mademoiselle.* With the breakfast!"

"Oh, thanks, Gaston." The girl in bed lay still until she heard the door of the suite close behind the waiter, and then got up yawning and went into the sitting room, pulling on a yellow satin wrapper as she went.

"It's a gorgeous morning, Linda!" she called, and grinned when she heard her room-mate groan. She poured half a cup of *café au lait*, drank it at a gulp, and went back to the bedroom to pull the faded green taffeta curtains apart.

"Oh Nancy, don't make such a racket! I was having such a lovely dream."

"I'll bet. You want me to bring you a cup of coffee in bed?"

"No, I'll get up. In just five minutes . . ."

"That gives me ten in the bathroom, *and* first go at the hot water." But when Nancy Macpherson came out of the bathroom, tubbed and brushed, she found the other girl sitting at the breakfast table, pensively spreading her ration of butter on two halves of a small brioche.

"What time did we get in last night?" said Linda Lee.

"About half past one. But I didn't sit out here with Jack Macey after that," said Miss Macpherson virtuously. "I went to sleep at once, and slept till three, when you came clumping in!"

"Oh, *Nancy!*" Linda self-consciously twisted the very new engagement ring on her left hand, and gasped. "I forgot to wind my watch. What time is it?"

"Must be nearly nine." Nancy got up, carrying a fresh cup of coffee and a croissant from which some thin honey dripped dangerously, and looked out of one long window. Above the courtyard, along two sides of which ran glass arcades lined with potted plants and basket chairs, two clocks were set in elaborate coils of white painted metal.

"Quarter to nine," said Nancy, "and not a soul to be seen but old Joseph hosing down the yard. They don't get up early in the Hotel de France et Choiseul."

"We've got lots of time, then."

"No, we haven't really. Don't you remember, we're going to see the big parade before we go on duty?"

"Oh my God, so we are!" But Linda made no attempt to hurry. She poured herself some more coffee and joined Nancy at the window, pushing back her long hair and tying the belt of her white wrapper tightly.

"Here comes Mitzi and her mistress."

"Mitzi and her slave." A young woman wearing a bright red coat had appeared at a door on the left of the courtyard, escorting a little grey Persian cat on a leather lead. She looked up at the two American girls, smiled slightly, and waved her free hand.

"The mystery woman," said Nancy. "Paris is full of them."

"Oh don't; she probably understands English."

"The Mata Hari of the France et Choiseul, taking her cat for a walk in the Tuileries. Or maybe Mitzi's going to see the big parade too."

"You're crazy this morning, Nancy. Why don't we get dressed?"

But Nancy continued to look dreamily out of the window. A pleasant scent came up from the wet boxwood set in wooden tubs round the paved courtyard.

"Fourth of July!" she said. "Where were you last Fourth, Linda?"

"Back home in Wilmington, Delaware. Give me Paris, any day!"

"Me too. Do you want that last brioche?"

"Go ahead and eat it."

While Linda was in her bath she heard her room-mate singing "Roses of Picardy" and a new favourite called "Let the Great Big World keep Turning", with whistled variations which made Linda smile as she brushed her hair and coiled it up. When she emerged from the bathroom she found Nancy in her olive drab uniform skirt, knotting her tie and whistling still.

"You *are* in good form this morning, Nan!"

"Am I?"

"You think I don't know why?"

"Why, then?"

"Because Tom Fleming's coming in to town today."

"Maybe."

"You mean you're not sure?"

"I won't be sure until I hear from him."

Linda reached her own uniform down from its hanger.

"There's an awful lot of 'maybe' about that guy, isn't there?"

"What do you mean?" asked Nancy, busy with the buckle of her Sam Browne belt.

"Well, *maybe* he was going to take you out to dinner in London, and *maybe* he was coming back from Finland in February, and *maybe* he'll be in Paris today, and what's it all about?"

"That's what I'd like to know. But let's hurry, Linda, I want to see General Pershing, and I don't believe we'll get anywhere near the reviewing stand."

The American commander was to take the salute from his troops at a point far up the Champs Elysées, and as soon as the two girls emerged on the Rue St. Honoré—already bright with the flag of the Stars and Stripes—it was clear that they were going to get nowhere near the Rue de Berri. The Parisians were hurrying up the Rue de Rivoli and down the Rue Royale, across the bridges, converging from all points on the great avenue where the US Expeditionary Force was holding its Fourth of July parade. Linda and Nancy pushed their way, as best they could, across the Place de la Concorde.

It was an emotional moment in the fourth summer of the war called Great. For weeks on end the fate of the Allies had hung in the balance. In April General Foch had assumed the supreme command of all the armies, and still Ludendorff smashed ahead on his remorseless course. On May 27 he opened the third battle of the Aisne, took Soissons two days later and on May 30 reached the Marne river less than forty miles from Paris.

It was then that the US 2nd Division went into action at Château-Thierry. In their first major effort of the Great War, they joined forces with the French to stem the German advance, forcing Ludendorff to break off the action and regroup his weary troops. A few days later, after bitter fighting and heavy losses, the US Marines took the German strong point of Belleau Wood. The relief in Paris was profound. The Americans were in the field at last and performing the long-expected miracles. Their unimpaired strength and spirit had come to the rescue of their exhausted allies, and on the Fourth of July, their Independence Day, all of surviving Paris turned out to cheer the new heroes of the war.

"Et mon Dieu, que de matériel!" said the Parisians who chose the way along the Seine to reach the Champs Elysées, for the quays from Bercy to the Point du Jour had become parks for the mechanised vehicles of the United States Army. The French, accustomed to troop transport by train and horse-drawn field kitchens and ambulances, were deeply impressed by the long lines of mechanised weapons carriers, oil and gasoline tankers, trucks for personnel, and even tanks. On ordinary days there were always old men and boys loitering near the tank parks, staring at the American guards, who gave the youngsters chewing-gum, but on the Fourth of July it was the soldiers, not their tanks, who were the star attraction, and the men and boys were standing ten deep along the most splendid avenue in the world.

If any Finn who watched the parade of Mannerheim's young victorious army down the Esplanade had stood on the Champs Elysées that day, he might well have been amazed at what was not so much a parade as a human tide, irresistible, breaking from the Place de l'Etoile and stretching all the way to the Horses of Marly. There were soldiers in that procession who were touchingly young, and the older, black-clad Frenchwomen greeted them with murmurs of compassion, while young girls waved bright handkerchiefs or threw flowers. There were others whose faces were seared with vile experiences, the veterans of the Mexican War, the ex-convicts; half-disciplined desperadoes whose grim stare made small boys gasp as if they saw the badmen of the cinema screen in flesh and blood. But all were united in a common purpose, and as the brass bands played they sang,

> Over there, over there!
> Send the word, send the word over there,
> That the Yanks are coming, the Yanks are coming,
> The drums rum-tumming everywhere!

"Oh, isn't this something!" screamed Nancy Macpherson. She had to scream to make herself heard above the noise, for she was separated from Linda by a big French infantryman in horizon blue, who had already celebrated his first day's leave in a litre of red wine. He had his arms round the girls' shoulders, having pushed them to the front of the spectators with a cheerful bellow of *"Vivent les petites américaines!"* When the French crowd broke through the police barriers and ran into the roadway, trying to shake hands with the Americans, patting their shoulders until the whole Place de la Concorde was filled with an hysterical crowd, the big *poilu* obligingly acted as a battering ram, and took the girls back to the quiet of the Avenue Gabriel.

They let him kiss them on both cheeks outside the American Embassy, and ran giggling up a side street, back to their canteen. "Peabody'll be having a fit!" predicted Nancy when she got her breath back, for the elderly New England supervisor was strict about punctuality. The canteen was in the basement of a big hotel in the Boulevard des Capucines, a hot airless place where the girls worked by artificial light, and every girl was ready to leave as soon as her relief came on duty. Joanie and Peggy-Ann had been watching the clock; they'd been doing a land-office business in coffee and doughnuts, they said, since the boat trains came in at six o'clock.

"There was a call for you about ten minutes ago, Nancy," sniffed Miss Peabody. "If you hadn't been tardy, you could have taken it yourself."

"Was there any message?" said Nancy. She looked quickly at Linda Lee. "Did the caller leave his name?"

"Oh, you guessed it was a gentleman, did you? It was a Mr. Fleming; he'll be in touch with you later in the day."

"He didn't leave a number where I could reach *him*?"

"He was speaking from a post office near the Champs Elysées. Now get your aprons on, girls, and don't waste more time. You're not supposed to receive private calls at the canteen anyway."

Linda muttered "Sourpuss!" as she went to hang up her blouse, but Nancy's colour was bright and she tackled her job in high good humour. It declined a little during the long day, when the canteen was thronged with the boys from Pasadena and Evanston and Hoboken, asking for soft drinks and ice-cream, and

173

telling the girls that gee, the French kids were cute, and gosh, they sure were friendly. Linda thought her own friend tired, and certainly quieter than usual, when they came out into the boulevard at six o'clock and found it a sea of flags, the Tricolore and the Stars and Stripes floating side by side from balcony windows, above the dusty tops of the plane trees.

"A letter for Mademoiselle Macpherson," said Monsieur Adolphe, the elderly concierge, coming out of the *loge* at the France et Choiseul and raising his gold-laced hat politely. "Also some flowers arrived. I told Simone to arrange them in water in the ladies' sitting room."

"Oh, thank you, Monsieur Adolphe," said Nancy. She pulled Linda round the corner, into the arcade with the basketwork chairs, and opened the envelope with her thumb. "It's from Tom. He's going to call at eight and take me out to dinner. Oh Linda, my God, the party!"

"Honestly, he's got his nerve," said Linda. "Are you supposed to be sitting here waiting for him to show up, when you haven't seen him for over six months?"

"Oh, that doesn't matter, Lin, it's just — I kind of hate to have him crash the party. And he did try to reach me in the morning—"

"Does he say where he's staying now?"

"The Grand Hotel."

"Why don't you call him, and put him off till tomorrow, Nancy?"

"I can't do that," she said decidedly, and put Tom's letter in her satchel. "Let's go upstairs, now. Those people'll be here in an hour and a half."

The girls seldom used the old-fashioned lift, installed in the 1880s, and preferred to run up one wide shallow staircase to their suite. The sitting room with its Empire furniture, all lyres and sphinxes and imperial bees, was already shadowy, but in a Baccarat vase on the centre table stood Tom's flowers, thick blooms of forced white lilac, filling the room with fragrance.

"How lovely," Linda said.

"Tom's very good about sending flowers," said Nancy. She went straight to the bathroom and poured herself a glass of water. "You get changed first, if you like," she said persuasively. "Maybe I will call Tom, after all. We *do* have a dinner date with Jack and What's his Name, haven't we?"

"Sure." Poor Lieutenant Novak, he's What's his Name already, Linda thought. This Fleming must be really something. And then she forgot Nancy's problems in the excitement of getting ready to see her own fiancé, whose leave from the new Tank Corps was the real reason for the Independence Day party at which Tom Fleming looked like being the fifth wheel. But Nancy sat on in the stiff Empire sitting room, re-reading a letter which had come from St. Michel many weeks before.

They've given me another medal, and I found it was for going on night patrol as well as for the fight at Tammerfors. What a laugh, Nancy—one medal for losing my own men and another for losing Boris Heiden. Because I let him slip through my fingers, and now I'm quite sure Charlie Keiller's dead, just as I know Sophie is dead. Everything I try to do turns sour on me somehow. Thank God we're going into action in the morning.

It was not the only letter from Tom in Nancy's satchel. There was a later one from Helsingfors and one from London, both cheerful, affectionate and ordinary, and she had begun to look forward fervently to seeing him in Paris. But knowing he had been near the Champs Elysées while the big parade was taking place, she wondered how it had affected him. He must surely have noticed, as she had, that all along the avenue and the boulevards the Tricolore and the Stars and Stripes were flying side by side, with very few Union Jacks, and no sign at all of Canada's maple leaf. Then at the party he was bound to meet Lieutenant Alfred Novak, MD, whose obsessional topic of conversation was the treatment of shell-shock. Linda heard her talking and the phone bell ringing as one call after another went through the switchboard. When she herself was ready, and Nancy in her brief petticoat and lace camisole, Linda asked casually:

"Did you call Tom?"

"No, I decided not to. But I called a lot of other people, and asked them to the party." She repeated the names of half a dozen friends.

"Safety in numbers, eh?"

"Something like that."

"Nancy, what *is* it?"

"I'm just afraid Tom'll be mean to somebody. Say something

mean about the Americans coming in to the war late, or—oh, I don't know. I told you how changed he was when I saw him in London—so bitter, and sneering and snarling at everything—"

"But he was just out of hospital then, wasn't he?"

"Yes, and what he's going to be like after fighting in Finland, tell me that? Oh Linda!" said Nancy, subsiding on to her high white bed and picking at the frilled pillow, "it breaks my heart to think of Tom disfigured and in pain . . . when I remember him as he was the day his regiment left Vancouver, with all the kilts swinging and the band playing 'Hielan' Laddie' . . . and then now."

"Don't, sweetie," said Linda, sitting down beside her. "It'll be all right. You'll see. And the others will all be here long before he comes—"

"Sure," said Nancy resolutely. "Which reminds me, we'd better get on to room service and get this party organised. Just let me put on my dress, and I'll call the switchboard."

James J. Macpherson's only daughter could afford to buy as many Paris dresses as she pleased, and the pale blue chiffon Nancy took off its hanger had cost a lot of money. It was too bad, reflected Linda—petite and dainty Linda, whom everything suited—that Nancy, so neat in uniform, so unconsciously sexy in short petticoat and long silk stockings, should look all wrong in evening dress. The shade of blue, this time, was wrong, the puffs of silver lace replacing sleeves, and broadening her shoulders, were a definite mistake.

"It doesn't do much for me, does it?" said Nancy ruefully.

"You ought to take off maybe six, seven pounds."

"I know it. Oh hell, I'd rather wear my uniform—"

"Not if we're going to Maxim's, you can't."

"Tom would laugh, anyway."

She took up her comb and gave some vicious tugs at her rough dark curls.

Linda said gently: "You're really stuck on him, aren't you?"

"I guess I am."

"More than on any of the others?"

"The others don't count. Tom's different. Maybe it's because he's been there always—"

"You know I don't really go for the childhood sweetheart stuff," pronounced the experienced Miss Lee. "You get to know

176

each other far too well, too soon. You miss the romance, the glamour of a first meeting—"

It was impossible for Nancy to be solemn for long. Now she giggled, and glanced over her shoulder at Linda.

"You know you're only thinking of the day you met Jack Macey!"

14

BY HALF PAST SEVEN everything was ready for the party. Gaston, the waiter, had arranged champagne in coolers on the mahogany table which held Tom's flowers, its marble top supported by two gilt caryatids, and a tray of *foie gras* sandwiches was placed on a console table between the two long windows. It was so warm that the windows were wide open, and a pleasant hum of conversation came up from the courtyard. The hotel was popular with Americans, who thought the flower-decked courtyard quaint, and others besides Nancy and Linda were celebrating their first Independence Day in Paris, France.

The heat of the July afternoon had been caught and held by the white walls of the hotel, which the sunset had stained to the colour of grapes, and other open windows gave views like theatre sets of young men in the new uniforms drinking to victory in these old surroundings. By tradition, the France et Choiseul was opened in 1812 as a transit hotel for Napoleon's officers on their way to the campaign in Russia, and when Nancy and Linda had rearranged the sofas upholstered in a velvet of the true Bonaparte green and the stiff chairs with brocade seats of imperial violet, the two gilt mirrors with eagles springing from their tops might well have reflected young cuirassiers and hussars on their last Paris leave before the burning of Moscow. The only recent additions to the room were a little upright piano with wax candles in its bronze brackets, and the electric lighting in the ceiling, where three weak lamps were protected by glass shades like tortured lilies, in the worst style of art nouveau.

"If we light the floor lamp and the candles, that should do," said Linda. "It isn't dark outside."

"And it won't be, with all those lights in the hotel," Nancy agreed. She pulled the faded gold satin curtains, swagged and draped, as far open as their brass rings and rods would allow. "Linda, here's Jack."

She disappeared into the bedroom as Linda Lee, looking like

a bride in her white evening dress, went into the arms of her tall fiancé. She and Lieutenant Macey had known each other for exactly two months, and intended to marry as soon as the war was won. They had a few minutes alone together, and then Lieutenant Novak arrived, a thin young doctor with impressive spectacles from Base Hospital 117 at La Fauche. Nancy had no time to whisper "Al, please don't talk about neuropsychiatry tonight!" before Joanie, their canteen colleague, arrived with her current admirer, followed by two Red Cross girls with theirs. Hot on their heels, and all together, came six young officers from the leave hotels near the canteen, all of whom had been invited by Nancy in her last-minute telephone calls.

The corks were popping, and what the girls called the party roar was growing louder when another guest came to the door. He stood there hesitantly, looking at Nancy Macpherson surrounded by laughing young officers with champagne glasses in their hands, and Linda, sitting on one of the formal sofas with Jack Macey, stifled a giggle.

"This must be Mr. Fleming," she whispered, "and just look at Nancy. 'Safety in numbers' indeed! The little minx means to show him she's got plenty of beaux—Nan!" She raised her voice and got up. "Here's another guest!" Tom Fleming, his hesitation gone, walked into the room.

"Oh, hello, Tom, thanks for the lovely flowers! I'm so glad you could make it!" Nancy smiled up at him as if they had met the day before, and Tom blurted out, "Gosh, Nancy, I didn't mean to butt in! I didn't know you were having a party!"

"It's the Fourth of July," she reminded him. "Come and be introduced," She began with Joanie, nearest to the table, poured Tom a glass of champagne, and began to pilot him gracefully round the room.

"And this is my room-mate, Linda Lee."

"Pretty name!" said Tom, taking Linda's hand with a look that said "pretty girl!"

"How about Melinda Macey?" said her fiancé possessively, and Tom said, "Better still!" without waiting for the introduction and explanations which followed. Then Peggy-Ann burst in, late as usual, with a young Texan lieutenant in tow and both very noisy and apologetic. Nancy turned away to welcome them.

"Say, Nancy!" Peggy-Ann exclaimed, "Tex and I ran into

Irving Greenbaum just outside the Opera. I asked him to look in and say hello after he filed his cable, you don't care, do you?"

"I sort of wish you hadn't." It was so like Peggy-Ann to drag in an uninvited guest, and Greenbaum, an American war correspondent, was apt to be a liability at any party. His paper, the Chicago *Clarion*, was anti-British, and had become fanatically so since the American victory at Château-Thierry. "Yankees die to Save King George's Men" was a fair sample of its recent headlines, and the big parade of the morning was likely to stir Mr. Greenbaum to even higher things. I hope he doesn't get across Tom, and upset him, thought Nancy, and looked at Tom's reflection in one of the gilt mirrors. Chatting with Jack and Linda, he looked very relaxed. He was the only man present in civilian clothes, but his dark blue suit had been made for him in Savile Row, and if his face was no longer the boy's face, smiling beneath the Highland bonnet on the day the pipes played "Hielan' Laddie", neither was it the ruined face of last December. The dark moustache suited him very well. The weather in Finland, first winter-harsh and then brilliant, had given Tom a suntan across which the scar, once a swollen welt, had subsided into a thin white seam. It would mark his cheek for the rest of his life, but it was not disfiguring. It only made his face look older and more purposeful than the bland faces of the untried men around him.

With half an ear, while refilling glasses, she heard Jack Macey telling Tom, "I've a forty-eight hour pass from the tank training centre at Bourg. It's a great outfit, and boy! have we got ourselves an instructor! He was the first officer enrolled in the Tank Corps, and he's loaded for bear every day and all day!"

"What's his name?" asked Tom.

"Captain George S. Patton, junior. Junior for his grandfather, a Civil War general," said Jack. "No tanks in Finland, I suppose?"

"No tanks, no gas, no ack-ack. Say, Linda, I see a gap in the crowd round Nancy. Will you excuse me if I go talk to her?"

"Certainly." When Tom moved away she whispered to Jack Macey, "What do you think of him, darling?"

"Nice guy."

The nice guy, having his glass refilled by a rather flushed Nancy, asked with a smile: "You wouldn't be avoiding me, by any chance? You've hardly given me the time of day since I got here."

"We've got a lot of guests to look after, Tommy."

"Then let Linda take her turn. You stop being a hostess for a bit, and be a *femme fatale*." He drew her away from the table towards one of the open windows.

"I don't think I'll ever qualify as a *femme fatale*," said Nancy.

"You'll do." *Fatale*, never, with that round face and those unruly curls, but there was something in Nancy's eyes and the quick lift of her breast that was entirely *femme*.

"I don't have much luck with my dinner invitations, do I?" he said. "Last time I had to leave London unexpectedly, and this time I find you in the hands of the US Army—"

"Oh, but this party's been arranged for ages. I'm just so glad you turned up in time to meet my friends."

"I should have called you back this afternoon—"

"The supervisor might have fired me if you had."

"—But I was held up for hours at the Swiss Embassy, and couldn't get near a phone."

It was on the tip of her tongue to ask, "What on earth were you doing at the *Swiss* Embassy?" but Nancy had taken a vow not to "push him around", as he had accused her of doing in December. No questions about his plans, no allusions to his parents and their increasing need to have him at home; she said "That was too bad", vaguely, and expressed a hope that he had enjoyed his stay in London.

"It was fine, but I was only there for about ten days. I stayed in Finland till the end of June, you know."

"I thought you might've been able to leave sooner."

"I wasn't demobilised for three weeks, to begin with. You can't create an army out of nothing and then disband it in a day, eager as Svinhufvud's government was to see the last of the foreign volunteers. Except their beloved Germans, of course."

"The Germans are still in Finland, aren't they?"

"Living off the fat of the land—or what little fat is left. Of course the farming has been knocked to hell for this year, and the timber exports too. I stayed on with Mr. Baker until the end of the month—I told you in one of my letters, didn't I, that he came back to Helsingfors?"

"Yes, you did. What did he say about your joining the army?"

"He was rather bucked, as a matter of fact. He's a great admirer of Mannerheim." So bucked, that there had been no word of reproach for Tom's requisitioning of his flat. He had made a clean breast of that, and got nothing but a gruff "Glad the place was of some use, my boy," from Mr. Baker.

"And then you went right back to London, from Stockholm?"

"I stopped over in Gothenburg for a day or two."

"Oh, good!" she said, nodding at the piano, "Dicky Hallowell's going to sing."

Lieutenant Hallowell, who had the enviable talent of playing by ear, was being dragged to the piano, and from the keys, yellow and tinkling with age, he began to coax the current hits from "The Bing Boys" and "Chu Chin Chow". Just so, in the summer of 1870 when the mother-of-pearl inlay in the little piano was new, might a young man wearing the blue and silver of the Imperial Guard, excited by the coming war with Prussia, have played a sugared melody of Offenbach, or the patriotic strains of "Partant Pour la Syrie", with a glass of champagne and a pretty girl at his elbow. Joanie and Peggy-Ann were leaning devotedly over the piano now.

"How did you find a swell place like this, Nancy?" said Tom.

"Linda's father told us about it. He and Mrs. Lee spent their honeymoon here."

"What does Linda's dad do for a living?"

"He's with du Pont at Wilmington."

"I bet you like this better than your Earl's Court hostel."

"I love Paris."

The lights were going out across the courtyard, and the big room was dim. Nancy's blue and silver dress had faded to the colour of the twilight. And the pianist played "Let the great big world keep turning, never mind now I've got *you*", while the subalterns and the Red Cross girls drew closer, and the group round the piano began to sway gently to and fro.

"Sing 'First Love', Peggy-Ann."

"She's got a lovely voice," said Nancy. It was a sweeter soprano than might have been expected from the boisterous Peggy-Ann:

> My first love   was my last love
> and that's the best love   of all.
> The new love   was never the true love
> It's only   you that makes me want you—

182

"Look at Nancy," whispered Linda in Jack Macey's ear. "Darling, you *must* ask Tom Fleming to come on to Maxim's with us. Make it seem as if the invitation came from you."

"What, because of Nancy? But how about Al Novak—is that all off?"

"I don't think it was ever on."

"He did, and he's going to break this up, you watch."

They both saw that as soon as the song was over the young doctor moved up to Tom and Nancy and began an amiable, rambling conversation, leading nowhere in particular, which gave Nancy an opportunity to pass round the sandwich tray and tell Peggy-Ann how well she sang, while Linda followed filling the champagne glasses. The party roar broke out again, to a gentle accompaniment from the piano. "First Love, Last Love, Best Love," sang the keys, and Tom Fleming observed to Lieutenant Novak that it sure was a beautiful song.

"Hey!" bawled a loud voice from the door, "whaddya all doin', sittin' in the dark?" The ugly ceiling lights came on with a click.

"*Irv!*" shrieked Peggy-Ann and her Tex in unison, and Nancy, with a wry glance at Linda, went forward with her hand outstretched.

"Good evening, Mr. Greenbaum," she said, "how nice of you to stop by for a minute," and Linda, coming up beside her, said insincerely, "We're very glad."

"Party manners, huh?" said the uninvited guest. "Mighty nice to see you, gals. What you got there? Bubbly? Gimme, gimme, gimme, Tex. I sure have had one sonofabitching day."

This was scarcely news, every day being a sonofabitching day to the war correspondent, and also to those who had to deal with him, but the Texan lieutenant took his cue immediately. Pouring Greenbaum a large glass of champagne he asked eagerly:

"What was the trouble today, Irv?"

"A bastard called Kerensky," said Irv, with a noisy swallow. "Alexander Kerensky, late of Petrograd. He had the nerve to keep the entire press corps waiting while he ate a four-hour lunch—"

"Is Kerensky in Paris?" said Tom Fleming abruptly. Mr. Greenbaum looked him up and down.

"He sure is, do you know him?"

183

"Never set eyes on him in my life. I heard quite a bit about him when I was in Finland, though."

"Yeah, that's right, he did hide out in Finland. Got out through Murmansk, a while back. You been to Murmansk?"

"No."

"Say, what part of the United States do you come from?"

"Vancouver's my home town."

"Canuck, hey? This your first time in Paris?"

"First time since my last Paris leave," said Tom, and Nancy was able to interrupt at last.

"Mr. Greenbaum, I'd like to introduce you to Captain Fleming," she said. "He served with the Canadians in France for three years, and won the Military Cross at Sainte Elodie."

"Cut it out, Nancy!" said Tom, and "Where the hell's that?" said the war correspondent.

"On the Scarpe."

"Never heard of it."

"Don't apologise," said Tom, "it was long before your time."

For the life of her, Nancy could not resist giving Tom a look of triumph at this proof of what she always said, that the artificial sensation of Sainte Elodie would quickly be forgotten. But she realised that the doctor from La Fauche was listening to every word that passed between the two young men.

"So did Kerensky show up at his press conference at all?" asked Tom.

"Oh sure, he showed up. 'You must excuse me, gentlemen,' he said, 'it's so nice to be back in Paris I forgot the time. I was sitting eating peaches until a quarter of five.' The boys roasted him, I hope to tell you, little swollen-headed bastard, excuse me, gals."

Tom grunted. He remembered Mr. Baker's living room, and the British agent, made up to look like Kerensky, lying bleeding on the floor. He remembered the first appearance of the Red Guard who shot Sophie Sandels, and her face of terror at his knock. It had been a big price to pay for Kerensky's freedom to enjoy a basket of peaches.

"Say, what were *you* doing in Finland, bud?" said Greenbaum, working on his second drink.

"Serving in Mannerheim's army."

"But not in combat?"

"I fought in Wetzer's corps, the whole goddamned way from Seinäjoki station to Viborg," burst out Tom, and Novak laid a restraining hand upon his arm.

"Take it easy, Mac," said Greenbaum with a grin. He was a slovenly sight, with two buttons of his blouse undone, and his shirt collar open behind a loosely knotted tie. Tom looked at him with loathing.

"Mannerheim ran a pretty good little sideshow, but he didn't last long," said the war correspondent. "They kicked him out at the end of May, didn't they?"

"He resigned his command when the government wanted him to take orders from an officer of the German General Staff," said Tom. "That's okay with you, isn't it? We're fighting the Germans, right?"

"Dick," said Peggy-Ann, "play something!"

But Irving Greenbaum had backed down before the anger in Tom's face. "Well, gee," he said, "he sounds like quite a guy. Maybe I should've gone up there myself. I cabled my boss, Red Donnelly, about it, but he said there wasn't a story in Finland."

"Look," said Jack Macey, "some of us have got a table reserved at Maxim's—"

"Play 'Till We Meet Again'," cried Peggy-Ann.

> Smile the while   I kiss you sad adieu,
> When the clouds   roll by I'll come for you

"Oh, don't, Dick," said Linda suddenly. "That song gives me the creeps."

*   *   *

Maxim's, still in its *Belle Epoque* décor of dark wood and lacquered brass ornaments, was so crowded that Jack Macey's argument to make Tom join the party—"they'll be putting extra chairs at every table tonight"— was seen to be valid as soon as they entered the restaurant. They were in fact eight instead of the original foursome, for Joanie and her escort Captain Oliver had been co-opted along with Dick Hallowell, who walked along the Rue St. Honoré with Nancy. Behind them, she heard Tom chatting easily and pleasantly with Lieutenant Novak, and began to breathe more freely. Irving Greenbaum had been spirited away to a bistro dinner with Peggy-Ann and Tex, and Tom's only comment on him had been a general demand to know how a bum like that got a job on a paper at all. The evening, with a few sticky patches, was turning out splendidly.

Thus optimistic Nancy, as she took her place at the table between Novak and Jack Macey, and beamed at Tom on the opposite side. He seemed delighted to be back in Maxim's, now livelier, he said, than on any of his Paris leaves. The place had been going downhill since the war, when the old turn of the century grace and style had vanished, perhaps for ever, but the maître d'hôtel and his waiters were smiling on this Fourth of July night, which was like the great days come back. There sat *messieurs les américains*, the new conquerors, with their *demoiselles*, so obviously ladies but without a chaperone in the lot, and some of them even in uniform. The elderly Parisian gentlemen who came to Maxim's for old sake's sake were conspicuous by their absence, for as usual when danger came too near, the rich Parisians had decamped from the capital and were enjoying the summer sunshine at La Baule or the Cap d'Antibes. And danger had been very near Paris ever since March 23, when the German gun called Big Bertha began shelling the city. On Good Friday, hundreds of worshippers were killed in the very heart of Paris, when the Krupp gun, firing from a distance of over fifty miles, dropped a shell on the church of St. Eustache. That, and the inconveniences of cellar life as the German air raids increased, chased the rich and timorous from Paris, but the American officers were bigger and better spenders, and the restaurant keepers were delighted with the change. The band leader at Maxim's played "The Merry Widow" only once, but "Over There!" six times between half past nine and eleven o'clock.

> So prepare, say a prayer,
> Send the word, send the word to prepare,
> We'll be over, we're coming over,
> And we won't be back till it's over, Over There!

There were bars and cafés in the city that night where the gay, arrogant song was being bawled or whistled by all the doughboys on leave. In Maxim's, where an American general was giving a dinner for three French and two English officers of the same rank, the celebrations were more dignified, and the only noisy customer, a major from Tennessee who broke a plate by beating time upon it with his spoon, was quietly assisted from the table by his friends. Perhaps the presence of the French girls was a little oppressive. They were all, of course, *poules de luxe*, beautifully dressed in black, with aigrettes or tulle veiling sweeping their bare shoulders, show girls whether on or off the stage, but their disdainful interest in the American women distracted their attention from the colonels and majors who had bought their favours for the night. Their gaze swept the young women in uniform. Never, the cold eyes seemed to say, would a Parisienne make such an object of herself, and their judgment was severe, too, on the girls who had changed into evening dress. It was an article of faith among the Americans in Paris that Our Boys liked to see bright colours, a change from all that olive drab and the dreary, eternal French black, and so the guests at Maxim's looked and sounded like a cageful of many-coloured parrots. Nancy's blue, Joanie's scarlet and an assortment of pinks and lime greens at the table behind them were clashing and aggressive, Linda's white charmeuse the most attractive dress of all.

"Isn't she pretty?" said generous Nancy, when the orchestra began to play "If You were the Only Girl in the World", and Linda got up to dance with her fiancé.

"So're you, Nancy," said Tom. "Let's dance."

She wanted to dance with him, to be in his arms at last, but Nancy was determined not to be too forthcoming, and the waiter, offering a dish, provided a ready-made excuse.

"I'd like to dance, after I've eaten this," she said pertly. "It's *ris de veau Clamart*, I can't let that get cold!"

"Joanie?"

"Love to."

Nancy kept her eyes on her plate. The sweetbreads were good, and so was the Beaujolais ordered by Lieutenant Macey, a Philadelphian who flattered himself on his knowledge of wine. When her plate was removed she danced with Dick Hallowell and then Lieutenant Novak; Tom danced with Linda before inviting Nancy to dance again.

" 'The Blue Danube', come on, Calamity, let's show 'em."

She rose at once, smiling at the old nickname, and he swung her out on the crowded little floor. They had always danced

187

beautifully together, and now after a moment's hesitation they found the old rhythm and harmony.

"When was our last dance, Nan? Dominion Day at the Country Club?"

"No, it was at the Hotel Vancouver, after Dorothy's wedding," she said too quickly, and bit her lip. She felt Tom draw her a little closer in his arms.

"Wonderful to dance together again . . . It's been a great day, hasn't it? That was a swell parade this morning. I was proud of your lot."

"Thank you, Tom."

Their eyes met and held. Back at their table Linda, watching, whispered to Dick Hallowell, who grinned and sent a message to the band leader. A few minutes later "The Blue Danube" ended in a cadenza, and with a flourish of his baton the leader took his musicians into another tune:

> My first love   was my last love
> And that's the best love   of all

Nancy lowered her head. Not for worlds would she have allowed Tom Fleming to see what that song meant to her, the perfect expression of all she felt for him.

> Doesn't matter where I chance to be,
> No one else can be the same to me,
> For my first love   was my last love
> And that's the best love   of all.

"Let's sit the next one out, shall we?" said Tom when the music stopped.

"Tom, you're crazy! There's no conservatory at Maxim's!"

"Finest conservatory in the world, right on the corner. Come on, before they start looking for us and waving."

In the press of dancers coming off the floor they slipped through the lobby and into the Rue Royale. Before them the Place de la Concorde stretched wide and almost deserted, illuminated more by the nacreous light of the summer sky than by the clustered lamps dimmed as an air raid precaution. On the far side, beyond the Seine, the Tricolore hung motionless above the lighted Chambre des Députés.

"Looks like an all-night sitting," said Tom. "Well, they've got plenty to talk about . . . You're not going to be cold, are you?"

"Cold hands, warm heart," she said, slipping her hand into his, and Tom flinched.

"What's the matter? Tom, are you all right?"

"Of course I'm all right. Will you look at the roses, though?"

The statue of Strasbourg, still draped in black, was heaped with flowers; not wreaths, as in the early days of mourning for Alsace-Lorraine, but bouquets of triumphant summer flowers.

"I've never seen that before," said Tom. "So now they're putting flowers at the foot of the statues in Paris too."

"Too?"

"I've seen it done in Helsingfors." They walked out into the centre of the square, looked up and down, right and left, at the astonishing vistas, the Arc de Triomphe, the Madeleine.

"Interesting man, your friend Novak," said Tom.

"They say he's a very clever doctor."

"Did you know he spent a week at Dykefaulds last February?"

"He—I believe he did mention it."

"I told him I was a Dykefaulds graduate."

"Oh, Tom!"

"He went there on a course before the AEF hospital at La Fauche opened on the first of March. I don't think he was impressed by Colonel Henderson's ideas on occupational therapy for shell-shocked patients. He says the Yanks are way ahead of us in neuropsychiatry, and they're trying out a whole new technique at La Fauche. Early rising, heavy manual work out-doors, no sympathy from the staff—the return-to-duty concept, it's called. I told him I'd gone one better than La Fauche. I joined another army and started fighting."

Tom laughed quite naturally, but Nancy shivered. "Shall we go back to the restaurant?" she said.

"No, let's stay out here. Only ten minutes. Please!"

"But we can have a long talk tomorrow, Tom—"

"That's just it, we can't. I may be going to Switzerland tomorrow. If I can get a visa."

Two gendarmes, capes slung over their shoulders, were eyeing them curiously. Nancy moved away. "Pretend we're looking at the fountain," she said.

The fountain opposite the Crillon was still playing, lamplight and starlight reflected in the flying drops. Tom put his arm round Nancy's shoulders and drew her gently to the side away from the water. "Let's sit down a minute," he said, "sit on my handkerchief."

"Is it something to do with Helsingfors, Tom?"

"Yes. You guessed that, I suppose, from that crazy letter I wrote to you at Saint Michel."

"It wasn't crazy. It *was* about people I didn't know. Sophie Somebody, and Charlie Keiller, and Boris Heiden—"

"Especially Boris Heiden."

"Tom, tell me something. Is Heiden an unusual name? A Russian name?"

"It's a Baltic German name, originally. This fellow's father was a Baltic baron."

"In Finland?"

"No, in Russia." And Tom began to tell his story, his voice hardly louder than the plash of the fountain, so that the few passers-by on the Rue de Rivoli heard nothing, saw nothing but a young man with his arm round a girl, a sight repeated on that Independence night in every doorway, on every park bench throughout the warmly-breathing city, attracting nothing but a sympathetic smile. But what Tom said was terrible, a tale of hatred, perhaps of treachery and espionage, a revelation, more terrible than all, of his obsession.

It was not the whole truth he told her. The Chief's request, the plot to save Kerensky, were omitted from Tom's narrative, and he stressed Sophie's devotion to the White cause and Mannerheim as the reason for her black-listing and her death. But Nancy was perfectly conscious of the omissions. She had always suspected Tom's plan to go to Finland, or rather the people behind it. Mr. Ballantine's proposal that he should spend some time in Helsingfors was just too pat, it tied in too neatly with Tom's discharge from Dykefaulds to be convincing. She had heard enough careless talk at London parties to realise what a close network of organisation there was both in and outside the army, and how many men in Intelligence were moving other men like pawns on a chessboard. They used him for something, she thought. My poor old Tom!

"So it was quite by accident you met this Heiden first?"

"Quite by accident. I told you he was hanging round the younger Sandels girl."

"And you made up your mind at once he was a Russian spy?"

"Not at once, no. The second time we met I began to have suspicions. And then when he turned up in the Russian lines at Vilppula—"

"Yes, I agree, that looked very bad. And you've no idea what happened to Captain Keiller?"

"I called on his family in Gothenburg on my way back to London. They hadn't heard from him since he left to go to Finland. I must say they were very cool about him. Said Karl was a bit of a rolling stone, and he'd show up when it suited him."

Nancy thought that was precisely what Tom Fleming's family might be saying about him. But she went on:

"Look—let me be absolutely clear about this, Tom—you denounced Heiden to the Finnish officers on the ground that his brother Igor was a known anarchist?"

"Yes, and I couldn't make it stick. Think, Nancy, we didn't even search him properly! We took his gun, but nobody checked to see if he had a knife in his belt . . . Alone in that freight train with Charlie Keiller . . ."

"Yes, I understand how you feel about that. But look, I asked you just a minute ago if Heiden was an unusual name?"

"Sure, but what— ?"

"Remember I told you, that day we had tea at the Ritz, that my university instructor, Kathleen Donovan, got fired from her job because she'd concealed her marriage to a Russian revolutionary?"

"I remember."

"Igor Heiden was the man she married."

They stared at each other, pale in the light of the Place de la Concorde.

"She was *his* widow?"

"They met as students in Geneva and were married there."

"*My God!*" said Tom slowly. "To think that was the first thing that put me on to him—when he spoke about Seattle, and how I might have read some of his brother's stuff in the magazines. It was his brother's widow he was thinking of, not me." And then, in a rising tone of exultation, "So he made a mistake! I know he makes mistakes! He thinks he's so goddamned intellectual with his Kropotkin and his Pavlov, but he's not so smart after all!"

"Tom, what are you going to *do*?"

"You *are* cold now: here, take my jacket." He stripped it off and laid it round her shoulders, crushing the unbecoming silver lace.

"Do? I'm going after him to Switzerland, as soon as I can get a visa. That's why I was hanging round the Swiss Embassy, all afternoon."

"But why? What good can you do now? Wouldn't it be enough if you—you reported the whole thing to somebody in London, so they could watch out for him, and . . . Tom! How do you know he's *in* Switzerland?"

"I don't know for certain. It's just a hunch I have. And I know his mother lives in Zürich, maybe I can get a line on him through her."

"If he's gone to Russia you'll never be able to get at him."

"At least I can find out if he took Lisa Sandels with him."

"Is that so important?" asked Nancy with a touch of impatience.

"It is to me. The last words Sophie spoke to me, she asked me to look out for Lisa, and I'm going to."

"Are you in love with Lisa Sandels, Tom?"

"Lisa? I didn't even like her very much! But she told a friend she was going to marry this bastard, and I want to be sure they *are* married—"

"Heiden doesn't seem to be much of a catch," said Nancy drily. ". . . Tom, was it Sophie Sandels you—came to care for?"

"I told you, Sophie's dead."

"But you'd fallen in love with her? You meant to marry her?"

"We never talked about marriage. Sophie and I. We were only together for two weeks before she was killed."

"Together? Then you—"

"All right, if you want it in plain language, we were lovers. We went to bed together, every chance we got. And I'll never forget Sophie, I'll always be grateful to her, is that enough for you?"

It was enough and too much for Nancy's sore heart. And even as he said it, Tom knew it was no longer true: the gratitude

192

was fading with the memory, Sophie belonged to the past, and the present was his hatred of Boris Heiden.

"Was she very pretty?" said Nancy with an effort.

"That's girl stuff, I suppose. She asked me the same thing about you."

"You discussed me with *her*?"

"I didn't discuss you, I just happened to mention you one night."

"In bed or out of bed?"

"Oh, quit it, Nancy! I just happened to say you were patriotic, like she was patriotic, and then she asked if you were pretty."

"What did you say?"

"I said you were very pretty."

"Thanks very much."

"I didn't mean to make you mad," said Tom humbly.

"I'm not mad. I—I should be glad you found somebody to be—kind to you," said Nancy painfully. Then, with a rush, "Oh Tom, please don't go to Switzerland!"

"Why not?"

"Because you've done enough. Three years in Flanders, and then the war in Finland—"

"Heiden's special. You can't measure the Heidens by years of active service, any more than you can measure the Lenins. But sooner or later he'll make another mistake—"

"You said he'd made more than one already. What was the other?"

"The first was what he said about Seattle. The second was at Vilppula, when he told the Finns I'd been in a mental hospital in Scotland—that wasn't true, of course, but it did mean he'd had access to my records. Sainte Elodie, well, he could have read that in the papers, even Mr. Baker just might have known, and told the Sandels girls, but Dykefaulds, that's classified information, and Heiden could only have got it through some intelligence network of their own."

"Or through Lieutenant Novak," said Nancy calmly. "He told you himself he was at Dykefaulds last winter. How do you know he's not a Russian agent in the US Army? Or else some nurse at the hospital could have given your name to Heiden. Or why not some clerk at the War Office with access to the classified records? Why not me?"

Tom stared at her. "I'm beginning to catch on," he said. "The Communist conspiracy. We don't know where it begins or ends, do we?"

"And you think you can beat it, by going after Boris Heiden?"

Tom's answer was to pull her to her feet and fold his arms round her, jacket and all, bending his head to hers.

"I've got to, Nan," he said. "It's such a slender thread, and it runs right across the world, but I've got to follow it. And you'll help me, won't you? You'll be on my side?"

Nancy knew when she was beaten. She looked into his face, strained in the light of what was now the first intimation of the summer dawn, and heard the birds begin to murmur in the chestnut trees across the square.

"If you need me I'll be there," said Nancy Macpherson. "But don't kiss me. Not just now."

15

I N July 1918, the frontier zones between France and Switzerland were officially described as "nervous", and so, unofficially, were the Swiss themselves. The war had gone on too long for a neutral country whose boundaries marched with the belligerents, and Swiss hospitality had been not only used but abused as the killing years went by. Especially at Basel, where the frontiers of France, Switzerland and Germany met, the Swiss immigration and customs officers went on duty accompanied by special police and the military, ready to arrest on suspicion any presumed deserter from either army, any political agitator or agent, any currency trafficker and any person likely to threaten in any way the peace and dignity of the Helvetic Confederation. The Swiss had had enough of foreign intriguers on their peaceful soil. Years before they had expelled Prince Kropotkin, the anarchist dedicated to dynamite, gun and dagger, but since that time Switzerland had been a snug refuge for his fellow revolutionaries, notably Lenin and Trotsky. The despatch of the Bolshevik leaders in a sealed train from Switzerland, which with the connivance of the Kaiser's ministers had crossed Germany into Russia after the Czar's abdication, had been so bitterly criticised in the American and Allied press that the Swiss were almost tempted to close their frontiers to all foreigners for the duration of the war. Certainly it was made very difficult for a foreign national to obtain a visa and entry permit for Switzerland at any Swiss embassy or consulate abroad.

So Tom Fleming had discovered. In London they had sent him on to Paris, which suited his plans quite well: in Paris they washed their hands of him and advised him to go to Lyon. He had hoped to go direct by train from Paris to Basel, but this at once brought him into conflict with the French, who treated his request as a crime against the Republic: no one without a diplomatic pass, they said, could travel through the Territoire de Belfort at this crucial moment of the war. Tom had no doctor's certificate of ill health, no business references, he was merely a Canadian who wished to visit Switzerland on vacation: his was the lowest name on all the priority lists at the Swiss consulate in Lyon.

Eventually, however, his papers were in order, and on the night of July 18 he ended a slow train journey at Thonon, where he caught the lake steamer for Geneva. The trip was too short for cabin accomodation and too long for sitting up in a saloon which smelt of tobacco smoke and sausage, so Tom got a steamer chair and a rug on deck. The air was damp but not cold, and at dawn he was rewarded by the magnificent sight of Mont Blanc rising above Lake Geneva and the prospect of breakfast in a neutral country.

After an interrogation by the immigration men which the Helsingfors Red Guard could not have bettered, he went straight to the Gare Cornavin to have breakfast in the first-class buffet. But first he bought a newspaper; he could read the *Tribune de Genève* well enough, and certainly the lead story was set out very simply on the front page.

The Allies had taken the initiative at last. On July 15, Ludendorff had launched another attack on the Marne, although without the vigour of his great March offensive. And this time he was faced by nine US divisions, fresh and disciplined, under the supreme command of General Foch. With their support Foch passed to the attack, and the Germans began to retreat on July 18.

Studying the news story and the accompanying map, Tom Fleming realised that the action on July 18 might prove to be the turning point of the war. The thought added zest to the best breakfast he had eaten for years. Not even in neutral Stockholm, where the morning menus leaned too heavily on cold meats and cheese for his taste, had he enjoyed such good coffee and cream, boiled eggs, assorted breads and a delectable roll called Weggli, of which he ate three. He even asked for a glass of milk, and got it; he hadn't had milk at breakfast since he left Vancouver, where there was always a big pitcher on the sideboard at Rubislaw House. The abundance and the quality of the fare made him think the war was as good as over, and that brought a brief temptation to yield to Nancy's arguments and persuade himself that he had done enough. Done enough—without a showdown with that bastard Heiden! He boarded the 9.30 train for Zürich, thinking of the nine American divisions thrown into the Second Battle of the

Marne. He had heard that a US division was twelve thousand strong. That meant one hundred and eight thousand men, about four times as many as Mannerheim had mustered for the final attack on Viborg. Wear the fir sprig for Tammerfors! He wished he had an American patrol in support right now.

The train reached Zürich about one o'clock. Tom carried his bag across the street to the Schweizerhof, was taken up to a bedroom of clinical cleanliness, and shaved. His mouth felt dry. After the huge breakfast he wasn't hungry, but telephoned for a bottle of mineral water, and as he laid down the handset had the idea of looking for an address in the telephone directory. It was there all right: Heiden, Baroness; Villa Heiden, Dolder Allee, and then the phone number; the fellow had given the correct address on his passport.

"Can you direct me to the Dolder Allee?" he said to the hall porter.

"But of course, sir, the Dolder Allee is on the Dolderberg, one of the hills outside the town."

"Far away?"

"Only ten minutes in a taxi, or if you like you could go up by tram and funicular. It's quite a tourist attraction."

"I'll do that."

Tom got the exact directions, and left the hotel. A ten minutes' trip was far too short, he couldn't walk in on the Baroness Heiden at a time when any middle-aged lady might be taking a siesta. He came to a tram stop and found he was at the corner of the city's principal street, the Bahnhofstrasse. It was planted with lime trees, or lindens as some Europeans called them, and smelled delightfully of lime blossom. Under the lindens walked calm, well-dressed people, the older folk too fat, the girls corn-blonde and slender, the babies pink and proud in their white perambulators. Picture of a city at peace. The shops along the Bahnhofstrasse were stuffed with consumer goods, eatables, drinkables, pastries, chocolates, silks and embroidered lawns. It was very hot, and some cafés had set tables on the pavement; these were crowded. Ancient fountains were decked with red and white petunias, the national colours. No statues draped in black here, no blue and white crocuses lying in the snow. Nine American divisions engaged along the Marne.

Tom felt his head beginning to spin. It was surely not possible to have an attack of vertigo while strolling along a sidewalk, and yet he suddenly felt as dizzy as when he clung to the rope rail above the Vuoksi river. No Mr. White on the other side of the torrent now, no friendly hand, no one—since he had refused Nancy's—to give him any advice. With a feeling of having burned his boats he stood for a little while under the pollarded chestnuts by the landing-stage, where the pleasure steamers left for trips up and down that blue lake with the white peaks of the Alps just showing, and then turned to find the tram the porter had told him to take for the Römerplatz.

The square was a little bourgeois world of its own, with all the Swiss prerequisites for comfort: a *Gartenwirtschaft* smelling of beer and lime blossom, a confectioner's shop, a dairy, an apothecary's shop. And the entrance to the Dolderbahn, the funicular railway, romantically reached through a thick stone archway where a little red mountain train was waiting.

In spite of his anxiety Tom enjoyed the ride. He was still boy enough to like seeing the town grow small beneath him, and the lake appear, and at the same time to catch glimpses of the tranquil domestic life in the pretty villas and cottages of the Dolderberg. He discovered too late that he should have got out at an intermediate station, was carried on to the terminal on the hill, and got his bearings from a waiter outside a hotel set among beechwoods, all thick dark green and silent in the oppressively hot afternoon. Tom started walking back downhill towards the Dolder Allee.

The Villa Heiden was not particularly impressive. It was approached by a short, straight drive with gates, but the gates stood hospitably open, and the walls which divided its lawns from the gardens on each side were only three or four feet high. The Allee, while private, was pleasant in the vistas it gave of well-kept rose arbours and trelliswork covered with clematis, and every villa had a smooth expanse of lawn, one covered with children's toys. Tom, after a close look at the houses on either side, went to the front door of the Villa Heiden and rang the bell.

He had to ring a second time before anybody answered. Then a man appeared, not dressed as a servant but opening the door with an untrained servant's rough nod, and he spoke to Tom in German.

"Is Mr. Heiden at home?" said Tom.

The man looked him up and down. He was wearing a suit of rough tweed, too warm for the weather, and there was perspiration on his heavy face and balding head. He again said something which Tom failed to understand.

"I want to see Mr. Heiden, if he's here."

The man shouted "Irene!" and beckoned to Tom to enter the front hall. A woman with dyed black hair appeared through a green baize door, hastily tying on an apron as she came.

"Can I help you, sir?"

"Thank you," said Tom, "my name is Fleming. I want to know if Mr. Heiden is at home."

"He's playing golf this afternoon. Is it important?"

There was an odd mixture of servility and arrogance in the woman's manner. Tom said, "I can come back later, now I know he's in Zürich."

"He's not very far away. What did you say your name was?"

"Thomas Fleming, from Vancouver."

"Better come in, then, and Hans can let Mr. Heiden know."

"Thank you." Tom gave his hat to the man, who turned it in his hands uncertainly, and followed Irene into a large drawing room on the right of the hall, where french windows stood open on a flagged patio from which two steps led down to the front lawn.

"Take a seat, Hans won't be long," said the woman, staring at Tom. "Can I get you a cup of tea?"

"No thank you." Tom turned away and looked out of the french window until he heard the door close behind Irene. Then he glanced quickly round the room. It was furnished without distinction, as if the chairs and sofas had been bought haphazard from some second-rate Swiss store, and somehow reminded Tom of a dentist's waiting-room. Although the windows were open there was a disagreeable smell, which he presently traced to the rotting stems of some yellow lilies in the stale water of a ceramic vase.

"*Vous venez de la cour, monsieur?*"

A lady dressed in black came in so quietly that she startled Tom. She appeared to be about sixty, with greying hair, but very slim, and had remarkable aquiline features and large dark eyes.

"I beg your pardon, ma'am," said Tom, bowing slightly, "it was Mr. Heiden I came to see."

199

"Ah! you prefer to speak English," the lady said. She came further into the room. "I thought you were a messenger from the Imperial Chamberlain. You are a friend of my son Igor?"

"Boris is the one I know best," said Tom.

"He has so many friends. But let me introduce myself: I am the Baroness Heiden."

"I'm honoured, ma'am." There was something as withered about her formal manners as the lilies in the vase, and yet she had a pathos that awoke Tom's chivalry. Poor old girl, he thought, she hasn't had much luck with the Heiden boys.

"Are you making a long stay in Saint Petersburg, sir?"

"Not very long."

"Long enough to be received at Czarskoe Selo, I feel sure," said Baroness Heiden, with a toss of her head. "Your Ambassador will take care of that."

"Perhaps he will." Tom's small talent for improvisation was failing rapidly. But just then a light step came rapidly across the patio, and Boris Heiden entered through the french doors. He was wearing country clothes, a grey flannel suit and a checked shirt with brown brogues, very different from the heavy garments he wore in Finland, but the greatest difference was in his appearance, for he had shaved off his beard, and his fair hair seemed to be several shades darker. He had even put on a little weight. He was just what the master of the Villa Heiden might be expected to be —a solid Swiss bourgeois, treating himself to a golfing half-holiday for the benefit of his health.

"Mr. Fleming," he said curtly. "Mother, you should be resting in your room." He jerked a bell-pull by the fireplace as he spoke, and the woman Irene came hurrying in. "Take your mistress upstairs and stay with her," he said.

"I wish you a prosperous return to Warsaw," the baroness said to Tom.

"Thank you kindly, ma'am," he said. Heiden waited until the door was closed, and then gave a short laugh. "Warsaw!" he said, "was my mother talking about Poland?"

"About Saint Petersburg. She thought I'd brought a message from the Imperial Chamberlain."

"Ah! Of course!" Heiden opened the sliding door of a small cupboard which stood between Tom and the hearth, and took out a bottle of whisky and a siphon.

"Drink?"

"No thanks."

"It's not poisoned, you know."

"I don't want to drink with you."

"As you wish." Heiden mixed himself a drink. "Didn't the servants offer you anything?"

"The woman offered me a cup of tea."

"Once a Cockney, always a Cockney. Hans is from East Prussia, I don't suppose you understood a word he said."

"*He* understood enough to fetch you in a hurry, though."

"Oh, we've been expecting you—I've been expecting you, since I heard you came safely through the fighting in Finland. I knew you'd have no trouble in finding me in Zürich."

"I'd have found you if you'd gone to ground in Vladivostok."

"What a fascinating study you are, Mr. Fleming," said Heiden. "Always so vehement and positive! Last time we met, you were holding a gun on me—"

"Last time we met, a good friend of mine went off as your escort, and was never seen again."

"You mean Captain Keiller? Really, Mr. Fleming, that's too bad! You've already accused me of espionage, and murder by proxy, and now you imply that I'm to blame for the vagaries of Captain Keiller! My guide and I persuaded him to cross the Kvarken with us; I've no idea what happened to him after that."

"So you did cross the ice to Sweden? I was sure you would."

"Not at all a pleasant journey, I assure you, but better than being shot down by the Butcher Guards." He changed his tone. "You know, I felt sorry for you that night at Vilppula. You did so well up to a point, but you were handicapped by that fat colonel and the other Finn, and of course the Swede was easy to get round. Look here, why don't we call it quits? There's nothing you can possibly do to me here, a Swiss citizen on Swiss soil, and I could have *you* run out of the country tomorrow if I wished. But why should I? I like you, Fleming, I've always thought we could be friends. And you think so too . . . or you would never have come so far to see me again."

"I only came here for one reason," said Tom. "I want to know what you've done with Lisa Sandels."

For the first time Heiden appeared disconcerted. "Lisa?" he said. "What do you want with her?"

"I want to know if she's here, and well, and happy—or as happy as anyone can be, in this house."

"But why should she—"

"Oh, come on," said Tom, "Lisa told the neighbours she was going to Stockholm to be married to you. That was when I knew for certain you'd gotten away to Sweden, that night last February."

"Dear Lisa," said Heiden softly, "always a chatterbox. I'm sorry I can't produce her immediately, to set your mind at rest, but she's in the city this afternoon."

"And you're married?"

"No, we're not married. As it turned out, there was no reason why we should be."

"What d'you mean by that?"

"Before I left Helsingfors for the front, Lisa told me she was expecting a child. That was why I arranged for her to come to me in Stockholm."

"And?"

"The oldest feminine trick in the world," said Heiden wryly. "There was no child coming. But Lisa refused to go back to Helsingfors without a wedding ring, so I brought her along with me to Switzerland. In fact, I found an interesting job for her in Zürich."

"In a bank, so she can give you the lowdown on the Swiss depositors?"

"Her German's not nearly good enough for that. No, she's working as a nurse's aide."

"In a hospital? Which one?"

"In a private nursing-home, and they don't encourage visitors. But she'll tell you all about it herself, I'm sure . . . I wish you would sit down, Mr. Fleming!"

"I'd rather go out of doors," said Tom. The smell of decaying flowers was oppressive. Heiden, with a faint smile, followed him out to the flagstones outside the french windows. Over the low stone walls of the garden they could be seen by a man in rough clothes mowing the lawn of the house on one side, and a lady swinging a child from a beech tree in the other. Along the Allee a group of older children were coming home from school.

"A pleasant place, isn't it?" said Heiden, reading his thoughts. "Why shouldn't Lisa be happy here?"

"I was wondering how she got on with your mother, who appears to be—living in the past."

"I'm sorry my mother forced herself upon you, but she must have heard a strange voice in the hall, and come to see."

"See if I was that messenger from the Imperial Chamberlain?"

"Perhaps I should tell you something of our family history, Mr. Fleming. It might help you to understand my point of view."

"Carry on," said Tom. "I hope it's as good a story as the one about your brother and Stolypin."

Heiden looked into his empty glass. In full sunshine the slight change in his appearance was less noticeable. Nothing could alter the shape of his blunt features or the neatness of his hands, and his body had still something of a boy's grace.

"My father, the late Baron Heiden, visited Warsaw about forty years ago," he said. "It was some time after the Polish insurrection, but there was still a good deal of unrest in the country. Baron Heiden was one of a pacifying mission sent to Poland by the Czar Alexander II, called the Good Emperor, whose statue you may remember in the Senate Square at Helsingfors."

"By 'pacifying' I suppose you mean they went with troops and artillery?" said Tom.

"No, this was a genuine mission of reconciliation. The members of the mission met with all classes of respectable society in Warsaw, and there, at some official reception, my father met my mother. He was already married and had a family. He persuaded my mother to put herself under his protection, as the saying goes, and return with him to Petersburg. My brother Igor was born there a year later."

"I see," said Tom.

"I must say for Baron Heiden that he treated us all very generously. I remember a house with a garden, and servants, and Igor was sent to an excellent school, and university. But my mother, alas, was never happy. She wanted to shine in society. To appear at court, where my father had a distinguished position. To be summoned to wait on the Empress at the summer palace at Czarskoe Selo . . ."

"By a messenger from the Imperial Chamberlain?" said Tom.

"Exactly. So, for all the luxury, our home was not a happy one. I know it was the sight of his mother's suffering which first

203

turned Igor's mind to social injustice. Then he joined the Maxi-malists, as the Bolsheviks were called in those days, and swore to destroy the world of tyranny we lived in."

"And so he brought suffering to others," said Tom. "I suppose you know Stolypin's young son and daughter were maimed for life in the attempt to kill their father?"

Heiden shrugged. "The innocent must suffer with the guilty before the better world is made," he said.

"You mean the Communist world?"

"If you like. But while I admired my brother Igor, you must believe that I disapproved of his solution. I dislike violence wher-ever I find it, and we can achieve our aims by more intelligent methods — in the long run."

"You were with a pretty violent lot that night on the Russian front."

"The front!" said Heiden, for the first time showing anger, "The Reds against the Butcher Guards! That totally unnecessary war!"

"Yes," said Tom. "You didn't expect that, did you? You for-got Mannerheim when the Reds planned to take over Finland!"

"I give you that point," said Heiden. "Some great planner at the Smolny overlooked Mannerheim. A colourless personality, a middle-aged cavalry officer stuck on the Bessarabian front — do you think he would ever have been allowed to leave for Finland if anyone had thought him dangerous? However, it's all finished now. Mannerheim's day of glory was soon over; long may he live to enjoy his Swedish exile."

"Tell me one more thing about your parents," Tom put in. "Did they ever marry?"

"No."

"Then that poor lady is Baroness Heiden only by courtesy?"

"She was a rabbi's daughter," said her son. "Her name was Miriam Rebowitz. Is there anything else you want to know?"

"No," said Tom, "I think that ties it up." He looked towards the house next door. The man who had been mowing was trimming the edges of the lawn. "Heiden," he said, "I don't want to call it quits, but I think we'll have to call it a day. I can't force you to marry Lisa, if that's what she wants, any more than your father could be forced to get a divorce and make you legitimate. And that's what you and Igor wanted, wasn't it, a damned sight more than your better Communist world? But I won't leave Zürich without seeing Lisa, and hearing her tell me herself that she's all right, and here of her own free will and choice."

"Very good," said Heiden. "Lisa shall telephone to you as soon as she comes home. Where can she reach you?"

"At the Hotel Schweizerhof."

"The Schweizerhof, about seven. Will that do?"

"Fine."

To the gardener next door and the lady playing with her little boy, the two young men were a model of Swiss politeness as they parted at the gate of the Villa Heiden. The householder, having retrieved his guest's hat and said goodbye, strolled round his own garden, picking off a few withered leaves before he went indoors. Tom walked off towards the funicular, and when his footsteps died away the quiet of July lay over the Dolder Allee.

But Tom, as the little red train carried him down the steep descent, was in a mood to jump at his own shadow. When they stopped at the intermediate station he was sure he saw Hans, the servant—or bodyguard—from East Prussia, among the boarding passengers, and once back at the Römerplatz he almost ran through the tunnel exit and jumped into a taxi.

*   *   *

Back at the hotel the wakeful night and the anxious day caught up with him. Tom lay down on the bed in his shirt and trousers and fell into a deep sleep. For the first hour it was dreamless, and then was filled with flickering images: of Heiden pushing Charlie Keiller out of the freight train at the knife's point, of a Red agent guiding them to Björkö island and then out on the solid ice of the Kvarken—so far, only, for one of the three. And there came an image of Keiller's body floating down the Gulf of Bothnia when the ice melted, hideously changed, so that the knife wound had vanished, as Heiden smiled and said "I've no idea what happened to him" . . . Tom struggled to wake up. But fatigue held him in the feverish sleep from which he only woke at half past six to a dull sense of having once again been worsted by Heiden. In spite of his bold words to Nancy, his purpose had diminished at the sight of Heiden's mother, and the story her son had told so well. Miriam Rebowitz's suffering, which had made an assassin of her son Igor! Miriam Rebowitz had done pretty well out of the deal,

205

thought Tom, hardening his heart as he looked for a clean shirt. That's a nice house, if it were tidied up a bit and Irene changed the water in the vases.

Then the idea struck him that Lisa Sandels could not possibly be in that house. He remembered the perfect order of the little flat in Helsingfors, the scent of Roman hyacinths and birch logs, and was sure that Lisa could not spend one night in the Villa Heiden, even as a guest, without getting fresh flowers from the garden and bringing some order into that slovenly Russian room. He looked at his watch anxiously. He wanted a drink badly now, but he was afraid to miss Lisa's call—if it came—by going down-stairs to the bar, or tying up the line by calling the floor waiter. He lit a cigarette instead. At five minutes past seven the phone rang.

"Tom Fleming here."

"Oh- h!" Her voice was very soft, hardly above a whisper. "This is Lisa."

"Lisa, how are you? Are you well?"

"Yes, I'm quite well."

"When can I see you? Where?"

"In the city. Will you meet me at ten?"

"Not until ten?"

"There's a wine bar on the Glockengasse—"

"What's it called?"

Her voice was so faint that he could just catch "only one," and then what sounded like "Gertie",

Tom said quickly, "All right, I'll find it. I'll be there at ten," and heard her hang up at the other end. He wondered if Heiden had been listening on an extension.

Tom went down to the bar at once. He drank a large Scotch, straight, with a little water on the side, and then asked the barman to mix him a second Scotch and soda, very long, in a tall glass. The men standing at the bar were discussing Foch's advance. Tom carried his glass to a table by the window. He had been deeply stirred, far more than he would have believed possible, by the sound of Lisa Sandels's voice. It had sounded so like Sophie's—like enough, by some trick of memory, to arouse in him the stirring of sexual desire. He wanted to punish Lisa, to take Heiden's girl away from him, to be reminded in her body of Sophie's tenderness. He wanted to hear her voice again. When he finished his drink he went out to the lobby, looked up the number of the Villa Heiden and called it from the public phone box. He let it ring until the operator cut in at last to tell him there was no reply.

The Glockengasse, he learned from the helpful porter, was in the Old Town of the city, only a few minutes away from the Bahnhofstrasse. The traffic on the main street was growing less, and the lime blossom smelled more sweet than ever as the dew began to fall; Tom walked up a hilly street under old bow windows dripping with striped petunias into the Glockengasse. There was indeed only one wineshop, with a fine cut-glass door opening into the narrow lane, and he realised what was meant by "Gertie", because the place was called the Goethe Stübli. He looked in at the door and saw three or four customers sitting in front of old-fashioned green glasses and tall bottles of wine. A charming tavern, a picturesque neighbourhood, and to a soldier's eye as fine a place for an ambush as he had ever seen.

The Street of the Bells led into a square running irregularly by the side of St. Peter's Church, the heart of the Old Town. The houses in the square, some of them four and five storeys high, bore dates from the seventeenth and eighteenth centuries. The façades were grey, picked out with white, the frilled curtains spotless, the flowers rioting from one window to another. It was the dead centre of calm in the storm in Europe, and Tom Fleming in another mood might have been charmed by its peace. But although he had walked the dark streets of Helsingfors in the nights when the Red Guards were arming, he felt more real alarm in the shelter of St. Peter's Church, on a summer evening, in peaceful Zürich. He thought of the pretty villas on the Dolderberg, and what one of them concealed. He looked at the nameplates on the ground-floor flats: a doctor, a professor, a notary. All so worthy and respectable.

But if there should be a madman looking out of an attic window?

The square was a thoroughfare, for several lanes and flights of steps led out of it, but there were not many people about when the great clock of St. Peter's Church struck eight. Tom found a restaurant, the Veltliner Keller, which the hotel porter had recommended, in a little alley called the Street of the Key, and there on a cushioned and beautifully carved wooden bench, he settled down to enjoy an excellent dinner. The waitress recommended Bündnerfleisch, the dried smoked meat of the Grisons, and then a delicate veal dish flavoured with fresh sage. It was a menu which enhanced the Veltliner wine, a strong red for which the restaurant was famous, and it induced in Tom a mellow mood. It was too good a meal to be eaten alone. He wanted a girl to sit beside him and look pretty and gay when he lifted his glass to her. He wanted to talk to Nancy.

But he was alone, by his own choice, and he looked so very grave that when the owner of the restaurant, whose name was given on the menu as Frau Maria Matter, came in from her supervision of the kitchen, she noticed Tom at once, and sized him up as an English guest. There were only eight other people in the ancient room, with its peasant woodcarving, and she knew them all: Frau Maria addressed herself to Tom, and hoped he had enjoyed his dinner.

"Very much indeed, thanks," said Tom, and smiled so pleasantly that Frau Maria determined to break down the well-known English reserve. In the old-fashioned Swiss way, she drew out the empty chair at Tom's table, where he had wished for Nancy to be sitting, and began to talk about the weather, the flowers, and the quality of the Luzern strawberries she suggested for Tom's dessert. It was very soothing, and rather like talking to the Goddess of Plenty, for Frau Maria was tall and strongly built, with a humorous face and abundantly coiled fair hair. Soon Tom was telling her that he was a Canadian, in Zürich on business, and yes, had been a soldier, and certainly, hoped the war would be over soon. When it was time for the coffee she got up with a graceful little bow, like someone who had granted an audience, and went to sit with her Swiss guests at the next table. The time had flown: Tom heard St. Peter's clock strike half past nine.

So now he was in for it. But when he paid his bill Tom asked the waitress to bring him a sheet of paper and an envelope, with a foreign postage stamp. The talk with Frau Maria, and her strong personality, had given him an idea: he addressed the envelope to Miss Agnes Macpherson, at the Hotel de France et Choiseul, 239, rue St. Honoré, Paris.

Dear Nancy [he wrote],
I saw Heiden this afternoon at the Villa Heiden, Dolder

Allee, Zürich, it's on the Dolderberg just outside the town. I hope to meet up with Lisa Sandels later tonight. Have been dining here, and can't help having a hunch that things won't work out too well. If you get this letter it will mean I've run into trouble, and maybe you could drop a hint at the British Embassy before I'm posted missing like Karl Keiller. I wish I could have stayed with you in Paris.

Love, Tom.

Frau Maria was just rising, with a swirl of her elegant black dress, as Tom put the letter in the envelope. "Madame?" he said interrogatively, as she was about to speak to the waitress, and she bent over his table at once.

"Can I help you in any way?"

"Please," said Tom. "Look, madame, it was a great dinner. I'd like to eat lunch here tomorrow, some time between twelve and two. If I don't come, and don't telephone to cancel—my name's Fleming—could you put this letter in the mail?"

She gave him an appraising look, and picked the letter up in one smooth movement under Tom's discarded table napkin. "You can rely on me, Mr. Fleming," said Frau Maria Matter, and he said,

"Thanks, I thought I could."

In the deep arched doorway of the Veltliner Keller, a doorway which went back to the Middle Ages, Tom took his pistol out of its shoulder holster and put it in the waistband of his trousers, with all but one button of his jacket undone. Then he walked up the Street of the Key and started to cross the square. All five great bells of St. Peter's clock were striking the hour of ten, and all the windows of the tall grey houses were shuttered for the night. On a seat beneath the huge linden in the middle of the square a man and a woman were clasped in a close embrace, their faces hidden, their breaths held as the stranger went quietly by. A reassuring noise of conviviality came from the open back window of the Goethe Stübli.

Tom looked behind him. The way into the narrow alley, the Street of the Bells, was clear, and so was the way ahead. And on the doorstep of the old wine bar stood a slender figure in a pale blue coat, with a hat of the same colour pulled down over the bright springing hair he remembered so well. The figure moved as he came towards it.

"Is it really you, Lisa?"

"Tom! Oh, Tom!"

Then two arms held him in a fierce embrace, pinioning his own arms to his sides in a grip stronger than any girl's, and a mouth was pressed to his own in a kiss that kept him silent. And the face so vilely close to his own was the face of Boris Heiden. That much he knew before the blow fell on his head, and the church and the linden and the madman in the attic exploded together in his brain.

16

WHEN TOM CAME BACK to his senses he was in a hospital bed, lying on his side and staring at a small clock on the bedside table whose hands said a quarter to twelve. He supposed it was night, for the bedside lamp was lit, and also there was diffused light coming from elsewhere in the room. He had difficulty in focusing his eyes, but could make out a grey-haired woman dressed in white sitting beside his bed.

"What happened?" he managed to get out.

The woman put her finger to her lips and rose to ring a hidden bell. Tom rolled over on his back, and groaned. He put up his hand to his head and felt a heavy surgical dressing taped between the nape of his neck and the crown.

Someone was leaning over the foot of the bed.

"Can you see me, Mr. Fleming? Clearly? Or only as a blur?"

"Blur."

The white shape came closer and resolved itself into the figure of a man in white jacket and trousers, who took the nurse's place beside the bed.

"Who are you? Where am I?"

"I'm Dr. Schmidt, Mr. Fleming. You were in a motor accident about two hours ago. This is Dr. Meyer's private clinic, where you will be well looked after. Is the pain severe?"

"Yes."

"But you can hear me quite clearly? You understand all I am saying?"

"Yes."

Dr. Schmidt felt Tom's pulse, examined his eyes with a tiny flashlight, and moved a stethoscope over his chest. Then he helped Tom to raise himself on the pillows, and examined the surgical dressing.

"Nurse has gone to fetch you a hot drink," he said, "to make sure you'll sleep well for the rest of the night. You'll be a new man in the morning."

The bedside light was extinguished. The nurse supported Tom while he swallowed a few mouthfuls of a drink tasting rather pleasantly of herbs, and then laid his head gingerly down on his pillow. The soft lights in the room faded and went out.

When he awoke again he heard a clock striking, very loud and near, and counted nine strokes before he opened his eyes. The room was lighted as though it was still the middle of the night, and he saw that the single window was made of frosted glass and curtained in thick white net. The furniture was white enamelled, the walls of the room and the two doors were painted grey.

"*Es ist Morgen oder Nacht?*" he said hazily, and a young nurse put down her magazine and laughed.

"I speak English, Mr. Fleming," she said. "It's morning. Would you like a glass of water before I change your dressing?"

It was so like his old hospital routine that Tom sat up obediently. The pain in his head had become endurable, and his brain extremely lucid, with a sense of elevation as if he were floating at least three feet above the bed. It was as though his power of vision had been enormously increased, for he saw the little bone stud in the nurse's collar sparkling like a cluster of diamonds, and a curl of fair hair escaping from her cap like a coil of manila rope on a ship's deck. He surprised himself by the poetry of his similes.

"Do you feel well enough to use the bathroom alone?"

"I sure do."

Tom got out of bed unassisted and went through the door she held open into a small bathroom with a barred window. It was set in the same wall as the window of his bedroom, he noticed, and both looked out on a narrow shaft about six feet square, driven between four walls of what was probably the same building. There was a new toothbrush on the washbasin in a cardboard container, but no razor and for some reason no mirror. He stepped back inside the bedroom, holding on to the door handle.

"I'd like a shave."

"Someone will shave you later, with your own razor." The nurse looked towards the wardrobe, and there Tom saw his own suitcase, unlocked and opened, standing on the floor.

"Hey, how did that get here?"

"You mustn't talk, Mr. Fleming. Please get back into bed again, your breakfast will be here in a moment."

As soon as the woman left the room Tom got out of bed again

and stumbled to the wardrobe. The sight of his suitcase had triggered off the dormant memory, and he now remembered everything that had happened. Motor accident be damned! He was Heiden's prisoner.

He hunted frantically through the wardrobe, where both his suits were hanging with his shoes beneath them. His wallet and keys had gone from the suit worn yesterday, and there was no sign of his gun. He felt in his open bag, it wasn't there of course, and nothing was left which could possibly be used for identification. He pulled back the net curtains; the window was protected by an iron grille. At that he almost lost his head and flung himself on the door, which was locked; he wanted to scream and beat on it with the flat of his hands, as Sophie had beaten on the library door before she was shot down, but he knew that would be a sure way to gratify Heiden, and sat down limply on a low chair, clutching his throbbing head with both fists. Then he heard the sound of a key being turned in the lock, and remembered the promise of breakfast. He got up, prepared to charge whoever came in and make a run for it, and he got as far as tearing the tray from the hands of the girl who entered and throwing it with a crash of crockery to the floor. Then she said "Tom!" and he was staring in dismay at Lisa Sandels.

"I was bringing your coffee," she said stupidly, and stopped to pick up the broken china.

"Leave that alone," said Tom. "You're a bit late for your date with me, aren't you? It was for ten o'clock last night, not ten o'clock this morning."

"But Boris said you had an accident—"

"Accident, hell! You know better than that. You set up the time and the place, but you never went near the Glockengasse yourself—did you?"

"No." Lisa hung her head. And now Tom, focusing his still blurred vision, could see her properly, in a white overall, stockings and shoes, with a white square of cotton tied tightly round her head. With her fair hair hidden she looked astonishingly like Sophie, with the same features, the same beautiful grey eyes, and her voice was the same, with the attractive lilt in it.

"Lisa, what are you doing here?"

"Boris said you wanted to see me, to be sure that I was well."

"And are you? You look a wreck."

Lisa flung her head up angrily, but it was true. She looked ill, and much older than the girl Tom Fleming saw first on a winter night in Helsingfors. "I'm well and quite happy," she said.

"Even though you can't get Heiden to marry you?"

"Boris says marriage is an outworn bourgeois convention, and that a man like himself, specially trained for work abroad, must not be encumbered by family ties," she said, as if she were repeating a lesson.

"But *you* work here?" he said, taking in the white uniform, "this is a real nursing-home, not just some set-up of Heiden's?"

"This is Dr. Meyer's private clinic, and I'm a nurse's aide."

"A clinic with bars across the windows? What is it, some kind of nut-house?"

"Bars?" said Lisa, looking uncertainly at the window, "I've never seen any—I've never been inside this room before. Dr. Meyer only takes lady patients, I believe. Ladies who appreciate discretion—"

"An abortionist, eh?" said Tom. "Oh, Lisa, what would Sophie say?"

"Don't talk about Sophie," she said, and there were tears in her eyes. Tom saw his advantage, and took her in his arms. "Lisa," he said, "do you realise that Sophie gave her life for you? If she'd stayed at home that morning, and waited till I came for her, I could have got you both out of Helsingfors to safety. But she only thought about you. She *had* to go out and telephone for a doctor. And she was thinking about you right up to the last. She said your name when she was in my arms, dying. She cared about you far more than she cared for me."

Lisa was sobbing now, and Tom tightened his clasp. He felt her young body relax in its white overall, and under the thin pyjamas the heat was rising in his own. "Lisa," he said again, and his voice was thick, "I saw the man who killed your sister. And I'd seen him once before, on the night he followed her from the office to—a place where she was meeting me. Do you know who set that man to hunt her down, and got her name put on the Red death list? Well, I can tell you. It was your lover, Boris Heiden."

She said "No!" so loudly that he closed her mouth with his own, and as Lisa writhed in his arms to free herself Tom Fleming felt his heavy limbs resolve themselves into one driving machine of desire, the desire to dominate, to punish, fusing into the desire for sexual satisfaction. He pushed Lisa down on the bed and flung himself upon her. But she was strong, and he was weakened by the blow and the sedative they had given him. With a shriek of "Boris! Boris!" Lisa Sandels struggled free, tripped on the coffee tray and fell on the floor as the door burst open, and the powerfully built, grey-haired nurse of the night before seized Tom's shoulders and held him pinioned to the bed.

"Don't be rough with him," said the amused voice of Heiden, "I thought that was a soporific you gave him yesterday night. It appears to have been a powerful aphrodisiac. Eh, Fleming?"

Tom found himself back in bed, panting, and staring at the ceiling.

"Lisa, get out of here," said Heiden. "All right, nurse, he's quiet and presentable now. We won't need a strait-jacket this time."

"Shall I ask Dr. Meyer to come, sir?"

"Not yet. But you might bring fresh coffee for the patient, I want his brain as clear as possible before I talk to him."

The coffee was brought immediately, and the nurse helped Tom to sit up on his pillow. The frantic drive which had possessed him was quite gone, and it was an effort to lift the coffee cup in his heavy hand.

"What sort of dope have you put in this?" he said.

"Nothing harmful. Now drink it quickly, and let nurse take the tray away." Heiden sat down on the edge of Tom's bed. He was wearing a dark blue suit, a white starched shirt, a gold Swiss watch on a morocco leather strap, and gold cufflinks engraved with a coat of arms. He might have been a young professor of medicine, called in for a consultation at Dr. Meyer's exclusive clinic. When the door closed behind the woman he said pleasantly:

"Feeling better now? How's the head? I'm sorry Hans was so rough, but we had to make sure of you—we were running on a very tight schedule."

"You made sure of me all right," said Tom. "Your Prussian plug-ugly coshed me, and now I'm in some sort of nutty hospital, but why?"

"For one reason because you're a nuisance, and I want you out of the way for a while, and for another, because certain people think you might be a useful subject to test some experiments my friends have been working on."

"What kind of experiments?"

"To control the subject's mind by the use of certain drugs. Nothing so vulgar as cocaine or hashish. We leave the drug peddlers to do our work for us in those particular fields. Ours are preparations developed in the Far East and brought to Russia from Tibet. They will help to bring 'pitiful isolated individuals' like yourself—to borrow a phrase from Comrade Trotsky—to the great norm of acceptance that the state is God walking among men."

"The Communist state?"

"The world state which will emerge when all other states and nations are merged through war and conquest into one global community. This was the doctrine of Karl Marx, developed from the Hegelian dialectic—"

"Heiden, you're as crazy as your crazy mother."

The hazel eyes gleamed hate.

"You intruded on my mother yesterday," he said. "I wish I could have disposed of you in my own house, but—"

"But there were too many witnesses on the Dolder Allee," said Tom.

"Yes, you were smart enough to think of that."

Tom nodded. He felt very smart indeed, even to arguing against the Hegelian dialectic, with the same kind of lucidity and sense of elevation as he had felt on first awaking.

"I was going to say: But it was my duty to report your arrival to Comrade Semenov, our Commissar in Switzerland."

"Aren't *you* the Commissar?"

"I'm just a humble *apparatchik*," said Heiden modestly. "With a few ideas of my own, which unfortunately don't always conform to the Party line." He settled himself more comfortably against the foot of the bed.

"Before Meyer comes," he said, "I want to tell you that I don't agree entirely with the course of treatment Comrade Semenov has ordered for you. Just at present all our Party leaders are rather too fond of violent action. It's natural, after such a long struggle to gain power, but I don't think we need mass executions, looting and burning, and drugging as our long-term policy. It's very tempting for born orators—I'm not one, and I envy them—born orators like Lenin to use their gifts to sway the proletariat into a great uprising. Personally I'm a little tired of the proletariat. I

216

think in one generation the great breeding ground for Communism will be the *bourgeoisie* itself."

"Never," said Tom.

"If not in one generation, then certainly in two. We shall begin with the students of Europe and the Americas, and make them revolutionaries like the students of Russia."

"You didn't do very well with the students of Finland."

"We shall spread sedition in the armed forces of the Powers— not by mutiny, not by shooting officers, nothing so noisy, nothing to provoke a counter-revolution, but by the weapons of satire and derision. We shall make patriotism laughable, and show the officer class for the arrogant oafs they are, and we shall destroy the pride in the regiment, in the national army, which is so strong in you, my friend. We shall destroy the power of the Christian church in all lands, merely by holding its ministers up to ridicule."

"Carry on," said Tom. "What else have you got in mind?"

"The subject really is limitless. Instead of spreading our ideas by rioting in the Nevski Prospekt, we shall spread them by the great new means of communication, notably the cinema. Wireless telegraphy, too, will be a great mass medium in a very short time from now. With those two weapons, the image and the voice, we shall reach millions who never heard of the Romanovs and their tyranny, but who'll be willing to rise against their domestic tyrants—when we tell them to. Take the disaffected peoples. The Irish were always ready to murder an undefended Englishman in the dark of the moon, but in 1916 they showed the world that they can mount a genuine rebellion. Take your French Canadians, who say they would rather leave your precious Confederation than submit to the Conscription Act. Take India—there is far more to be done there than the Czar's generals knew, when they laid their silly plans to infiltrate the North-West Frontier. We aim at the conquest of the mind, not of the territory, and what helpers we have in the world of science! Our own Pavlov, whom I mentioned to you in Finland, and the great Freud. He's teaching the world to throw away its inhibitions and repressions, its guilt complexes and its parent complexes; and within two generations, I predict, we shall see men and women copulating in the parks like the animals they are, with two thousand years of so-called civilisation thrown down the drain where it belongs."

"Do you think you'll live to see all this?" said Tom.

"I'm only thirty, why shouldn't I?"

"Somebody might knock you off first."

"Wishful thinking," said Boris Heiden. "But you're not holding a gun on me now . . . Dr. Meyer will be here in five minutes. I repeat, I'm not sure the drug treatment is right for you, but I admit I'm interested in some of your reactions. For instance, we may discover your latent homosexuality, which seems to me to lie quite near the surface."

"I'm not a queer, if that's what you mean."

"My virtuous lumberjack, you must have been a very handsome boy. I'm sure you had many close admirers in your logging days."

"Any punk who made a pass at one of the loggers got dunked in the Fraser, or any river that came handy," said Tom. "And even the gaycats never went around in drag, like you. Say, was that blue coat really Lisa's, or do you wear it with the wig whenever you go on the town?"

Heiden paid no attention. "Another thing worth investigating is your obvious dread of impotence. Last night you carried a gun in your trouser band, which Freud would see as the classic weapon substitute—"

"I wasn't quick enough on the draw."

It was no good, he couldn't keep it up much longer. Whatever stuff they had given him in the coffee had lost its effect now, as the soaring spirit relapsed into the body prone on the hospital bed. For the first time Tom felt a real pang of fear.

"What are you going to do to me?"

"There's just time to tell you," Heiden said. He looked at his wristwatch.

"Rasputin, the most powerful single influence in the downfall of the Czar," he began, "had a Tibetan wizard among his hangers-on, a fellow who went by the name of Bademayev. This wizard, or monk if you prefer the name, had a whole medicine chest of salves and balms and potions made from herbs in blends of his own invention. One of them could stop a haemorrhage, no matter how severe. Are you following me?"

"Yes," said Tom drowsily. "Stop bleeding, yes, I follow you."

Heiden got up and unobtrusively touched the electric bell.

"This was the secret of Rasputin's remarkable 'cures' of the Czarevich, who was a haemophiliac. But Bademayev had other drugs, one of which induced a form of mental paralysis." He did

218

not turn his head as a pale-faced man in white hospital clothes slid into the room. "Some people believed that after Rasputin had won the confidence of the boy's parents, he gave the Czar drops distilled from this drug, saying they would act as a stimulant in the difficult days of the war. Instead, the drug induced the indecision, the slowing-up of thought, which so many of his entourage complained of in our late beloved Little Father." Heiden leaned over the bed, raised one of Tom's eyelids and studied the dilated pupil. "At Comrade Semenov's orders, Dr. Meyer will try some experiments on you with a similar drug." He glanced at the hypodermic syringe in the doctor's hand. "Fleming, listen to me. *Rasputin had a Tibetan wizard among his hangers-on . . .* Repeat what I just said!"

Tom heard his own hoarse voice:

> "Infirm of purpose!
> Give me the daggers!"

Then there was darkness.

✻   ✻   ✻

There followed a period of which Tom Fleming was to remember very little. He knew that a male nurse attended to his needs as if he were a baby, and brought him food of different tastes and textures, usually in a feeding cup, but the man was not always kind, and teased Tom by pulling the cup away so that the contents fell on his nightshirt, or on the sheets. At intervals he felt the prick of the hypodermic needle in his arm; at others, the bedside light was turned full on his face, and from behind it a voice asked questions to which he never knew the answers. During this period his brain functioned independently in only one way: he could hear and recognise the sound of a peal of bells, chiming apparently above his head. Lying with his eyes shut, he reasoned that these were the bells of St. Peter's Church, as he had heard them striking in a place where there was white linen and red wine in a goblet, a place he had visited in the Street of the Key.

Every time the bells rang he tried to piece a little more of the story together. Beneath the bell tower there was a square, and in the square a linden tree with a seat below it, and that was where Hans waited with Irene's head on his shoulder and his on hers, like any courting couple. Then there was the Street of the Bells, the alley where Heiden waited, and where Hans came up behind him on rubber soles to strike him down. Tom knew that the bells, the alley, the linden tree were in Zürich, Switzerland, and that was where he was now held prisoner. He rejected the doubts, swirling up through the darkness, that Switzerland was a land of bells, and thus he might be anywhere, in any city, or even in a village near a church. Those loud and insistent bells were ringing from St. Peter's steeple, and nowhere else.

Then he had a completely lucid interval. It was obviously prepared for, because the hypodermic needle was withheld one night and the mild herbal soporific given instead. He had almost a normal sleep and next morning was given *café au lait*, rolls and black cherry jam which he ate to the last drop, and licked his fingers. "A special treat," the male nurse said. He was in a good mood that morning, and helped Tom into his blue suit, which now hung loosely on his shoulders. Wearing socks, and shoes from which the laces had been removed, he was propped up in a low armchair beside the electric fire, which was never lit.

Three upright chairs had been placed in front of him, and he waited expectantly for his visitors. They arrived together, Dr. Meyer in the lead, who shook hands with Tom, another man introduced as Mr. Semenov, and Heiden, dressed in the leather jacket and rough clothes of Finland, with his cloth cap in his hand.

"How are you today, comrade?" Heiden asked.

"Very well. Thank you. And you?"

"Quite well. You're staring at me. Why?"

"It's the way you're dressed. You're going on a trip?"

"My clothes look like clothes for a journey? Where?"

"Kouvola junction," said Tom promptly. "Where the Russian troop train halted, and you gave me tea."

"You see?" said Heiden to Semenov. "Always predictable!" He turned back to Tom. "Is there anything the matter with the clothes I'm wearing?"

"Shabby. Untidy."

"Indeed," said Heiden. "Take a look at yourself."

Dr. Meyer produced a mirror about twelve inches square and handed it to Tom. He saw a gaunt face, vaguely recognisable as his own but covered with a dark beard, and uncombed hair straggling down over the collar of a jacket unbrushed since he was struck down on the stones of the Glockengasse.

"That's Captain Fleming, MC," said Heiden. "You think he looks shabby too? Never mind. You're looking at the man of the future."

"Future?"

"The distant future. There will be no more silk hats and frock-coats in London when the war is over, just as there are no more white and silver uniforms in Saint Petersburg. The middle class will be induced to dress, first like the proletariat, then like tramps, then to wallow in their own filth like swine—"

"That's enough, Comrade Heiden," said Semenov. "Those are your own theories, and I've no time to listen to them. Get on with the subject of the experiment."

"Yes, Comrade Commissar." He spoke to Tom, taking the mirror from his hands.

"Do you know what day of the month it is?"

"The fourth of July."

"What is your name?"

"Tom Sandels."

"And who am I?"

"You're the German officer from Sainte Elodie."

"What did I say to you last time we met?"

"Don't make me tell! Oh, don't make me tell!"

"You must tell."

" 'My men have been . . . disturbed all night by . . . the screaming and moaning of your wounded.' "

Heiden looked at Semenov. "Always the same replies," he said, and Dr. Meyer murmured, "He has a very strong war fixation."

"Who was the German officer?" asked Semenov.

"The man who tried to get him to surrender on the Scarpe. That's one of the keys to his personality, the action at Sainte Elodie, but there are others. You notice he calls himself Sandels, the surname of his Finnish mistress. Obviously a case of female identification—"

"Now you're arguing from Freud."

"The madman in the attic," said Tom unexpectedly, and Heiden laughed. "That's quite a flight of fancy for you, my friend," he said. "Judging from Dr. Freud's preoccupations I should call him the madman in the cellar. But there's one more thing I want to ask you. What sort of man is General Mannerheim?"

"*Sans peur et sans reproche!*"

"That's what Sophie Sandels said, in my presence, when she planted the Butcher General's portrait on her mantelpiece," said Heiden. "Sometimes he varies that answer, and says 'Wear the fir sprig for Tammerfors!' just as he sometimes varies the date reply, and says it's the twenty-eighth of January."

"But the answers always deal with war and patriotism?"

"Except the first answer he gave me, the quotation from *Macbeth*. And that, because he was only under light medication at the time, was the most remarkable of all."

" 'Infirm of purpose—' Yes, I remember, you reported it. You quoted that when you were held at the Finnish command post at Vilppula?"

"When I was *his* prisoner," said Heiden with relish.

"So the response was still war-motivated. Doctor, I cannot see that this man's mind is paralysed. Subjected, possibly, but not destroyed."

"The resistance is certainly very strong."

"Can you increase the dosage?"

The little grey doctor looked unhappy. "I daren't take the risk, Herr Semenov, not at this stage in our knowledge of the drug. Already there are side effects—" he lowered his voice and said something about "*die Lunge*".

"It's not his lungs we're interested in, it's his brain. Which appears to me to be intractable."

"Intellectually, Fleming lives in the time of the Crusades," said Heiden. He took a metal case from his pocket and offered it to Tom. "Cigarette?"

Tom Fleming leant forward eagerly to the match which Heiden struck. With the first inhalation he began to cough, and falling back in the low chair coughed until the tears came to his eyes.

"You see?" said Dr. Meyer.

"That proves nothing. Except that the experiment has not, so far, been a success."

"Allow me to say, Comrade Commissar," said Heiden mockingly, "that I never believed the world state, 'God walking among men', could be arrived at by drugging half the world's population. Unless, of course, they take to using drugs of their own free will."

*   *   *

The darkness came down again, and worse than before. Even the sound of the bells seemed to be muted. The questions were put more often, and by more than one person; they were so confusing that Tom Fleming fell back on an answer he had been taught to give long ago. He gave it monotonously, steadily, even though he found it enraged his questioners beyond their control. Blows were struck, and there were subtler and more humiliating forms of punishment, from which he more than once recovered to find himself on his hands and knees on the bathroom floor, vomiting uncontrollably over the white tiles. But a time came when this ended, and he found himself being roughly dressed again, and taken out of the grey room at last, down in what appeared to be a service lift to a door where a car was waiting. Somebody said *"Schnell! Schnell!"*, and the car was driven furiously away, with all its blinds down, over cobbles and tram-lines, through the dark streets of the city. There was a gag in his mouth and a blindfold over his eyes which so effectively muffled his senses that Tom remembered nothing about being pulled out of the car. When he regained consciousness he was lying among stones and grass under a rainy sky, and heard water lapping not very far away. After a time he was lifted up by men in uniform and the questions began again. Theirs were almost similar questions to Semenov's (Who are you, where do you come from, do you know what day it is?) but they were put in German, and Tom continued to give his prepared answer, which he knew to be correct. Then he found himself back in bed, but this time in a large bright room with a view of trees through the window, and once again a girl was sitting by his side. He began to shudder, sure that he was back in the bell-haunted clinic, but the girl took his hand and spoke to him, and then he knew —

"Good Lord!" said Tom Fleming. "It's Calamity Jane!"

17

NANCY MACPHERSON ENTERED the lobby of the Hotel Baur au Lac at Zürich on a crisp September morning, when the first autumn wind was whipping the lake into cat's tails, and the big gingko tree in the hotel garden was showing its first yellow leaves. She went up to the head concierge with the crossed gilt keys on his dark frock-coat and asked, as crisply as the weather:

"Is Dr. Franzen still with his patient, do you know?"

"Yes, madame. He hopes you will wait for him in the salon."

"Thank you, I will." Nancy in her green tailored suit, her polished brown pumps and fresh white gloves, disappeared into the half-gloom of the great formal salon, and one of the hotel's regular guests, about to ask for mail, leaned over the counter and whispered to the concierge: "Who's the pretty girl?"

"Miss Macpherson, the American heiress."

"Another dollar princess?"

"One of the new style, sir."

Nancy had just time to make a tour of the salon, where huge oil paintings were lit from above and vases of mammoth gladioli were lighted from below, before she was joined by Dr. Franzen, middle-aged and balding, with a grey waxed moustache and rimless pince-nez which he used to point the rhythms of his speech. He greeted Nancy ceremoniously, bowing over her hand, but was merciful enough to say even before she asked him:

"Much, much better today. I find a great improvement in Mr. Fleming since last night."

"Oh, thank heaven for that!"

"In fact—let us sit down, my dear Miss Macpherson—his condition is quite amazing, considering that only four days have passed since he was found."

"I always knew he was as tough as old boots," said Nancy happily.

"I refer to his mental condition," said Dr. Franzen. "You'll find his head quite clear this morning—though you may, of course, be obliged to tell him once again about how he was found at the Zürcherhorn, and when. He knew today's date correctly, by the way—the first of September—what he can't quite compass is the lapse of time since the nineteenth of July."

"Do you wonder?" said Nancy. "I hope that brute Liptauer, or whatever his name is, gets a life sentence."

"Liptitz, or Meyer, or whatever name he is charged by, committed a very serious medical crime, if it's proved that he was guilty of negligence leading to the death of a patient."

"But Tom won't have to testify in court?"

"Not being an obstetrical patient, Mr. Fleming won't have to testify anywhere. He won't even have to appear in court on a charge of vagrancy, thanks to you, Miss Macpherson."

"I'm glad the police saw it my way, eventually. Of course that phone call from our Minister to the chief of police must have helped a lot."

"It did, but your handling of the police surgeon was very effective too. Between ourselves, he's an old enemy of mine; I enjoyed seeing him routed by a young lady."

"Well, I wasn't going to leave Tom in *another* horrible place," said Nancy. "But doctor, if Tom has begun to ask about the past six weeks, is it all right for me to tell him about the war, and anything else he wants to know?"

"Yes. He asked me one or two questions about the war today. Just be sure to confine yourself to telling, and don't ask *him* any questions. He doesn't respond well to interrogation."

"I won't."

Dr. Franzen coughed. "You understand, of course, that Mr. Fleming will have to remain under medical supervision for some weeks, until the after-effects of the drug administered to him can be determined? I can't detect any serious withdrawal symptoms, and my guess is that the dosage had been decreased rather than increased towards the end of last month. But if he was given one of the so-called 'hard' drugs, there remains the serious problem of addiction."

"But don't you *know* what it was they gave him?" said Nancy impatiently.

"Obviously a narcotic. If Dr. Liptitz, alias Meyer, had left a supply in his laboratory, an analysis would have been a simple matter, but as you know everything was destroyed before the police arrived."

"Wasn't Tom able to tell you something—"

"He fortunately remembered the name of Bademayev. At least he remembered it as Bade-Meyer, but we do know a little about Bademayev's preparations—he was one of Rasputin's clique. It's a clue—no more."

"But I thought you were so pleased with Tom this morning!"

"Yes, but—Miss Macpherson, perhaps you can tell me this: was Mr. Fleming ever in a gas attack while he was in the army?"

"Twice. Once at Second Ypres, before they had gas masks, and again at Vimy Ridge, but he said it wasn't very serious, either time."

"He wasn't hospitalised?"

"Only in the field hospital."

"H'm." Dr. Franzen polished his pince-nez with a large white handkerchief. "I'm not entirely satisfied with the condition of his lungs. That persistent cough may be the result of the early gas attacks, aggravated by the drug, or else of several hours' exposure to wind and rain last week. It's not serious at this stage, but if the season were right I should like to send him to the mountains for a couple of months."

"I think he's anxious to get out of Switzerland."

"Quite understandable. Then the French Riviera, perhaps? The September weather is very clement there."

"I told him nearly a year ago he should go home to Canada."

"I don't think he's quite up to the journey yet. Now, my dear young lady, don't worry too much about it. In all other respects he's making wonderful progress."

"May I go up to his apartment now?"

"Certainly. He's out of bed and dressed today. Oh, and, Miss Macpherson—you're determined to go on to Bern tomorrow?"

"It's the only way to set his mind at rest." Nancy shook hands with the doctor and walked with him to the front door. Her shoulders were drooping as she waited for the lift, but she was smiling brightly when Tom himself opened the door of his sitting room.

"Nancy, darling!"

The door was shut, he had his back against it, and she was in his arms, close held, with her face lifted for his kisses and pure delight rising in her heart. It was characteristic of Nancy that she quickly slipped away from him and said,

"Let's not get mushy."

"Oh, Nancy, you're so sweet and you're so prickly, and its so grand to be with you again!"

It was years since Tom had spoken to her so tenderly, and by his tenderness she was able to measure how hard the time had been as Heiden's prisoner. But she had taken a vow not to be "mushy", and Nancy said briskly, "What happened to your nurse?"

"Good Lord, Nancy, you don't think I need a nurse now? She's gone for good, and this afternoon you and I are going to sit in the garden. Lunch up here, and a stroll in the garden, how's that for a start?"

"Sounds wonderful." She let him lead her to the big window bay, where there was a circular, cushioned seat, and a table for meals now covered with papers and magazines. Through the boughs of the yellowing gingko the view ran over the private lawns and gardens, across a busy highway to the lake.

Nancy slipped out of her green jacket and laid it with her little hat on the windowsill. Tom tightened his hold on her waist.

"You've gotten thin, Nancy, d'you know that?"

"No wonder, running all round Europe trying to take care of you."

He kissed her averted cheek. "You were terrific."

"I saw Frau Maria this morning, Tom. You remember the lady at the Veltliner Keller? She sent you her best wishes. And honestly I could never have got you out of that police infirmary if it hadn't been for her."

Tom chuckled. He had forgotten about the police infirmary, where he knew he had been taken after he was found in the grounds of the Zürcherhorn, but now he remembered the first thing Nancy said when the police surgeon brought her into the ward. He also remembered Sophie's sweet compassion when he told her the story of Sainte Elodie, and the lovely maternal gesture with which she drew his head to her breast. "My love, my poor love!" she had said in Helsingfors. Nancy Macpherson in Zürich was a good deal less sympathetic. "Hello, Wild Bill, the Redskins sure scalped you this time!" was her friendly greeting. And yet she had more than responded to his letter, she had come all the way from Paris to help him when he needed help—

"You were very smart," he said, "to go to the Veltliner Keller first, and get Frau Maria to go to the police with you, and of course she helped you, speaking German, but if you hadn't been a sport and come to Zürich, nobody would have known where I was, or who."

"The police knew your name all right."

"How could they, dear? Those swine took everything, my wallet and my passport too; they even took the tailor's label and the laundry marks out of my clothes."

"But the police did know who you were, Tommy, because you kept telling them."

"*I* told them? How?"

And now for the first time he saw Nancy's lips quiver, and tears come into her eyes. "You told them over and over," she said shakily. "Your name, rank and serial number. Oh Tommy, your name, rank and serial number, over and over again!" She turned and buried her head on Tom Fleming's shoulder.

"What, in the Vancouver Seaforths?" he said, and by the sound of his voice she knew he was smiling. "Say, that wasn't bad, eh? . . . I remember repeating that, back there; it used to make Semenov mad."

He felt Nancy's body shaken with sobs. "Now who's getting mushy?" he enquired. "Come on, Calamity, that's not like you! It's not as bad as all that, you know!"

She sat up at once and blew her nose. "Sorry to be a fool," she said. "It's just—you had nearly six weeks of it, in that beastly room I made the police show me yesterday. If only I could have got here right away—"

"Didn't you?" he said, puzzled.

"I didn't get your letter for a long time. Remember our corps went forward after Soissons was liberated, and we opened a canteen there. A *mobile* canteen," she corrected herself, "we went as near the front line as we were allowed. Soissons is just a heap of rubble, there wasn't any place we could requisition there."

"You're a veteran now, Nancy, I keep forgetting."

"A veteran canteen hand, that's all."

"I've been looking at the magazines trying to catch up. We're winning the war, aren't we, Nancy."

"Sure we're winning now."

"But what the hell's been going on in Russia?"

"Oh Tommy, terrible things. Did you know about the Czar and his family?"

"What about them?"

"It must have been just about the time you got to Zürich. Of course the Bolsheviks held up the news as long as they could. But the truth came out as soon as the Czech Legion took Ekaterinburg, the town where the Imperial family was being held prisoner."

"Yes, I know about that, they were taken there from Tobolsk."

"They were at Ekaterinburg for—oh! over two months, I should think. And then one night the Bolsheviks took them down to the cellar of the house they were held in, and shot them all."

"What, *all* of them? The young Grand Duchesses, and that poor little boy?"

"All. Their bodies were thrown down a mine shaft and . . . destroyed."

"Where's it all going to end, Nancy?"

"In Russia? Or just the horrors of the world?"

"In Russia, for a start."

"Tommy," she said seriously, "you know I was always opposed to Czarism. I'm not a pinko now, as you used to call me, but I still think the Romanovs were bad rulers, and the Czar Nicholas and his wife dug their own graves. But when you think of their children—*they* were absolutely innocent—"

"I know."

"And Lenin was nearly murdered too."

"*What!*"

"A girl called Dora Kaplan fired two shots at him one night in the middle of August, when he was leaving some factory after giving an address. And she very nearly got him; they thought at first he was going to die—"

"But no such luck," said Tom. "Was she a White girl?"

"I think she belonged to some Socialist opposition party. Doesn't matter, it came to the same thing in the end, more arrests, more executions, the civil war spreading all through the country . . ."

"There really is a civil war in Russia now?"

Nancy hesitated. There was more to tell him, far more, but could he bear to hear it? She said cautiously, "The British landed a small force at Archangel about a month ago, in support of the Whites. I don't believe they've been very effective. But the Russians took reprisals in Petrograd. They invaded the British Embassy and killed some of the staff who'd stayed on . . ."

"God damn it," said Tom, "are we at war with *Russia* now?"

"Britain's in a state of war with Russia, whatever that may mean."

"It beats everything," said Tom. "The British Embassy invaded, and the Czar's family murdered, but Lenin recovers from his wounds, and of course the Heidens of this world go free . . ."

"If it weren't for all the worry and fuss for you," said Nancy, "I'd like to see him captured and brought back here to stand his trial for what he did to you. Have the police been to see you again?"

"Two men from their special branch were here this morning. I told them I wasn't going to press charges, and they really seemed to be relieved. I can't identify the place, except by the sound of bells—you know I was right there in Saint Peter's Square all the time? Anyway what's the point? Semenov and Heiden are over the hills and far away, and Meyer, I mean Liptitz, has been charged with criminal abortion—"

"But only because one girl of what they call a good family died in his abortion mill. Tommy, I don't want you to have to stay on here and get mixed up in a court case, but when I think you were kidnapped, and used as a guineapig for some horrible drug, and then thrown out of a car and left for dead, I honestly do get mad at the Swiss! They're so scared of any international scandal! They wouldn't even allow me to check Heiden's passport number in the Zürich records . . ."

"But you're going to Bern tomorrow to do that, aren't you?" said Tom anxiously.

"I'm going to Bern, and I'm going to their State Department, or whatever they call it here, but—look, Tom, let's be realistic. Suppose they won't talk to me? Suppose I draw a blank in Bern? What if Boris Heiden just disappeared into thin air, the night he had to get out of Zürich in a hurry? Could you accept it that you've really come to the end of the trail?"

I'm asking him questions, she thought in panic, the very thing Dr. Franzen told me not to do. But the pale, thin face she watched so closely showed no sign of distress. Tom Fleming said calmly, "No, I couldn't. The trail will end when either Heiden or myself is dead."

He felt the indrawn breath that shook her body.

"Listen, Nancy. I've thought a lot about Heiden, since I've been able to think straight again. I'm not smart, like him; I never even had a college education. But I've been trying to figure out what makes a guy like Heiden tick. You see, I know a lot more about him than I did before. I used to call him a bastard, and now I know he *is* a bastard—it's not supposed to make a difference, but it does. He started out in life with a grudge against society. And of course he inherited a lot of brains. From his grandfather the Polish rabbi, and his father the Baltic baron, one of the bright boys of the Czar Alexander's court. And maybe a streak of madness from his crazy mother."

"Was she crazy? You never told me that!"

"Give me time, and I'll be able to write a book about the Heiden family. Then brother Igor put in his two cents' worth. It can't be nice to have a brother arrested for attempted murder, and hanged in the public square. No wonder Mom and Boris wanted to get out of Russia. But what it all adds up to is that Boris has no family to accept him, and no roots."

"Have we? Roots, I mean?"

"Sure we have. What about Grandpa Fleming from Aberdeen, mining for gold at Cariboo, and Grandpa Macpherson, going all the way from Stranraer to Seattle with nothing but a bag of carpenter's tools to his name? They put our roots down for us—"

"Why did you never go to Aberdeen when you had a London leave?"

"Too far away."

"That's why I never went to Galloway."

"Maybe we should go together. But Heiden's rootless. He's not a Communist because he sympathises with the workers. He as good as told me he despises them. He wants power for Boris Heiden, power over minds, to make up for all he hasn't got, and never will have; and—I'm telling this so badly—it's young people's minds he'll go for first. Yes, what is it?"

The floor waiter came in with a little silver tray in his hand. "Excuse me, sir," he said, "you told me to bring the menu card at half past twelve."

231

"All right, just leave it here. But bring—sherry, Nancy? bring a glass of sherry for the lady, and a large Scotch with soda on the side."

"Very good, sir." The door closed.

"Scotch prescribed by Dr. Franzen?"

"Scotch not referred to Dr. Franzen. Come on now, Nan, I rate a drink—"

"I only hope it gives you an appetite. You've *got* to get some weight back on, you know."

"What about getting my moustache back on? Some excitable barber took it off along with my beard, when I didn't know if I was coming or going—"

"You don't need it any more." With a passion which surprised him Nancy Macpherson laid her cheek against Tom's scarred cheek, kissing the mouth where the distortion hardly showed, taking his eager kisses in return, and only drawing away when the tactless waiter came, far too promptly, with the drinks.

"May I go into your bathroom and wash my hands for lunch?" she said, when they had chosen from the menu.

"Why so formal? Of course you can. And that reminds me, you fixed me up with a very grand suite here! So I've got to get a cable off after lunch, to Cox's in London. You do know I haven't got a penny to my name in Switzerland?"

"They cleaned you out of everything, didn't they?"

"Cheque book and all. But my account's quite healthy, and Grandma Fleming's money comes in every quarter; Cox's can get a draft to me this afternoon."

"Oh," said Nancy casually, "then you can settle with my father. I got him to open an account for you at the Crédit Suisse on Monday, you only have to walk up the Bahnhofstrasse and write a cheque."

"You mean he cabled money to a new account here? How much?"

"Two thousand dollars."

"That ought to buy us another drink."

*   *   *

The journey from Zürich to Bern by express train took only an hour and a half, and Nancy had promised to dine with Tom on the evening of the day planned for her visit to the Swiss federal

232

capital. But as early as two o'clock Tom received her telegram saying "Slight delay here back tomorrow" and feeling unwarrantably depressed he decided to complete his new banking arrangements at the Crédit Suisse. It was the first time he had left the protection of the Baur au Lac, and although he walked up the quiet back street called the Talstrasse the crowd and the grinding of the trams on the Paradeplatz made his head ache. He remembered taking a tramcar from that square to the funicular railway on his way to the Villa Heiden. The villa was empty now, for the Swiss police had gone there at Nancy's insistence, and had found a shuttered house, and yet Tom Fleming looked over his shoulder more than once as he turned back from the Paradeplatz to the Crédit Suisse. He had lost his bearings completely in the dignified and prosperous city of Zürich, which hid so many ugly secrets. The sooner he was out of it the better.

With money in his new pocketbook, bought immediately at one of the handsome leather shops of the Bahnhofstrasse, he felt confident enough to shrug at Dr. Franzen's proposal, on his evening visit, to bring a consultant physician with him the next day. Yes, he felt a bit tired, he admitted, though he had only walked round one city block, and he did seem to have a summer cold, and a cough that was stubborn, but he would go to bed early and take it easy in the morning. He did take it easy, with breakfast in bed and all the new magazines: it was the *Illustrated London News* which shocked him into getting up and dressing quickly.

It carried the full-page drawing ("By our own Artist") of a man in naval uniform, standing on an ornate staircase, and emptying his revolver into the swarming crowd below. As a picture it owed something to the famous reconstruction of General Gordon in his last moments at Khartoum: the stair, the pose of the figure were the same, and the Cheka men were only the modern substitutes for Gordon's Arab murderers. But the artist, clearly working from a photograph, had drawn the face of the principal figure in great detail. "The gallant naval officer shot and trampled to death while defending the British Embassy against the Bolsheviks", the caption ran. The officer's name meant nothing to Tom. He had known the dead man as Mr. White, the British agent of the Byronic good looks who, in the forests of Imatra, had told him laconically that somebody had to stay in Petrograd to mind the shop. So

White had minded it, right up to the end, and that was another good man gone, while Heiden and his kind went free.

Tom's cough was rather more troublesome than the day before. But he went out after lunch to a shop he had noticed near the Crédit Suisse with its windows full of knives and firearms. There, after some deliberation, he bought a Browning .25 automatic pistol, the model brought out in 1910 by the Belgian Fabrique Nationale at Liège and never bettered since. The barrel was rather short for his liking, but the balance was beautiful, and the holster fitted very neatly into his armpit. Armed, he felt complete again, and wondered what Heiden and his friend Freud would have to say to that. He went confidently back to the hotel and waited for the doctors' visit.

*   *   *

The telephone rang in his sitting room just after seven.

"Tom? Nancy."

"Nancy! I was beginning to think you'd never get here!"

"I'm sorry it took so long, but I got what I went for. How do you feel tonight?"

"Pretty well, but what did they—"

"Will you meet me downstairs in your own lobby in about half an hour?"

"Anything you say."

Nancy laid down the handset. She knew he had a string of questions ready, and she had more answers than he expected: it was going to be the night of the big showdown, and even after two hours in the train she still needed time to collect her thoughts. One thing was gained: they were to meet downstairs, in a public place, "and we'll stay there," she said to herself determinedly. "Up in his apartment I'll let him kiss me, I can't help it, I want it; but I'm not Sophie Sandels, I'm not going to stay all night."

She rang for the chambermaid. Nancy had taken a room, for propriety's sake, in the other Baur, the Baur en Ville: the noise of the Paradeplatz was disturbing, but the service was first-class. A valet had already taken away her green suit, crumpled from the train, to be sponged and pressed. The woman brought it back, ran a bath, and took away garments to be laundered. She promised they would be ready for packing in the morning. Nancy had time to sit down and smoke a cigarette.

She was more tired than she would ever have admitted. The Bern experience had been testing to a girl of twenty-three, for the first time in her life in conflict with established authority, real power, instead of a Seattle policeman or a canteen supervisor. And though she had won, it was because she was James J. Macpherson's daughter—not because she was Nancy. Nancy didn't count.

She walked the short distance to the Baur au Lac. There were signs that a private party was beginning, probably a dinner dance, for motor cars were moving into the wide courtyard of the lakeside hotel and setting pretty women and their escorts down at the porte-cochère. Tom was sitting in the outer lobby, half hidden by the crowd but with his eyes fixed on the door; he jumped up as soon as he saw Nancy and came to her eagerly.

"Are you exhausted?"

"Not a bit. But the slow train was so crowded—"

"Lot of people here tonight, too. Sure you want to stay downstairs?"

"Let's have a drink first, I'm so thirsty," she said diplomatically, and Tom nodded. "I found a little room, in back," he said, "an old chap comes round with a drinks trolley. Shall we try that?"

It was exactly what Nancy wanted, private enough for their talk, but open on one side to a corridor down which the people in evening dress were passing to their party. From a room not far away came the first strains of a string orchestra. I hope they don't play "First Love" tonight, thought Nancy, or I'll never be able to say it all. "Here comes your drinks on wheels," she smiled, and asked for a glass of white wine and soda, half of which she drank too fast.

"Hey, you *were* thirsty," said Tom Fleming. "Was it awful in Bern?"

"It was worse than I expected. But your new papers are in order, Tommy, you can call at the consulate and pick them up tomorrow."

"Say, that's marvellous! When that vice-consul came to see me last Tuesday he said it would take at least a month."

"Red tape," she said indifferently. "The British in Bern are a lot of stuffed shirts, just like the Paris lot—which is one reason why I didn't do what you asked in your letter, and go straight to the Paris Embassy. But at least they're always polite, which is more than can be said for the Swiss."

"Tried to give you the brush-off, did they?"

"They not only tried, they did. I didn't even get to first base at the ministry. Some pompous little man showed me straight to the door, saying an American citizen (and you could see he meant a *female* American citizen) had no right to enquire into the status or whereabouts of any law-abiding Swiss national."

"Law-abiding, I like that!"

"Well, you did refuse to press charges, Tommy. I'm not saying you weren't right . . . So then I went to our place, and asked to see the American Minister. I thought I mightn't be too popular there either, after all that telephoning I made them do to the Zürich police, and sure enough I was told the Minister himself would be tied up all day. Oh, there were some striped-pants boys who fussed around repeating 'Can I help you?' but I didn't waste time on them. I went right out, checked in at the nearest hotel, and sent a cable to my father."

"You got James J. in on this?"

"I had to. It cost the earth, that cable, but it was worth it. I told him the whole story, and asked him to fix it for me with Washington, DC."

"*Not* with the White House?"

"I knew Dad would take it up to Presidential level if he had to. But his great friend in Mr. Wilson's cabinet is Newton D. Baker, the Secretary of War. So he got on the telephone to Washington right away, and first thing this morning there was a cable from Mr. Baker at the Bern Ministry that made the striped-pants set get on the job."

"Nancy, you're wonderful." He meant it, too; it was her determination that was wonderful, her inheritance of the grit which had taken a Scotsman with his carpenter's tools on his shoulder from the old port of Stranraer to the bouncing new port on the shores of Puget Sound. "You'd have made a great pioneer," he said.

"Thank you. Well, after that it all worked like a charm. I saw the Minister, and he sent one of the Secretaries, a career diplomat, back to the Swiss place with me after one or two phone calls cleared the air. Oh yes, and they called Zürich too. It was easier than I expected to get a check on Heiden."

"Nancy, how—"

"He applied for an exit permit for the Baroness Heiden on the twenty-fifth of August."

"You mean he left the country with his *mother*?"

"He left the country with his wife."

"*Married?*"

"The records show that Boris Aleksandrovich Heiden and Elisabet Lovisa Sandels were married here, in the City Hall in Zürich, on that same day, the twenty-fifth." Nancy added, "While you were still repeating your name, rank and serial number to Semenov."

He paid no attention to the sarcasm. "So Lisa got what she wanted after all!" said Tom. "I wonder how she talked him into it."

"He probably did it to prevent her giving evidence against him if the Meyer thing blew up."

"But what about the exit permit?"

"The man in the record office told Bern that the Baroness Heiden" (there was no mistaking the scorn in Nancy's voice as she repeated the title) "had only a one-way entry visa into Switzerland, stamped on some emergency document issued by the Red government in Helsingfors—not worth the paper it's written on now, of course."

"Where did they turn their exit papers in, Nancy?"

"They crossed into Italy at Chiasso."

"But was it possible to trace them after that?"

"Oh, Tom!"

"Don't hold out on me!"

"It didn't seem likely they would stay in Italy. So we checked with two port authorities, Brindisi and Genoa."

"Why Brindisi?"

"For the Near East—and the Black Sea. But they weren't heading for Russia. They sailed from Genoa on the twenty-ninth of August, on an Italian liner bound for Panama." Nancy sipped her wine and soda. "And that's all, Tom. That was absolutely all I could find out."

"And nobody on earth could have done it but you, Nan." He sat lost in thought, and Nancy watched the corridor, where the party guests were still assembling. Her story had not taken very long to tell.

"You make me feel an awful fool."

It was exactly what she had expected to hear Tom Fleming say, and yet the words gave Nancy pain. She said, "Does the news of Lisa's marriage make any difference to how you feel?"

"How *I* feel?"

"You told me in Paris that you felt responsible for her in some weird way or other. Because of her poor sister's dying words. But now it looks as if Lisa got what she wanted, she's the Baroness Heiden, for better or for worse, and where does that leave you?"

Tom said, "If they had married before I went to Paris, and I had known about the marriage, it might, it just might, have made a difference to me. Now it makes none. It's between Heiden and me; it always was. Only next time I won't behave like the bumbling fool I was six weeks ago."

"You're sure there'll be a next time? Where?"

"Don't know yet."

"Colon, Panama, is a pretty wide address. He's got a whole hemisphere to choose from there."

"By the time I'm ready to start it may be narrowed down."

"You mean you're not leaving tomorrow morning at first light?" she said drily.

"I've got to shake this cough first, before I make new plans. The doctors want me to go to the French Riviera for a bit."

"Why not?" said Nancy. "You can go anywhere you want after tomorrow, when you get your papers at the consulate. I'm glad to have got it all fixed up for you, before I go."

"*Go!*" said Tom. "Where the devil do you think *you're* going?"

"Back to Paris, of course." Nancy tried to smile. "I did myself a favour at the Ministry this morning, too. It took me three days to get here by Lyon and Thonon, but the Minister gave me a diplomatic pass for one journey, straight through via Basel. I've got a seat in the morning train tomorrow."

"But you *can't* go yet!"

"Can't I?" said Nancy. "What about the US Canteen Corps?"

"Well, what about it? You told me you got leave to come to Switzerland."

"I should have told you," said Nancy, relenting, "it was terminal leave. My contract with the corps was up on the thirty-first of August. They let me go a few days earlier, to come to you."

"I never knew you had a contract! I thought you enlisted, I mean enrolled, for the duration."

"I hoped it would be for the duration, didn't we all!" She struck her little clenched right fist into the palm of her left hand. "It kills me to have to quit right now, with the war so nearly won. But that was the bargain I made with Dad, when he gave his consent to my joining the corps at all, and he means to hold me to it. He's booked passage for me on a Swedish boat, the *Queen Christina*, calling at Le Havre. And as our dear Miss Peabody reminded me, nobody's missed. There are twenty American girls in Paris ready to leap at the chance to take my place at the Soissons canteen."

"You didn't tell me about this in London, about the contract, I mean."

"You didn't show much interest in my job, except to kid me about the uniform."

"Nancy, I'm sorry. Listen! Please don't go."

"But I must go, Tommy, Dad wants me at home. I know you're not interested in the North-west, but Dad's having trouble all up and down the Pacific coast, even as far south as Callao. He's lonely in that big house with only Aunt Edith to talk to— and *she* doesn't talk about much except the price of food in the Public Market—"

Tom Fleming got out of his chair and moved over to the little sofa where Nancy was sitting. He put his arms round her, and said, "Nancy, don't go away."

"People can see us, Tom."

"So what? Don't leave me, darling. Cancel that sailing, cable your Dad again and say you're scared of submarines. And come to the South of France with me."

He had her pinned against the end of the sofa, there was no way of escape. But Nancy was a hundred miles from Tom in spirit when she asked.

"As what? Your mistress or your nurse?"

"As my wife."

"Oh, no!" And this time she did free herself, as his arms relaxed, and stood up pulling down her jacket and straightening her skirt. "I won't be proposed to out of gratitude, or on the rebound from Sophie Sandels!"

"Nancy!" Tom got up too, furious, but trying to keep his voice low: "It's not out of gratitude, my dear."

"Oh yes, it is. You think I've done a great job, well, I know I have. Calamity Jane rides again! I fixed the police, and the hotel, and the bank, and the passport, *and* found out about Mr. Bloody Heiden. But what you really mean is what you just said, Tom: I've made you feel an awful fool. And by and by you'll think of me as just Little Miss Fix-it, who came after you to Switzerland, and got herself a proposal, after all those years!—No, don't interrupt," she said, "Let me say my say, and then I'm going. In Paris I begged you not to follow Boris Heiden, and you wouldn't even listen to me. I don't beg you now. Follow him to Panama or any damned place you please, for all I care. Get him out of your system in any way you like. But next time you ask me to marry you, Tom Fleming, it won't be because I've come panting along, tough little Nancy, game to the last, to get you out of whatever mess you've got yourself into . . . It'll be because you've come after *me*."

18

WITHIN A FEW WEEKS of his rejection by Nancy Mac-pherson, Tom Fleming was able to rationalise that trying scene in the little room at the Baur au Lac. He convinced himself that the last of the Bademayev drug was still in his bloodstream at that time, slowing up his reactions and making him seem, by contrast with Nancy's quicksilver energy, much duller and stupider than he need have been. He doggedly followed the diet and hours of sleep prescribed by Dr. Franzen and super-vised by his French confrère, and as his cough cleared up he began to put on some of his lost weight. He sent to Hachettes in Nice for books and began a course of study in the genesis of revolution. In his deckchair in the Riviera sunshine Tom, whose preferred authors were Stephen Leacock and John Buchan, grappled manfully with translations of Herzen, Marx, Plekhanov and Kropotkin in an effort to understand the mind of Boris Heiden.

He had been sent to Cannes, and this turned out to be the best therapy of all. Cannes was a leave centre for Allied officers, and among them Tom met old friends from the Canadian Expedition-ary Force and new friends ready to celebrate the victories which were bringing the Great War to an end. There were charming little French girls, too, willing for a price to help anybody forget any-thing, and in their arms, in the darkened rooms of the back streets behind the Croisette, Tom forgot many of the experiences which had preyed on his mind for so long. He began to sleep without dreaming. He wrote to his mother and asked her to get his room ready and be prepared to kill the fatted calf for the prodigal, because he was beginning what looked like the long process of booking a passage to New York.

In mid-September the Americans had won a great battle at St. Mihiel with the new Tank Corps in action, pinching out an entire German salient and taking fifteen thousand German prisoners. Soon after, an even greater battle opened with a gigantic pincer movement, the British crossing the Hindenburg Line towards Cambrai and Lille, the Americans advancing to the Meuse through the Argonne. General Foch, the supreme commander, threw nearly a million and a quarter men into this attack, which succeeded in breaking the iron nerve of Ludendorff. Behind the lines, across the frontier, the German people were sick of war, and Prince Max of Baden, the new German Chancellor, spoke for his people and for the Austrians in appealing to President Wilson for an armistice. But the Americans smashed on through the Argonne forests towards Sedan, the symbolic scene of the French surrender in 1870, and the British recaptured one by one the towns which for years had been the scene of bitter fighting. St. Quentin, Lens, Armentières; Roubaix, Lille, Valenciennes—the great historic names of French Flanders—were the names of victory at last.

In the early evening of November 10, Tom Fleming arrived in Scotland, by the day train from London to the city of Aberdeen. It had been a long, crowded and hungry journey, with nothing to eat but railway tea and sandwiches sold from trolleys at the various halts, and Tom was delighted to be taken in charge by a porter running alongside the London train as it came up to the buffers, with a cheerful shout of "Onybody here for the Palace Hotel? Onybody for the Palace?" There was the further sophistication of an elevator which took Tom, with two other first-class passengers, straight from the dark platform to the warmth of the Palace, which until then he had thought of as just one more hotel in his long wanderings, but which through some trick of accent and phrasing, some downright approach in the speakers, reminded him of his Canadian home.

"No chance of a sitting room?" he asked the greyhaired woman at the reception desk.

"I'm sorry, sir, it's taken; some foreign body, a general, cam' in and took the suite not long ago. But you can have a nice fire in your bedroom if you like."

"Yes, I would like that." The service was good, the fan of sooty paper in his bedroom grate was whisked away before Tom had time to unlock his suitcase, and a porter arrived with a shovel full of hot coals to supplement the fire already set. There was a good blaze in the chimney by the time he washed his hands and went down to have a drink.

He found a small news-stand beside the door of the lounge,

where half a dozen young officers in the Gordon tartan, the new intake, sat rather self-consciously in a room full of elderly civilians. Tom felt like patting them on the shoulder, and saying "You're all right, kids, it's over." He contented himself with giving them a friendly grin as he went to buy the town's two evening papers. These seemed to concentrate on local crime, for one had headlined its lead story "Theft of a Washing-tub at Inverurie", while the other announced "Peterhead Man found Guilty of Reset." Established in a saddlebag chair, waiting for his drink, he found a line in the stop press about the Kaiser's flight to Holland. That was it, then, the German Empire had crumbled about that man's ears, and the armistice would certainly be proclaimed tomorrow. It had been a foregone conclusion for a week, ever since the German Fleet mutinied at Kiel, and every German city from Hamburg to Munich rose in a sick revolt against the war, but now it was true: the war was over.

"What does this word 'reset' mean?" Tom asked the pontifical head waiter who put his Scotch before him.

"Receiving stolen goods, sir."

"Thanks very much." I must remember every word of this to tell Dad, thought Tom; but before it gets much later I ought to call up Cousin John.

He carried his drink into a telephone box at the back of the lounge and apologetically asked the hotel operator if she could call Mr. John Endicott at an address on Queen's Road.

"I'm sorry I don't know the number."

"Isn't there not a directory on the shelf, sir?"

"I'm sorry, I can't see one."

"They'll steal anything these days. Hold the line, please."

As the buzzing sounded Tom hummed a little tune. After four years he was going to speak to a kinsman, in the city from which his ancestors had sprung. In a jumble of thoughts, absurdly excited, he heard a woman's voice saying "Hallo? Hallo?"

"May I speak to Mr. Endicott, please?"

"Who'll I say wants him?"

"Mr. Fleming."

"I'll tell him." Sounds of receding feet, surely a servant's, and another female voice, querulous, in the background; then a man's tread.

"Is that Mr. Tom Fleming? John Endicott speaking."

243

"Good evening." He wanted to add, "Cousin John," but not to that uncompromising voice. "How are you?" he said, "I hope you got my letter."

"Oh aye, I got your *letter*," said the voice grudgingly, as if Tom's cables, telegrams and parcels were all missing in the mail. "We were quite interested to hear you were planning to pay Aberdeen a visit. Taking a look at the cradle of the race, eh?"

"That was the idea. Just a quick trip to the north before I go back to Canada. I've heard so much—"

"When are you sailing?"

"On the fourteenth, from the Clyde."

"Oh then," said the voice, much more cheerfully, "you'll not be spending much time in Aberdeen. You're at the Palace?"

"I'm speaking from the Palace now."

"You'll be quite comfortable there. Well now, Mr. Fleming, I'm quite disappointed that I can't ask you to come along and see us this evening. The fact is, we're at sixes and sevens in this house tonight, Mrs. Endicott appears to be coming down with the influenza, and we're both in terror that our girlie will be smit."

"I see," said Tom, baffled by the idiom, "there's a lot of 'flu going about just now."

"It's a perfect epidemic, the town's full of it, I've just been telephoning for the doctor. But look now, you and I must meet and have a chat. Would you care to lunch with me down town tomorrow?"

"Yes, I'd like that. Here at the Palace, do you mean?"

"Better make it the Fish Market restaurant. If their armistice is announced tomorrow it'll be a short day on Market Street, and I'll need to make the most of my morning. Would you pick me up at my office about half past twelve? You'll find the address in the telephone directory."

"They've reset the telephone directory," said Tom, and choked back a laugh. That absurd word had tickled his sense of humour, or maybe it was Mr. Endicott's delightful idea of hospitality.

"They've what?"

"Never mind," said Tom, "I'll find it. And I hope Mrs. Endicott will feel much better in the morning. Good night to you."

"Good night."

Tom hung up the receiver, feeling blank. It wasn't the sort of

244

welcome they gave to family in Canada! But if there was sickness in the house . . . He shrugged, and followed his nose in the direction of the dining room. Whatever the Fish Market restaurant might offer, there was an immediate promise of roast pheasant and bread sauce. And Brussels sprouts.

*   *   *

On November 11, 1918, local crime took second place to the war news in the Aberdeen morning papers. General Foch had received the German armistice commission in a railway carriage in the forest of Compiègne, and the Germans were obliged to accept an armistice on the very harsh terms put before them. All they had won in four years was now lost: territories, submarines, warships, locomotives, railway trucks, prestige and power. Alsace-Lorraine would be French again after nearly fifty years, long-suffering Belgium would see the departure of the grey invaders. Only the dead stayed dead.

Tom Fleming found a flower shop opposite the Palace, and sent chrysanthemums to Mrs. Endicott. He disliked the flowers, with their suggestion of graveyards, but there was nothing else to be had at the florist's on this steel-grey November day. The granite city was a study in silver point, pierced by the narrow Baltic spires he had come to know in Helsingfors, and the handsome main thoroughfare, he saw with a pang, was called Union Street. Battlemented towers at either end, and domestic architecture drawn with a sure hand, but no Senate Square, no Empire façades by Engel . . . also no House of the Workers, no Red mob raging over the Long Bridge to shoot the bourgeois down. Tom walked west. The doubledecker tramcars passed in a steady stream. They had coloured lanterns fore and aft, which must be pretty when they were lighted after dark. Queen's Cross, Mannofield, Bridge of Dee, and then one going to Rubislaw, which made Tom stare and smile.

He walked on to a road fork, and boarded the next Rubislaw tram that came along. "Does this car go to Rubislaw Quarry?" He wanted to say "My home in Vancouver is called Rubislaw House," but he'd been long enough in Britain to know that wouldn't do. As it was the conductor snarled, "Aye, it gings tae th' Quarry, or near eneuch. And you pit oot that cigarette, mister, or ging up the stair. Nae smokin' doon here, A'm tellin ye!"

"Beg your pardon!" said Tom politely, and climbed to the upper deck. It was the right place for the view, and the houses grew handsomer as the tram went west, past another couple of those evocative spires, and then into Queen's Road, where John Endicott lived. Tom had time for a good look at the house, which was beside a tram stop: it was built of the local granite, with a circular carriage sweep leading up to the porticoed front door, and a monkey-puzzle tree on a small lawn in the middle. There were four bay windows, two up and two down, with dormer windows on the top storey, and a side wing which might have contained a morning room or library. "He's got plenty of space," said Tom to himself, "he could easily have asked me to come along for a chat without disturbing his wife." And he thought of the lavish Canadian hospitality, and the kind of table his mother would have set to welcome any relative, no matter how distant, who came to Vancouver from what they called the old country.

Now he was in the old country, but Tom felt strange and lonely as, following the conductor's grudging directions, he walked away towards the Rubislaw Quarry. There was more than one quarry now, the man said, and those still in operation were hedged round with barbed wire and ferocious warnings about trespassing, but at the end of a rough path overgrown with bramble bushes Tom at last came on a great granite pit, the silver shale sparkling through weeds and mosses, which might have been the very one where his grandfather worked as a young man. Sandy Fleming, whose wandering foot took him from the shores of the North Sea to the Pacific! And I don't know a damned thing about him, thought his grandson, staring down into the silent pit. If Grandpa Sandy had been half as good a story-teller as Granny Bell, I might have known today what sent him away from here to London, and then to Fort Garry and Cariboo. But she only talked about the Tarras family, and Brand Endicott.

He stood for a long time by the abandoned quarry, hearing faintly the voices of the quarrymen from another working, while a late bird sang a November song. This was the cradle of the race, all right. Somewhere on his journey across the prairies Sandy had begotten Arthur, and in a pleasant villa in a new city Arthur had begotten Tom, and Tom—? Had he proved himself in four years of fighting half as good a man as his grandfather?

He walked thoughtfully back to the tramcar terminus. A

246

driver and conductor, waiting to start the run back to the Castle-gate, told him what he knew already, that the cessation of hostilities was to take effect at eleven o'clock. They all synchro-nised their watches and stood talking about the war. Both the Scotsmen had been with the Gordons in the retreat from Mons. The lads, they said, would be fine pleased the day, to be bye wi't. We bate him, though, yon Kaiser. Aye.

The maroons went off just as the tram stopped at Queen's Cross, where the hands of a church clock were standing at eleven. There was the distant sound of bells tolling, and sirens from the harbour, and then a total silence. Nobody moved inside the tram. When it moved on past the grounds of what appeared to be a military hospital Tom saw a group of men standing inside the railings, dressed in the bright blue suits and red ties of the wounded which he had once worn himself, and some of them had their medals up for the occasion. Very solemn, the Jocks, just as he had known them in Flanders! Further along, on the opposite side of the street, a crocodile of schoolgirls in navy overcoats and hats were walking quietly into town, he supposed on their way to a thanksgiving service. There was no cheering, no dancing in the streets such as Tom had seen in Paris on the Fourth of July. Just the grave acceptance of the fact of peace, as there had long been the grim acceptance of the fact of war.

Perhaps it was the name of Union Street which triggered off his memories of Helsingfors. Certainly Tom Fleming, walking down past his hotel to the Aberdeen harbour, had a sense that he was back in Finland, in a less classically perfect Helsingfors, with the office buildings on Market Street taking the place of the houses on the South Quay where he had often gone with Nikko Hirn, and the red-brick buildings of the Aberdeen Fish Market looking like a larger version of the covered market in the Finnish capital. The grey wintry skies were the same, with the gulls wheeling above the greasy harbour waters, and the smells were the same, of tarry ropes and ship's chandlers' stores. And something in the faces was the same, something square and durable, with here and there a fisher girl's face beneath her shawl with an elusive beauty in it—like Sophie's face beneath the silk scarf, as she ran to her death up another Union Street.

The Fish Market, as far as Tom could see, was empty, but the pubs on Marischal Street and Regent's Quay, when he walked back towards the town, were doing a roaring trade. He felt a strong desire to go into any one of them and have a drink, to drink to excess even, to celebrate Armistice Day and the ending of the war, anything to forget that gaping hole in the ground not two miles away on the verge of the city, like the pit in the graveyard of the curious crosses that had opened to swallow Sophie's body. He knew if he did that he would never find his way back to the offices of the Tarras Line.

And there they were, he had missed them when he first went along Market Street, because they were so inconspicuous, not in the least like that ten-storey building in Portland, Maine, of which his grandmother had shown him a photograph. TARRAS-ENDICOTT was the name above the Portland building, in letters six feet high picked out in electric lights, while these Aberdeen offices, where the firm was founded, were distinguished only by a little wooden sign which announced in Victorian lettering:

TARRAS LINE

It even took some time to find the front door, which was modestly hidden between a newsagent's and a haven called Maggie's Dining-room, smelling of frying fat; nor was there any trace of the Tarras-Endicott millions, or even of the luxury of the mansion on Queen's Road in the linoleum-covered staircase leading to what a painted hand in a stiff dress cuff indicated as the Main Office. Tom pressed an electric bell. After a few minutes a glass partition shot up, and he found himself looking into an anxious face adorned with a red moustache beneath a scanty head of red hair, turning grey.

"Mr. Fleming?" said the owner of the face. "Come away in. I'm John Endicott, you'll need to excuse me for answering my own office bell. I let my clerkesses off at twelve o'clock; there was no getting any good out of them after they heard the news. Come ben to my private room."

"I hope you didn't stay on yourself just on my account," said Tom, following him into a square room with a roll-top desk, an old-fashioned letter press and a massive safe. A very small fire burned in the grate. "How's Mrs. Endicott this morning?"

"Some better, oh, a lot better, and the girlie went away to her school in fine spirits, which is the main thing. Sit ye down, Mr.

248

Fleming, and we'll have a dram. I'm not one for drinking in the office, but since there's nobody here to tell tales, we'll just treat ourselves to a wee nip to toast the armistice. D'you take water?"

He produced a half-pint bottle of whisky and two small tumblers from a corner cupboard.

"Straight is fine, thanks," said Tom Fleming. He watched Mr. Endicott pour a very small measure of whisky into the tumblers, and they solemnly raised their glasses to the victory. "Though I doubt it's come too late for a lot of folk," said the judicious host, "there'll be a lot of sore hearts the day, Mr. Fleming."

"I wish you'd call me Tom. After all, we *are* related! Third cousins, aren't we, or something like that?"

"Aye, well, when it comes to third cousins we're just what the Aberdeen folk call 'far out friends'," said John Endicott with a smile. "But take a look above the mantelpiece and you'll see our common ancestor. That's our great-great-grandmother, Isabella Tarras, the first chairman of the Line."

In the November light (for Mr. Endicott was economising on electricity) Tom had hardly noticed the picture, but he now got up and looked at it attentively. "I haven't seen this one," he said. "Granny Bell had a daguerrotype, but it wasn't the same."

"That was done from a daguerrotype, and a right mess they made of it."

"It's foxed a bit." In fact a bar of foxing, like ectoplasm, lay across the reproduction; above it the intelligent square face of a bright-eyed old woman seemed to be sizing up her two descendants.

"And here's my girlie," said John Endicott, handing a snapshot from his wallet to Tom. "She's very like the old lady, isn't she?"

"I'll say she is," said Tom, for the solemn little face in the snapshot was almost laughably like the founder of the Tarras Line above the mantelpiece. "What's her name?"

"Sandra. We called her Alexandra, after Skipper Endicott's wife, my grandmother. I like the family names the best."

"So do we. Granny Bell's real name was Isabella, after Mrs. Tarras, and my older sister's called Isabel too."

"She's married to a Mr. Trumper, isn't she?"

"Why, you've really kept up with us," said Tom in surprise.

249

"Old Mrs. Fleming used to pass on all the news to our branch of the family. She and my grandfather, Brand Endicott, were quite fond of one another in their young days; I believe that lady up there" (nodding at the portrait on the wall) "had some idea they might make a match of it, 'Bell Tarras was a fine girl', I often remember him saying to me but of course from the time he met the Finnish lady she was the only one for him . . . There's not much of the Tarras about you, Mr. – er – Tom. You'll take after the Flemings, I suppose?"

"They say I'm like my father." He wondered who the little red-haired man "took after"; certainly not "after" any of the very handsome Tarrases and Endicotts he remembered from the family album. Somewhere back along the blood lines there must have been a forebear as completely forgotten as the young man who had toiled in that granite quarry on the rim of the expanding city. "You were born in America, weren't you?" He was trying to remember the man's age.

John Endicott supplied the answer. "Yes, I was born in Portland, Maine," he said. "I spent the first twenty-one years of my life out there. Then the old Skipper brought me to Aberdeen and started me in this office, and here I've remained for nearly twenty years more."

"Ever thought you'd like to go back to America?"

"Oh, I don't think Mrs. Endicott would fancy that very much. Her friends are all here, you see, and Sandra goes to a very nice school—no, I couldn't uproot them, just to go back to Maine."

"Was Mrs. Endicott a local girl?"

"She was a Miss Violet Sangster," said the husband respectfully. "They're a very well-known family. Her father's in the running for Lord Provost."

"But you're still an American citizen?"

"Oh, as far as that goes, yes. But you get accustomed to a place and a way of living, Mr. -er- Tom. And I've been through a lot with the Aberdeen folk in the war years. Two of our passenger steamers were torpedoed on the Norway run, with a heavy loss of life. The *Hazelhead* was sunk in '16, just before the battle of Jutland, and the *Ferryhill* went down off Bergen last July. Aye, the Kaiser has a lot to answer for. I hope he's enjoying his dinner in Holland this armistice day." He sighed. "And speaking about dinner, or lunch I should say, maybe we should be on our way."

"Yes, sure," said Tom, rising. "You don't want to be late home today."

"Not too late, because the doctor's going to look in on Mrs. Endicott about three." There were still two drams of whisky in the little bottle, but the ship-owner rammed the cork home and replaced it in the cupboard. With his back to Tom he said awkwardly, "Mrs. – er – Violet telephoned to me about an hour ago. She said you'd sent her some beautiful flowers this morning."

"It was a pleasure."

"You shouldn't have bothered."

Mr. Endicott being satisfied with the condition of the office fire, which was now reduced to ashes and clinkers, the two men walked together down the linoleum-covered stair.

"Is this your restaurant?" said Tom.

"Oh fie no, that's Maggie's Diner, it's chiefly for the fish salesmen and the boys. We'll get a better dinner at the Fish Market over the way."

Unfortunately the restaurant above the windy sheds where the fish boxes had been laid out for sale that morning was almost empty of customers on this day of low-keyed celebration in the port of Aberdeen. The food was good, thick Scotch broth and a dish of lemon soles fried in breadcrumbs, golden on the outside and melting to the taste. "Part of this morning's catch," said Mr. Endicott with satisfaction. "The fishermen'll be able to go to sea now without the fear of a German sub. on their tails, poor lads." He continued to talk about the heavy losses at sea, his own and other people's, both in lives and vessels, as if he wanted to excuse himself to Tom for not having joined a fighting service. Mr. Endicott had been a Special Constable, patrolling the Queen's Road area. Not dangerous, he said, but once he had walked into a lamp standard in the black-out and got a nasty cut on his brow.

Tom was rather amused than otherwise. He was warming to his "far out friend", and not because of the thimbleful of whisky: he was amused by this American's complete adaptation to the land of his fathers, even to the Scottish speech patterns and the Scottish thrift. And he had enjoyed the family talk, the reminder that names and characteristics were handed down from generation to generation, that there was an interlocking awareness and interest among those who shared some of the same blood. He was even

251

better pleased when John Endicott began to talk about Finland, the first person to do so voluntarily since the day Tom sailed from Helsingfors.

"I was quite interested," he said, "when you mentioned in your letter that you'd been in the fighting in Finland. I was always interested in the Grand Duchy on account of my grand-parents, and I followed the struggle for independence from day to day. We get *The Times* here, though it comes in pretty late in the afternoon, and the war was fairly well reported after it actually began."

"I've heard it called a sideshow," said Tom. "But I'm proud to have been in it."

"Maybe you can tell me what possessed the Finns to let Mannerheim go, and keep the Germans?"

"I think some of the Senators were jealous of General Manner-heim," said Tom. "They've certainly had their bellyful of General von der Goltz. I've a correspondent in Helsingfors, a man called Nikko Hirn, and he writes me that von der Goltz gives grand dinners every night at the Society House Hotel, with the orchestra playing 'Deutschland über Alles' and 'Die Wacht am Rhein'. Now that can't go on, John! The German troops under von der Goltz's command looted Finland this summer. They sent all the iron and copper ore they could lay their hands on back to Germany to the munitions factories, and they sent the butter and other foodstuffs too, out of a country already on the verge of starvation. We didn't fight the War of Independence for that!"

"No, but the Finnish government is still pro-German," said John Endicott. "The Diet too. It's just a month since they elected a German to be King of Finland—"

"Do you think Prince Friedrich Karl of Hesse will ever reign?"

"Not after this week's turn-up in Germany. But the Finns must be mad to think they would get any help from the Allies, the French especially, if they crown the Kaiser's brother-in-law as king."

"I agree with you, it's crazy; and it shows Svinhufvud and his cabinet are completely out of touch with the Finnish people as I knew them. I don't think the men who fought in Wetzer's corps would want a German prince to be their king."

"Very patriotic, were they?"

"Very—like your grandmother, Alexandra Gyllenlöve."

He pronounced the name correctly, Yillenleuve, and Endicott nodded approbation. "I see you know the story."

"Know it? We were brought up on it! How Alix and her husband, Skipper Endicott, fought the contrabanders in the *Duchess of Finland*, in the old Baltic war, and how they blew up a Russian frigate off the fortress, Sveaborg—"

"It was a Russian three-decker," corrected their grandson. "Something maybe easier to do in 1856 than it was last winter, eh, Tom?"

"The Russians were there in greater strength last winter, but the Finns hadn't changed."

"I wish my grandmother had lived to see them win their independence," said John Endicott. "She was a real Finnish patriot. I don't think she was ever happy in America, devoted as the Skipper was to her. She went into a decline, as they called it then, and died quite young."

"That Sandra girl of yours won't go into a decline," said Tom with a smile. "She's the picture of health in that snapshot."

"Isn't she, though?" Cups of strong tea were brought by way of ending the Fish Market lunch, and after John Endicott had kindly enquired after every separate member of Tom's family, the Canadian got up to take his leave.

"It's been good to meet you, John," he said, and now he meant it. "You and Violet and Sandra will have to visit us in British Columbia one of these days."

"I don't think Mrs. Endicott will ever cross the ocean, she gets seasick on the Bieldside ferry," said her husband. "But I know she'll be quite pleased to see you at the house next time you come to Aberdeen . . . It was an awful pity about the influenza. But good luck to you, Tom, and haste ye back!"

The ship-owner, now in a mood for reckless expenditure, went off in the direction of the station yard to pick up a cab, and Tom continued his exploration of the harbour. The wind had risen, and the day had turned much colder; even the watchmen aboard the trawlers lying at their moorings had gone below. The clock hands on a distant steeple stood at two, and already, as in Helsingfors at that hour, the grey of twilight had begun to veil the city. It held nothing for Tom Fleming, except an evocation of Sophie Sandels, who like a girl called Alix had believed in "Finland's world's dream": neither one of them had lived to see the dream come true.

Aberdeen held nothing for Tom, but he was very glad to have been there. In some subtle way the grey city had knotted his old ties with the past and spun the filaments of new. He was nearer than he had ever been to Nancy's plea that he give up the pursuit of Boris Heiden, accept his defeat in Zürich for what it was, and going home to Canada begin a family life in the sensible old pattern of affection and prosperity. He almost regretted that he had arranged with Colonel Henderson to visit the hospital at Dykefaulds on his way to the homebound liner in the Clyde.

He turned and started up Guild Street, back to the hotel. There was a youngish policeman on point duty at the corner, wearing medal ribbons: Tom was too far away to make out which. He thought of the decorations which, as his mother embarrassingly wrote, were now in the glass display case in her drawing room, along with a gold nugget brought back from the Yukon by Graham Fleming, and other family treasures. The silver MC, and the white enamel Liberty Cross of Finland, and he had neither one in his possession to wear today. I should have picked a bit of evergreen in the quarry woods, he thought. "Wear the fir sprig for Tammerfors!" He entered the hotel and without removing his overcoat went straight to the news-stand to buy the evening papers. A tall man, even taller than himself, was turning away with the two newspapers in his hand. Tom glanced at him casually and then stiffened to attention. It was General Gustaf Mannerheim.

19

THE GENERAL WAS THE first to speak.

"It's Captain—Fleming, from—Vancouver, isn't it?" he said in his stiff English. "How pleasant to meet an old comrade-in-arms in Aberdeen!"

It was the same form of address which had delighted Colonel Holsti in the railway transport office, the "two old soldiers, two old comrades-in-arms" approach, and Tom Fleming experienced his own moment of gratification. That slight hesitation over "Fleming" and "Vancouver" made the feat of memory all the more remarkable. No doubt about it, the general was wonderful with troops.

"I can hardly believe my eyes, sir," he said, and Mannerheim laughed.

"I too am a little surprised to find myself in Aberdeen," he said. "I expected to be in London this afternoon, but that turned out to be impossible. Are you alone here? Would you care to come up to my sitting room for a chat or have you another engagement?"

"I only had one engagement in Aberdeen, sir, with a distant cousin of mine. We were talking about you, less than an hour ago."

"Come along, then."

They walked up the broad shallow staircase, while Tom reflected that the foreign general in the sitting room was the soldier he had least expected to meet in Scotland.

"My aide-de-camp and I crossed from Bergen in the *Prince Arthur*," General Mannerheim was explaining, "and a miserable crossing it was. We hoped to proceed on the night train to London, but it wasn't possible to get a berth or even a first-class seat last night; we're travelling this evening, on the night sleeping-car train."

"I'm glad you got fixed up, sir. I understand the night sleepers are booked solid to and from Thurso, for the naval officers at Scapa Flow."

"So I was told." They arrived at the sitting room, large and comfortable, with a roaring coal fire in the big grate and a fine view over the railway yards and the harbour to Girdleness lighthouse and the open sea. A side table was arranged with a vase of chrysanthemums, a drinks tray with two bottles and some glasses, and a file of newspapers from that day and the day before.

"Come in, Captain Fleming. My aide-de-camp is in his room. He was quite unwell on the North Sea, and I advised him to rest this afternoon before the next stage of our journey."

"The North Sea can be pretty rough," said Tom.

"You've used the route, of course?"

"Never from Bergen. From Gothenburg, last June."

"I forgot to ask you—have you had luncheon?"

"Yes, thank you, sir, with this cousin of mine, down at the Fish Market."

"Ah!" said the general, "the Market! We walked that way this morning. In fact we were on the old quay, beside the Customs House, when the bells rang out for victory." He smiled. "It made me think of Helsingfors."

"You too, sir?" said Tom eagerly. "I thought it was only my imagination."

"No, it is very like. I think if Scotland had become the sixth Scandinavian kingdom, Aberdeen would certainly have been its capital."

He stood looking out of the window at the harbour and the sea, the Baltic spires and the plain old houses of grey granite. It was the first time Tom had seen General Mannerheim out of uniform, immaculate as ever in a conventional dark blue suit, a blue tie with a narrow pin stripe, and black shoes. The last time Tom had seen him, on the day of the victory parade, he was mounted on Neptune, with the blue and white banners and the Lion of Finland floating above him, and the cheers of his followers ringing up and down the Esplanade. But in this anonymous hotel room in a foreign land Mannerheim was still the "seer-king and passionless warden" of poor Sophie's poem. Calm and unruffled in exile as he had been in triumph, he turned to a table in the centre of the room and laid down the newspapers carried beneath his arm.

"Let's see how London received the news of victory," he said.

London, said the Scottish papers, had gone mad. The king and queen appeared on the balcony of Buckingham Palace at eleven

o'clock, the official time of the cessation of hostilities, and again
when the massed bands of the Guards played the national anthems
of Britain and her allies. Huge crowds . . . wild enthusiasm . . .
statue of Eros . . . Trafalgar Square . . . drive through the City
planned for the afternoon. The characteristic Scottish note of
deprecating such excitement was clearly to be read between the
lines.

"I hope this will mean a favourable atmosphere for my
mission," said Mannerheim.

"You're on an official mission, sir?"

"Yes." The general's handsome face relaxed in an almost mis-
chievous smile. "Believe it or not, I'm now the accredited representative of Finland to the governments of the United Kingdom
and of France."

"And high bl-" Tom caught back the oath—"high time too,
sir."

This time there was no doubt about the smile. "You're a loyal
supporter, Captain Fleming," he said. "Do sit down, and let us
talk comfortably."

They pulled up heavy velvet armchairs to the brass fender, and
the general looked dubiously at the fire.

"Should I ring for the maid?" he said. "I understand stoves
and logs, but not coal fires—"

"She would set the chimney on fire if she put more coal on now.
I'll keep an eye on it."

"Thank you. You don't smoke a pipe? There are cigarettes in
the leather box beside you."

The general filled his own pipe thoughtfully. "When did you
leave Finland?" he asked.

"At the end of June, sir."

"Oh! About a month after I did."

Tom was silent. He was perceptive enough to realise that
Mannerheim was going to talk confidentially, perhaps for the first
time since he gave up the command of the Finnish Army, and
certainly because his confidant of an hour was a man from another
country, whom he would probably never see again as long as he
lived. Talk might even be a relief for a man so reserved, who must
have acted the part of indifference all summer long, even with his
relatives in Sweden. Tom watched the pipe being lit, and the
match thrown in the direction of the fire.

"It's a curious experience," said General Mannerheim reflectively, "to lead a national army to victory, when victory means the freeing of the nation on its own soil, and then to be told exactly two weeks later that a German officer of the General Staff is to work out all the schemes for that army's future organisation, my signature being appended to the German plans like a—how do you say? a rubber stamp. This news was broken to me in the Senate chamber where Senator Svinhufvud had welcomed me on the sixteenth of May and thanked me officially for what I had done to save my country. Of course I laid down my command at once, and asked the government to appoint my successor. Nobody spoke a word as I went out, and not one of those men rose to offer me his hand."

"But now, sir?" said Tom Fleming.

"Ah, now six months have passed, and the government has had time to repent of its pro-German policy. A hungry people, a land torn by civil war and pillaged by the German occupants, the prisoner-of-war situation desperate—over ninety thousand of them still awaiting the mass trials on which the government insists, and very lucky not to be sent to Germany as forced labour!—all that amounts to rather more trouble than our worthy Senators are equipped to handle. I wasn't in the least surprised when my friend Minister Enckell, a man I've known since the old days in Petersburg, turned up in Sweden to beg me to undertake this mission to the Allied capitals."

"Nobody but you could undertake it, sir," said Tom. "I suppose it's still the question of getting Britain to recognise Finland's independence?"

"Exactly; and in Paris it's an equally delicate matter: the restoration of the diplomatic relations France broke off over all that nonsense about Prince Friedrich Karl's election as king. Above all I'm going to ask for food from America, beginning with the release of the grain already stored up for Finland in the granaries of Denmark. But it won't be easy. I realise myself that it's difficult to gain sympathy for a small and distant country, which was unwise enough to back the loser right up to the end."

"I'm glad they had the sense to appeal to you at last," said Tom.

" 'At last?'?" said Mannerheim. "As time is reckoned by the calendar I hadn't very long to wait. It only seemed a long time to me. Believe me, I never was a politician, or aspired to govern any country, even my own. But the victory we won last spring was won from nothing, nothing but the courage of the best men I ever commanded, and I—what's the word?—I *chafed*, over there in Sweden while I watched the results of our victory being frittered away. And yet I realised that I was luckier than many general officers who have been obliged to give up their commands. I only had to wait. My earthly possessions could easily be contained in a couple of suitcases, so I could go wherever I pleased; and I chose, of course, to go to my brother and sister in Sweden. We've always been a close-knit family, and my summer with them was very valuable to me."

The coals fell together, and Tom Fleming bent forward and took up the poker. The flames leaped up again, and the firelight brightened all the room. General Mannerheim took note of the strained attention on the younger face.

"Your own family is still alive, in Canada?" he said.

"Very much so, sir, three generations of family! I'm looking forward to seeing them all quite soon."

"So you're going home at last? I'm glad to hear it."

"That's very kind of you, sir. I had to spend rather longer in the doctors' hands than I expected. They were worried about a whiff of gas I got at Ypres, and sent me off to the South of France at the beginning of September."

"And you're all right now? You look well. Better than when I decorated you at St. Michel."

"When you said 'Wear the fir sprig for Tammerfors!' I was thinking about that this morning . . . Yes, I'm all right now. But—sir, could I ask you a very personal question?"

Mannerheim knocked out his pipe. "You may *ask* it," he said.

"It's not an easy one to ask. I mean—when you took the command at Vasa at the beginning of the year, were you preparing to fight *for* Finland, or *against* Bolshevism?"

"H'm," said Mannerheim, "that's not an easy one to answer. Perhaps I should say yes, both *for* and *against*, but the liberation of Finland of course came first. I would never lead an army against the Bolsheviks, though every opposition newspaper in Finland says that's just what Mannerheim the warmonger intends to do. By that I mean, to lead an army against the Bolsheviks in Russia. We *were* fighting Bolshevism in Finland, though sometimes we called it by another name."

259

"Forgive me, sir, I didn't quite mean that. I meant, do you think it's more important to fight *for* a nation's liberty, like we went to fight for Belgium in 1914, or *against* a movement on the international scale, out to destroy the whole world?"

Mannerheim brushed his moustache with the familiar movement of his forefinger. "In the one case the fight would be waged with men and weapons, in the other with ideas, agitation, propaganda—what the Bolsheviks themselves call *agitprop*."

"But suppose it was just one person who was doing the agitprop, and who could be eliminated?"

"By homicide, you mean?"

"By murder, yes."

Mannerheim smiled, but his eyes were sombre. "You have to be a very good shot for that," he said. "Dora Kaplan's attempt to eliminate Lenin was unsuccessful."

"I think I mean, is there ever any justification for cold-blooded murder?"

"What you really mean is that you have some particular person in mind."

"I have."

"A Russian?"

"Whom I met in Finland."

"Was it on his account you volunteered to join the White army?"

"No, it was to avenge a girl. A Finnish girl, shot on the day of the coup d'état. I believe this man was morally, if not actually, responsible for her death."

"Is he still in Finland?"

"When I last heard of him, he was on his way from Genoa to Panama."

"What chance have you of ever finding him now?"

"Only one."

"And you intend to take it?"

"Sir, until about an hour ago I was ready to give the whole thing up."

"And now?"

"Meeting you again has made a difference."

"In what way?"

"It made me remember how you fought a war and won it, and then right away you were defeated—because it *was* a defeat, what

260

the government did to you—and you never complained. You went abroad and waited, and when you were offered another chance you took it. You'll make a big success of your mission to the Allieu governments, and that won't be the end of it. You know you'll go on from here to something bigger still, and I guess you know what it is. I'll never be sent on a great diplomatic mission. But I've waited, like you, and I'm going back to my family, like you, and if I don't get another chance I'll make it—like myself."

Mannerheim chose his words with care before he spoke. "Are you superstitious, Captain Fleming?"

"No, I don't think so."

"Do you believe it was chance, or fate, that brought us across each other's path today?"

"Chance, I suppose."

"Let me tell you a story. It has to do with myself, but it has a bearing on all that you've been saying. I've never told it to a living soul because I used to think it was a foolish story, and I was a fool to have played a part in it. Because, like you, I'm not superstitious, and I certainly never believed in fortune-telling."

"Neither do I, sir."

"Good. One day last year, before the Bolshevik revolution, but while Kerensky was in power, I had a riding accident when I was on active service in Bessarabia. It wasn't a serious fall, but I sprained my ankle badly, and the doctor said I would be confined to bed for a couple of months. Chance, eh? Blind chance. But I used it to get a medical permit to go to Odessa for treatment. I was there when Lenin seized the power, and from Odessa, as you may know, I made my way back to Finland.

"All that was chance, or luck as some would say. But one night while I was still in Odessa a very charming English lady, staying in the same hotel, gave a little party to amuse her friends for an hour in such anxious times. She engaged the services of a clair-voyant—or so the good woman called herself. I thought she was a gipsy, the kind of fortune-teller who reads girls' hands at country fairs.

"She told me some things, which happened to be quite true, about my personal life. That didn't impress me: the facts were public knowledge, and any fortune-teller who knows her trade acquires a few facts about the people she expects to meet. But this woman said some curious things. She said I was to travel a long way, receive the command of an army, and lead it to victory. I was to lay down the command of my own accord, but very soon I would go on an important mission to two great Western countries. I thought it was a pack of rubbish. I could hardly keep from laughing when I told Lady Muriel what the fortune-teller said."

"Two of her predictions have come true already," said Tom Fleming. "Was there more?"

"That I should return to a higher position than the one I had when I resigned my army command. That my honours would be of short duration, but that after many years I would come to them again."

"I've always thought there was only one man fit to rule in Finland," Tom said quietly, "and that was you."

Mannerheim laughed, and stretched his long legs comfortably across the hearth rug. "Even if my rule is fated to be short?" he said. "The best of the good lady's prophecy seems to be that I've a long life ahead of me. But whatever she said, remember, chance or fate still played its part. It was chance that made my horse stumble and throw me, chance that brought us face to face today, chance—I'm sure—that brought you and your enemy together, whoever he may be. My advice to you is, if chance brings you together again, take it—all the way."

A brisk knock at the door announced the arrival of a porter with a scuttleful of coal.

"You're sittin' in the dark in here," said the porter cheerfully. "Will I sort yer fire to you, sir?" Without waiting for permission he shovelled coals half-way up the chimney, switched on the electric chandelier, drew the curtains close, and saying "That's mair like the thing!" took his departure.

"Not only the city is like Helsingfors," said Mannerheim with a laugh. "The citizens as well . . . Captain Fleming, I'm a very poor host. We must drink together to the triumph of the Allies, and though I can't offer you akvavit or vodka, the hotel cellars produced some excellent brandy, which I recommend. And of course there's the wine of the country, if you prefer Scotch."

"May I have brandy, general?" Tom watched apprehensively while the steady hand filled two glasses to the brim. He knew he was in for the terrifying "Mannerheim's *skål*", the ordeal in which many a subaltern had disgraced himself by spilling a drop from the overflowing glass as he raised it to his lips. He prayed that his own hand wouldn't shake as he took the glass from Mannerheim's.

"To the Allied victory!" said Mannerheim, "*Skål!*"

"*Skål!*" Stiff-wristed, Tom raised his glass without mishap, and emptied it in a single swallow. Russian-style, the general at once refilled both glasses.

"Will you propose the next toast, Captain Fleming?" he said in his courteous way. "To the Canadian Expeditionary Force, perhaps?"

"Thank you, sir," said Tom Fleming, "I'll give you another one. To the fortune-teller's prophecy. To chance and fate."

20

THE FORTUNE-TELLER'S PROPHECY came true for General Mannerheim while Tom Fleming was on his way home to Vancouver. Finland had found the right man to speak for her in the councils of the Allies, and his reasoned arguments won Britain's long-delayed recognition of Finnish independence. The conditions attached were entirely to Mannerheim's liking, for they included the immediate departure of the German troops and military instructors from Finland, and the dropping of the royal candidature of Prince Friedrich Karl of Hesse. The first cargo of grain was despatched to Finland, and the attention of Herbert Hoover, directing American Relief in Europe, was attracted to the country's needs.

The Svinhufvud government, once brave enough to declare for independence and make war on the Reds, was now brave enough to admit its errors of judgment and recall the man who six months earlier had preferred exile to taking orders from a German general. On December 12, while he was still abroad, Gustaf Mannerheim was appointed Regent of Finland, and on December 22, after landing at Åbo, he asked the blessing of the Lutheran bishop on his future task. Received in state at Helsingfors, he was installed in the beautiful Residence which the Reds had seized on that fateful Sunday, the Feast of the Kings.

Helsingfors was decorated again that day, and so, on the other side of the world, was Rubislaw House at Vancouver for Tom Fleming's long-delayed homecoming. His father was driven alone to the station to meet him, Mrs. Fleming, a self-indulgent person old before her time, having announced that she would faint if she had to greet her baby boy in public. But she was hovering in the front hall long before the train's scheduled arrival, supported by her elder daughter Isabel, who had come from Victoria for the occasion, and Isabel's boy and girl. Isabel's husband, Daniel Trumper, was studying what he called statistics in the library, a pose he thought suitable for a member of the Provincial Government, but Dandy and his sister Jo were hopping about the gravelled driveway, wildly excited at the combination of the Christmas holidays and Uncle Tom.

"Now, mother, not a word to Tom about Nancy Macpherson," warned Mrs. Trumper at the last moment.

"We'll have to tell him sooner or later, dearie."

"We'll have to tell him about Peru, but not about her engagement, at least not right away. Let him get accustomed to *us* first."

"Get accustomed to his own folks! The very idea!"

"Here they *are!*" yelled Dandy. The limousine was purring up the drive. Mrs. Fleming burst into tears as her tall son got out. There was an awkward moment of hesitation, and then he said "Mother!" and lifted her off the ground in a big hug, while Isabel hung on his arm and Daniel Trumper burst out of the library, bellowing a welcome.

"Well, here he is, mother, what d'you think of him?" said Mr. Fleming jubilantly. He thought the boy looked well, besides being cheerful and glad to be at home, and that scar there'd been all the fuss about really didn't amount to much. "This is something like a Christmas, isn't it?" he said, shepherding them all inside to the warm hall, hung with holly wreaths and mistletoe. "Come, Josephine, kiss your uncle. Dandy lad, shake hands."

Dandy shook hands enthusiastically, but Jo, who wished to be taken for a boy and despised kissing, hung back and allowed Tom to ruffle her short hair instead. Mrs. Fleming, who was weeping hysterically, begged her husband to support her into the drawing room, while Isabel took Tom upstairs. "You're in your own old room," she said. "Mother's been fussing over it for days."

"It looks great. Good to see you, Isabel, it was nice of Dan and the kids and you to come over from the Island."

"We couldn't keep away," she said affectionately. "Wonderful to have you back, old boy!"

"What about Dorothy and Harry? Are they coming up from Seattle?"

"Why no, didn't mother write you?"

"I didn't hear from home for weeks before I sailed."

"There's a whole slew of letters waiting for you now. But the Carlsons are staying home this Christmas, if you please. Dorothy's expecting her first baby in May, and the doctor says she mustn't travel."

"Well, good old Doss! Five years, isn't it, since they were married?"

"I know, she was getting terribly worried. But everything's going well, and they'll probably call up on Christmas Day to say hallo."

"Fine. Isabel, what time's dinner?"

"Seven o'clock, like it always was. Hurry on down, dear, there's such a lot we want to hear about."

"Just let me have a wash." When he was alone Tom threw himself on the pile of mail. Christmas cards, welcome home cards, even a card with an invitation to a New Year dance. Vancouver must be getting back into its old form for the first New Year of peace. But nothing from Nancy, not even a greetings card, though he had written her a long letter from Cannes, and a short one from shipboard. Here he was, having come after her, just as she'd demanded, and he'd very nearly gone to Seattle first, instead of coming home. Only the thought of his parents had brought him straight on to Vancouver. And the sight of his parents, after four years, had been a shock. Dad so grey and shrunken, Mom so small and fat! He took his jacket off and undid his cufflinks. The bedroom was just the same, with immaculately laundered organdie curtains, and his sports trophies polished and shining. The boys' books were all there, rows of Ballantyne and Henty, and some of his sisters' books mixed up with them, probably in the course of a wartime spring-cleaning, for he could see *Anne of Green Gables* and *The Youngest Girl in the Fifth*. It was the home room, and out on the big landing was the home smell, beeswax and turpentine mixed with lavender floor polish. He ran downstairs to join the party in the drawing room.

In spite of what Isabel said, there wasn't much they really wanted to hear about. The war was taboo, although his mother did enquire if he had ever met up with the son of a church friend called Mrs. Robertson, who had been on active service at Gallipoli. His visit to Aberdeen aroused some interest, which waned when the ladies found he had not been inside the Endicott house, and so could describe none of the furnishings or ways of serving food, and what was most earnestly discussed was his visit to the Graham Flemings at Toronto on the way west.

"They made you welcome, Tom? Julia looked after you properly?"

"They couldn't have been nicer. Graham gave a little dinner for me at his club one night, and young Colin came along, all togged up in a dinner jacket for the occasion."

"What did you think of the lad?" That was his father, and Tom, who knew Mr. Fleming was fond and proud of his elder grandson, resisted the temptation to say "a proper little pipsqueak!" and replied, "I couldn't get over the change in Colin. He was only about Dandy's age when I went away, and now he's almost a man. Acts like one, too. That must be a very posh boarding-school he's at."

"Julia's idea," sniffed Mrs. Fleming.

"It's the best boys' school in Ontario," said her husband, "and Colin's doing very well there. Graham thinks he'll make a fine businessman one of these days."

"Good for him." Tom got up and began to examine the Christmas cards arranged round the room. This was family life and family gossip, precisely what he was supposed to have missed during four years of war. They were all working hard at making him welcome, with pre-dinner sherry to drink his health—even Dandy and Jo were given small glasses of the stuff, which Tom detested, to celebrate the occasion. He turned from the display table, where the Christmas cards hid his war medals, and said,

"Where's the Macphersons' card? It usually comes in early, with a gift for you, Mom. Hasn't it arrived yet?"

His mother looked nervously at Isabel.

"We can't tell about the mails this year, dearie. We haven't worked out how long it takes to get a letter to Peru . . ."

"*Peru?*"

"Mr. Macpherson and Nancy went off to Peru at the beginning of November. They may spend a few months there, it isn't certain—"

"James J. has run into labour troubles on the Callao waterfront," explained Tom's father. "He has his hands full in Seattle, come to that, but he's got Harry Carlson there, and other good men to carry on while he's away. The situation's more difficult in Lima, or so he says."

"But why'd he have to take Nancy with him?"

"Those Peruvian officials are always looking for a kick-back," said Daniel Trumper. "Mr. Macpherson has a lot of wining and dining to do down there. Nancy went along to act as hostess for her father."

"I'm really disappointed in Nancy Macpherson," began Mrs. Fleming, and was quelled by Isabel's warning glance. ". . . I think she might have paid us a visit, just to tell us about meeting you in Europe—"

"Dorothy saw Nancy in Seattle, mother."

"Yes, but it's not the same. You met in Paris, didn't you, Tom?"

"In London too, Mom." And also, of course, in Zürich. He remembered the girl in white at the police infirmary, in that ward of drunks and muggers and sex deviates, saying "Hallo, Wild Bill Hickok!" smiling and cool. He remembered her defying him in the little room at the Baur au Lac—

The Japanese butler beat the gong for dinner.

*   *   *

The next two days Tom devoted almost entirely to his father and mother. They had planned it so between them, Mr. Fleming taking Tom to the firm's offices in Granville Street, to the saw-mills at New Westminster, even into the forests, to the logging camp nearest the city. Mrs. Fleming asked for his escort to tea at The Hotel, where he had to shake hands with half the Garden Club, and also on a drive round Stanley Park in the automobile, for the exciting purpose of looking at the Big Tree. She was very proud of Tom's good looks and his amiability. So many of the returned ex-servicemen were surly, got into bar-room quarrels or demanded hard liquor at home, and hung about Chinatown or the blue light district of Vancouver's twenty mile long waterfront, while Tom's chief pleasure seemed to be in playing with Dandy and Jo. They had accepted him completely on the day after his return home, when Dandy had got over his disappointment at Tom's not wearing the kilt and Highland bonnet of his photographs in uniform, and Jo recovered from her affront at the present of a doll. They were the only people in Rubislaw House who wanted to hear about the war, especially the war in Finland and the fighting in the snow. Dandy was cast as General Mannerheim and Jo as Lenin in their make-believes, and Tom, obligingly standing in as the whole of Wetzer's corps or the Red Guards at Viborg, observed that the world had progressed since the days of Wild Bill Hickok and Calamity Jane.

"I just don't know what to make of him," said Arthur Fleming to his wife, when they were enjoying an early cup of tea in their bedroom on the morning after a cheerful family Christmas Day. "I said to him yesterday when the bairns were outside playing and he and I happened to be by ourselves in the library, I said: 'Tom, I don't want to hustle you, but I think it's time ye took just one decision: are you going back to the Toronto office or would you rather stay here with me?' And d'you know what he said? 'Oh, Dad, it's hardly worth my while to go back to Toronto, young Colin'll be ready for my old job any day now' — "

"What nonsense," said Mrs. Fleming. "Julia wants her boy to go on to McGill."

"Yes, but it was the principle of the thing, just as if he wants to shuffle his job off on to Colin."

"He never got on too well with Graham. Wouldn't you *like* Tom to stay on here and help you?"

"I would if I thought he was interested. But all the places we went to, he seemed so apathetic, as if he was hardly taking in what was going on."

"You'll need to give him time, Arthur, time to settle down again. That's what they all need. I'm sure the minister gave a beautiful talk about it at the last Ladies' Guild meeting, and Mrs. Robertson was telling me about her experience with her own boy—"

"Yes, but ye'll need to remember it's over a year since Tom was out of the army, if ye don't count that daft-like caper up in Finland. Lily, I can't help wondering if he's quite all there."

"Arthur Fleming, that's an awful-like thing to say about your own son!"

"Oh, I don't mean he's not rational enough, it's just that his mind seems to be set on something else . . ."

This conversation preyed on Mrs. Fleming's mind. She had been an excellent stepmother to Graham Fleming, whose mother died when he was born, but she had no intention of seeing her own boy "ousted", as she thought of it, from the company in favour of Graham Fleming's son. During the forenoon she asked Tom to take "a wee turn" with her round the beautifully landscaped garden, where in that temperate climate the first bulbs were showing their tips of green, and drew his attention to the freshly pointed stonework and painted window sashes of Rubislaw

House. The place had been built to the plans of a Canadian architect, a disciple of Frank Lloyd Wright, and stood three storeys high, with walls already dignified with ivy, and an imposing tower with a flag-staff from which the Union Jack was flown on Dominion Day and the birthday of the Sovereign.

"Daddy's looking forward to having you in the office here, Tom," she began diplomatically. "He was saying to me just this morning what a big help you would be to him."

"Was he, Mother?"

"He was greatly impressed by the letters you wrote about the timber trade in Finland when you went there first. Said you showed a real grasp of—of conditions. Or was it conservatism?"

"Probably conservation, the Finns are way ahead of us in that. But you know what I'd like before I finally decide what I should do? I'd like to spend a few days in Seattle with Doss and Harry."

"But you've not been home a week, you restless laddie!"

"It's still holidays, isn't it, up to the New Year?"

"Well . . . I know poor Dorothy would be very pleased to see you, and Harry too. But don't stay long, dearie, I do want you to do your best for Daddy." Mrs. Fleming played her trump card. "Remember, Rubislaw House and all the Vancouver property will be yours someday."

"Mine? But what about the great man in Toronto?"

"Graham Fleming's done very well out of the business already," said the stepmother. "Daddy's arranged for your share with his lawyers. But don't tell him I told you."

He was too kind to tell her that Rubislaw House, run by a Japanese staff in 1919, would be a white elephant by 1929, and that he had no ambition to be the master of the place or any place like it. Tom had won his point about going to Seattle, and spent the rest of the day at the Fleming offices, to so much purpose that his father came home cheered and encouraged about the future. It was not until dinner was over, and the family drinking coffee in the drawing room, that he asked abruptly:

"Exactly how long are the Macphersons going to stay in Lima?"

Nobody cared to say. But Isabel took the bull by the horns, and encouraged by a wink from her husband, said, "They talked about a few months, that could mean until March or April. I suppose it depends on the date fixed for Nancy's marriage."

"Nancy?" said Tom. "*Marriage?*"

270

"You didn't know she was going to be married?" Isabel saw that Tom was beyond speech. He set his coffee cup, with infinite care, on a small mahogany table.

"I thought you might have met the gentleman in France," said Mrs. Fleming, for whom the European theatre of operations was one vast Garden Club where all genteel persons met each other sooner or later. "That's where Nancy met him. A Dr. Novak, from Chicago, I believe."

"That little runt with the spectacles?" said Tom.

"Oh, then you do know him?"

"I saw him once at a Fourth of July party."

"And was he very attentive to Miss Nancy?" That was Trumper, making the best of a bad job.

"She had the men round her that night like bears round a honey pot," said Tom angrily. "Novak! Nancy Novak, what kind of name is that? Sounds like one of Dad's Galicians—"

"Don't be a name-snob, Tom," said the politician's wife. "I believe he's a very clever doctor."

"Some of my best voters are Galicians, ha! ha!" said Daniel Trumper.

"I'm sure I was very sorry to hear about it," said Mrs. Fleming, whose tactless sentimentality had been kept in check too long, "I always hoped you and Nancy would make a match of it, Tommy dear. You were such a cute pair of little sweethearts, right from the beginning. Remember the first time her dad and mother brought her here for Christmas? She was just about three years old, with that lovely mop of curly hair tied up with a big pink ribbon bow, and you were seven, Tom. You were *infatuated* with her. Remember how you stood up on the rug in front of the fire and sang:

Nancy is my fancy
And I'm still true blue!"

"Sure I remember," said Tom. "And at suppertime she crawled beneath the table cloth, and bit me on the leg."

Under cover of the relieved laughter which followed, Tom asked his mother to excuse him, and left the room. When he had been gone for ten minutes Daniel murmured to his wife from

271

behind the evening paper "Now what?" and she whispered back, "I wager I know." Neither of the Trumpers looked at all surprised when Tom returned, and said briefly: "I just talked to Dorothy, she sent you all her love. She's expecting me tomorrow. I'm going to Seattle on the morning train."

*   *   *

The young Carlsons lived on First Hill, in one of the pleasantest districts of Seattle, and from her front windows Dorothy could see the splendid view of Elliott Bay with the snow-capped range of the Olympics beyond it. In one of the burning sunsets bringing the year 1918 to its end, she had eyes for nothing but her brother's troubled face.

"I blame Nancy's aunt for starting all this talk of an engagement," she was saying earnestly, "with very little to go upon, indeed."

"This Novak never showed up in Seattle?"

"How could he, Tom? He's still on the staff of that American Base Hospital in France, where they've done such wonderful work with—with—"

"Yes, I know, with shell-shocked patients. Don't worry, Doss, I know all about it; I was talking about their work to the MO at Dykefaulds just before I left Scotland."

"You went back to that place of your own accord?"

"Yes, I did, there was something I wanted to find out. But if Novak's in France and Nancy came back to Seattle, how did it get about that they intended to get married?"

"You see, I think Dr. Novak *was* very much in love with Nancy. And he wrote to her father to tell him so, and ask his permission for them to be engaged."

"And then?"

"It hasn't been announced yet. But James J. told the whole story to Aunt Edith, and of course that was just as good as putting an ad. in the *Post-Intelligencer*—"

"She told the world."

"Some people believed it, some said they'd wait to hear from Nancy herself."

"What did Nancy have to say to *you*?"

"I didn't see very much of her between the time she came back from France and went off with James J. to Peru."

272

"I wrote her twice since last summer, but she never answered my letters."

"What a shame," said Dorothy Carlson, "one of the Equator steamers left for Callao yesterday. You could have sent a special letter by the captain's hand, and he would have given it himself to Nancy when he went ashore. It's not ten miles from Callao to Lima, and the captains always report to Mr. Macpherson direct."

"Maybe if I wrote care of the captain, special delivery, it would reach him at San Diego. Which steamer was it?"

"The *Mount Rainier*, Captain Jensen. I'll give you Nancy's address in Lima." She crossed the pretty room to her writing desk. "They've rented a furnished house, the Casa Luza, in the old part of the town."

Tom looked at his sister's altered figure, still not clumsy but curved and gracious, and said to himself: "I wish I could see Nancy looking that way, carrying my kid."

"Do you want a boy or a girl, Doss?" he said teasingly, as she handed him a slip of paper.

Dorothy laughed. "Just so it's got all its fingers and toes and senses, we don't care," she said. "It's wonderful to have a baby coming at all, after five years."

"It's the kids that make me begin to feel old," said Tom seriously. "That Colin Fleming, what a pain in the neck! He treated me like some old derelict, called me 'sir' with every breath he drew, and explained the action at Vimy Ridge to me till I was fit to murder him. Seems they've a class in military history at this punk school he goes to. They wear blazers and sing 'Land of Hope and Glory' after prayers every morning—more British than the British, you know the sort. But Dandy and Jo are a grand little pair. Jo was upset because I brought her a doll from Toronto. I had to sneak down town in the car and buy her a bow and arrow."

"Poor old Uncle Tom," said Dorothy fondly. "Time you were married and had some nice kids of your own."

"I did ask one girl to marry me, but she turned me down."

"Nancy Macpherson?"

"Yes."

"In Europe last summer?"

"Yes. I made an awful mess of it—"

"That's probably why she's been avoiding me," said Dorothy. "I think you'd better write her one more letter and try again.

273

Because I don't believe you have to worry about Dr. Novak, Tommy. Nancy never cared for anyone but you."

Harry Carlson's key was heard in his front door at this point, and Tom set himself to be an agreeable guest in the married home which he had never seen before. He knew that in one way he was imposing on the Carlsons, that there was an unexplained reason for his visit to Seattle, and the least he could do was listen to Dorothy's happy chatter about names for the expected baby, and answer Harry's questions about the war in Finland and the courage of the Swedish Brigade. For Sweden was the old country to Harry Carlson, and his plump, rather smug face grew taut with feeling as Tom described the resistance of the Swedes on the plateau of Kalevankangas, and their leading part in the capture of Tammerfors. "I've heard Finland called 'the bloody shield of Sweden'," said Tom Fleming, "but by God! the Swedes made up for it there and at Viborg. Mannerheim knew it, too, he praised them every chance he got—especially the army officers on the active list who ruined their careers by going off to fight for Finland's independence."

Dorothy had gone to bed before the talk turned to the war, and over a final beer it was agreed that the two young men should lunch together in the town next day, so as not to put a strain on her housekeeping. Dorothy made no objection, but she raised her eyebrows when Tom appeared dressed for the street next morning in an old red and black checked mackinaw from his lumberjack days, with a shabby felt hat and hobnailed boots.

"Did you bring all that junk with you from Vancouver?" she demanded. "I hope you're not going to lunch with Harry at the Olympic dressed like that."

"We're going to eat ourselves silly on geoduck chowder and halibut in one of the waterfront joints," said Tom. "We're not going to disgrace you at a posh hotel."

"Waterfront joint indeed!" said his sister. "Is that why you've given up shaving too?"

"Didn't do a very good job this morning, did I?"

"Didn't begin to do a job at all. Honestly, Tom, I was going to suggest you take a cab and go along to Queen Anne's Hill and call on Nancy's Aunt Edith, if you really want to get this Novak business cleared up, but you can't do that dressed like a Skid Road bum."

"Don't worry, Doss, I'm only kidding. I'll come back around twelve and make myself respectable for lunch with Harry. Just feel like poking round the waterfront a bit this morning, dressed to blend with the background."

"Once a logger, always a logger," said his sister affectionately, as Tom let himself out at the front door. He was delighted to be called a Skid Road bum. That was precisely the character he intended to sustain in his last attempt to find out Boris Heiden's whereabouts. The thin thread which stretched across two continents and an ocean from Kouvola junction had come to its terminal in the city of Seattle. Tom Fleming was going to try to establish contact with Igor Heiden's widow, whom he had once known— and luckily from photographs only—as Dr. Kathleen Donovan.

Avoiding the fashionable Queen Anne's Hill where James J. Macpherson's stately home was situated, Tom began the descent from First Hill to the waterfront. It was not as steep as it had been when he first knew Seattle as a child, for the major work of regrading the cliffs beneath which the Seattle pioneers laid the foundations of the city had been done some years before the outbreak of war. The cliffs had literally been washed away, and while regrading was still going on in some districts the new centre of the city had been made viable for the automobile. Between First Hill and the old artery for which he was heading, called the Skid Road, there were still vacant lots and tracts of ground waiting to be built over like the land behind the National Museum in Helsingfors where Tom had seen the fierce little children playing a year earlier. He turned into one of them, picked up a stone and bruised the flesh round his finger nails, biting them to a jagged rim and rubbing dirt into the skin of his hands. He thought they were the only detail which might give him away in his impersonation of a Skid Road bum. They had been calloused and frostbitten when he fought with Wetzer's corps, but for more than six months he had done no manual work at all.

The Skid Road, in Seattle's vigorous beginning, was just that— the road down which the oxteams skidded logs to Yesler's mill on the tide-flats near the mouth of the Duwamish river. It was also known as the Deadline, the frontier between respectable, fashionable, up-and-coming Seattle to the north and the red light, deadbeat, down-and-out district to the south. It was somewhere in this area, as Nancy told Tom in London, that Kathleen Donovan had worked on a little pacifist paper, which closed down when America entered the war, and here Tom Fleming hoped to pick up news of her.

He had a hunch the woman was still in Seattle. It was too vital a nerve centre to be deserted by a revolutionary, unless of course the comrades had called Igor Heiden's widow to her spiritual home in Russia. But even though Kathleen Donovan had failed in her assignment at the university, he knew enough of the way the system worked to be confident that, going underground and working with professionals, she could do her modest part towards disrupting the American economy. Seattle was one of the keys to the North American continent, with ships and trade reaching out across the Pacific to Japan, where James J. Macpherson was still hoping to extend his steamship line, with military installations and a booming industry. For Seattle, barely seventy years old, had always been a boom town, and in 1918 the war in Europe had sent its economy rocketing. There were government contracts for the shipyards, the beginning of aircraft construction, and for the timber and building trades a bonanza as new cheap houses were hastily thrown together to house the workers. There was also, as a result, an augmented labour force in and around the city, ripe for what the Russians called agitprop when the wartime wage controls were relaxed.

Tom Fleming slouched the whole length of Skid Road before he began his search for Dr. Donovan in the back streets. He came out on the waterfront near the pier where the Washington State ferries ran to Bremerton across the Puget Sound, where a US Navy Yard had been in operation for nearly thirty years. There was a naval installation further north at Whidbey island, and Tom thought of the damage a few well-placed bombs could do at either of these places. A US battleship could be blown up in the dry dock at Bremerton by means no more sophisticated than those Skipper Endicott and his Finnish wife had used to blow up the Russian three-decker at Helsingfors in the old Baltic war. It was not an immediate danger, unless Kathleen Donovan was a bomb expert, but as Tom looked across the beautiful bay to the peninsula where the Navy yard was located and new communities were springing up, he visualised as he could never have done before his life in Finland the menace which constantly hung over such a vulnerable area.

He walked back up Skid Road, from which the glamour of the turn of the century had long departed. The dance-halls of the gold rush days, when Seattle had another great boom as the nearest port to Alaska, had disappeared with the houses which made Seattle one of the great centres of the white slave traffic: all was dull and dingy, though still far from respectable. Even the Indian totem pole in Pioneer Square had a raffish look: the Raven and the other symbols in the primitive carving had a disturbing resemblance to the human primitives hanging round the sleazy barber shops and pool rooms on the ground floors of the old red-brick hotels. Tom crossed into Washington Street, once a strong-hold of the Wobblies, and worked his way up and down the alleys connecting it with Skid Road. It took him half an hour to find anything that look promising, because in the usual hit-or-miss way of his pursuit of Heiden, he had never asked Nancy the name of the socialist weekly where Kathleen Donovan had worked. At last he found something that looked possible: two dirty windows in an unoccupied first-floor flat, on each of which a word had been inscribed in fading white paint

THE SPARK

That might be it. He had read so much about Lenin and the origins of Bolshevism in his attempt to understand Heiden's mentality, that he knew the Russian leader in his London exile had edited a little propaganda sheet by that name, *Iskra*, the spark. Tom looked about him. At street level in the house next door there was a foul little restaurant, where one old man in a dirty apron was listlessly stirring a pot of beans on the back of an iron stove. Tom went in and asked for coffee.

He was no actor, but he had decided to try to pass himself off as a Swedish sailor. His height, some knowledge of the ports of Sweden, and a few seafaring phrases picked up from the drunken freighter captain on his voyage out from Hull to Stockholm were his scanty equipment for the part, but on this his first attempt none of the props happened to be necessary. The grey-haired short-order cook was in the hazy state brought on by a thorough wine drunk, and when he brought Tom's coffee, half slopped into a cracked saucer, he was quite willing to help in the search for Mrs. Donovan. Yes, she'd worked on the paper next door, often came in for coffee, very fine woman. "What you want with her, Mac?" he asked, with a dim flicker of suspicion. Tom's incoherent words about jumping ship seemed to satisfy him, and while swabbing the counter with a filthy rag, lowering his voice not to be heard by a sleeping customer at the other end, he bent towards Tom and said,

"You know the Public Market, Mac? You go along and try the office above Joe's Curiosities, maybe you'll find out something about the lady there."

The Public Market, Tom remembered, lay on a bluff above the bay and some blocks to the north. He walked along the waterfront again, hurrying now, past the old Schwabacher dock where the s.s. *Portland* had berthed in July 1897 with the first ton of gold from Alaska, past James J. Macpherson's Equator Line piers. The *Mount Olympus* was in her berth, and he thought of the *Rainier* on her way south to Peru while the *Mount Vernon* and the *Mount Baker* were probably hailing each other in mid-ocean. He climbed the long wooden stairs to the Public Market, past the trinket shops and chop-suey joints underneath the main market, where even in December the stalls were laden with fruit and vegetables brought into town by Japanese truck gardeners. Many well-dressed women were moving up and down between the stalls, for the Public Market was the place for bargains, and the fresh-caught fish, the good red meat on the butchers' stalls, were as tempting as the greengrocers. A tasty smell of cooking shrimp and freshly baked bread ran through all the market, and there were lunch counters with piles of doughnuts under glass covers which looked far more appetising than Tom's discovery near the former office of *The Spark*. One or two of the bigger eating-shops had upstairs rooms, very simply furnished with benches and wooden tables like an indoor picnic ground, and Tom saw that there was an upper storey, not all of it in use, running above the stalls and shops all round the market. He found Joe's Curiosities after a while, a dusty little shop selling corals and Indian headgear and what it claimed to be a dried mermaid in a bottle. A narrow staircase beside the booth led to an equally narrow landing with one closed door, across which was written:

Workers' Advice Bureau
Mrs. Hyde

278

He knocked, and heard a chair pushed back inside the room. A little wooden shutter in the upper panel opened, and two rather watery eyes looked out at him. A woman's voice said, "Yes?"

"Sven Larsson, from Stockholm. For advice, please."

Two bolts were pulled back; the stronghold of the Workers' Advice Bureau was open. "Mrs. Hyde?" said Tom. He knew quite well it was Kathleen Mavourneen, although the wild Irish rose of 1912 had become a flabby woman with greying hair, carelessly dressed in a tweed skirt and a knitted jacket loosely belted at the waist. Her spectacles were pushed above her brow.

"Yes, I'm Mrs. Hyde," she said impatiently. "Sit down, Mr. Larsson. You're a Seattle resident? Having difficulty in adjusting to the new wage scale? Give me your union card and affiliation number, please."

"No resident," said Tom. "I am Svensk sailor" (and he hoped the Svensk lilt in his voice was convincing, he was trying to imitate the volunteers of the Swedish Brigade), "My ship is in port here on the way to Chile."

"What ship is that?"

"The *Valkyrie*." He had noticed the name on a smart Swedish cargo vessel, lying next to the Equator piers.

"Well?"

"I was hoping to know the address of Comrade Boris Heiden in Valparaiso." It was only a venture; it might work.

"You know Comrade Heiden?"—greatly surprised.

"I was with the Red army in Finland last winter. I was with Comrade Heiden at Kouvola and Vilppula fights. He is a good man, I would be glad to meet with him again."

"I remember the story of his escape from Vilppula," said Igor Heiden's widow.

"Over the ice of the Kvarken—very brave."

The woman actually smiled. "And you fought with the gallant Red army, Comrade Larsson?"

Tom touched the white seam on his left cheek. "This is my memorial of the Butcher Guards," he said. "I was lucky not to be taken prisoner."

"Yes, but we would be glad to have details of the White horror camps . . . What made you think Comrade Heiden was in Valparaiso?"

"He told me he might be going there from Panama."

279

"At Colon he was ordered to Lima. There is much to be done there at the University of San Marcos, and you might hear of him at Callao, if your ship calls there. Ask at the headquarters of the Seamen's Union. Will the *Valkyrie* call at Seattle on her voyage home?"

"Yes, comrade."

"Then come back and see me here. You may find us in the middle of a general strike by that time, if the unions disregard the orders of the AFL. That's what this office was set up for last fall: to organise relief for the workers' families if necessary, and the distribution of essential supplies while the strike continues."

"Yes, I understand. I will come back."

He got up and made an awkward, he hoped a not too bourgeois, bow.

"And you'll bring me news of Comrade Boris. Was it he who told you that you'd find me here?"

"He told me everything," said Tom significantly. "I am proud to have met you, Comrade Heiden."

There was moisture in the eyes which looked like a stupid dog's. "Thank you," she said. "Living in a police state as we do here, it seemed wiser to change my name to Hyde. But it's good to know that Igor's memory is still green among our comrades."

"You bet," said Tom. It was just what a Skid Road bum would have said, and Sailor Larsson was only one degree better than Skid Road. But he meant it, *you bet* he meant it, Igor's memory was green all right, but not the way Mavourneen thought. With a final effort of control Tom slouched back along the road beneath the Public Market until he was well out of sight of the window of the Bureau, which looked straight out across the bay. Then he hailed a passing taxi and had himself driven to the railway station.

There was a large timetable on one wall of the waiting room giving the times of all the trains in and out of Seattle. He studied it, washed his face and hands and telephoned Harry Carlson at his office.

A girl's voice announced that Mr. Carlson was in conference, and before he came to the phone Tom Fleming had time to panic. The name of Lima had hardly registered when he heard it first: he was so intent on his impersonation that he could not at once associate it with Nancy. But now the thing had hit him amidships.

Heiden and Nancy were in the same South American town where, whatever its size, any foreigner must be conspicuous, and Tom had no doubt that watchers left behind in that secret city, Zürich, had noted all Nancy's activities at the time when he was rescued from the Zürcherhorn. Would her involvement with himself earn her the same fate as Sophie Sandels? "Come on, Harry!" he groaned aloud, and the same moment heard Carlson's cheerful voice on the wire.

"Hey there, fella, you're early, aren't you? I won't be free for lunch for over an hour yet."

"Listen, Harry," said Tom. "The *Mount Rainier*—what day's she due at San Diego?"

There was the ruffling of the leaves of an office calendar, and then Harry told him. "And from Diego to Callao in Peru, how long's the run?" asked Tom.

More ruffling. "Eleven days, with say half a day ashore in the Zone. Why d'you—"

"Just let me do the talking," said Tom. "Harry, I'm going right through to Los Angeles on the noon train, and then on to San Diego. Wait! Don't say anything to worry Dorothy. Just tell her I've been thinking over what we were talking about, and I'd rather go and see Nancy in Peru myself than write another letter. She'll understand."

"You mean you're going just like that, in the clothes you stand up in? Doss called up a little while back, she said you'd gone off to town dressed like Paul Bunyan—"

"Doesn't matter, I can buy a new outfit in California. It'll be summer in Peru anyway."

"Right," said Harry Carlson, dazed. "But you're sure you're fit for the trip, Tom? Hell, you only just got back from Europe, and you were hospitalised—"

"I'm fine," said Tom impatiently. "Give my love to Doss and ask her to square it with Dad and Mother. Just tell them I said 'Nancy is my fancy' and they'll be perfectly happy."

"Sure," said Harry. "I guess that's the way to do it. Well, good luck, buster, give our best to Nancy. And my respects to the boss, of course. Are you going to let them know you're coming?"

"Going to get a cable off right now. So long, Harry!" Tom had an idea, as he hung up the phone, that Harry Carlson was saying something about money.

281

He had just time to get to the Western Union cable office. As he ran, he was composing the cable in his head:

Reason to believe Dolderberg friend in your locality stop please be careful stop I am on my way to you love Tom

But he wasn't worried about money. He had money in his belt, and a bank draft clipped to his passport. And when he pressed his left arm gently to his side, he could feel the comforting outline of the Browning.

21

THE PATIOS OF THE Casa Luza lay empty and silent in the summer warmth of a January afternoon in Lima. Outside, in the network of narrow streets laid out nearly four hundred years earlier by Francisco Pizarro, some of the homeless and the beggars lay sleeping in the shadow cast by heavy wooden doorways, the men with bright striped ponchos pulled up to their chins. In bedrooms hung with oriental silks imported long ago in exchange for Peruvian silver, the ladies of Lima lay relaxed in the siesta. In every bedroom except in one of the principal bedrooms of the Casa Luza, where a yawning maid was helping her young American mistress into the dress which a *Limeña* lady had worn nearly a century before.

Nancy Macpherson was having her portrait painted to please her father, and in the traditional dress to gratify his Limenese associates. When it was finished the picture would hang in his new offices in the capital, and the artist had been commissioned to make a copy for the mansion on Queen Anne's Hill at Seattle. He was a Peruvian, and worked so slowly that Nancy doubted if the portrait would be finished during her stay in Lima, let alone the copy made, and she told him she was prepared to give him extra sittings, ruthlessly arranging them for the sacred hour of the siesta. The man was late this January afternoon, but then he was always late: there was plenty of time for the sleepy maid to pull the obligatory corset strings a little tighter, and ensure the perfect fit of the *saya y manto*.

Nancy had worn it for the first time in the house of a Peruvian lady who had organised a "young girls' afternoon" of refreshments and charades. Entertaining young girls was a problem in a city still fighting in 1919, after a hundred years of independence, to preserve the etiquette of a colonial society which had lasted since the days of the Spanish viceroys. Girls obviously could not be exposed to young men before their arranged marriages, so kindly mothers planned the afternoon parties, and even included a young woman like Nancy Macpherson, alarming though some of her ideas were. Nancy enjoyed the charades and guessing games, although she sometimes wondered what Joanie and Peggy-Ann would think if they saw the canteen hand who could cope with the roughest of the battle-weary men who passed through Soissons, romping with the sheltered girls of the Peruvian aristocracy.

When she wore the *saya y manto* for the first time there was a murmur of genuine admiration from the watchful girls. Nancy had found the style to suit her at last, and her hostess was very willing to lend her family heirloom for a modern portrait. The white lace bodice and underskirt had to be altered only a little to fit Nancy, the *manto* not at all. It was a sleeveless hood of black taffeta, falling to the waist, where it was fastened, and the *saya*, which was scarlet, fell from Nancy's waist to her ankles. The material was closely pleated and shaped to the body in such a narrow cut that a woman wearing the *saya* could only take short steps, but even so Nancy flitted round her sombre bedroom too quickly for the maid to follow her. There was a fan and a lace handkerchief to be taken from the top of a carved chest, and a freshly-cut red rose from a glass on the dressing table, and there was Tom's cable from Seattle to be looked at one more time. She knew, of course, that he was aboard the *Mount Rainier*, for he had cabled from San Diego and later still from the Pacific port of the Panama Canal, but the first cable was the one that mattered, that said "I am on my way to you." There was not much longer to wait now, for the *Rainier* was due at Callao at five o'clock next morning.

"The artist is here, señorita," said a manservant at the door, and Nancy said "Good! Now you can finish out your nap, Manuela!" as she disappeared in a rustle of skirts down an open stone gallery from which a flight of stone steps led to the inner patio of the Casa Luza.

James J. Macpherson's taste in art inclined to the chocolate box lid or the magazine illustration, and Nancy had at first rebelled at a composition which was to show her on a cushioned stone seat against a bank of flowers. But it was an easy pose to hold, with the handkerchief and fan in one hand lying on the cushions, while the other held the red rose to her lips, and restless Nancy tried hard to look like an indolent Peruvian lady, basking in the January sunshine. The flowers behind her were canna lilies, red and yellow, and all round the patio stocks and carnations of every shade bloomed at the foot of green myrtle trees.

There were days when the artist found his subject talkative, and anxious to practise her rudimentary Spanish on him, and then her lively face changed expression so often that he was obliged to concentrate on the floral background, but today, to his relief, she was willing to be tranquil. He thought she might even be a little drowsy, for more than once he saw the blue eyes close, and he took advantage of her silence to paint with concentration, while the afternoon sun drew heat from the adobe walls of the Casa Luza.

That was how Tom Fleming saw her, when he followed a soft-footed servant through the outer patio and paused by the wrought-iron inner gate: as a Peruvian, in a dress from the past but vividly alive, and he held out his arms to her with a single gesture which told Nancy he was hers at last. She ran across the patio to take his kisses, heedless of the artist and the scandalised manservant, with the rose crushed between them, and the black *manto* falling from her curls.

"Nancy, you're so beautiful!" was the first coherent thing he said to her, and even in her joy Nancy had to be matter-of-fact, and tell him it was just the fancy dress.

"It's not the dress, it's you. You're sitting for your portrait?"

"Oh, yes, but—senor, I have to end the sitting for today," she said to the smiling artist, who was already putting his brushes and palette away. "Perhaps tomorrow—no, I'll send you word . . . Tom, we didn't expect you until early morning!"

"Captain Jensen broke all the records for the run after we left Balboa."

"And did you go to the Equator office in Callao?"

"Not I! I grabbed the first taxi I could find and offered the man double fare to get me to the city fast."

"Come into the sala, Tom. But where's your luggage?"

"I dropped it off at a hotel the driver recommended."

"Oh, but Dad expects you to stay here! You can't possibly stay at a hotel!" Nancy hardly knew what she was saying. She led him through an open door into the casa's vast reception room, furnished with long sofas and armchairs covered with Cordoban leather, and wooden chests on which Nancy had placed bowls of flowers. Religious pictures in thick dark paint hung on the walls. Until the hovering manservant rolled up the sunblinds the place was gloomy, and Tom hardly waited for the man to go before he took Nancy in his arms.

"Are you glad to see me?"

"Oh *Tommy*, yes!"

When he raised his head from that long kiss Tom said, "You told me to come after you, and I did."

"Why did you stay so long in Europe?"

"I had to wait for a sailing, and then, I thought you were in Seattle, not thousands of miles away. Why didn't you answer my letters?"

"I only got your shipboard letter last week, after I knew you were on your way."

"But I wrote a ship letter *to* you, and sent it to Havre, to the *Queen Christina.*"

"Oh!" Nancy bit her lip. "I'm afraid that letter's lost. You see, I didn't sail on the *Christina.*"

"Didn't?"

"Come and sit down." Nancy moved out of Tom's embrace but kept tight hold of his hand as she led him to one of the Cordoban sofas. "I delayed my sailing for three weeks so's I could take care of Linda on the voyage home. You didn't know—of course, you couldn't know, that her fiancé was killed at St. Mihiel?"

"Oh *no!*"

"On the first day of the battle. He was in the 304th Tank Brigade, you know, and they led the attack. Jack Macey was one of the very first to be killed."

"Oh hell," said Tom helplessly. "I only saw him that one time, but I liked him a lot. He was as keen as mustard about the Tank Corps, too, and some fire-eating commander they had—Captain Patterson, was it?"

"No, it was Patton—Major George S. Patton now. He was badly wounded himself in the Argonne, but he came through." And Nancy laid her cheek on Tom's shoulder, running her hand up his arm, as if to reassure herself that he had come through too. "We're two of the lucky ones, aren't we?" she said.

"I know I am." And Tom kissed her, deeply, fervently, from her parted lips to the hollow in her throat above the ruffle of white lace. "And nothing can come between us now, can it, Nancy?"

286

"I hope not," she said, wide-eyed, while the words neither wanted to be the first to speak hung in the air between them.

"Poor little Linda," said Tom with an effort. "Was she terribly cut up?"

"Tom, she was heart-broken. They were so in love, and just right for each other, and their families so pleased about the engagement. I never left Linda until I got her home to Wilmington, but I don't think I could have got her out of France if it hadn't been for Al Novak. He was a tremendous help'"

"Well then, how *about* Dr. Novak?" said Tom aggressively. "It was all over town that you were going to marry him."

"That was rubbish, Tommy. He did ask me to marry him, before we left France, and of course I said no."

"Of course," agreed Tom, tightening his clasp round her shoulders.

"And then he wrote a crazy letter to my father, repeating his proposal, and saying the fact that I'd refused him the first time only proved that I was suppressing my desire for him—"

"Freud again, I suppose. You know," said Tom, "next time we go to war I hope we put the Psychiatrists' Brigade in the front line. They're a lot more dangerous than the troops."

"Oh, Tommy, don't even talk about another war! But Al's letter made my father furious, and he told some of it to Aunt Edith, and of course that did the trick . . . Tom, let me go, dear, here comes Luis."

The Peruvian butler came in solemnly, carrying a large silver salver which he set on a low table and placed beside Nancy. It held a variety of iced drinks, orange and lemon made with fresh fruit, with one made of wine like Spanish sangría, and also maté in silver-banded gourds called *bombillas,* as well as plates of marzipan pastries and small cakes.

"Luis is a real tryer," said Nancy, when the man had gone, "he knows I loathe maté, but he serves it every afternoon. Señora Luza always drank the stuff, and he's trying to make me be a lady, just like her."

"D'you have a feast like this every day at four o'clock?"

"I only drink orange juice when I'm alone. But try the wine cup, Tom, it's very refreshing, while I go up and change my dress."

"Oh no you don't," said Tom, laying hold of the pleats of the scarlet *saya* as she rose. "You look so lovely in this thing, whatever it may be called."

"The *saya y manto*. But it's too hot to wear indoors in summer. They wore it when they went to church, and then they were called *tapada*, covered up, but the real *tapada* style was to show one eye, like this." With a deft movement of both arms, which a Peruvian girl had taught her, Nancy pulled the black *manto* over her hair and part of her face, until only one bright blue eye sparkled out of the taffeta folds at Tom. It was the ideal costume for flirtation, and Tom thought she was enchanting. Pushing the table of refreshments aside he jumped up and seized her in his arms.

"You've got to be so little," he said stumblingly. It was not what he had meant to say, but the other words were still too hard, and Nancy stammered too as she said it was the s-slippers, the slippers for the dress had to be heelless, and he prob'ly remembered her with high heels—

"Little Nancy." Last time, in Zürich, she'd been bossing the show, but Tom was in command now, and he meant to make her realise it. "You're my girl, aren't you?" he said.

"Yes, Tom."

"And you're—all right? You haven't been worried about anything, or frightened, or—"

"How could I be? You see the way I live here, like a princess in an ivory tower. With an army of servants, and two guards at the gate, as well as a policeman?"

"I saw the policeman," said Tom, "what's he in aid of?"

"Security. Some kids threw stones at Dad's Pierce-Arrow last week and broke a window."

"You don't drive the Pierce, do you?"

"I don't even drive my own car! Dad gave me a roadster for a coming-home present, and we shipped it down here with the Pierce, but it's never been out of the stables. Benito turns the engine over every day."

"What did he give you?"

"A Stutz Bearcat."

"Wow."

Nancy laughed. "That's better," she said. "Tom, don't worry so. I never go out alone, I never see anybody more alarming than Dad's Peruvian friends, I *know* nothing, I've *heard* nothing"—and Tom knew what the emphasis meant.

288

"If anything happened to you I would go mad," he said. "I tormented myself the whole way south in the *Rainier* . . . Nancy!" and as his voice grew deep she closed her eyes, "I want you to — to give me the right to look after you, always, all the time. Look at me, darling! I want you to marry me. To be my wife. Because — "

"Because — "

And the words came at last. "Because I love you, my own darling girl."

*   *   *

An hour later they were walking across the Plaza de Armas, on their way to the hotel where Tom had left his luggage. Nancy was wearing a plain white dress with a black lace mantilla over her hair, and Tom thought she looked nearly as pretty as in the *saya y manto*. The great wave of emotion which had spent itself in kisses, promises, and broken words had not left them exhausted, but calm and serenely happy. They had known each other for so long and so well that the past meshed smoothly into the happy present, and their future seemed as bright as the late afternoon sunshine gilding the cathedral towers. They were crossing the square where Pizarro had founded Lima, the City of the Kings, one Epiphany day long past, and dragoons in white and scarlet uniforms which might have been copied from the Chevalier Gardes of Mannerheim's youth were on sentry duty outside the low-roofed adobe presidential palace in its warren of courtyards and added wings. The Indian faces were impassive under the plumed brass helmets, and each man's white gloved hand rested lightly on the scarlet knot at the hilt of his sabre. The cathedral and the headquarters of the municipality faced each other on opposite sides of the plaza, the fourth side being lined with shops and offices which were slowly taking the place of the town houses of the rich. Lima was still a Spanish colonial city in appearance, with the low roofs of its streets and alleys dominated by the tiled belfries of its many churches, and clung to its Spanish way of life. It was close on the hour of the *paseo*, and a few horse-drawn carriages were moving slowly round the plaza, past gardens set out with cassia trees and hibiscus, both yellow and white, above beds of frangipani and poinsettia. "It's a wonderful town," said Tom.

"You should have seen the plaza at the time of the armistice

289

celebrations," said Nancy, "they were still celebrating when Dad and I got here."

"The *Peruvians* were celebrating?"

"Yes, they were on our side, didn't you know?"

"I can't say I did."

"I don't blame you, I didn't know myself. But after a Peruvian ship was torpedoed by a German submarine, they daringly broke off relations with the Central Powers. So that makes them allies, and of course they've a great admiration for President Wilson, too."

"I don't envy him his job at the peace conference."

"No more do I. Shall we stop by Dad's new office and have them telephone to say we're on our way to pick him up?"

"You don't have a telephone in the house?"

"The Luzas made it an absolute condition of the lease, that we wouldn't do anything as modern as put a phone in."

"How does your father like that?"

"Sometimes it drives him nearly mad."

The office was on the fourth side of the plaza, where some of the houses still had the old Moorish balconies and screens of carved and fretted work, between which its new plate-glass windows looked astonishingly modern. There were three rooms, occupying the whole floor above a bookseller's shop, and the outer door bore the simple inscription in gold lettering, MACPHERSON ENTERPRISES OF PERU.

Two Peruvian clerks in the outer office stood up as Nancy and Tom entered, and a middle-aged American in a thin grey suit came quickly from an inner room. "Good afternoon, Miss Macpherson," he said, "what can I do for you?"

"First say hallo to Mr. Fleming, our visitor from Vancouver," she said brightly. "Tom, this is Mr. Simpson, Dad's office manager in Lima."

"Very glad to meet you, Mr. Fleming. Your arrival was made known to us by Captain Jensen, when he telephoned from Callao."

"Oh good," said Nancy. "And here's the second thing, could *you* call up my father and tell him we'll pick him up at six o'clock?"

Mr. Simpson hesitated. "At Callao, Miss Macpherson?"

"At the Equator offices, as usual. Why?"

"There just might . . . be a bit of trouble at the port this afternoon."

"The stevedores again?"

"Plus a contingent of the San Marcos students, who went down to Callao by train and electric tram about four o'clock."

"Pooh!" said Nancy, "another student demonstration; there's nothing new in that. Won't you show Mr. Fleming round the offices?"

Tom was impressed by what he saw, and said so when he was out in the plaza with Nancy. "I heard your father was branching out in Peru," he said, "I didn't know it was to quite that tune."

"Who'd you hear that from?"

"My father for one, and Harry Carlson for another. Oh, don't worry; Harry and Captain Jensen are very loyal employees, but I somehow got the impression that James J. was playing a pretty sharp game of politics in Peru."

Nancy smiled. "I think I'll let him tell you about that himself, darling. This isn't Seattle; the Limeña ladies don't discuss politics."

"*You* don't discuss politics?"

"Not with the gentlemen who come to dinner, the New Men, Daddy calls them. But I watch, and listen, and one thing I do know, my father is spending a lot of money on good causes in Peru. He's making a gift of a new drinking water system out at the old Paseo de Aguas, for one thing, and proper sewage too. Which may not be very romantic, but it surely is worth while. This way, Tom, we go down the Jirón Union—Union Street."

He wondered, as they turned the corner, how many cities in the world had chosen Union Street as the name of a principal thoroughfare. But this Union Street had nothing in common with that snowy street in Helsingfors. Already far too narrow for the traffic of 1919, it was crowded with men and women, with children offering shoe-shines, with flower-sellers peddling bunches of the perfumed Lima roses at every street corner. It also held the finest shops in the city, their windows showing luxury merchandise from silver turkeys to vicuña cloth, and there was one fine jeweller's which Tom silently noted as he passed as a possible place to buy a ring for Nancy. She stopped to point out the crowds entering and leaving the church of Santa Maria de las Mercedes.

"I think this must be the church they love the best," she said, "it's always full of people."

"Can we go in for a moment?"

"Of course we can."

The altar of the Lady of Mercy was decked in silver and set round with tall white lilies in silver vases. Tom and Nancy stood by a pillar, hand in hand, watching the changing faces of the multi-racial crowd, mestizos, cholos, zambos, all the mixtures of the Indian, Spanish and Negro strains, and the eagerness, the almost gaiety, with which they bent their knees to the statue or touched the votive offerings on the wall, like people paying a quick visit to a familiar friend. "Is she their patron saint?" Tom whispered.

"Yes, the patron saint of Peru, and she was made a Marshal of the Peruvian Army in the Independence time." Nancy smiled up at him: in that church, so foreign to them both, their promises were being made again.

The church of Las Mercedes was so full and so active that it seemed almost a part of the busy street. But as soon as they were back in the Jirón Union Tom saw Mr. Macpherson's Pierce-Arrow standing by the kerb, big enough to form a minor traffic block, with Benito the Peruvian chauffeur in his grey summer uniform and leggings standing proudly beside it. Tom uneasily remembered what Mr. Simpson had said about the possibility of trouble at the port.

"Sure you don't want to be driven back to the house, darling, and let Benito and me go down alone to get your father?"

"You don't suppose I'm afraid of a pack of students, do you?"

As Benito had been sent to the hotel ahead of them, Tom's California-bought bags were already in the lobby, and his offer to pay for the room he had only used to change his clothes in was courteously refused.

"I only hope Emilio Concha D. won't lose his commission," he said to Nancy as they drove away.

"Who on earth's he?"

"My taxi driver. Very up-to-date fellow—look, he even gave me his card."

"Could he speak any English? A bit? Well, good for him." Nancy took the grimy piece of pasteboard. "*Emilio Concha D. ofrece taxi moderno,*" she read aloud. "How *moderno* was it?"

"One of the first-ever Model Ts. Say, that's a fine-looking old place."

"That's the University of San Marcos. I asked Benito to take us a round-about way, so you could see it before we hit the Callao road."

"It looks peaceful enough."

"Oh, well, if the kids are all down in Callao!"

It was one of the oldest universities in the Americas, Nancy said, but there had been more student violence than exam-passing for the past few years. The protest had two sides to it: the one internal, voiced by a call for *cogobierno*, which meant a sharing by the students in the university government and programme of studies, with student right to censure and dismiss incompetent professors. The other, which was the more violent, was external, and had begun about the time of the Mexican revolution against Porfirio Diaz and his dictatorship, being greatly fanned by Peruvian police brutality in the mass demonstrations of 1911.

Nancy forbore to add that the real revolutionaries among the students of Lima had been far more affected by the triumph of Lenin than by the overthrow of Diaz, and Tom made no comment. He twisted round in his seat to look back at the low two-storey buildings of the ancient university, remembering what Igor Heiden's widow had said to him at Seattle about her brother-in-law's finding much to do at the University of San Marcos. He was determined to get through this day, of all days in his life and if it were humanly possible, without mentioning the name of Boris Heiden. He took Nancy's hand and kissed it, and watched while the big car turned west through streets less prosperous than the Jirón Union and came out on the Callao road.

"Why doesn't your father keep a car and a driver down at the Equator offices?" he said.

"I guess because he prefers to have Benito take him and bring him back."

"And you go down to pick him up every afternoon?"

"Every second afternoon. He works at the Lima office on alternate days."

"At least it's not a lonely road for you to travel." It was one of the best roads in Peru, although still cobbled in places, and a few years earlier the installation of electric tram-lines had made it possible for a body of office workers to live in Lima and travel daily to the port. There was very little automobile traffic, but Benito overhauled two trams with a lordly blast on the Pierce's horn, startling a family of Indians camping by the side of the highway. They were roasting grains of corn over a little fire.

"Look at them," said Nancy, "that's the saddest sight in Peru. The rich are so rich, and even richer since the war, and the poor are so very poor."

"I saw a lot of them on the way up to Lima," said Tom. "What are they—nomads?"

"They're Indians from the Andes, come down to the city hoping to find work. Because there are new industries since the war, of course; but these poor creatures aren't skilled workers, and nobody tries to teach them or to care for them."

"Doesn't the government look after them?"

"The government doesn't want to be bothered with them yet."

They were driving through a flat country to the sea, with the brown Andes foothills at their back. The fields near the road were hardly cultivated, but the oleander and hibiscus, growing wild, were covered with blossoms. A goatherd with a little flock of goats waved to them as they went by.

"Tom," said Nancy, "what did you think of when the *Rainier* came into Callao today?"

"Only that I was getting very close to you."

Her look, and the tightened clasp of her fingers, showed Tom that he had said the right thing, but Nancy's face was so serious that he asked, half as a joke, "Was there something special I should have thought?"

"I don't know. I thought about New York myself, and the day I got back from Europe. Linda was asleep, poor darling, and I slipped out of our cabin and went up on deck about daybreak. And it's such an amazing sight, the towers of New York coming through the mist . . . isn't it, Tom? You sail for seven days, maybe more, and there's nothing but the sea, and then you come to a whole new continent, where men have done such wonderful things and built such cities . . . I felt so proud that my grandfathers were two of them—the makers of America."

"So you should be."

"But when we came to Peru, that was an even longer voyage. Nearly two weeks it took us to get here from Seattle. And Callao's nothing to see compared with the New York skyline. Just the two round towers of the old fortress, the Real Felipe, built of that yellow-coloured brick, and half the Peruvian Navy lying out in the roads, and the Pacific breaking on the rocks and shingle. But it made me think how there was nothing but sea, westward, until you come to Polynesia, and here was a new Republic men had struggled to make . . . I thought it was exciting. Until we went ashore, and then I saw it was the same old story. One law for the rich, and another for the poor. A big power struggle to get back two provinces Peru lost to Chile in the War of the Pacific, just like the French lost Alsace and Lorraine. Violence and strikes, just like the revolution began in Russia—just as it began, you know better than I do, in Finland before Mannerheim. This is where I came in, I thought. Back in Skid Road with K. Donovan."

"What are we going to do about it, Nancy?"

"That's what I don't know . . . There's a road block ahead!"

There was an electric tramcar, lying on its side at the entrance to the Callao suburbs, with all the people from a street market overflowing from the tram-lines to their own merchandise lying on the unpaved sidewalk, a chaos of melons, vegetables and pottery wine jars. Two or three policemen, in soiled white uniforms, were keeping back the crowd, and one waved the Pierce-Arrow to a stop.

"What's the matter, Benito?" Nancy exclaimed.

"Trouble on the waterfront, señorita. The officer suggests we turn the car round and go home."

"Señor Macpherson is waiting for us," said Nancy. "Drive on!"

"Wait!" said Tom, "is it the stevedores, as Mr. Simpson said?"

"Yes, but he says the police are there in strength. We must go on, the worst they can do is rock the car again—"

"But you're inside it this time."

The car crawled round the capsized tram. Tom sat forward, looking from side to side. There was no sign of any further disturbance until they came within sight of the sea. Then they heard the roar of an angry crowd.

"Nancy, I wish you'd get out, and wait in one of these cafés till I can fetch your father."

"It's all right," she said, as coolly as ever, "they're nowhere near his place. Look, it's the Standard Oil offices they're going for—".

The plate glass windows of the Standard Oil Company were falling out of their frames in a shower of splinters, and Benito looked round with an anxious face.

"What does he say, Nancy?"

"He's says they're shouting 'Down with the American imperialists!' "

"The waterfront's completely blocked," said Tom quietly. "Is there any other way of getting to your father's office?"

"Up Cock Alley . . . I can't help it, Tom, that's what the sailors call it . . . Turn right, Benito!"

The prostitutes of Cock Alley had closed and barred the upper halves of the doors of the wretched box-cribs where they plied their trade. The broken glass in the alley had no political importance, coming merely from beer bottles smashed in the nightly rows which broke out between foreign sailors boozing in the filthy bars, but there was enough of it to make Benito call on the Lady of Mercy to protect his tyres, and sigh a prayer of thanksgiving as he turned the car into a cobbled yard behind the Equator offices.

"Up the back stairs!" said Nancy . . . "Dad, what's going on around here?"

James J. Macpherson was looking out at the Callao waterfront from the window of his private room, chewing an unlit cigar. He was a short, strongly built man, whose hair had once been curly but was beginning to recede, and with bright blue eyes under shaggy dark brows. It had often been said in Seattle that Miss Nancy Macpherson was a chip off the old block, and he greeted her now with perfect calm.

"Hallo, Nancy, hallo Tom, glad to see you, boy," he said. "Those dockyard peons are acting up again. Just the usual, shouting for less work and more wages, but a bunch of the *señoritos* from San Marcos came down from Lima this afternoon, and they're egging the fellows on. I'm going to phone the Real Felipe and tell them to send troops."

"We were told the police were out in strength," said Tom.

"They turned tail and ran when the shooting started. What's needed now is the military." He picked up the telephone. "Get me the Real Felipe fortress, please."

"It's not a quarter of a mile away," said Nancy. "They could be here in ten minutes."

The noise was coming along the waterfront in their direction.

"What's that?" said Mr. Macpherson into the phone. "*Señor Coronel*, let me remind you, it's the army's duty to protect the lives and property of foreign residents—" He cupped his hand round the mouthpiece and flung at his daughter:

"The garrison commander won't act without authority."

"I'll get the *alcalde* on the other line," said Nancy. With relief, Tom saw her disappear into a back room. He pushed open the balcony door and went out cautiously, followed by the ship-owner. and the reek of burning tow rose up immediately beneath them.

"They've set fire to the rope carts," said Macpherson. "It'll be outright arson next."

Tom Fleming made no reply. On the fringe of the crowd of well-dressed youths and wharfside labourers yelling round the Standard Oil offices, he had seen a young man standing. A nondescript young man, unnoticeable in any crowd, and in that Peruvian mob typical, with his crumpled white linen suit and pencil-thin line of dark moustache, of a hundred Latin-American clerks employed by the port authorities. But Tom recognised the blunt, slightly Slavic features: he was looking once again at Boris Heiden.

It was only the recognition of a moment, for the crowd surged forward and swallowed Heiden up, and now the few taxis still standing by the dock gates seemed to be about to share the fate of the rope carts, from which the drivers were frantically trying to cut their struggling mules.

"There's my friend Emilio Concha, trying to shift his taxi," said Tom. "Wait a minute."

"Where the hell do you think you're going?" shouted Nancy's father. Tom was rushing down the front stairs and across the cobbles to the entrance gate. Mr. Macpherson, cursing, saw him giving something to one of the Peruvian taxi drivers, first pointing across the crowd and then waving directions to the man to get his vehicle into Cock Alley and round to the Equator backyard. All the chauffeurs were gunning their engines, trying to make their way through the roaring crowd.

"Dad, where's Tom?" said Nancy, on the balcony.

"Down there. He went out for a breath of fresh air," said her father grimly. "How about the *alcalde*?"

"I got through. He's going to give the order."

297

"Good girl."

They saw Tom helping the Peruvian doorman to close and bar the entrance gates.

"Fat lot of good that'll do," grunted Macpherson. "Matchwood, if they can lay their hands on iron bars."

"Down with the American imperialists! Down with Macpherson's gold!"

"Our turn now," said the ship-owner, as Tom reappeared breathless on the balcony. "Bloody Peruvian military, where the hell are they?"

"Captain Jensen and the crewmen are on their way," said Tom. "Nancy, go back to the other room and stay there. Have you a gun, sir?"

"Sure."

"Then you take care of Nancy. I hear horses, the troops must have taken time out to saddle up."

He pushed the father and daughter ahead of him into the back office as the yard gates gave way with a crash. Tom jerked the Browning from its holster as the crowd, now armed with torches, burst across the yard towards the main door.

"Back!" yelled Tom Fleming from the head of the stairs. "*Soldados! Muerta!* Back!"

"Down with the American imperialists!"

The stones flew, the torches were thrust forward to the wooden stairs, the glass of the windows on the yard was shattered.

"Back!" cried Tom again, and emptied his pistol over the heads of the shrieking crowd.

*　　　　*　　　　*

"That's quite a man you've got yourself there, Miss Nancy," said her father, coming into Nancy's bedroom when dark had fallen over Lima. "Got a lot of guts. I like a fellow who can make a snap decision and follow it right through."

"He's had a lot of practice, Daddy. Now I suppose you want me to tie your tie?"

Her father looked at her proudly as she arranged the black silk tie. So pretty, and so composed, dressed for her engagement dinner as carefully as if she had not been delivered from fire and violence, so short a time before, by a detachment of Peruvian cavalry.

"Are you happy, baby?"

"Terribly happy." Nancy laid her cheek against her father's, and whispered, "*Terribly.*"

"He was always the one, wasn't he?"

"Always."

"Well, well," said Mr. Macpherson, "I'm delighted it's turned out this way. I admit you had me worried for a while back there, the two of you, but now everything's going to be fine . . . I always thought a lot of Tom Fleming; never did believe Arthur and Lily knew the right way to handle him. I mean to have a long business talk with him tomorrow, in the office."

"But *weren't* you talking downstairs, for over an hour? I heard you in the patio when I was getting ready for my bath."

"Oh then! We were discussing politics."

"I should have thought you'd had enough of Peruvian politics for one afternoon," said Nancy drily.

"Seattle politics. Sharp lad—he found out more in one fore-noon than Harry Carlson could find out in a year. A Red cell in the Public Market, of all places, with that crazy instructor of yours running it! I'll give the Seattle police the tip-off right away, and if that woman steps one inch out of line they'll have her behind bars before she knew what hit her."

"Oh, Daddy, please, no politics tonight!" said Nancy, stepping away from him. "Can't we talk about something happy, for a change?"

"Like a wedding, eh?" chuckled her father. "Get this: my future son-in-law is trying to push me around already. He wants to marry you right here in Lima, in the English church of all places, without any fuss and feathers was what he had the nerve to say. I said to him, Son, I said, when you marry James J. Macpherson's only daughter you stand right up beside her in the Presbyterian kirk in her own city, with all your family and hers looking on, and the biggest wedding-cake ever baked to be cut with your own sword—"

"I don't think he ever *had* a sword," said Nancy. "Now listen here, James J. You may be the greatest fixer in North and South America, but don't try to fix up anything for Tom and me. He doesn't fix easily, as I should know."

"And that makes two of you," said her father, and gave her an affectionate little push. "Go on down to the patio, Nannie. He's waiting for you."

He was waiting for her, and in Tom's arms it was easy to think and speak only of happy things. For he found it easy, too, to repeat that he loved her; the words so long unspoken came in a dozen tender forms. He adored her, he was crazy about her, mad about her, he loved her, loved her, loved her—all this in the dark patio, with the moon rising above the myrtles, and the voice of the watchman coming regularly from the distant street, assuring the City of the Kings that all was well. No one came near them for an exquisite half hour, although there were lights behind them in the sala and the dining room, where servants were setting the table, until at last Mr. Macpherson came to join them, preceded by Luis carrying a candelabrum as ceremoniously as if he were ushering in a royal personage.

"It's warm tonight, we'll have drinks in the patio," said the master of the house. "That all right with you, Nancy?"

"Of course."

The servants had already arranged some light garden furniture in the patio where Nancy posed for her portrait. Luis set down the candles on a small table, and went indoors to fetch a tray of pisco sours, one of which he presented to Nancy with his usual expression of disdain.

"Luis thinks I'm a lost cause," said Nancy, sipping the cocktail. "Do you like it, Tom?"

"It's very good. What's in it?"

"Peruvian grape brandy, lime juice, egg white, a little sugar syrup and crushed ice."

"Very refreshing," said her father. "Drink up, Tom, and have another."

"You're not going to tell me this is the first drink you two have had since we came back from Callao," said Nancy.

"We thought we rated a little Scotch when we came home," said her father, with a wink at Tom. "We're having champagne at dinner, for our celebration."

"Wonderful." Tom laid his head on the cushioned back of his chair. "This is really great. I feel as if I'd been running for a year, non-stop."

Nancy knew exactly what he meant. But whether he had been running to, or from, she couldn't say.

Presently they went in to dinner. The Luza dining room was no more cheerful than the sala, with a huge refectory table and chairs of carved oak, and particularly dismal religious pictures on the wall. The light from a chandelier, swung high from the ceiling, hardly pierced the darkness of the room. But there were a dozen candles on the table, set between bowls of the sweet-scented Lima roses, and in their light Nancy Macpherson glowed. Because Tom had admired her in the *saya y manto* she had come down to dinner in the white Peruvian dress she wore beneath the Limeña scarlet and black. The skirt, of white China silk, was quite short, and from half-way below the knee a flounce of white lace fell to the tips of Nancy's white satin slippers. The bodice, made entirely of bands of lace, had wide lace sleeves sewn in a circular pattern and worn thrown back across the shoulders, so that in the dusky dining room the transparent flounces had the shimmer and flutter of a pair of wings. Nancy's father saw that Tom Fleming could hardly take his eyes away from his future bride.

The champagne was opened, and Mr. Macpherson drank ceremoniously to their future happiness. From her place at the table Nancy saw that two or three of the maids were peeping through the service door for a glimpse of the señorita's *novio*. The master of the house had told Luis of the engagement, saying Mr. Fleming was to be addressed and obeyed as Don Tomaso, and of course ripples and waves of excitement were going through the kitchen premises. Nancy smiled at the peeping maids. She was proud of her *novio*, so handsome in his white dinner-jacket, tanned from the Pacific voyage, and the two of them had come so far, in time and distance, to this happy hour!

The dinner, by Peruvian standards, was simple, but it was excellent. It consisted of shrimp soup, a dish of chicken with rice and fresh vegetables, and then a platter of exotic fruits, pineapple, the very ripe bananas called *plátones*, and *chirimoyas* whose pale green and black skin contained a delicious milky cream. "Now that's what I call a good dinner," pronounced Mr. Macpherson. "Tasty, but not too spicy, and digestible. You're getting a wonderful housekeeper, Tom."

"I only ordered dinner, Dad, I didn't cook it."

"I'm getting a wonderful girl, sir."

He couldn't quite realise it yet, that Nancy was going to keep house for him, have his kids, go out to parties with him in a world at peace. She looked so different in that white lace get up, with the curly fringe which had not suited her brushed back to show her brow and held in place by the Spanish comb which gave her the dignity Calamity Jane had never known. He raised his glass to her and drank in silence.

The talk at dinner, as Nancy had wished, was all of happy things, and the events of the afternoon were not so much as mentioned. The only slight breaks in the pleasant hour occurred when, twice, the heavy gate bell rang and there were steps and voices in the outer patio, and each time this happened Tom Fleming felt a tightening of his muscles, a moment of anticipation. But each time it was to Mr. Macpherson, not to himself, that Luis brought a letter on a silver tray, and Mr. Macpherson, after reading it with a word of apology, put the letter in the pocket of his dinner jacket and said, "No answer." The third message came while they were having coffee in the patio, and this time the envelope had a heavy red seal on it, and the letter took longer to digest. But once again Mr. Macpherson shook his head at the butler, and went on calmly with an amusing story of himself and Tom's father in their young manhood, camping out in the Snoqualmie forest, and their confrontation with a she-bear and her cubs. He finished his cigar after the story was ended, before saying casually to his daughter:

"Nancy, my dear, I may not be able to exercise my paternal authority much longer. So before I hand you over to your husband I'll take the opportunity, tonight, of telling you to go to bed. You've had a big day, and it's past eleven."

"I think I will," said Nancy, rising with unusual docility. "I really am rather tired—and we breakfast early, Tom!"

"Right!" He waited while Nancy kissed her father's cheek, and then walked with her to the foot of the stone staircase. There were lighted candles, he saw, along the coping of the balcony. When he walked back down the patio he saw that Mr. Macpherson, too, was on his feet, and heard him say:

"I hear Luis in the dining room. Would you ask him to speak to me?"

"Certainly."

The butler came at once and bowed to his master.

"Tell Benito I want the car at the front gate in five minutes. Get one of the yard boys and make sure he's dressed properly; I'll want him to come too."

"At once, sir."

"You're going out this late?" said Tom.

Mr. Macpherson showed him the envelope with the red seal. "I must," he said. "This is a rather pressing invitation from Señor Pardo, the President of the Republic. He wants to see me at the Palace, and I can't refuse. It's only a few blocks away, but I don't want to walk through the streets alone tonight."

"I'll come with you."

"No, I'll be all right in the car. No need for you to get further into the mess we're in already. No need to alarm Nancy, either, that's why I didn't say anything in front of her. See you in the morning, son. Sleep well."

Tom walked with Mr. Macpherson to the great front door. It opened and closed quietly, the big car purred away, the distant watchman proclaimed the safety of the night. The candles were already extinguished along Nancy's balcony.

Tom had been given one of the bedrooms with a door, Peruvian style, on the patio. It was prepared for the night, with a lamp burning, and a bottle of mineral water on the bedside table. He poured himself a glass. His mouth was burning from Nancy's kisses as he held her to his heart at the foot of the old stone steps. His body was on fire at the thought that he was under the same roof with her tonight.

His desire for her was so strong that when the light tap fell on his bedroom door he felt himself stiffen with the assurance that, against all imagining, she had come to him. But it was Luis who stood there, still holding his silver tray, still wearing his disdainful face.

"I beg Don Tomaso's pardon," said the butler, "but a—a person, a . . . taxi-chauffeur, left this letter at the kitchen door. I regret that the—person did not wait for an answer."

"Thanks, Luis," said Tom curtly. The envelope he lifted from the tray was badly smudged; the writing, when he studied it by the lamplight in his bedroom, was hard to read. But the sense was clear enough:

"Señor," the letter ran, "I followed the man in the white suit from Callao back to the city. He moved about much through the evening. But he lives below the bridge, in Rímac. He has a room in the house with a pink front, next to the San Lazaro church. Respectfully, Emilio Concha D."

303

22

"WE'RE GETTING A BAD press this morning, Tom!" was Mr. Macpherson's cheerful greeting, as Tom Fleming entered his office in the Plaza de Armas.

"So Mr. Simpson was telling me."

"And I'm afraid there's more bad news, sir," said the manager, who was close behind Tom. "We couldn't get off Mr. Fleming's cables to Vancouver and Seattle from the general post office. The postal and telegraph workers are out on strike."

"The hell you say!" exploded the ship-owner. "The cables *from* Seattle came in all right this morning!"

"The strike was declared about ten," said Tom. "They're keeping the telephones in operation for the time being."

"I wonder for how long. Mr. Simpson, you'd better call up the Equator office and find out what's doing at the harbour. Sit down, Tom. Sorry you couldn't cable to your family."

"Good news will keep," said Tom. "And I did get Nancy's ring."

"First things first," grinned Nancy's father. "Was Simpson any help?"

"He was a great help at the jeweller's. Not only for speaking Spanish, but he seems to know a lot about precious stones as well."

"He's a pretty knowledgeable fellow all round. Can I have a peek?"

Tom produced a little white leather box from an inner pocket and sprang the lid open. James Macpherson whistled.

"That's a beauty!"

Tom had chosen a Colombian emerald of the first water, almost half an inch square, set on each side with six diamonds, arranged by three, two and one to join the narrow band of gold.

"Green fire," said Tom. "I thought it looked like her."

"It looks like the devil of a lot of money. See the size! She'll be able to use it for a knuckleduster."

Tom laughed. "I hope it fits," he said. "She absolutely refused to come to the shop with me."

"Ah, they get skittish when it comes to that. Her mother was just the same, poor dear—I remember taking the size of *her* finger with a bit of string."

"Maybe that's what I should have done."

"Come to think of it, it does seem a bit small," said Mr. Macpherson, fitting the emerald ring on the tip of his little finger.

"Nancy's gotten so slim, I thought a small ring would be all right."

"But she's got strong hands, Tom; not like the Lima ladies, they've got tiny little paws, and the jewellers calculate accordingly . . . It's a beautiful ring, Tom. Nancy's a lucky girl."

Tom put the ring back in his pocket. "I'll try to make her a happy one," he said soberly.

"I know you will, son. Now we ought to think about the future. Have you any plans?"

"About what I'm going to do, and where we're going to live, and all that?"

"Especially what you're going to do."

Tom hesitated. "Well," he said, "My father wants me to join him in Vancouver. I don't know how much that would appeal to Nancy."

"Does it appeal to you? Come clean, Tom, this is important."

"Not particularly."

"Why not?"

"Because from all I heard in Toronto, when I was staying with my brother Graham, and all I saw in Vancouver—of course I was only there a week—the timber industry has changed a lot since I was a kid. We tore the heart out of the forests, and now the whole forest zone is smaller, and the saw-mill's more important than the logging camp. Probably that's as it should be, because timber will be in great demand for the next few years to repair the war losses, especially in the actual war zones. Maybe my friends in Finland will have a chance to make a big profit out of their green gold."

"You're not considering going back to Finland, are you?"

"*Never!*"

"All right, all right, I only asked."

"But my father, and Graham too—they're looking beyond the war damages. They think the new cheap motor cars will bring in a whole new way of living. 'The flivver is the answer!' Dad told me more than once. He sees new camp sites opening, new summer homes for more people, new cheap housing for the new immigrants from Europe, and all in all, a great new market for his timber."

"Very good," approved Mr. Macpherson. "Arthur always had a shrewd eye for the future. But you don't quite cotton to his programme?"

Tom shrugged. "I'd be keener if our timber were to go to housing developments for ex-servicemen. I don't see much reward in selling planks for tourist camps."

"I think I could offer you something more adventurous, if you came in with me."

"With you, sir? But I don't know the first thing about shipping."

"I wasn't thinking about the shipyards or the Line. I meant MEP—Macpherson Enterprises of Peru."

The head of MEP put his elbows on the desk and looked earnestly at Tom. It was a look of such concentrated sincerity that Tom was reminded of his father's often-pronounced judgment, that if Jim Macpherson weren't so completely honest he would be the finest con man on the Pacific Coast.

"You've come to Peru at a great time, Tom, when the old stranglehold of the oligarchy seems to be broken for good. The days of the military junta and the soldier president are over, and the businessman is coming out on top. Pardo has had a rough passage in this term of his presidency, and maybe we'll have to replace him by a better man next May, but there's no doubt he's done something to open Peru up to American know-how and technology."

"While concerns like MEP supply the capital."

"Exactly. Now, Tom, I know you British Columbians are heart and soul for the old country, so don't take offence if I just mention that the British began to skim the cream off Peru nearly a hundred years ago. They were first in the field with the railroads, with London and Pacific Oil (that's in the hands of International Petroleum now, of course), with British Sugar, with the textile mills. I'd like to see American capital getting its innings now."

"And where does MEP come in, sir?"

"We've made a very promising start in developing the mineral resources. Mind you, I don't think we'll ever be a threat to

Cerro de Pasco, but there's a lot MEP can do with lead and zinc, and I've good reports from my copper prospectors in the south. I've bought fairly heavily into the coffee interests and other export lines. What most Peruvians don't realise is that the old guano and nitrate days are gone for ever; it's cotton, oil and sugar that have to be exported on a large scale now. In one word, that's what MEP stands for: diversification."

"It's an empire," said Tom.

"Yes, but the ruler's not prepared to abdicate, don't run away with that idea. I suppose I seem like an old fogey to you, but I'm younger than your father, fifty-eight last birthday: I should be good for another ten years before I begin to think of retiring . . . I wish I could believe I wouldn't have to wait ten years for an air service that would get me from Lima to Seattle in fifteen hours instead of fifteen days!"

"What are we waiting for?" said Tom. "Macpherson Airlines sounds all right to me."

"It could be Macpherson-Fleming in a few years' time, Tom," said Nancy's father, getting up and sitting informally on the side of the desk, "I don't want to rush you. Take your time and think it over. Consult your father if you like. He'll probably think I'm poaching on his territory. But—well, I've always wanted a son of my own. Nancy's the apple of my eye, you know that, but I've always wanted a young guy to work with me, and carry on where I leave off. I've hoped for quite some time that that guy would be Nancy's husband, and that her husband would be you. Because I suspect that you'll do well at whatever job you set your hand to."

"Thanks, Mr. Macpherson. Nancy's the one I'll have to consult first."

"I think she'll see it my way, Tom."

"Maybe. Of course the whole thing is a new idea to me, I'd have to think it over carefully. Could I say just one or two things now?"

"Fire away."

"I've had quite an education in the past twelve months. I've heard about people and books and ideas I never even knew existed. Until today I never heard of London and Pacific Oil, or the Cerro de Pasco mines. But I did know one thing about a Peruvian empire, we used to discuss it in high school."

"The Incas, I suppose?"

"No, not the Incas. The rubber empire of the Putomayo."

Macpherson looked annoyed. "That was a bad business," he said. "The treatment of the Putomayo Indians and the negro labour scandalised the world. But it's all over now, it ended with the natural rubber boom, and I can assure you no Indian in my employment is ever likely to be maltreated—"

"I wasn't thinking of maltreatment, just of plain hunger. Those poor wretches by the roadside, roasting their grains of corn—"

"The government does nothing for the Indians, because they're illiterate and therefore have no right to vote."

"Teach them to read."

"That's a pretty tall order, Tom . . . What was the other thing you had on your mind?"

"Just a question. Who are you backing for President?"

The ship-owner's grim look melted into a smile. "Former President Leguía," he said. "He has the right idea about the good old USA."

"But you had a conference with the present incumbent, late last night?"

"I did, in the presence of a senior official from the US Embassy. Pardo had the gall to have me on the carpet for that affair at Callao yesterday afternoon. The *alcalde* was censured for calling out the military at my request. I told Pardo straight he'd be calling out the troops himself if the present wave of strikes continues. The labour unrest has been much worse lately, the peons have got new encouragement from somewhere or someone, it's my belief. Pardo was in a blue funk last night. He even tried to duck out of appearing with me when the new water system's opened at the Paseo de Aguas, tomorrow morning. I told him he had to toe the line, or else."

"We're the heavies for what happened at Callao, Mr. Simpson said?"

"According to the press. I've got the translations here. *El Comercio* calls you an American, heavily armed and desperate, and so does—no, that's funny, the Callao paper calls you a Canadian."

"Somebody got his facts right," said Tom lightly.

"Yes. Well, there you are, Tom; whatever you decide to do, we're in the riot business shoulder to shoulder, American imperialists one and all . . . We'd better start back to the casa now. Nancy probably told you, we're having guests to lunch."

"Yes, she did."

Mr. Macpherson rose to get his hat. "Oh, by the way," he said casually, "I've been thinking over what you said about the wedding. On second thoughts, I think a wedding in Lima could be a mighty pretty affair. That's if you decide to stay on here, of course. Then I could turn the Casa Luza over to Nancy and you and get back to Seattle."

        ✻   ✻   ✻

It was not until the luncheon guests—two charming, cosmopolitan and excessively rich Peruvian couples—had been driven away that Tom and Nancy had a chance to be alone together. Her father so far conformed to the custom of the country as to take an hour's nap: the two young people retired to a little room which Señora Luza had decorated with English chintzes and flower paintings, and which was the most attractive apartment in the stiff Spanish Colonial house. There Tom produced the emerald ring and had the chagrin of discovering that it was indeed too small.

"Oh, darling, it's the most beautiful thing I ever saw, and I'll adore wearing it, but it really doesn't fit!" said Nancy in distress.

"What a fool I am," said Tom, "I should have asked you if you had a ring the right size, to show the jeweller." He kissed the square, heavy-knuckled little hand. "Your father says you have one that does fit."

"I'll go get it." She went to her bedroom and came back with an old-fashioned diamond half hoop, which Mr. Macpherson had given his wife when Nancy was born.

"Even mother's engagement ring's too small for me," she said, handing it to Tom, "but I know this one's all right."

"Sure you won't come to the shop with me? You might see something you like even better. We could stop in on our way back from this art show, or whatever it is we're going to." There had been talk at lunch of an exhibition of paintings opening that day in a small palace of the Spanish Colonial time, called the Torre Tagle.

"Please don't make me, Tom! I just couldn't try on engagement rings in public. You chose this one, and it's perfect."

"But what about the wedding ring? Do you want it broad or narrow, or carved, or plain? I'd better ask the man to send a selection along here, for you to choose."

Nancy burrowed her head in his shoulder. "That makes it seem so real," she said in a muffled voice. So she feels just as I felt last night, thought Tom, as if she can't quite believe we'll have an ordinary life together.

Nancy sat up and put the emerald ring carefully into its velvet setting. "I can't wait to wear it," she said. "How I wish I could wear it at the Torre Tagle this afternoon! Most of the people we know at the embassy will be there."

"I'm sure they can enlarge it in a day," said Tom comfortably. "You can have it by dinner-time tomorrow night."

"When we're entertaining two dreadfully dull Peruvian politicians."

"Two of what your father calls the New Men?"

"Has he been telling you about that?"

"Just a little. But those two chaps at lunch, they aren't New Men, are they?"

"No, they're potential investors in MEP, I think. They, or their wives, I'm not sure which, inherited two of the big guano fortunes from their parents. They're part of the oligarchy, which has always been against Leguía."

"Your father asked me to join him in MEP today."

"What did you say?"

"I told him it needed thinking about, and talking over with you, too." Tom stretched his long legs over the parquet floor. "There hasn't been much time to think, of course. But I keep remembering what you said yesterday, that we're two of the very lucky ones. Not only because we came through the Great War, but because we're able to choose our own way of life. We can live in Canada or the United States or even here in South America: which would you prefer?"

"It's up to you, Tom. You've got to do the job that suits you best. And I think you'd really like to go back to the forests, wouldn't you?"

"How can I, darling? I'm too old to be a lumberjack again, I've done that part of my timber training. No, I was thinking of the place to live. When I was in Vancouver, my mother told me all the property there would be mine some day. How'd you like to be the mistress of Rubislaw House?"

He smiled at her fleeting expression of dismay. Nancy said diplomatically, "Your mother's so proud of Rubislaw House,

Tom, I hope she lives to enjoy it herself for many, many years to come."

"I know exactly how you feel," he assured her. "I felt absolutely stifled in the house myself. Gee, Nancy, if you'd been there on Christmas Eve you'd have run out of the place screaming. All mother's relatives were there—and you know what a tribe the Stuarts are—and all Dan Trumper's, trumpeting away like himself, and I was just killed with kindness, swamped in family, all so nice and all so deadly dull. No, the people I envy are the Carlsons. They started out on their own in Seattle, without a bunch of in-laws breathing down their necks and butting in, just the two of them alone together."

"That's what I'd like too, but where?"

"You know what I'd really like to do? Put the old Fleming homestead in order, down by Burrard Inlet. There's a lot of room if you take in the barn space, and a huge garden, and even a slip- way for a boat—"

"And would we keep a cow?"

"Well, no, we wouldn't need a cow . . . You're laughing at me!"

"No, I'm not!" said Nancy indignantly. "I'll keep house for you in Gastown if that's what you want. Or if you'd rather take a job in Alaska I'll go along and cook flapjacks in bacon grease for breakfast and learn to make sour dough—"

"You're thinking of the gold rush, darling. All that was twenty years ago."

"I know it was," said Nancy softly. "What I'm trying to make you see is, we can't put the clock back. We can't escape into the Fleming homestead, because it's only a museum piece now. We're what our old folks made us, and we're rich, Tom. Rich and young and strong. We can't duck out on our responsibilities."

"I suppose that means you want me to go in with your father?"

"Not necessarily."

"Do you want to go on living here?"

"In Peru or in the Casa Luza?"

"Right here in the casa."

"Goodness, no!" Nancy sat bolt upright in surprise. "Why, Tom, it's not our house, it's the Luzas' house, it isn't like a home at all! . . . Oh, when we came here in November, I thought it was marvellous. And it was, too, with summer beginning, and all the sunshine and the lovely flowers. But the life was beginning to stifle me before you came—just as *you* felt, surrounded by the Stuarts and the Trumpers! I don't want to spend my days playing charades with sixteen-year-old girls, or ordering meals for idlers whose fathers made their money out of birds' droppings! It's a lovely, lazy life for a rich woman, Tommy, but it's not nearly demanding enough for me!"

"That's what I hoped you'd say," said Tom. "Because, you know, if I did go in with your father, I'd have to learn whatever branch of MEP I start in, from the bottom up. How would you take to life in a mining town in the Andes, or in one of those dreary little ports Captain Jensen told me about, where your father's freighters are going to put in for the ore? Or on a coffee plantation, with nobody to talk to but the under-manager's wife, who doesn't speak anything but Spanish?"

"You once told me I'd be a good pioneer, and that would be pioneering in a way. And then—don't you think—we could do something for the Indians?"

"We could try."

"Oh, Tom, it might be a great sucess!"

"Your father paid me a compliment today, and I'm not sure it's true. He said I could do well at anything I tried . . ."

"So you can."

"But I've got to do better than well, Nancy. Because of the men who didn't come back from Sainte Elodie."

*　　　*　　　*

The palace built by the Marqués de Torre Tagle in the middle of the eighteenth century was only a few blocks from the Casa Luza, but Mr. Macpherson insisted that Tom and Nancy should go there in the car. He was decidedly anxious about conditions in the streets, for the strike had spread to the drivers of the electric trams which went to Callao, and it was predictable that there would be further unrest if the San Marcos students came out to encourage the men of the Lima terminal. But the narrow streets in the San Francisco quarter were as sleepy as ever, although the honour guard of policemen at the great door of the Torre Tagle was as large as if the President of the Republic were expected. But President Pardo remained in his own palace, and the most distinguished persons at the *vernissage* were the French and Portuguese ambassadors and a group of minor diplomats from the embassy of the United States.

The Americans made a little group in the outer patio of the ancient house, looking about them uncertainly as if in search of a host. No one seemed quite to know who had sponsored the exhibition, organised by an art gallery in the Jirón Union, although a large portrait of the fifth president of the United States, James Monroe, which was prominent among the Peruvian paintings, caused one or two knowing whispers of *"Panamericanismo!"* Nancy introduced Tom to all the Americans she knew, blushing delightfully as she murmured "my fiancé". One of the striped-pants set, as she liked to call them, annoyed Tom by asking sarcastically if he were the *señor americano* who distinguished himself at Callao yesterday. He was glad to reply that no, he was the *señor canadiense*.

Some of the other invited guests lingered in the outer patio of the Torre Tagle palace, of which few people had ever seen the interior. It had been untenanted for a long time, and had fallen into considerable disrepair, and there was now a movement on foot to restore it for government use, or for any practical purpose which would renew the glory of the city's choicest example of the pure Spanish Colonial style. Even the dilapidations were less apparent in the summer sunshine which added lustre to the decorations of blue glazed tiles from Seville, and brought out the scent of the roses planted among clumps of gladioli along the walls. Like all the old houses of Lima, the Torre Tagle had two patios, each with balconies, and lattice-work balconies in the Moorish style overhung the street, carved from cedarwood and the wood of the cinnamon tree. Inside, in the rooms bare of furniture, the intricately carved ceilings were a decoration in themselves.

Glasses of wine cup and sweetmeats were offered to the guests, who strolled round the room where the paintings were hung exchanging slightly puzzled remarks. The purpose as well as the sponsorship of the exhibition remained in doubt, although the pictures were described in a short catalogue as belonging to the school of Cuzco. The ancient capital of the Incas had given its name to an art form which was essentially Spanish but marked by the Indian tradition, a cross-pollination which produced, at its most original, something engagingly like the Italian primitives. There were a number of religious paintings, showing a Christ, a John the Baptist, a Magdalene with the impassive faces of the half-breed Indians, and some excellent paintings of Peruvian animals. In this sense the display seemed to have the appeal of folklore, of an Indian culture, but the Cuzco School petered out, three quarters of the way round the room, into more modern pictures of a decidedly political nature. There was a portrait of Simon Bolívar, the great Liberator of South America, and a vast canvas showing General San Martín proclaiming the independence of Peru from a balcony in the Plaza de Armas, prominent among other pictures of the period in which the Liberators themselves were indistinguishable in their stiff Spanish uniforms, with their stiff Spanish faces, from the former masters of the land. Finally there were two contemporary portraits, astonishing in that company, of two men with pince-nez and starched wing collars: the President of the United States, Woodrow Wilson, and the former President of the Peruvian Republic, Augusto B. Leguía.

"Your dad doesn't miss a trick, does he?" whispered Tom to Nancy, and saw by the amused little quirk of one eyebrow that she had understood.

"Very interesting," she said demurely. "Is that the whole of it? Or are there more paintings in the room next door?"

She said afterwards that she had only wanted to see a little more of the Torre Tagle, without actually trespassing, and expected the room next door to be quite empty. But the smaller room beyond the impoverished gallery, with the same ornate ceiling and panelled walls, held a modern table desk at which a fair-haired girl sat writing. And when she looked up at them both with a start of surprise, Tom recognised Lisa Sandels.

He felt the blood come into his face with a rush as she got slowly to her feet. He could remember nothing but that he had nearly raped her in that barred bedroom in the Zürich clinic, and he knew by the answering blush which coloured her own pale face that Lisa was remembering too. But she had more presence of mind than he had; she held out her hand with a "How do you do, Mr. Fleming?" and that was all.

"How are you?" he said. "Nancy—er—this is Sophie's sister. I mean, it's Mrs. Heiden."

"How do you do, baroness?" said Nancy with awful clarity. Lisa shook her head. "I'm *Mrs.* Heiden—unfortunately."

Tom managed to say, "I'd like you to meet Miss Macpherson, Lisa . . . She and I are going to be married." It was gauche in the last degree, but it was better than that terrible start: this is Sophie's sister. He dared not look at Nancy. Lisa murmured something about congratulations, with her eyes anywhere but on his. In her office uniform of a white shirt-blouse and a long black skirt, with the office table and writing materials behind her, she looked amazingly like Sophie Sandels as Tom saw her first on a winter night in a city on the other side of the world. Even the bright hair seemed to have darkened, and was smoothed into wings by brown tortoiseshell combs.

"Have you been organising the exhibition, Mrs. Heiden?" Nancy asked.

"I work for the gallery which collected the paintings," said Lisa. "I mean, I work for the owner in the afternoons, and for one of the hotels in the evenings. The hotel where I'm living, that is; I keep their books."

"Your Spanish must be very good."

"I remember telling T—Mr. Fleming, the first time he came to our home in Helsingfors, that we Finns have to be good at languages."

"How's your Russian?" said Nancy.

Lisa lifted her chin. "I gave up learning it," she said. "My husband left me, about two months ago . . . Mr. Fleming, could I possibly speak to you alone?"

"Say anything you like in front of Miss Macpherson," Tom told her. "She knows all about the Meyer clinic, and how you helped to put me there."

"Oh, but do excuse me," said Nancy. "I'm sure two such old friends must have a lot to say to one another. Just tell me one thing, Mrs. Heiden: is your husband in Lima now?"

"He left me to go to Arequipa. As far as I know, he's still there."

"Thank you," Nancy said. "Goodbye."

The door shut behind her with a decisive click, and Lisa sighed. "She's angry with me," she said. "I'm sorry, Tom. I only wanted to ask your pardon for what I did in Zürich. The telephone call, I mean."

"He made you do it, Lisa."

"I wouldn't do it now."

"There's really a split, for good, between you and him?"

"I hope I never see him again."

"Then what are you doing here in Lima?"

"Trying to earn enough money to get away. Oh, Tom, he sent his mother back to Petrograd with those two awful servants, the day before we were married; how I wish I'd had the wits to go with them!"

"What, to Petrograd?"

"No, no, to Helsingfors . . . I want to go home, so much."

Tom Fleming wondered how he had ever desired to punish, savagely and sexually, that drooping figure which now aroused only his pity. He said, "You were very much in love with him, I know. What happened to make you change?"

"I think it was what you said to me in Zürich, about his responsibility for Sophie's death. I simply couldn't stop thinking about it. And one night after we came here, it must have been about the end of October, I challenged him with it, and he only laughed and said yes, he'd had her name put on the Black List, and that was one White less."

"The cruel devil."

Lisa caught at the word. "Yes, he *is* cruel, he was cruel to me and – not normal, and the whole Party machine is cruel, I know that now, although I never joined it, never! . . . Tom, what am I going to do?"

"Let me talk to Nancy's father about it," he said. "He's a terrific fixer. Maybe he could do something about travel papers for you, that's going to be the real difficulty. The money part's quite easy."

Lisa's lips set, she looked exactly like her sister when Sophie refused to accept his expensive presents. "I'll pay back every penny that anybody lends me," she said, "but the travel visas! Oh, Tom, I've felt so trapped in Lima—"

"We'll work something out," he said, more confidently than he felt. "Tell me the name of your hotel and I'll be in touch with you."

She wrote the address on a slip of paper with the letter-head of the art shop which employed her and gave it to him with an earnest word of thanks. "You mustn't keep your fiancée waiting," she said wistfully.

"No, I'd better go, Lisa, I'll see you soon."

"Goodbye," she said. And then, when he turned to smile at her before opening the door, Lisa added,

"Sophie would have wanted you to be happy."

Tom nodded; there were no words. He found Nancy chatting with the American diplomats. She had a glass of water in her hand.

"I think I'd like to go home now, Tom."

"Yes, it's getting late." There were a few goodbyes to say, and then they were going through the huge doorway of the Torre Tagle palace, wide enough to admit a carriage and horses, under the carved, enclosed balconies, so engagingly irregular, and the richly decorated entablature above the pillars.

"Well, what had Mrs. Heiden to say for herself?" Nancy demanded, as soon as they were seated in the car.

"She only wanted to tell me about the break-up with her husband, and how much she wants to go home to Finland."

"She should have thought of that before she married him."

Tom was silent, and Nancy burst out:

"What a busy girl she is! Working for an art shop in the afternoons, and bookkeeping at a hotel in the evenings! What does she do in the mornings—blow up trains?"

"Don't be like that, Nancy. She's working to earn the money for her passage home."

"If you can believe that you'll believe anything." The car turned into the narrow *calle* where the Casa Luza stood. Then Nancy said, "Is she very like her sister?"

"More so than she used to be." A servant opened the nail-studded door of the casa: the flower-decked outer patio was inviting and cool.

"I think I'll go on to the jeweller's now, and see about the ring."

"Oh, the ring; yes, of course. Tom, I've got a headache coming on, maybe I've been missing my siesta. I think I'll stay in my room till dinner-time, or until Dad comes home. He said something about having dinner earlier tonight, maybe about eight."

"Right. You have a good rest, dear."

Benito and the car were still waiting by the door, and Tom allowed the man to drive him to the jeweller's shop on the Jirón Union. There, over Benito's protests, he told the chauffeur to go home. He knew his way back to the casa now, he said, and preferred to walk. But when the two rings were handed over, and the man willingly agreed to make the emerald ring the same size as the diamond half hoop, Tom Fleming asked directions to the San Lazaro church.

It was sunset when he crossed the Plaza de Armas again, and the guard was being changed outside the presidential palace. It was a sight, however familiar, which always drew a crowd to the railings, beggars and shoeblacks, idle young men, women drawing lace mantillas over their faces like the *tapadas* of an earlier day. Tonight there seemed to be a sullen movement among the crowd, and there were troops lining the pavement outside the railings in addition to the two guards completing their evolutions inside the great court-yard. Tom looked back at the lighted windows of the MEP offices above the *portales* on the far side of the square, and wondered if inside his palace President Pardo knew that James J. Macpherson, that careful planner who even sponsored an art exhibition as a means of propaganda, was planning to replace him at the earliest possible moment by that disciple of Panamericanism, ex-President Augusto B. Leguía.

The pigeons were circling round the cathedral towers in the last flight of the day, and the sunset light was red on the water bubbling from the fountains. The red sabre-knots swung in rhythm with the horsehair plumes as the jackbooted guards went through their paces. Tom stopped to watch them; they were well-trained and smart, and he thought how odd the Indian faces looked above the European uniforms of a style and swagger surely no European armies would ever imitate again. Wear the fir sprig for Tammer-fors.

It was of Finland that, inevitably, Tom Fleming thought as he came up to the Stone Bridge which would lead him to the place where, a deep inner conviction told him, he would meet again with Boris Heiden. The encounter with Lisa had not aroused remorseful thoughts of his dead passion for Sophie Sandels. That belonged to the past, and now he had engaged himself in heart and soul to the only girl with whom he could truly live and have his being. He was even inclined to smile at Nancy's transparent jealousy of both the Sandels sisters. But seeing Lisa had brought back very vividly the memory of Finland and his impulsive decision to join Mannerheim. "Take your chance, as I did," Mannerheim had said at Aberdeen. Now chance, or fate, lay on one side or the other of the Stone Bridge.

The river flowing underneath the massive arches was called the Rímac. The name went back to Inca times, and in their language meant "He who speaks", meaning an oracle of the Incas whose shrine stood on the river bank; but the watercourse itself was not impressive. Flowing from the Andes, the Rímac was narrow as it flowed through Lima to the Pacific, although just below the Stone Bridge it fell in a miniature waterfall and became a wide sheet of water, not very deep. Tom went as far as one of the bays of the bridge, and stopped to look about him.

For three hundred years this bridge had carried all the traffic from the seat of power on one bank to the impoverished, sprawling but vigorous life on the other. It had been a favourite place for assignations between the gallants of Lima and the *tapadas* whose black mantles flirtatiously concealed all but one sparkling eye, and the bays above the huge stone buttresses were still a rendezvous for paid love, as Tom found when he was solicited twice in five minutes by street-walkers not much more inviting than the Cock Alley drabs. The girls, being politely refused, did not insist. There was something withdrawn about the tall stranger who stood looking from the shallow grey river to the teeming suburb beyond.

The crowd went by him, workers going home, discussing the probability of no work tomorrow if the strike call spread, and children, with a coin or two to spend, choosing sweetmeats from the vendors whose baskets were opened invitingly round the farthest coping of the bridge. In the warm summer evening all were lightly dressed, and some indeed in rags. No scene could have been more different from the dark streets of Helsingfors, and yet in its own way it appealed to Tom. He was in a mood, like so many returned soldiers, to make a complete break with the past, and take his chance in a new land.

The only reservation he had against accepting Mr. Macpherson's offer—and it was a very strong one—was the older man's obvious involvement in Peruvian politics. Macpherson the Kingmaker, he thought whimsically, and wondered what it would be like to work with a man who made presidents, in his own words, toe the line. Tom was convinced that the future President Leguía, with American capital behind him, would be a vigorous champion of what Peruvians who shared his opinions called the Colossus of the North. Against the political wheeling and dealing, so obviously the breath of life to James J. Macpherson, could be set the great opportunity for himself and Nancy to do something, no matter how little, to improve the lives of the Indian labourers. Unconsciously straightening his shoulders, Tom Fleming thought there would be no danger of a Putomayo scandal in any enterprise he was going to run.

It might all work out well—if the shadow which once fell across a quiet living room in Helsingfors could be kept from the Casa Luza patio.

There was nothing for it but to go and find out. Tom crossed the bridge, as he had crossed the falls of Imatra, and went up the narrow Calle de San Lazaro.

It was the principal street in the suburb called for long 'Below the Bridge," but now more generally known by the name of the river, Rímac. Here the houses were still, as in the grander quarters, only two storeys high, but with lines of washing hanging from the wooden balconies where the glass was often broken in the windows, and the ground floors had been turned into shops selling everything from the sweet corn, bananas, chick peas and sweet potatoes which formed the basis of the national dish, *puchero,* to bales of violently tinted cotton and tinsel scarves. There was enough ornamentation in the woodwork above the pink and green and gamboge façades of the houses and on the frontage of a shabby theatre to remind the passers-by that in the days of the viceroys Below the Bridge had been a pleasanter district, where gardens and carriageways led to the bullring and the promenades favoured by the grandees and their discreetly mantled ladies. But now the pavements were crowded with inhabitants whose faces were of every shade from white to black, the *mestizos* of the capital, and there were quarrels and arguments, bursts of song and the spanking of children to enliven the evening in every block of the narrow street. Tom was glad to smell cooking beef and pork, and something his nose identified as mutton, from the pans on top of a hundred cooking stoves. There would be some meat in Rímac's *puchero* as well as cabbage and cereals.

The church of San Lazaro stood at the north end of the *calle,* almost where the arid open land began. As with all the Spanish churches of old Lima, there was a tiny square in front of it, with two stone benches on which idlers were lounging and smoking in the swiftly falling darkness, waiting for their women to call them to the evening meal. Emilio Concha's message had said Heiden lived in the pink house next to the church, but this was not easy to identify at first, because the little church itself was coloured pink, and what Tom took for a presbytery was in fact a rooming house.

Aware that he was an object of interest and dislike to the loungers, he went in quickly after he was certain of the door. It was a taller house than most of the others in Rímac, being three storeys high, with no balconies, and there was a dingy inside stair on which doors opened and heads peeped out as Tom went by. He looked into each room as he passed. There was only one closed door, right at the top of the stair, and there Tom knocked and entered.

"Come in," said Boris Heiden, "I've been expecting you."

As he spoke he smiled slightly, and Tom Fleming knew the twisted smile was reflected on his own face. They had come to understand each other so well that there was no need for any explanation or accusation; Tom said, "I saw you down in Callao," and that was enough.

"I saw you too, brandishing your pistol in defence of the Yankee slaver. Will you sit down?"

"Thanks. Did your students enjoy their demonstration on the waterfront, setting fire to rope carts, and the taxis decent men use to earn their living?"

"It was good practice for them. A general strike will be declared tomorrow, and the students will pass to direct action then."

"Oh, it's been settled, has it?"

"We settled it this afternoon."

"Here? Is this the Party headquarters?"

Heiden smiled again. "Hardly," he said, "this is my private residence. How does it appeal to you?"

"It's not as classy as the Villa Heiden."

"I'll be going back to the Villa Heiden eventually."

"I wouldn't count on that if I were you."

Tom looked about him. Heiden appeared to be living in a single room, with peeling wallpaper and an evil-smelling sink in one corner. There was a narrow bed against one wall. The table at which he sat held nothing but a thick notebook and writing materials, and a dingy curtain did duty for a wardrobe, and hid his clothes. Above the sink a shelf held a shaving brush and other odds and ends, among which Tom saw a pair of white gloves and something coloured red.

In this drab setting Heiden's talent for fading into the background was once again fully demonstrated. He seemed to have sunk even further down the social scale than the Latin-American clerk he had appeared to be on the fringe of the Callao riot, and there was little to distinguish him from the men idling in San Lazaro's square outside. He wore nothing but a white shirt and trousers, neither very clean, and with the dyed black hair and thin moustache he could have passed for any of the *mestizos* running the women who solicited on the Stone Bridge. Only his eyes, of the true Russian hazel, hinted at another blood: the blunt Slavic features were partly disguised by the long Spanish sidewhiskers still in fashion in some parts of Lima.

"Well," he said to Tom, "what have you come for? Surely not for the pleasure of my company?"

"No."

"Revenge for Zürich?"

"Zürich's only part of the score," said Tom. "It's no thanks to you I'm not a raving lunatic. I owe you for six weeks of drugging and indecencies, which ended only because your abortionist friend had to face a charge of murder—"

"You owe me for your life," said Boris Heiden. "You fool, don't you realise how easy it would have been to kill you, before we dumped you in the grounds of that restaurant at the Zürcher-horn? Semenov was all for cutting your throat, the night we had to get out of Meyer's clinic in a hurry. He took a great dislike to you, did Comrade Semenov, after he heard your name, rank and serial number for the five hundredth time. It was my intervention, and mine only, that saved your life."

"So I was never on your personal Black List, was I?"

"No."

"Why not? Why Sophie Sandels, and Charlie Keiller, but not me?"

Heiden said slowly, "Because there is a . . . very . . . close relationship between us. It began, perhaps not that first night in Helsingfors, but when I helped you into that rail shed at Kouvola junction. We met only once after that, at Vilppula, before you came to find me—remember, you sought *me* out—in Switzerland; but you thought about me, I know . . . as I thought of you."

"I thought of you as something to be exterminated."

"But you could never bring yourself to do it. You're armed, this evening, I suppose?"

"I am. And I bet you've got a gun convenient to your hand, in that table drawer."

Heiden got up at once and moved back to the wall beside the sink. His head was close to the red material at the corner of the makeshift shelf. Tom saw now that it was a piece of braid.

"I'm at your mercy."

"For God's sake, Heiden, you don't deserve mercy from me or anyone. How many murders have you on your conscience, if you have a conscience? How many people are going to be killed or injured in the riots you're planning for tomorrow?"

"Tomorrow's riots are going to usher in a new era for Peru. The students and the workers together will destroy the whole oligarchy, the whole miserable structure of society. Even in Moscow they'll have to admit this was my finest achievement. They'll have to admit that the Heiden way was best."

Tom noticed, not for the first time since he entered the room, that Heiden had developed a curious tic, a sideways jerk of the chin which punctuated the kind of speech which, as when he spoke to the Finns at Vilppula, he had previously delivered with so much confidence. It was as if he were listening to himself, and punctuating his declarations with a little jerk of approval, the approval he desired so much from the Soviet leaders.

"The students of San Marcos are the very finest raw material I've ever had to work with," he went on. "Some of them, and one in particular, deserve to be sent, and will be sent, to Moscow for a complete indoctrination in revolutionary tactics. They're far, far better than those pig-headed clods in Helsingfors, who declared in the end for Mannerheim—"

"Whose exile didn't last long, incidentally. He's the head of state in Finland now."

"— But the San Marcos boys completely bear out my theory, which some people at the Smolny were too high and mighty to listen to, that we must infiltrate the middle class rather than the bone-head proletariat. The San Marcos boys are all drawn from the middle class; they've received some education, however reactionary their professors may be; they were absolutely ripe for the influence of a man like me."

"Your sister-in-law said they would be."

"My—"

"Mrs. Igor Heiden," said Tom calmly. "She told me where to find you, when I visited Seattle."

He had never before seen Heiden disconcerted. His jaw dropped, and he seemed literally to fight for words.

"But how did you find *her*?"

"You gave me the clue, Heiden, when we talked at Kouvola junction. You've always been so busy, spouting about Freud and Pavlov, you didn't realise you'd made the one mistake that helped me to find you out."

"Perhaps it was a Freudian slip," said Heiden. "Perhaps I subconsciously wanted you to find me again."

"Oh, for God's sake, cut out the Freudian junk," said Tom disgustedly. "You asked me why I came to you tonight, I'll tell you. I want you to get out of this country and go back to Russia. You say you spared my life; I'll give you yours."

"Leave this country at the very moment of our victory? Are you completely crazy?"

"All right then, I'll have you run out of town, which is what you threatened to do to me at your villa on the Dolderberg. You're not in Switzerland now, with your precious passport, and a green frontier to cross into Italy, and disciplined officials waiting at every check-point to wave you on. You're just one of the bums of San Lazaro, and I can get the police to pick you up in half an hour and railroad you down to Callao and aboard the *Mount Rainier*. She's sailing in the morning for Seattle, you can stop by and say hallo to your sister-in-law."

"That stupid Irish bitch," said Heiden. "What Igor ever saw in her!"

"You didn't like the marriage, eh? Wanted to keep the big hero all to yourself, maybe? Well, that's the way it is, Heiden, go willing or go in handcuffs; I'll take damned good care to see the handcuffs on."

"I believe you really think you could," said Heiden. "Do you imagine you can buy anything you like in Lima with Yankee gold?"

"I'd rather Yankee gold than Russian blood."

"You sound like Macpherson, the enemy of the people—"

"I've known Macpherson ever since I was born," said Tom. "He's a decent man, and he means to do well by this country. He may be your enemy, but he's not an enemy of the people."

As he said the words, Tom remembered the Helsingfors Black List, and the words the Red Guard shouted as he shot Sophie Sandels down.

"He's the power behind the reactionary Leguía, who's waiting tamely in Panama until Macpherson gives him the signal to return. Everything Macpherson does is propaganda, even that charade he's staging at the Water Promenade tomorrow. Leguía, who was general manager of British Sugar before his last presidency! Leguía the lackey of western capitalism! I'll rally the whole proletariat and sack the presidential buildings as we sacked the Winter Palace, before Leguía and Macpherson destroy democracy in Peru! Do you know what the people are going on strike *for*, tomorrow? For an eight-hour day. For a decent labour code. For the food they've been denied for years, because the oligarchy cut food production in favour of cotton and the other riches of war. For the health and education of the Indians. Are these unworthy aims? Are these—"

"No, not unworthy, but you can't achieve them by killing and violence—"

"Oh, go away, Fleming, you weary me to death. Go away and think over what I've said. Then, if you must, go to the *cabildo*, and turn out the police, they're always glad of the chance to make an arrest. But Rímac's a big place, and looks after its own; I won't guarantee your flunkeys will find me here when they come."

Tom went down the creaking stairs in silence. He knew that he was still infirm of purpose, even now; that all Heiden's arguments and dialectic had not shaken him like that simple appeal to hunger and decency. He thought of the homeless Indians by the roadside, crouching over their tiny fires. New laws, new measures, even those who called themselves New Men, were desperately needed in Peru. Was that enough excuse for handing over the country to Heiden and his friends? Give me the daggers, he said to himself in despair. I wouldn't even know how to use them.

Unless—

Unless Heiden made one mistake more. Tom had learned to analyse his talk, to look for the same slips as had betrayed him in Finland, and he knew there was the germ of a thought, just out of reach, in what had been said in that dingy room. And there was something more, something teasingly connected with the piece of red braid close to Heiden's head. The association did not come to him until he was again passing the presidential palace on his way back to the Casa Luza. There was a powerful lamp above the side entrance, which brilliantly lit the two sentries on guard. They had their sabres over their shoulders, an unusual position which made Tom look twice, and then he saw that the red braid knotted in the sabre hilts was the same as the hank of braid on Heiden's shelf.

325

23

"TOM, I'M SORRY I was so bitchy this afternoon," said Nancy contritely.

Dinner was over at the casa, and James J. Macpherson, remarking with forced good humour that two lovebirds didn't really need the old man around, departed to a meeting called to discuss the measures to be taken in the event of a complete stoppage of work at the docks. He was extremely anxious about the *Mount Rainier*, which had a heavy passenger list for the United States and now might well be prevented from sailing. Tom and Nancy were in the patio, from which Luis had just removed the coffee tray.

"Are you angry with me, Tom?" she repeated. She had purposely not come downstairs until she heard her father talking to Tom in the patio as they drank their pisco sours, and she was sick. of sulking. It was not in Nancy's nature to sulk for very long.

"How could I possibly be angry with you, darling? You know I adore you—" He bent above her and kissed her, and Nancy sighed with pleasure.

"You were so quiet at dinner," she said.

"Sorry. I was thinking about something, trying to get something straight in my mind. But I think I've worked it out all right."

"Don't you know?"

"I believe I'll know tomorrow morning."

"Was it something to do with MEP?"

"Connected with MEP, yes."

"Did my father say anything more about that, before dinner?"

"He seemed to have Seattle on his mind tonight," said Tom.

"Oh, did he ever! Dad and the Shipbuilding Adjustment Board and the uniform national wage scale, what a drama!" In fact Mr. Macpherson's discourse on the iniquities of the SAB had more than covered Tom and Nancy's silence at the dinner-table.

Nancy looked sideways at the man she loved. His mouth was

set, and the white scar stood out on his brown cheek. He was thinking about something, and she was pretty sure it wasn't her.

"I just acted plain jealous this afternoon," she confessed, and was delighted when Tom laughed. He took her face between his hands and kissed her again.

"You mustn't be jealous of the past," he said. "I might have to see Lisa Sandels some time, because I want to help her to get back to Finland and make a new start, but you don't have to be jealous of poor Lisa. She made one bad mistake, as don't we all, and now she's paying for it."

"I'd like to help her too, if I can."

"That's my girl."

"But why do you always call her Lisa Sandels, never Lisa Heiden?"

"I don't know."

"Do you think Lisa was really telling the truth, when she said Heiden was in Arequipa?"

"At the time they separated, yes."

"But he's not in Arequipa now, is he?"

"How should I know?"

"Tommy, you do know." Nancy rose up from her garden chair. She was not a tall girl, but her long black chiffon dress gave her the effect of height, and her face was grave and sad as she looked at Tom. "You saw him today, didn't you?"

"Yes, I did. How did you know?"

"I was hoping you'd tell me yourself . . . I knew by instinct, I suppose. You look different, you sound different, when you're thinking about him. Did you see him this evening, after the Torre Tagle?"

"Yes. I did. At a room he has in Rímac."

"Did *she* tell you where to find him?"

"No, she didn't. I saw him on the waterfront at Callao yesterday, while you were telephoning. I paid somebody to follow him home."

"And you didn't tell me?"

"I could see, as soon as I got here, you didn't want to talk about it."

"I should think not indeed," said Nancy bitterly. "I tried to tell myself it was for me, me alone, you came to Lima. But I couldn't forget that you mentioned Heiden in your first cable, the one you sent off from Seattle—that you were looking for him as well as coming after me."

"I was coming after you anyway, darling."

"Why did you go after *him*, this evening?"

"I thought I just might have the guts to kill him. I couldn't do it in cold blood."

Nancy stifled a cry. With her hands over her mouth, she stared aghast at Tom.

"You wouldn't *murder* him? Tom darling, I know he deserves it, after all he's done, but this is Lima! Even if you shot him in self defence, you would be put in jail, and held months waiting to stand your trial. You're a Canadian; the American diplomats wouldn't even interfere. I knew today at the Torre Tagle that they're furious with all of us for calling out the troops at Callao, they think it might create an international incident! Tom—"

"Don't worry, Nancy," said Tom wearily, "Heiden's alive and kicking, and I'm here."

"Yes, but—darling, are we never to be done with these people? Are our lives going to revolve for ever round Boris Heiden and the Sandels girls? Now, when we ought to be happy, and we've got everything going for us, must we go through all that again?"

"My dearest girl, you know I want you to be happy, more than anything else in the world."

He was on his feet beside her now, wrapping her closely in his arms, and Nancy, feeling the excitement in his body, knew her power over him and opened her mouth to his kisses. And between the kisses she whispered, "Promise me! Promise me!" hardly knowing what she was saying, but meaning Promise me you'll give up this insane pursuit, which may destroy us both.

"Nancy, you don't understand. This Heiden is mad, I'm certain of it now. I went back to Dykefaulds, and talked to the doctors there about him—"

"Oh no! Oh no! I don't want to hear about it! Please!"

He lifted her in his arms, right off the ground, and the black chiffon straps of her dress slipped off her shoulders, which she allowed him to kiss while her own mouth found the scar on his cheek and clung there. And Tom's hands cradled her hips and clasped him to her.

He could feel the heat spreading through her limbs.

"I'm sorry, Nancy—"

"Don't be sorry, darling—"

Her mind was suddenly made up. Nancy was ready to make her own bid against Tom's obsession by the offer of her love. She allowed herself to go limp in his arms, leaning back until she felt the full strength of his body pressing towards her own, and then Tom groaned.

"Nancy, I must—I must have you—"

"Yes, oh yes!"

The door of his room was only a few steps away. He swept her up and laid her on the bed. The black chiffon dress was easy to undo. For a moment Nancy felt him hesitate, and wondered if he was afraid to take a virgin, but in her love she did not falter nor even close her eyes. It was Tom's flesh which was discovering her own, and she was proud of the young breasts and taut slimness which she was offering up to his scarred limbs. They came together in true love and mutual fulfilment, and Nancy only gave one sob when he first entered her body.

A sob which, later in the night, turned to happy sighs.

24

"NANCY ISN'T COMING DOWN to breakfast, she seems a mite peaky this morning," said Mr. Macpherson, arriving in the solemn dining room.

Tom took a gulp of coffee, which burned his mouth. "I'm sorry to hear that," he said, "she had a bit of a headache yesterday."

"I can't understand it," said her father, "Nancy's usually as fit as a flea. Oh, don't worry, she's not in bed, she was having coffee on the balcony when I looked in. She had Manuela walking up and down, showing off the new green dress she's going to wear at the Water Promenade."

"You haven't been able to talk her out of that, have you, sir?"

"You try talking to the wind," said Mr. Macpherson briefly. "A messenger from the presidential palace arrived an hour ago, and I thought Pardo was going to duck out at the last moment. However, it was just to say he wanted to advance the ceremony by one hour. Ten o'clock, it is now, because he plans to hold a cabinet at eleven."

"I thought he might have cancelled the whole thing now that the general strike's begun."

"Yes, well, that project cost too much to cancel," said Mr. Macpherson. "I sent a message back saying I would cut my speech to two minutes, and gently hinted he might do the same. Damnation, what have I *done* with that speech? I want to practise reading it in Spanish. Finish your breakfast, Tom; you'll find me in the library."

Tom left half his papaya uneaten and went out to the patio. He lit a cigarette, and looked up at Nancy's balcony. Was she really all right, or was she too shy to face him over the breakfast table in the presence of her father? Would she be angry with him in the cold light of day?

Tom's heart was a tumult of love and gratitude. The experience with Nancy had been like no other experience in his life, and it was only the beginning! He was frantic to take the bribe her father offered, of holding the wedding at once, in Lima, in exchange for Tom's joining Macpherson Enterprises of Peru; he wanted to buy a wedding ring for Nancy that very day. But before that could be done there was the ceremony at the Paseo de Aguas, when President Pardo was to cut the gilt ribbon holding the key of the new fountain of pure drinking water, Mr. Macpherson's gift to the grateful inhabitants of an area too completely cut off from the town, and whatever Tom's heart said his mind was absorbed by the problem of Boris Heiden.

Colonel Henderson had said that the Russian's state of mind, as described by Tom, presented one of the finest cases of paranoia known to the new psychiatry. There was a strong delusion of persecution, inherited from his mother and her race, and at the same time a delusion of grandeur which made Heiden seek to assume power over the minds of men. There was a desire for the approval of his superiors in the Communist hierarchy, and a strong fixation on the memory of his dead brother which might, sooner or later, drive him to emulate that brother in an imitated, but this time successful, political assassination. Finally, in dressing as a woman and embracing Tom before his accomplice struck the Canadian down, he had revealed a more than latent homosexuality. Tom, in Lima, was certain that this was one of the reasons for Heiden's separation from his wife.

"What a case history!" Colonel Henderson had said at Dykefaulds. "It would take Professor Freud himself to write it up."

"I have to hand it to Heiden for one thing," Tom had replied. "He has the nerve of the devil. It took guts to cross the Kvarken ice at all, let alone with a prisoner in tow, to be disposed of before they reached the Swedish shore, and then at Zürich! There were people in that wine bar, I heard them talking and laughing when I went up the alley. Half a dozen honest Switzers could have come out of the back door while they were dragging me back across the square. 'Operating on a tight schedule,' Heiden called that. Tight, I'll say it was."

"That kind of nerve may push him over the edge some day," the doctor said.

And so they had come to this day, and from Heiden's compulsive references to the "Water Promenade charade" and the storming of the Winter Palace Tom had come to the conclusion that he would try to assassinate the President of Peru. Then in the ensuing confusion in the city the students would try to seize the power, under whichever of their leaders Heiden saw as a suitable case for further indoctrination in Moscow. The one thing he couldn't fit into his assumption was the red sabre knot in Heiden's room. He thought it had probably been left behind by some trooper whom Heiden was using to subvert the president's bodyguard. Or for more personal purposes.

He walked up and down under the myrtle trees, thinking what he should do, and very much aware of the Browning pistol, out of its holster and handy in the pocket of his linen jacket. He had smoked two cigarettes before he heard light steps on the stone stair, and looked up to see the girl he loved.

Tom was at her side in an instant. He knew even before she spoke that she was happy, her smile said everything, and some words of a rubric he had last heard at his sister's wedding came into his mind. With my body I thee worship, he knew now what that meant, and when he took Nancy into his arms Tom said, "I worship you."

"I love you, Tom."

When he released her from that long kiss Tom told her she was beautiful, and perhaps she was, in her pallor and her shadowed eyes. "What a pretty dress," he said. "Did you wear green to match your emerald? We'll pick it up at the jeweller's when we come back."

"I'd love that."

"Ah, there you are, Nancy," said her father, coming out with two pages of typescript in triple-spaced capitals in one hand. He had changed into morning dress, and carried a silk hat in the other. "I'm just off to the palace. You two don't need to start for half an hour."

"I'd rather go out to the reviewing stand, or whatever they call it, and have a look round first," said Tom definitely. "Nancy, is that all right with you?"

"Sure." She had her gloves and bag, and her black lace mantilla ready to put on.

"I don't see why not," her father said. "Just remember this is a for men only ceremony, Nan, and keep well in the background."

"But won't there be women at the fountain? I thought the new sewage system and the laundry were meant for them."

"I don't know how the palace has set it up, I'm sure," said the hero of the occasion, "the president's doubled the honour guard, I know."

"I'll look after Nancy," promised Tom. "We'll start out now, if Benito's ready."

It was not possible to speak of tender things behind Benito's listening ears, for the chauffeur knew some words of English, but Tom kept Nancy's hand in his as the Pierce-Arrow swept across the Stone Bridge, down the narrow *calle*, and past the square of San Lazaro. Tom looked up at the windows of the rooming house. He wondered if Heiden were inside, or in the city.

"One thing I'm looking forward to," said Nancy, "is getting the Bearcat out of the stables and going driving our two selves."

"I am too." That would be great, driving with his girl in a Stutz Bearcat! "I feel like a president myself, when we go rolling around in a limousine."

"But these roads were never meant for tyres," said Nancy. They were bumping over cobbles new in the days of the viceroys, when the farthest suburb, beyond the arid land which separated it from Rímac, had been the scene of pleasure parties for high society, and once a year, when the yellow narcissus, the *amancaes*, flowered on the bare brown hill beyond, the ladies of Lima made a day-long excursion to gather them. Now a cross stood on the summit of that hill, the last outpost of the Cordillera, and at the foot, one or two families of homeless Indians had contrived to set up little huts.

"What a queer place," said Nancy, when the car came to a stop. "I've never been here before. Where are we, Benito?"

The chauffeur made them understand that the long avenue of diamond-shaped paving, with rather shabby flowerbeds and broken statues on each side, led to the monastery of the Barefoot Friars. The *padrón* had said the car was to wait here, he explained: no cars except the presidential cortège would be allowed near the Water Promenade. "See, the honour guard has halted here already," he pointed out. Young men in white uniforms were jumping down from an army truck.

The seventeenth-century glory had long since departed from the avenue of the Descalzos, the Barefoot Friars, at the moment frequented only by beggars and poor women nursing little children, and so, somewhat to Nancy's dismay, it had departed from the Paseo de Aguas built by the Viceroy Amat. Two stagnant pools in dry grass led up to a Moorish structure in terracotta, with fretted pillars above and three arches on each side of a central arch. It was inside this arch that Mr. Macpherson's new fountain had been installed, and the turning of the key by the president would not only start the waters playing, but activate the invisible sewers and the supply of water to the new laundry. Several rows of gilt chairs were already occupied by prosperous-looking men, some of them the city fathers, others merely the presidential claque, in front of the new fountain. The inhabitants of the district, in shawls and ragged trousers, were standing humbly behind a wire barrier.

"Don't let's sit down," said Tom, and Nancy nodded. They strolled nearer to the arch, and Tom scanned the rows of seated men. The soldiers from the lorry were being marched into place in front of the arches in seven groups of five. They were dressed in a theatrical uniform Tom had not yet seen, white tunics and trousers, strapped beneath light shoes, with shakos which covered half their faces, and wide chin straps. They carried dress swords and wore white gloves. "Smart but not very soldierly," said Tom.

The presidential car came up, with Mr. Macpherson sitting beside the president, and a guard of mounted troops riding beside the cars containing members of the government. "What a day for Dad," said Nancy, "they're really doing him proud!"

The national anthem was played, rather too fast, as if the president was in a hurry to get on to his cabinet meeting, and he at once began his speech, talking quickly, without notes. Mr. Macpherson stood beside him. Tom caught some of the easier expressions, "friend of Peru . . . generous donor . . ." His hand was in his right pocket and his eyes moved steadily among the faces of the listening crowd. They were Peruvians to the last man.

The president's speech was nearly over when awareness came to him. The guards carrying dress swords wore the same red braid on the hilts as the palace sentries wore upon their sabres. And one of them, moving very slightly out of line and fumbling at his belt, had a dark moustache and sideburns beneath the peak of his shako—

"*Heiden!*"

Tom's shout, and Heiden's movement, came at the same time. The Russian dagger flew through the air at Mr. Macpherson's back. The American fell headlong to the ground. And Tom fired once, he dared not fire through the milling crowd again, at a slim

334

man in a white uniform, who was running for his life towards the avenue of the Barefoot Friars.

Macpherson not Pardo, Macpherson not Pardo, of course that was the target. Tom's awareness was alert on all levels, he knew that Nancy had screamed and rushed towards her father's body, that every Peruvian among the invited guests had his pistol out, that every trooper standing by his horse was trying to mount and surround the president. But Tom Fleming was running, faster than he had run for years, in pursuit of the man who at last had done the deed of violence which should put him on the same pedestal as his brother Igor.

Heiden was running fast up the Descalzos. Some of the women were shrieking and pulling their children behind the broken columns, and Tom Fleming risked a shot at the man in white. It missed, but Heiden turned and fired back: there was a scream, and a young woman fell. A beggar had the courage to run towards Heiden, and was shot down. And Tom was running still, with a stitch in his side, and a pain in the old wound in his stomach, waiting for the fools to get out of the way and leave him a field of fire. Heiden turned and fired at him again.

Then, mercifully and at last, the way was clear, the killing of the innocent came to a stop. Tom halted and fired two shots in quick succession. He saw Heiden fall and lie writhing on the ground.

He lowered the pistol and walked towards his enemy quite slowly. There was no breath left in his exhausted body. And Heiden was screaming, the thin high screams that Tom Fleming had not heard since the shell hole at Sainte Elodie.

The screams stopped as he came up, and he saw why. Blood was pouring from between Heiden's legs and from his face; his left cheekbone was all but shattered. But he was still alive, lying on his right side and in agony, with the fingers of one hand curving towards his side. The hazel eyes, clouding over now, looked up at Tom Fleming with a mute appeal. He was unable to speak, but he was asking for the mercy stroke.

"Yes, Boris," said Tom Fleming with compassion, and shot him dead, a clean shot through the brain, and dropped the pistol on the ground. There was still one bullet left in the chamber.

He looked behind him down the avenue of the Descalzos. There were people lying on the ground, there was screaming, there

335

were men in uniform and even horses struggling through the crowd. But there was someone in a green dress who had come to him again, and with a last effort Tom ran to meet his love.

"Tom—"

"Your father?"

"The doctor—the doctor says he'll live. His shoulder—the bone—" Her breath gave out.

"It's all over, darling," Tom got out, "Heiden's dead."

"The police are coming—"

"I know. Nancy, will you wait for me?"

"Always."

The sound of the police whistles and the running feet came nearer.